W9-BCJ-357

THROUGH STONE AND SEA

The Noble Dead Saga—Series One

DHAMPIR

THIEF OF LIVES

SISTER OF THE DEAD

TRAITOR TO THE BLOOD

REBEL FAY

CHILD OF A DEAD GOD

The Noble Dead Saga—Series Two

IN SHADE AND SHADOW

THROUGH STONE AND SEA

Also by Barb Hendee

The Vampire Memories Series

BLOOD MEMORIES

HUNTING MEMORIES

THROUGH STONE AND SEA

A Novel of the Noble Dead

Barb & J. C. Hendee

A ROC BOOK

ROC
Published by New American Library, a division of
Penguin Group (USA) Inc., 375 Hudson Street,
New York, New York 10014, USA
Penguin Group (Canada), 90 Eglinton Avenue East, Suite 700, Toronto,
Ontario M4P 2Y3, Canada (a division of Pearson Penguin Canada Inc.)
Penguin Books Ltd., 80 Strand, London WC2R 0RL, England
Penguin Ireland, 25 St. Stephen's Green, Dublin 2,
Ireland (a division of Penguin Books Ltd.)
Penguin Group (Australia), 250 Camberwell Road, Camberwell, Victoria 3124,
Australia (a division of Pearson Australia Group Pty. Ltd.)
Penguin Books India Pvt. Ltd., 11 Community Centre, Panchsheel Park,
New Delhi - 10 017, India
Penguin Group (NZ), 67 Apollo Drive, Rosedale, North Shore 0632,
New Zealand (a division of Pearson New Zealand Ltd.)
Penguin Books (South Africa) (Pty.) Ltd., 24 Sturdee Avenue,
Rosebank, Johannesburg 2196, South Africa

Penguin Books Ltd., Registered Offices:
80 Strand, London WC2R 0RL, England

First published by Roc, an imprint of New American Library,
a division of Penguin Group (USA) Inc.

First Printing, January 2010
10 9 8 7 6 5 4 3 2 1

Library of Congress Cataloging-in-Publication Data:

Hendee, Barb.
Through stone and sea/Barb & J.C. Hendee.
p. cm.
ISBN 978-0-451-46312-8
1. Quests (Expeditions)—Fiction. 2. Vampires—Fiction. 3. Dwarfs—Fiction. I. Hendee, J. C. II. Title.
PS3608.E525T47 2010
813'.6—dc22 2009029241

Set in Adobe Garamond
Designed by Alissa Amell

Printed in the United States of America

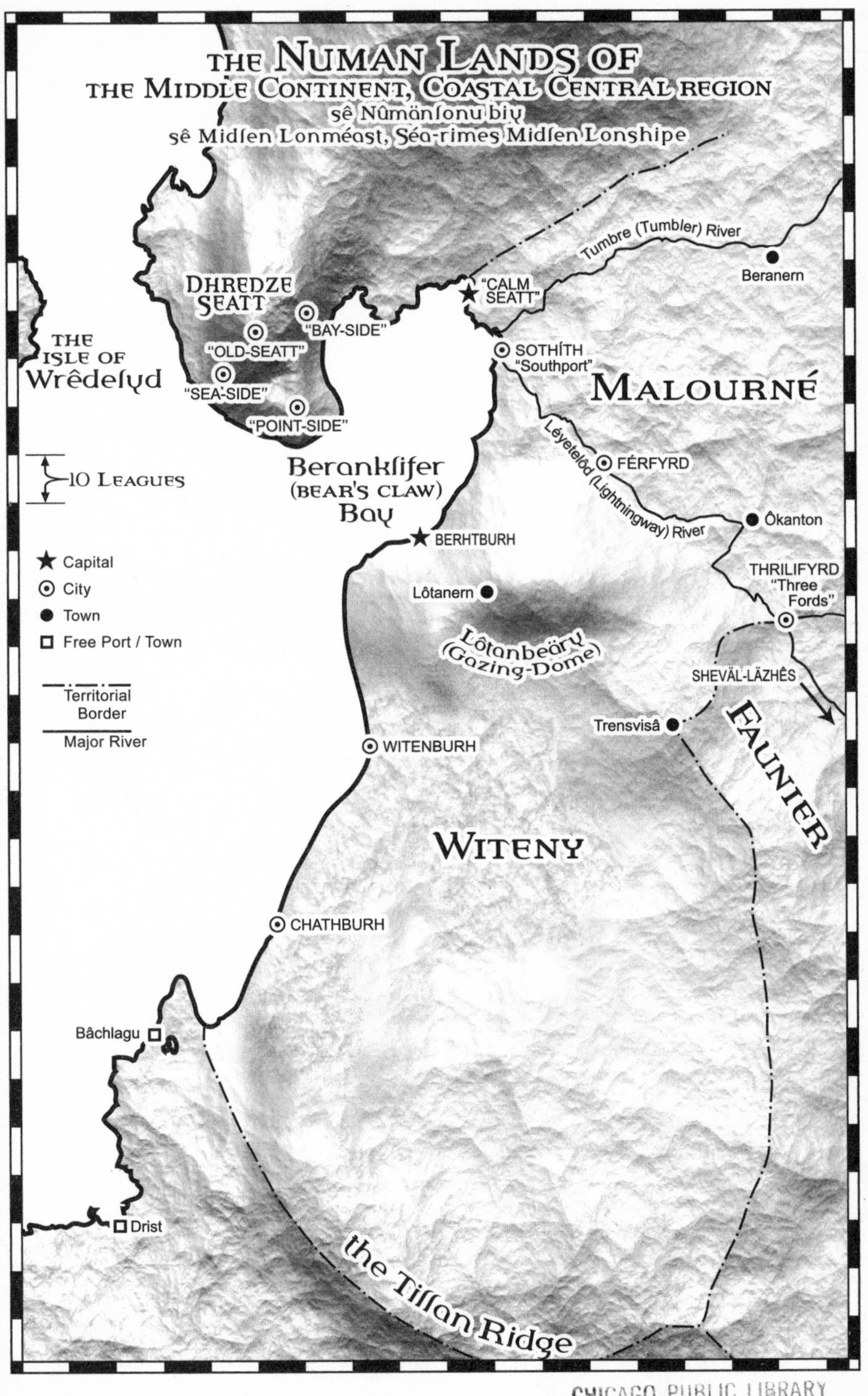

THE NUMAN LANDS OF
THE MIDDLE CONTINENT, COASTAL CENTRAL REGION
sê Nûmânſonu biy
sê Midſen Lonméast, Séa-rimes Midſen Lonshipe
Tumbre (Tumbler) River
Beranern
"CALM SEATT"
DHREDZE SEATT
"BAY-SIDE"
"OLD-SEATT"
"SEA-SIDE"
"POINT-SIDE"
THE ISLE OF Wrêdeſyd
SOTHÍTH "Southport"
MALOURNÉ
Léyetelôd (Lightningway) River
FÉRFYRD
Ôkanton
10 LEAGUES
Beranklifer (BEAR'S CLAW) Bay
BERHTBURH
Capital
City
Town
Free Port / Town
Territorial Border
Major River
Lôtanern
THRILIFYRD "Three Fords"
Lôtanbeäry (Gazing-Dome)
SHEVÄL-LÄZHÊS
Trensvisâ
FAUNIER
WITENBURH
WITENY
CHATHBURH
Bâchlagu
Drist
the Tiſſan Ridge

THROUGH STONE AND SEA

PROLOGUE

Dusk settled over the harbor below Chemarré—Sea-Side—the western settlement of Dhredze Seatt, home of the dwarven people across the bay from Calm Seatt. A two-masted Numanese ship drifted up to its docks. As the crew cast lines to dwarven dockworkers, the vessel settled, with five cloaked figures waiting near its rail.

Three of the quintet wore polished steel helms gleaming pale yellow under the deck's lanterns. A glimpse of glittering chain vestments beneath crimson tabards showed through the splits of their cloaks. Each wore a long sword sheathed upon a wide belt of engraved silver plates. These three were Weardas—the Sentinels—personal guard to the Âreskynna, the royal family of Malourné in Calm Seatt.

Behind them stood one of the other two, easily as tall as they were, but slighter of build. This one's earthy-colored cloak with full hood hid his face but not the hem of a white robe around his tan felt boots.

The last of the five, standing before all the others, was much shorter.

Hidden beneath a hooded cloak of deep sea green, small gloved hands and a slight frame marked this one as female. She gripped the rail and peered over the ship's side and up the dock, as if looking for someone.

The crew gave these five a wide berth and hurried to unload a paltry cargo, as if their vessel had left its last port not fully loaded. By the time they finished, night had settled in.

The ship's captain strolled past the quintet and stopped a ways off. The broadest and tallest of the Weardas nodded curtly. That brief movement exposed the tuft of a dark beard on his squared chin. The ship's captain shook his head and turned aftward toward his quarters below.

And still the five waited—until heavy footfalls barely carried from shore.

The woman in sea green rushed down the boarding ramp.

She reached the dock before her panicked guards caught up and encompassed her once more. The tall one in the earthy cloak pushed close behind her as she searched the night for those footfalls. But all she saw were warehouses, other smaller buildings, and a trio of dwarves settled down to pipes and low talk.

Yet those footfalls never broke rhythm.

At first, the dockworkers gave no notice. Perhaps they thought it was one of their own coming on for evening duty. Then something passed through the edge of their lanterns' dim light.

It stomped onward like a broad piece of night on the move, and then vanished from the light's reach.

The closest dockworker jerked to his feet, overturning his heavy cask stool. His companions rose, but he turned the other way, peering shoreward and all around the port. Only then did he stare after those footfalls, as if the shadow heralded something worse he hadn't spotted.

Slowly, the steady steps breached the edge of the light from the ship's lanterns. Illumination exposed the silhouette of a broad dwarf.

At first, the light only caught on wild, steel-streaked black hair around a grim, wrinkled face. The rest of him remained lost, as if night clung to his massive form. An indignant hiss rose from the tall Weardas with the chin beard.

"You're late!" he growled. "I don't like my *charge* being forced to wait in the dark!"

"*You* are early, Captain," replied the new arrival, his voice like gravel crushed under a boulder. "And I do not care to be seen by my people . . . any more than necessary."

He drew closer, stepping into full view.

Standing as tall as the small woman, he was easily twice as wide and three times her bulk. Wild locks hung to his shoulders, framing the hard line of his mouth within a beard of short, steely bristles. Over char-gray breeches and a wool shirt, he wore a short-sleeved hauberk of oiled black leather scales. Each scale's tip was sheathed in ornately engraved steel, and two war daggers in like-adorned black sheaths were tucked slantwise in his thick belt.

This dark juggernaut stopped three paces off and blew a long exhale through his broad nose, full of disdain for his challenger. Then his black pellet eyes settled upon the small woman ringed in by her taller entourage.

"The new moon comes, this time with the year's highest tide," he rumbled. "Welcome again . . . Princess."

The woman raised gloved hands to her hood.

The movement opened her cloak, exposing a forest green skirt. The skirt's front was split around her dark brown breeches and calf-high leather riding boots. The hilt of a small horseman's saber poked out above her left hip. She pulled the hood back, revealing a mass of dark chestnut hair around a dainty face of even features that some would call fetching.

"Duchess . . . Master Cinder-Shard," she corrected him, but her voice quavered and broke. "Always . . . duchess."

Reine Faunier-Âreskynna, Duchess of Faunier and princess by marriage to the royals of Malourné, nodded respectfully—almost reverently—to the dark dwarf.

"Toying with titles changes nothing," he returned. "It disrespects heritage. It is a princess of the Âreskynna who comes to the Hassäg'kreigi."

A soft laugh, like a lark in the woods, rose from the brown-cloaked attendant.

"Oh, spare us, Smarasmôy, you old ghost tender!" that one whispered, using the newcomer's dwarven name. "Preference of title will not crack the walls of propriety."

Master Cinder-Shard's dour expression flattened. He raised those black pellet eyes to the tall and slight figure.

"Chuillyon?" he asked with a forced scowl. "What impish prank did you pull this time . . . to end up on guardian duty?"

His caustic tone didn't hide an elder's shake of the head at some suspected mischief by a youngster.

"Not a thing, I swear," answered Chuillyon innocently. "I chose this duty."

At that, Cinder-Shard turned serious, almost worried. "Why not assign one of your order instead?"

Duchess Reine remained uncomfortably quiet, and Chuillyon pulled back his earth-toned hood and the white cowl beneath it.

Lantern light spread over a male elf's triangular face with the large amber eyes of his people, but he was no youngster to be chided. Chuillyon's golden brown locks, hanging past his oversharp chin, were faded in streaks. Prominent creases lined the corners of his eyes set around a narrow nose a bit long even for an elf. More lines framed his small mouth, perhaps as much from mirth as advanced age.

"How fares the Order of Chârmun," Cinder-Shard asked, "without your mischievous guidance?"

Chuillyon, whose name meant "holly," lost his soft smile. "As well as the Stonewalkers, I imagine . . . with such unknown times ahead."

Duchess Reine cringed, clasping her hands tightly together. She tried to breathe slowly, normally, but her effort was plainly visible. One Weardas, with a face too boyish for his stature, leaned around his captain's shoulder.

"Sir, we draw too much attention."

Reine's gaze slipped to the dockworkers down the way. Three dwarves stared with anxious wonder at Master Cinder-Shard and the gathering on the dock.

"Enough talk," growled the captain. "We go now."

"Tristan!" Reine admonished sharply, and then lowered her voice. "You will show respect for the master of the Stonewalkers!"

At her strained tone, everyone fell silent. Chuillyon laid a hand lightly upon her shoulder.

"Apologies," the captain said. "No offense intended."

Cinder-Shard nodded and glanced briefly at the gawkers far behind him.

"You are correct, Captain," he agreed. "Will you lead with me?"

Cinder-Shard turned a hardened gaze upon Reine as the captain stepped beyond him to wait. A look of sadness or deep regret passed across the dwarf's craggy face. Reine set herself, every muscle rigid, as his gravelly voice declared . . .

"Time again, Princess . . . to return to the underworld."

CHAPTER 1

The racing lift rolled over a shelf lip on the sheer mountainside and lurched to a halt at the way station. Wynn Hygeorht stepped off the lift's platform, arriving at Cheku'ûn——Bay-Side—one of four main settlements for Dhredze Seatt, the nation of the dwarves, overlooking Beranlômr Bay. Even at this dizzying height, the bay below looked wide and vast. Calm Seatt's pinprick lights marked its far shore as the glow of encroaching dawn rose in the east.

Wynn pushed back her hood and brushed away wisps of light brown hair that the breeze pulled across her oval face. Beneath her cloak, she wore the light gray robe of the Order of Cathology in the Guild of Sagecraft.

"We're finally here," she said.

When she turned back, glancing up the stone loading ramp, any matching relief on her companions' faces had nothing to do with reaching their destination.

Shade, taller than a wolf and with a shimmering coat of charcoal black, whined sharply as she wobbled out of the lift's railing gate. The dog swallowed hard, as if her last meal of mutton might come up, and drool ran from her mouth.

Chane Andraso was little better. Tall and lanky but muscular, with solid shoulders, he didn't release the railing until he stepped onto the stone ramp. His raggedly cut red-brown hair ruffled in the wind as he followed Shade down to join Wynn.

He was shivering.

He couldn't have been cold, not as an undead, and she'd never seen him frightened of anything. The barest relief spread through Chane's narrow features. Then he glared back at the lift's massive wheels resting level at the station.

Wynn sighed. "Oh, for goodness' sake—it wasn't that bad."

Chane looked down at her, dumbstruck and aghast. Shade tried to growl, but only gagged, and shook herself all over as if trying to shed the entire experience.

Wynn headed off, shaking her head.

"After all we've been through," she muttered, "such fuss over a simple ride up a mountain!"

A chain of extraordinary events had brought the three of them here.

Two years before, she'd found an ancient castle atop the highest mountains of the eastern continent. An immense decaying library within it held texts written by ancient Noble Dead, perhaps the oldest of vampires. One vampire was still there after a thousand or more years. Wynn had taken away a pittance of that treasure, only what she and her companions could carry. She'd hoped her selections, written in lost dialects and dead languages, might illuminate theories on the Forgotten History . . . and the great war that some believed had never happened.

When she returned to the small beginning of a new guild branch on the eastern continent, she'd been given the task of carrying those priceless tomes home to Calm Seatt, Malourné, and the founding origin for the Guild of Sagecraft. She'd boarded a ship and crossed the eastern ocean and the central continent, eager to finish a long, arduous journey and begin translation with her fellow sages.

But nothing in Wynn's recent years had ever turned out as she'd hoped.

Upon her arrival, the texts and her own travel journals had been confiscated and locked away. Only a chosen few of her superiors ever saw them. At least until sages began to be murdered in the night over bits of translation work sent out to local scribe shops for transcription. She came to realize she had to regain those texts and solve whatever mysteries they held.

At first, she'd believed they were stored somewhere on guild grounds. Later she suspected they were hidden elsewhere. She'd spotted dark-clad dwarves at the guild, but they vanished without a trace of how they came or went. She learned what they called themselves only by chance.

Hassäg'kreigi—the Stonewalkers.

And now, here she was with Chane and Shade in Dhredze Seatt, a place close to home and yet she hadn't seen it in years.

A pair of humans bundled in winter attire, perhaps merchants from Calm Seatt, waited with crates of goods at the larger cargo lift. But no one was waiting to take the smaller passenger lift that had brought Wynn up. More people bustled about the main street here than in any of the lower way-station settlements.

Wynn gazed about the small stone city built into the mountain's sheer side.

She'd been so young the last time she'd come here. Just shy of apprenticeship, she'd been overjoyed that Domin Tilswith had chosen her to assist him. Well, that and trying to keep up with her old master and not get lost amid a foreign place and its people.

She stepped around the way-station's crank house into the narrow stone street, and everything before her seemed to stretch *upward.*

The main road snaked back and forth up the mountain between buildings of stone and scant timber. Only short and steep side streets aimed directly upward, and most were built of wide stone steps and multiple landings. All of it was behemothlike—rather like the dwarves themselves. Dying moonlight barely revealed roofs of slate tiles, stone blocks, and shakes and planks of oak on smaller structures. Everything else was carved from granite so precisely that little mortar was ever used.

Something bumped Wynn's leg. Shade whined and pressed closer. Young and wild, Shade didn't like crowds. Her blue eyes—flecked with yellow—grew wide as she looked around. Wynn reached down to stroke her ears.

"Daunting," Chane rasped from behind.

Wynn was accustomed to his maimed voice, but it still startled her in the dark predawn.

"It can be a little disorienting at first," she replied.

And it was. Dwellings and inns, smithies, tanneries, and shops all spread out, around, and above them in a melded maze.

She shifted her pack to relieve pressure on her shoulder. Chane seemed oblivious to the weight of his own two packs. Gripping her tall staff, a leather sheath covering its top end, Wynn led the way farther up the main street. When she glanced back, she paused, spotting a great open archway in the mountain's side behind the crank house.

The entire lift station could have fit through it with room to spare. The orange light of the dwarves' heated crystals spilled from its interior over people coming and going. But she had no time for a closer peek and instead looked eastward.

The star-speckled night had lightened farther along the distant horizon, and urgency took hold.

"We must find the temple," she said.

Any visitor in a foreign place had to find lodging, but in Chane's case, it was foremost. She needed to get him inside before the sun rose.

"Find?" he echoed. "You do not know where it is?"

"Of course I know. It's just . . . been . . . a long time."

Wynn hurried up the street's gradual slant, deeper into Bay-Side, and quickened her pace. In spite of her assurance to Chane, she wasn't certain of the temple's location. It was still the best place to take shelter, away from other travelers at an inn. It was also a place where a visiting sage would be welcomed.

Dwarves practiced a unique form of ancestor worship. They revered those of their own who attained notable status in life, akin to the human concept of a hero or saint, or rather both. Any who became known for virtuous accomplishments, by feat and/or service to the people, might one day become a thänæ—one of the honored. Though similar to human knighthood or noble entitlement, it wasn't a position of rulership or authority. After death, any thänæ who'd achieved renown among the people over decades and centuries, through the continued retelling of their exploits, might one day be elevated to Bäynæ—one of the dwarven Eternals. These were the dwarves' spiritual immortals, held as the honored ancestors of their people as a whole.

Wynn sought lodgings at the temple of just such a one.

Bedzâ'kenge—Feather-Tongue—was the patron of wisdom and heritage through story, song, and poetry, their paragon of orators and historians. For as long as any history remembered, the dwarves kept to oral tradition rather than the literary ways of humankind.

As Wynn hurried along, she noticed faint shadows upon the granite street stones. Another glance eastward, between stout buildings on the settlement's outer edge, showed the horizon growing ever lighter.

"Are we near yet?" Chane asked.

He didn't sound concerned, but Wynn knew better. If they didn't find the temple soon, they'd have to knock on some random door and beg admittance to get him out of the coming dawn.

"We're in the right area," she half lied. "I'll recognize the street when I see it."

But she wished she'd paid better attention as a girl while visiting with Domin Tilswith.

Wynn stopped between wide steps on both sides. Another thick four-sided stone pillar stood in the intersection. Atop it, steam leaked around a huge raw crystal casting orange light and warmth about the street. Oral or not, dwarves had an ancient writing system, and columns often served the same purpose as street signs in human cities.

She circled it, scanning for engravings upon its smooth faces—not for names of streets but for places found in the direction the column's sides faced. She could read the common dialect reasonably well, but the temple of Bedzâ'kenge wasn't mentioned. Either it didn't lie along any of these routes or it was more than one level up.

Along the higher staircase, she spotted a mapmaker's shop on the first landing, its tan banner flying above a wide front door.

"There," she breathed in relief. "I remember that from the last time I was here."

She hurried up the steps past the mapmaker's shop and others, all the way to the main street's next switchback.

"I know where we are," Wynn exclaimed.

Chane raised one eyebrow. "I was not aware you were in doubt."

"Oh, just come on!"

She broke into a jog, heading the other way. At the next intersecting stairway, she turned upward again. She stopped halfway, catching her breath on a landing with sculpted miniature fir trees planted in large black marble pots. She knew she had the right path, but Chane's brow wrinkled as he glanced east.

"Almost there," she said in a gasp, and hiked her robe as she climbed again.

Shade bounded ahead, reaching the street's next switchback first. Wynn hoped at least one shirvêsh—a temple attendant—was up and about this early.

A deep tone echoed between the buildings.

Wynn pulled up short on the steps and held her breath.

"What?" Chane whispered.

She raised a hand for silence and waited, listening and hoping for more tones to come, but none did.

"Night-Winter is over!" she whispered in panic. "Day-Spring begins!"

"What does that mean?" Chane demanded.

This was no time to explain dwarven measures of night's and day's phases. She grabbed his sleeve, jerking him onward.

"Dawn is coming!"

"I do not need bells to know that," he answered.

Wynn reached Shade at the main street's next crossing. Across the way, before the next intersection pillar and its steaming crystal, was a massive structure emerging from the mountainside. Its double doors of white marble were set back beneath a high overhang supported by columns carved like living trees. But quick relief vanished.

Faint shadows from the columns began to appear upon the doors.

Wynn had to get Chane inside right now.

A dark column, like smoke thickening in shadow, grew in a small street-side terrace. It coalesced before an old fir tree nurtured in that place. And a heavy black cowl sagged across a cloak layered over a long black robe.

Sau'ilahk watched his trio of quarry scurry up the steps to the columned and roofed landing.

The sky grew light, and he could not remain for long nor risk going closer. The wolf might sense him. But he now knew these three better, having followed their nightly journey all the way from Calm Seatt.

Wynn Hygeorht, journeyor sage, kept company with a savage, tall wolf she had named Shade. But the pale one called Chane was more suspicious. He gave off no sense of *presence* at all. In Calm Seatt, both of Wynn's companions had been difficult to deal with face-to-face, as neither succumbed to Sau'ilahk's life-consuming touch. But Wynn frustrated and angered him most.

If not for her meddling, he might have acquired more translation folios—and perhaps a hint to the remedy of his long misery.

She did not know his name, never would, and instead referred to him as something out of her people's quaint old folklore—a wraith. She even thought him destroyed by the staff's crystal. Oh, she had injured him worse than he could remember and driven him into dark dormancy. The crystal's flare had torn him up like sunlight. But she had no notion *what* he truly was, *whom* she had interfered with. In centuries of searching, he had never come close to what he sought until the ancient texts had appeared at the guild. And now . . .

Sau'ilahk slid back through the massive fir and into its deeper shadows, feeling the life in its branches pass through him as if he were *nothing*! That worthless tingle of life was too removed from his once living nature. It did not feed him and only made him ache for one precious thing lost an age ago.

Flesh.

By dear, deceitful Beloved, the one true deity, how he ached to have flesh once more. That singular desire might have been all that had kept him from fading into nothingness over more than a thousand years. And there was Beloved's more recent promise, given one dusk upon the edge of Sau'ilahk's dormancy.

Follow the sage . . . urge her, drive her. . . . She will lead you to your desire.

That temptation of hope ground against doubt-fueled rage. Could he ever trust his god again?

Sau'ilahk sighed, though his "voice" was nothing more than conjury-twisted air, allowing him to speak if needed. It was smothered like a weakened hiss in the mountain breeze.

Word of his supposed death—or second so—had spread through the sages' guild and beyond. Yet their leaders still chose not to send folios out to scribe shops. And it had become too risky to search farther on guild's grounds. Beloved's whispered words and this sage were all he had left.

It would be so much more pleasing to just kill her.

She thought she knew so much. It was twice as galling that in part she was correct. She knew more than her confederates, though so little of the actual truth.

Sau'ilahk would make her efforts come to nothing, once she led him to what he wanted. He needed her to find the writings of Li'kän, Häs'saun, Volyno, and others of Beloved's "Children." Wynn Hygeorht was his one and only tool for finding a way to regain flesh. But why had she come here, to this temple?

And the first bell of day sounded.

Sau'ilahk could not face the dawn any more than other undead. He let go of awareness and began slipping into dormancy. He faded from the physical aspect of all Existence to the far edge of its spiritual side—to that thin place between life and death. As he sank into dormancy, into dream, he whispered only in thought . . .

My Beloved . . . bless me again . . . this time in truth.

He would hunt Wynn Hygeorht once more when the sun set. Time was the one thing Sau'ilahk possessed in endless quantity.

Chane jerked up his cloak's hood, not daring to glance eastward. Perhaps his clothing would shield him if the sun came too quickly, but he had never tested this outright. He peered up the steps rising to the temple.

The building's frontage emerged from the mountainside and twin granite columns carved like large tree trunks framed the landing's end. Even so, the structure hardly seemed large or deep enough to house these shirvêsh, as Wynn called them, be they monks, priests, or whatever tending some long-dead ancestor.

Wynn hurried upward with Shade, but Chane followed more slowly.

"Don't worry," Wynn assured him. "I'll have you inside in a moment."

The panicked edge in her voice was less than reassuring.

A heavy oblong arc of polished brass hung between the columns like a gateway. Suspended from the roof's front by intricate harnesses of leather, its open ends dangled a shin's length above the landing's floor. It was so tall he could have walked through and not touched its top with an upstretched hand.

Chane climbed closer and noticed its metal was formed from a hollowed tube and not a solid bar. Wynn grabbed a short brass rod from a bracket on one column as Chane looked through the strange gateway to the shadowed front doors.

The emblem of a tablet was carved into the white marble and would split down the middle when the doors opened. Harsh-stroked characters were chiseled inside the tablet's shape as if it held some ancient epitaph or edict. Or was it a warning?

Chane took the last step onto the landing's edge with sudden reluctance.

Was this a true holy place?

He had heard the tales—undead could not enter a sanctified space. There were many such superstitions concerning his kind. Some were true, such as sunlight, the essence of garlic, and fire. Others turned out to be false. He had uncovered a few of those in frightening, accidental ways.

"What's wrong?" Wynn asked.

She was watching him, as if aware he feared more than just the sun. How could he explain if she did not already know? He shook his head at her. With nowhere to hide, and no way to distinguish this truth, Chane stood trapped between sacred ground and the coming dawn.

"You are certain this is the place?" he rasped.

She didn't answer and instead struck the rod hard against the great brass arc..

Chane's whole body clenched as a baritone clang assaulted his ears. Wynn struck twice more, and the sound vibrated inside him, sharpening the prickling sting growing upon his skin. The tones rolled along the street like an orator booming for attention.

"Someone should be up," she said, but too much nervousness leaked into her voice.

The brass arc's tones died, and Chane was uncertain what to hope.

What would happen when—if—he stepped across the threshold? Would he burn as in fire; would that be what the sun did to him if he did not cross over? Or would he merely drop dead beyond the threshold like a corpse finally lifeless?

One door began to open without even the grating of metal hinges.

Wynn sighed audibly, and a solid, white-haired dwarf leaned out of the opening.

He studied the trio upon the landing, his face rather flat and wrinkled, like a half-dried grape. Wavy hair flowed down and broke over his wide shoulders, becoming one with his thick beard, though no mustache sprouted below his broad nose. He was dressed in brown breeches and typical heavy dwarven boots, his muslin shirt overlaid with a hip-long felt vestment of fiery burnt orange.

Not typical attire for any clergy that Chane had ever seen.

At the sight of Wynn's robe, the dwarf's eyes widened a little. Before he spoke, Wynn grabbed Chane's sleeve.

"May we enter?" she asked quickly.

At her anxious tone, the old dwarf stepped aside, raising an ushering hand toward the interior. Shade trotted ahead as Wynn pulled on Chane, but Chane jerked free at the last instant.

He would not have her touching him when . . . if something happened.

Wynn looked up, startled and frightened, cocking her head toward the door as she sidled through it. When he crept to the threshold, he forced his eyes to remain open but quickly lowered them, watching only his dragging feet until . . .

His left boot toe slid from the landing's granite onto a tiled mosaic floor.

Chane faltered. He stepped onward, waiting for . . . something, until a dull thump echoed all around. He stopped and looked up when the door closed. The first thing he saw was Shade sitting before him on the tile floor. She was watching him, her unnatural blue eyes slightly narrowed.

Shade could sense any undead but him. While he wore the arcane "ring of nothing," it blocked his nature and presence from all unnatural awareness beyond normal senses. Shade had no idea of his true nature, though she made her dislike plain enough.

She finally huffed and began padding about the entry room.

"What is the matter with you?" Wynn whispered, and Chane flinched.

He stood inside a temple, and nothing had happened to him.

"Thank you, Shirvêsh Mallet," Wynn said to the old dwarf. "We just arrived, and winter mornings are far too cold up here. It's so good to see you again."

The old dwarf—this shirvêsh—squinted. He had recognized her robe but not her. Eye-to-eye with short Wynn, he fixed upon her face. One bushy eyebrow crept upward until his eyes widened again.

"Little Apprentice Hygeorht?" he said in perfect Numanese.

"Of course! You remember me?"

"Remember?" The old one snorted.

Shirvêsh Mallet grabbed Wynn's shoulders in his bear-paw hands.

Chane was so shaken by entering unharmed that he was taken by surprise. The dwarf could have tossed her about like an empty robe. But she never even teetered as the shirvêsh leaned in and kissed her cheek.

"My hair may be white, but my mind has not turned to ash," he said. "And

I warrant it is sharper than yours . . . with your obsessive need to write everything down!"

Chane frowned, uncertain what the last comment meant.

Wynn cleared her throat, or perhaps choked down a giggle, as if the old one's words were a common welcome. She pulled a folded tan paper from her pocket and held it out.

"I'm a journeyor now, here on assignment. Domin High-Tower sent this for you."

The shirvêsh took the paper, unfolding it as Wynn gestured to Chane. "This young scholar is Chane Andraso."

"A bit of a tall, pale one," the dwarf muttered, not looking up from the letter. "Perhaps not from around here?"

"From the Farlands, on the eastern continent," Wynn quickly explained. "He'll be assisting my research. And that's Shade."

Shade's ears pricked at her name.

"Can you spare two rooms?" Wynn asked. "I don't know how long we're staying."

All this familiarity left Chane further out of place. One did not walk into a temple and request rooms for an indefinite period. Yet here he stood in a sacred place, not quite believing he did so. And Wynn carried on as if she and the old one had stumbled upon each other at some public house. It was too casual . . . too presumptive.

The shirvêsh finished the letter and folded it up.

"Yes, yes, you need not ask," he returned. "Any from the guild are welcome, and it is good to hear from Chlâyard . . . I mean High-Tower, as you would say . . . though that pup could have written more than once in a decade!"

Chane had seen High-Tower, and the elder domin was certainly no puppy. How old was this shirvêsh?

"Have you eaten?" Mallet asked. "We are preparing breakfast. By the Eternals, what drove you to our doors before dawn?"

The two prattled on as if sudden visitors requesting what amounted to charity were commonplace. Chane had been born into a minor noble family in a world where no one made unannounced visits. Since rising as a Noble Dead, he had paid or fought for the smallest comfort or refuge.

"I think we're too tired to eat," Wynn said, hefting her pack again. "Could we just join you for dinner? We've been traveling all night."

"By night?" The old dwarf blinked hard. "Now I am curious about such a rush along the bay road. And with a foreigner from . . . where did you say?"

"Belaski," Chane rasped.

Shirvêsh Mallet nodded, giving Chane's maimed voice no notice, and ushered Wynn onward.

"Let us be off, child, and find you rooms."

The two led the way toward the open arch across from the doors, and Chane's attention wandered around the surroundings.

From the outside, the building had looked as if it would barely accommodate the entryway. But beyond the next arch was so much more. The opening was likely positioned where the building's frontage met the mountainside. It revealed a wide corridor heading deeper into the mountain, into this . . . *temple*. Even thinking that word left Chane unsettled with every step across the entryway's mosaic floor.

Colored thumbnail tiles created the image of a stout, dark-haired, and bearded dwarf bearing a tall char-gray staff. He wore a burnt orange vestment, somewhat like the elder shirvêsh. In the image, the figure appeared to step straight toward Chane out of the floor along an open road leading away from a hazy violet mountain range in the background.

Chane raised his eyes and quickened his pace to catch Wynn and their host, already a good way down the corridor.

Other dwarves in burnt orange vestments, male and female, appeared now and then. All nodded, waved, or spoke in their own tongue, some yawning as if just roused. They went varied ways through side arches and heavy wide doors along the broad main corridor.

Chane had encountered few dwarves in Calm Seatt, a city so named to honor these stout people who had helped build its castles and major structures. He had not yet grown accustomed to the sight of them. His homeland's folklore spoke of such beings as diminutive creatures of the earth found only in wild and remote hidden places. In truth . . . well, the lore was so far off the truth.

Though shorter than humans, most dwarves looked Wynn straight in the eyes. What they lacked in height, they made up for in breadth. Chane had once seen a dwarf turn sideways to get through a shop door in Calm Seatt. It had been a tight fit.

He trailed Wynn and Mallet until the corridor met with a wide archway opening into a cavernous round chamber. Wynn stopped there, looking back for him, but Shade trotted straight in, sniffing about a bright floor of octagonal marble tiles.

"This is the temple proper of Bedzâ'kenge . . . 'Feather-Tongue,' " Wynn explained. "One of the Bäynæ."

Chane immediately halted, not nearing the opening. There was a reason he had made it across the outer threshold.

He could just make out the chamber's far wide and curved wall beyond the arch. Strange characters of harsh strokes, as in the door's tablet emblem, were carved in what he assumed was Dwarvish. The engravings were sparse and austere, arranged in spaced vertical columns.

On the road to the seatt, Wynn had told him of the dwarves' oral tradition. What little they wrote was "carved in stone," or sometimes metal, and only when the meaning innately deserved the implied permanence. Interaction with human culture had led to some use of paper, parchment, and other portable records, but old tradition remained dominant.

Chane noticed six engraved symbols over the chamber's entrance.

Each pattern was octagonal in shape, its tangled carved lines too complex for single letters. They looked similar to a few finely lined ones among the chamber's engravings.

"*Chuoynaksâg Vîônag Skíal . . . Skíalâg Vîônag Chuoynaks,*" Wynn uttered.

Chane's gaze dropped to her slightly smiling face.

" 'Remember What's Worthy of the Telling; Tell What Is Worthy of the Remembering,' " she added, and then glanced at Mallet. "Yes?"

The old dwarf pursed his lips, trying not to laugh, but chuckled out, "Close enough . . . though it is better in my tongue."

Wynn rolled her eyes and waved Chane forward. Reluctantly, he drew closer, gazing past her to where Shade padded around the chamber's most prominent feature. On a round platform at dead center stood a gargantuan stone statue, perhaps two or more stories tall.

A dwarf, with a full beard and flowing hair framing serene features, had his eyes open in fiery joy. He appeared to look into the distance, but his lips were slightly parted, as if he were about to make some proclamation of import. In one hand he gripped a long staff, taller than himself, which appeared made of solid iron. His other hand was outstretched, palm upward, as if offering something—but that hand was empty.

It was the same figure as in the entryway's mosaic floor.

Once again, every muscle in Chane's body tightened. Perhaps he had not yet entered a sacred space.

Wynn and the shirvêsh raised their hands in unison, with palms pressed together. They touched fingertips briefly to their foreheads, then their lips, and finally opened their hands, palms up like the statue. When they spoke, Shirvêsh Mallet uttered Dwarvish, though Wynn echoed him in Numanese. Their voices resounded, far less like a prayer, and more like orators beginning a tale, loud and clear for all to hear.

"Thanks be to Bedzâ'kenge, poet eternal among the Bäynæ. . . . Thanks be to Bedzâ'kenge, preserver and teacher of heritage, virtue, and wisdom."

Chane did not follow their example—neither of them noticed; then his vision flickered.

His arms felt heavy and his legs weighted. Weariness surged over him like a sudden illness. Normally he would be in dormancy by now—and was the wide chamber growing brighter around that towering statue?

Only two oil lanterns hung from iron hooks on the chamber's walls, yet there was far too much illumination for those. The statue appeared to brighten amid a widening fuzzy pool of light.

A tingling sting grew on Chane's skin. He inched carefully closer, peering into the chamber's heights.

Shield-size polished metal disks hung in the chamber's upper reaches amid complicated clusters of interlaced iron half hoops. Attached cables ran from these through rings in the ceiling and the side walls. They came down to be tied off at waist height upon ornate iron fixtures.

Chane lurched back, much to the puzzled glance of Shirvêsh Mallet.

The temple chamber was filling with *sunlight*. Those cables adjusted the angle of the high polished panels. Somewhere above, light entered from the outside to be reflected into the temple's interior.

"Wynn . . . ?" he rasped anxiously.

She glanced into the chamber's growing glow, and her happy expression melted in alarm.

"Are the rooms far?" she asked Mallet. "I'm sorry to be poor guests, but we're ready to drop."

"Of course," answered the old dwarf, puzzlement on his wrinkled face softening with sympathy. "This way."

He led them into a side passage that curved around the temple chamber. Twice they passed openings into that sunlit space.

Chane kept to the way's outer wall, as far as he could from that light. They finally veered away down an intersecting wider corridor illuminated only by sparsely placed oil lanterns. Chane's steps became more sluggish.

They met no one along the way, and the shirvêsh turned down another narrow passage lined with stout oak doors. He finally halted and opened one, ushering Chane inside, then pushed open another across the hall for Wynn.

"Find me in the meal hall at Day-Winter's end," he instructed, and then grinned with large yellowed teeth. "High-Tower's letter did not speak of your pending research. I am anxious to hear what you seek."

Wynn nodded tiredly, and the shirvêsh headed back the way he had brought them.

Chane stumbled into a sparsely furnished room containing a very wide and low bed with no foot- or headboards.

"Don't worry about joining us for dinner," Wynn mumbled tiredly from the door. "Rest—I'll come for you later."

Chane nodded as she closed the door.

Dropping his two packs, he unbuckled his sword and leaned it against them. He carefully laid his cloak over the room's single stool, made from a whole round of a tree trunk. The ancient scroll he had taken from the icebound castle's library was still stored in its inner pocket. But he left it there and stumbled toward the bed. One strange object stopped him.

A large iron vessel, like a shallow, wide bowl on legs with a domed lid, rested atop a short stone pedestal. The lid's handle was insulated by a wood fitting, and slots around the lid's top let dim orange light escape.

Chane lifted the lid, its handle warm even through the wood, and the light erupted into the room.

A smattering of thumb-size glowing crystals rested inside the basin in a bed of steaming sand. Unlike the sages' cold lamp crystals, these looked raw and rough, as if taken straight from the earth, and gave off heat as well as low light.

Chane was too near collapse to puzzle over small wonders in a strange new culture. He lowered the lid and fell across the bed. The jarring impact made his eyes pop for an instant. The mattress was as stiff and hard as bare ground beneath a blanket. Wide as it was, the bed was too short. Still, he closed his eyes, drawing his feet up to lie curled sideways. The last thing that came to him before he sank into full dormancy was nagging hunger.

Like a beast with hands, chained in the dark, it whined and rumbled inside of Chane.

Wynn would not stand for his killing a sentient being in order to survive, and he would not risk doing anything that might cause her to send him away. Yet how else was he to feed in this place, under these new circumstances?

Dormancy smothered hunger and the rumbling discontent of the beast within him.

CHAPTER 2

Wynn awoke in late afternoon with a stiff neck and aches, remembering they were in the temple. She hadn't slept on a dwarven bed in many years. Its mattress was little more than layered wool blankets upon a stone platform. The design might be comfortable support for a heavy dwarven physique, but it was hard as packed dirt to anyone else.

Shade stirred on the bed's end and hopped off as Wynn sat up, rubbing her throbbing shoulder. A pewter water pitcher and plain ceramic cup rested on the stone table near the door, and she realized her throat was dry.

"Thirsty?" she asked Shade.

She got up and filled the cup for Shade, taking a sip for herself straight from the pitcher. She was glad to be away from the guild, her superiors, and other sages, though that thought brought regret. Answerable to no one but her chosen companions, she was journeying once more.

As a girl, she'd loved life at the guild. Then she'd traveled with Domin Tilswith and others across the continent and the eastern ocean to what the sages called the Farlands. Their purpose had been the beginning of a new guild branch. But in Bela, the coastal capital of Chane's homeland, Wynn's life became entangled with two rough strangers and a dog.

Magiere, Leesil, and Chap had come hunting an *upír*—vampire—one of the highest of the undead they called *Vneshené Zomrelé*—the Noble Dead. When this trio finally left, in search of an artifact sought by a vampire named Welstiel, Domin Tilswith had sent Wynn along on her first solo assignment—and not a typical one for a freshly titled journeyor sage.

Their travels took them through Droevinka's dank lands, Stravina's foothills, and into the Warlands, then on to the Elven Territories of the an'Cróan.

The journey ended far south from where they started, in the high frozen range of the Pock Peaks. There they finally uncovered the artifact—the "orb"—and the ancient texts Wynn had brought back to her guild.

But when she got home to Calm Seatt, nothing turned out as she'd expected. Nobody believed her stories of dhampirs, undead, and necromancers guarded by ghosts. Her superiors took over the texts and ordered her into silence, and "Witless" Wynn Hygeorht became the shunned madwoman of her cherished guild branch.

Then, less than half a moon past, four sages had been murdered in Calm Seatt, drained of life by what she labeled a "wraith." This previously unknown spiritual form of Noble Dead had been hunting translations from the texts penned by vampires who'd long ago served the Ancient Enemy of many names. And this enemy once used hordes of the undead like weapons in battle against the humans, dwarves, and elves.

In Wynn's journeys, she'd been exposed to fearful portents that this enemy might be returning. The appearance of the wraith, more terrifying and powerful than any vampire known, had driven her into her current search. She had to learn more of the history lost a thousand years ago, what signs to look for should war come again . . . or how to stop it from happening at all.

She had to find the texts, for there must be something in them. She had to believe this, for she had nothing else in which to place her hope.

Wynn donned her gray robe over her shift, and then stroked Shade's head.

"At least finding supper will be easy," she whispered.

By answer, Shade whined, and Wynn's head filled with sudden sights and sounds of a bustling city street. She knelt beside the dog, though Shade was much more than that in both breed and heritage.

Shade's father, Chap, had once been one with what the sages called the Fay, eternal spirits or beings behind all of Existence. He'd chosen to be "born" into the body of a majay-hì, one of the elven dogs descended from Fay-inhabited wolves during ancient times. His dual-layered nature, Fay spirit in Fay-descended body, gave him the ability to see rising memories in anyone within his sight line. He'd met Shade's mother, a true majay-hì whom Wynn had named Lily, during the journey through the Farlands' Elven Territories. Majay-hì communicated via memories transmitted while touching. Wynn called it "memory-speak."

Shade had inherited a mix of her kind's memory-speak and her father's memory-play, though not his ability to "speak" with Wynn via thought. Shade had her own twist on her father's gifts. Not only could she dip rising memories, she could send her own to Wynn when they touched. To Wynn's knowledge, no other majay-hì and human could do this.

Memories of city life called up by Shade made Wynn want to offer comfort to her young companion.

"I know . . . you don't like crowded places," she said gently, "but our search begins here."

Rising, she spotted her pack and leaning behind it by the door was the staff, its long sun crystal hidden beneath a protective leather sheath.

She fumbled in her pocket, making certain the protective spectacles made by Domin il'Sänke were still there. These pewter-rimmed glasses were essential once the staff's blinding sun crystal was ignited. The lenses would darken, protecting her eyes but allowing her to see.

Reticent to leave her other belongings, she almost opened the pack to check its contents, but her things were safe here.

Wynn stepped toward the door—one step only—and stopped.

The staff's sun crystal was irreplaceable, her only weapon against the Noble Dead. But carrying it about in the temple would only draw questions. Wynn forced herself out into the corridor, leaving the staff behind, and held the door until Shade followed.

Chane's door was still closed, and he would "sleep" until sunset, so she didn't disturb him. He and his belongings would also be left in peace, and Chane carried another of their most important possessions within his cloak's inner pocket.

As he'd left the library where she'd found the texts, he stumbled upon an old tarnished case containing a scroll. It was the very one that Li'kän, one of the oldest vampires to walk the world, had tried to make Wynn read. More baffling was that Wynn wouldn't have been able to read it at all.

The scroll had been painted over with black ink.

When Chane had later caught up with her in Calm Seatt, she'd glimpsed bits of the scroll's content with her mantic sight. A long passage of verse in obscure metaphors had been recorded in the fluids of an undead, written in an old dialect of Sumanese. She'd managed a partial and flawed translation of glimpsed fragments that told them nothing at first. But she and Chane both suspected the scroll was linked to whatever the wraith had sought.

And why would an ancient Noble Dead write something in its own fluids and then cover the words with ink? Why not just destroy it, if in afterthought, the content should not be read? And why had Li'kän wanted Wynn to see it?

Turning down the corridor, Wynn pushed aside such questions and forced herself back to the task at hand. Her present peace suddenly felt unnatural, even wrong, amid trying to locate the confiscated texts. And she had very little to go on, only one word overheard in Domin High-Tower's study. . . .

Hassäg'kreigi . . . the Stonewalkers.

Two black-clad warrior dwarves had visited the dwarven sage in secret. One, the younger, had called him "brother." By the conversation, both visitors belonged to this unknown group. If she could learn of them, perhaps find this brother through High-Tower's family, she might find a clue to where the texts were hidden. For as much as the wraith had killed for folios of translation work, and had been able to pass through walls at will, why hadn't it simply gone after the original texts? The answer was obvious.

The texts weren't stored on guild grounds.

Apparently, they were always available for a day's work by the chosen few and then removed each night. And two black-clad dwarves had appeared in High-Tower's study, but no one had seen how they came or went. Stonewalkers—that one word—was all Wynn had to work with, and in a dwarven seatt her scholarly training in research was nearly useless.

Dwarven tribes, clans, and families possessed few documents of personal or group value. For the most part, they relied upon their orators—poets, troubadours, keepers of history and tradition—and memory of things deemed worthy to preserve. She would have to practice new methods of seeking.

Wynn found the curving passage around the temple proper, pausing as she reached its outer main arch. The wide and round chamber within was still aglow, sunlight transferred in by the polished steel mirrors in its heights. She craned her head back, staring up at the giant statue with one hand reaching out, palm up in an offering . . . of what?

Domin Tilswith once told her that Bedzâ'kenge—Feather-Tongue—was the closest thing to a saint of sages the world would ever know. A nice notion, though she wasn't certain how it mattered. Sages were people of reason, not faith.

Shade rumbled, and Wynn found the dog staring the other way.

"Ah, Mallet mentioned we had visitors."

Wynn spun about, coming face-to-face with a female dwarf in an orange vestment.

"Oh . . . *banê*," Wynn greeted her. "Could you direct me to the meal hall? I'm supposed to meet him for supper."

Wynn had read some ludicrous Stravinan folklore in the Farlands. Dwarves—by other terms—were described as gnarly earth dwellers. Some tales claimed it was impossible to tell a female from a male because both wore beards.

What nonsense!

The female shirvêsh looked her up and down, and cocked her head at the sight of a "wolf" standing guard before a small human. She had long, shiny black hair draped down over her vestment's shoulders. Some might not care for the stout structure and wide features of a dwarven woman, but to Wynn's mind this one was perfectly alluring. A bit stern and severe-looking, until her expression broke with a wide grin.

"Follow me," the shirvêsh said. "I am headed there myself."

Wynn fell into step. Only a little way to the front doors they turned into a left-side passage. Loud, cheerful voices booming in Dwarvish echoed off the walls. Before Wynn even stepped inside a long hall, she smelled the aroma of mushrooms sautéed in herbs and butter.

Six shirvêsh were gathered at the nearest table, boisterously filling mugs and chattering away. Two more long tables with wooden benches filled the room on either side, and the one on the right, near a another archway, was laden with platters of mushrooms, spiced lumpy goat cheese, boiled root vegetables, and a little stewed venison.

Wynn realized how hungry she was just as she glanced down to find Shade salivating.

"Young Hygeorht!"

Shirvêsh Mallet rose from a stool at the food table's far end and waved her over. His white beard spread with his smile of welcome, and Wynn hurried toward him, pausing at the late-afternoon repast.

"This all smells wonderful," she said, ladling mushrooms into a wooden bowl and preparing another with venison for Shade.

"Where is your young man?" Mallet asked.

"He is *not* my . . . He is still sleeping. I didn't wish to wake him yet."

The shirvêsh grunted as he settled and lifted a small pitcher. Before Wynn could intervene, he poured some steaming brown liquid into a mug, sliding it over as she sat down. She peered hesitantly into the mug, smelling its vapor, and found that it was only heated broth.

"Thank you," she breathed in relief.

At the guild, most sages sipped wine only on special occasions, and tea was Wynn's normal preference. Dwarves often drank beer or ale, sometimes heated, in place of water. They weren't nearly as affected by alcohol as humans and even drank distilled spirits from wood—a beverage deadly to other races. Mallet's gesture was most considerate.

Wynn barely got Shade's bowl on the floor before the dog began snapping up the venison.

The shirvêsh swallowed a mouthful of mushrooms and washed it down with foaming ale.

"Tell me of your project," he asked. "What are you seeking to scribble in your journals?"

Wynn tried not to grimace. She was well acquainted with dwarven opinion of humans always writing everything down. It was common for dwarves to live two hundred years. But in addition, they found sages to be "funny little people" who spent their short lives hoarding tidbits of information, regardless of any practical purpose these served. To a dwarf, gathering more knowledge than one could remember, let alone use, seemed a waste of years. Better to pursue personal excellence or the enrichment of daily life and one's culture.

But for three nights Wynn had been contemplating exactly what she would say in this moment. She had to depend upon dwarven bias to make the old shirvêsh believe her.

"It's a delicate matter," she began, and leaning closer, she lowered her voice. "Our guild's Sumanese branch recently completed biographies of all their domins for their archives. They felt such records would be beneficial examples to future sages. The premin council of our branch decided to follow suit . . .

but it's not seemly for domins to write their own accounts. I've been assigned to research and write the biography of Domin High-Tower."

Shirvêsh Mallet stopped chewing and stared at her. With a great gulp, he appeared to make great effort not to smirk at the absurdity of such a task.

"And so, you have come here," he said with forced seriousness, "where Chlâyard sought his first calling."

It took a moment for realization to set in. Wynn sat dumbstruck and then cleared her own throat.

"Chlâyard—I mean Domin High-Tower—was here . . . to become a shirvêsh to Bedzâ'kenge?"

Mallet's brow furrowed in puzzlement. "Is that not why you came, to seek the tale of his life?"

Recovering quickly, Wynn nodded. "Yes, but journeyors assigned to this project were given no information and simply sent off. The biographies must be unbiased and come from a variety of sources. We are to seek the stories ourselves."

"*A'ye!*" Mallet barked, slapping his hand firmly on the table. "That, at least, was a wise decision!"

Wynn's guilt welled over lying so easily. More bad skills learned in Leesil's company, no doubt, but she had to continue the ruse.

"I didn't know High-Tower sought to become a shirvêsh."

High-Tower was a private individual. He would be mortified at such information landing upon Wynn's ears.

"He was my acolyte for only a short time," Mallet replied. "But I can introduce you to a few who knew him better. We were all stunned by his decision to . . . to become a scribbler of words."

Again, Wynn ignored the slight.

"I prefer to start with his earlier life," she corrected. "Can you direct me to his family?"

At this, Mallet straightened on his stool as if thinking carefully.

Wynn grew worried that she'd asked the wrong thing but had no idea why it was wrong. Had she made Mallet suspicious?

He looked her straight in the eyes. "I do not know an exact location and can only point the way. He hails from the Yêarclág—the Iron-Braids, in your tongue. A small family, and the last I knew, they lived in Chemarré . . . in its underside."

Wynn faltered once more. "Underground?"

Shirvêsh Mallet didn't answer.

Chemarré, or "Sea-Side," was one of the seatt's four main settlements, situated on the mountain's far side facing the open ocean and the Isle of Wrêdelîd. "Underside" was a polite reference for those living in the deepest—poorest—levels below the surface.

"Go back to the Cheku'ûn market and take the tram to Chemarré," Mallet instructed. "I do not know that settlement's underways, but someone at the Chemarré way station can start you off."

His tone had changed, as if speaking of something embarrassing, but Wynn wasn't finished.

"Shirvêsh, while I'm here, I wanted to conduct research for the guild's archives on the Stonewalkers. So little is . . . known of . . ."

Wynn trailed off as Mallet's eyes stopped blinking. His black pupils looked like hard pinpoints.

"Young Hygeorht . . ." he began, voice lowered, "your guild has ferreted out more than I realized . . . or did High-Tower mention this to you? How do *you* know of the Hassäg'kreigi?"

"I've heard the term only a couple of times," Wynn replied. "I know little other than they are a sacred sect among your people."

"Little more is known by my own people," he countered, but the way he spoke implied that he knew more.

Mallet sighed through his nose, plainly resigned to an annoyance he couldn't politely escape. This chat clearly covered much different ground than he'd expected.

"The Stonewalkers, as you call them, are guardians of our most honored dead." He paused, either for emphasis or to weigh his words. "Only Thänæ, who wear the thôrhk around their necks, so marked for their great achievements, are tended by the Stonewalkers. When a thänæ dies . . . and is to pass into earth . . . Stonewalkers may come to take him or her to the underworld. In their care, a thänæ of the greatest renown might one far day become known to the people as one of the Bäynæ—what you call our Eternals—and an ancestor to all of us, like our blessed Bedzâ'kenge."

Wynn's fascination didn't stop her from blurting out the obvious questions.

"This 'underworld,' where the Stonewalkers live . . . this is a real place? Where can I find it?"

Mallet rolled his eyes and rose, and this time his sigh *was* disapproving.

"That is not a question to be asked, let alone answered . . . or recorded!" His tone softened as he patted her shoulder like an indulgent grandfather. "What I have told you is all you need to know. Now, finish your supper, perhaps walk that beast of yours—outside, please! Then focus on your biography of High-Tower. Only the Eternals know if something useful will come of it."

Wynn knew that in his kindness, Mallet had no idea how condescending he could be. She'd pushed the limits of good judgment with her questions, but who knew when she would be granted his undivided attention again? She rose, halting him before he left.

"Shirvêsh, forgive me, but one more question. In all your remembered tales, do you recall anything of a place called Bäalâle Seatt . . . and someone named Thallûhearag who—"

A rushing pallor flooded Mallet's wrinkled features, and Wynn stiffened in silence.

He looked as if her words had struck him ill. Revulsion spread across his broad face. A long moment followed before his calm finally returned. Wynn grew frightened under his silent scrutiny.

Mallet glanced sidelong over his shoulder, but none of the other shirvêsh had looked up. Either they hadn't heard or they didn't know what Wynn spoke of. Mallet turned on her, leaning into her face as he whispered through clenched teeth, "Where did you hear that *title*?"

It was so sharp and abrupt that she flinched as she struggled for an answer. She could think of only one.

"Domin High-Tower must have mentioned it to me."

Mallet settled back.

"I am disappointed in my former acolyte," he said. "No one, especially one so young as you, should be told of such a *thing* . . . let alone seek it out! It is all but dead in my people's memories, and lives on in fewer by the years . . . I will not resurrect it!"

The meal hall had grown too quiet.

Barely a murmur passed among the others at the far table. Wynn found herself the object of blank and puzzled stares. She was an outsider who'd given some serious offense.

"Thank you for the meal," she said quietly. "I should check on Chane."

Wynn backed away under Mallet's intense scrutiny, passing her hand over Shade's head to bring the dog along.

"We'll head to the station tonight," she added, "and take the tram to Sea-Side, as you suggested. We might not return for a couple of days."

"You are always welcome," Mallet answered calmly.

But as Wynn hurried toward the main corridor, she grew obsessed with his reaction. Mallet had said nothing of Bäalâle Seatt, and she wasn't about to ask him again anytime soon. But as to Thallûhearag . . .

Mallet had called that a *title*, not a name—and a *thing* not to be remembered. That was a serious condemnation for an oral culture, where loved and honored ones lived on in remembered stories. Why was he so repulsed at the mention? He even wished to deny its immortality in memory . . . yet whatever, whoever, it was had been given a title, raising it above the common.

It was all very confusing, and try as Wynn might—and she'd done so before—she couldn't decipher the term. Perhaps it was some older form of Dwarvish, one of the most changeable languages known to her guild. As Wynn rounded the temple chamber, her thoughts drifted to Chane.

She and Shade weren't the only ones who needed sustenance. Chane's "food" wasn't pleasant to consider, but she couldn't just let him go hungry. It was unkind, if not dangerous. Wynn looked down, uncertain how much to share with Shade.

Wynn spun about and hurried to the front marble doors.

"Come, Shade. We have an errand to run before dusk."

Chane opened his eyes to a dim glow escaping through slits in the iron pot's lid. A moment's disorientation passed, and as he sat up, the previous night came back to him. He was in a room in the temple of a dwarven "Eternal," and he had fallen dormant while still dressed, creasing and rumpling his clothing.

Rising, he tried to brush out his attire. Without even thinking, he went to check his cloak's inner pocket.

The old scroll case was still there. This action had become a nervous habit.

Deciphering the scroll's mystery was what had brought him to Wynn. It had given him a justifiable reason to seek her out. Losing it would be like losing any chance to stay within her world, aside from the puzzle it held.

His other worldly possessions sat on the floor where he had dropped them, including his cloak and sword. Both packs were lightly stained from a night two years ago when he and Welstiel had abandoned a sinking ship and swum for shore. His own pack contained mainly personal items but also a small collection of texts and parchments acquired from a monastery of healers. They too were water damaged, though he had wrapped them carefully before jumping overboard.

Wynn had not seen these. Considering what Welstiel had done to the monks who had first possessed them, Chane was uncertain whether he would ever show them to her. But it had seemed wrong to abandon them in high, barren mountains.

Most of the works were written in old Stravinan, which he could read somewhat. One often stuck in his mind. It was the thinnest one, an accordion-style volume of thick parchment folded back and forth four times between grayed leather cover plates. The title read, *The Seven Leaves of*. . . something. The final word was obscured by age and wear.

Though Chane had taken these texts from others, he saw himself as their keeper now. There was no one else left to care for them. This sentiment did not carry to the second pack's contents, which had once belonged to Welstiel.

Chane had stolen it the night in the ice-bound castle when he had betrayed Welstiel to Magiere. He crouched to flip open its canvas flap and look inside. The pack contained an array of arcane and perhaps mundane creations. Though technically they were now his, Chane never stopped thinking of those items as belonging to his old companion. Perhaps he never would.

Hunger flushed through him, and he began digging into Welstiel's pack. Aside from two arcane journals, with scant Numanese writings scattered amid pages of indecipherable symbols and diagrams, there were odd objects and boxes.

Chane eyed three unmarked rods, each a forearm's length and as thick as his thumb. One was red brass or copper, the second gray like pewter but harder, and the last looked obsidian, though it clinked like metal. Lying against them was a thick, polished steel hoop the diameter of a plate, with hair-thin etchings that smelled of char.

Two boxes lay in the pack's bottom.

He ignored the long and shallow one bound in black leather and wrapped in indigo felt. Instead, he pulled out the other walnut box. Inside of it, resting in burgundy padding, were three hand-length iron rods with center loops, a teacup-size brass bowl, and a stout bottle of white ceramic with an obsidian stopper.

Chane had partially fathomed the steel hoop, but he had not learned its full power. Welstiel had been able to pick it up while it was still searing hot, and Chane could not. He understood the brass cup as well, though he could not use it. Welstiel used it to drain and trap a mortal's life energy in thrice-purified water from the ceramic bottle. This had allowed him to go for long periods without feeding otherwise.

Chane had drunk that burning, bitter fluid more than once. The draft was revolting, devoid of the hunt's joy and feeding's euphoria. But as he was Wynn's companion among the living, feeding had greater risks. Foremost that she would learn how he continued to survive—to exist.

So far, the cup's actual usage remained unfathomable. But his intellect and knowledge of minor conjury made him long to learn the secrets of Welstiel's creations, including that filthy little cup. If he could feed only once per moon, it would be one less obstacle to remaining at Wynn's side. But he would still have to keep such an act from her awareness, for the victim still died in the process.

A knock sounded at the door.

"Are you awake?" Wynn called from the other side.

"One moment," Chane rasped loudly.

He hurriedly returned the cup's box to Welstiel's pack, went to open the door, and then froze.

Wynn carried a glazed clay urn. She looked visibly queasy, a thin sweat leaving a sheen on her face.

"Are you ill?" he asked.

When she did not answer, his gaze dropped to the urn. A familiar scent began to reach his nostrils.

"What is that?" he asked.

Wynn swallowed audibly and pushed past him into his room. Before Shade could follow, she kicked the door, slamming it shut. Shade began barking and scratching outside, but Wynn ignored her.

"It is . . . is . . ." But she never quite finished, and Chane already caught the coppery, salty scent.

"Blood?" he whispered.

"Goat's blood," she blurted out, nearly squeaking. "I went to a butcher . . . so it's . . . it's fresh."

Wynn swallowed again, or rather gagged. Chane quickly snatched the urn out of her grip, horrified at what she had done.

"I told the butcher it was for . . . blood sausage," she whispered, then wiped her mouth with the back of her hand. "I'll come back in a while," she mumbled. "I have things to gather before we set out tonight."

She quickly turned for the door and slipped out. Shade finally ceased barking.

Chane just stared at the urn.

Wynn must have realized his hunger had grown each night of their journey here, though he thought he had kept that much from her. He had come as her protector—or that was what they both professed. In truth, he would have sworn anything to remain close to her. Now she had requested—perhaps watched—a goat be slaughtered, so she could purchase its blood as fresh as possible.

It had sickened her, and worse . . . it was a wasted effort.

Blood was sweet and salty all at once, but it was not what fed him. Blood was good, but only for what laced it as it rushed from a thrashing victim's flesh in the last moments.

It was only a medium of transference.

Chane had learned this too from Welstiel, another truth of the Noble Dead: Bloodletting was a method by which a victim's life was released furiously enough to be consumed by a vampire's inner hunger and close proximity. Aside from Welstiel's cup, there was only one source of this to sustain Chane—the living.

This blood was as dead as the goat it had come from.

The urn grew heavy in Chane's hands. Wynn's naïve sacrifice, her attempt to "feed" him, left him only humiliated. He never felt self-loathing, but it now stretched between his need for her and what his true nature desired.

He could never tell her why her effort was useless. Better to let her think she had helped and be certain she never did so again. He would see to his own needs.

Chane placed the urn beyond the bed, out of sight, and left his room. He found Wynn's door across the way cracked open. Her back was turned as she checked her belongings.

"Best pack up," she whispered.

Only Shade watched him steadily from where she lay curled upon the bed.

"Where are we going?" Chane asked.

"Through the mountain."

CHAPTER 3

Wynn trudged by tall pylons. Large raw crystals steamed in the night, casting pools of fuzzy orange radiance upon the street. She was silent the whole way, not saying a word to either Chane or Shade. As she approached Cheku'ûn "Bay-Side" way station, a cluster of fishmongers with emptied carts boarded the cargo lift headed back down the mountain. But that wasn't the way she was taking.

Her thoughts churned over Mallet's vague directions for finding the Iron-Braids. She'd always pictured Domin High-Tower coming from a family of rank, perhaps even with an elder clan relation in the conclave of the five tribes. Why had she imagined this—because of his pride, his arrogant demeanor? But High-Tower's closest kin lived "underside," well beneath the settlement's surface community, or even its upper tunnels and halls. Wynn knew so little of her old teacher.

She quickened her pace.

Just behind the way station, she saw the cavernous archway in the mountainside. A dull glow flooded from that place over the round crank house's backside along with a thrumming murmur, like a massive furnace mouth yawning in the dark.

"That's the main entrance to Bay-Side's underground," she said.

Chane walked close on her right, but Shade trotted a little ahead, as if knowing where they headed.

"Have you been inside before?" he asked.

"No, but Domin Tilswith told me about the trams. They're the quickest way between settlements, besides the lifts to the mountaintop and Seattâsh—Old-Seatt. But we're going all the way through the mountain to reach Chemarré . . . Sea-Side."

Chane stopped, forcing Wynn to pause.

"Even in a straight line, that will take days . . . nights," he replied, watching the mountain's glowing maw.

"No," she countered, and patted her leg to call Shade back. "We'll make Sea-Side before dawn."

Chane glanced doubtfully at her. "It is fifteen, maybe twenty leagues away. Nothing moves that fast."

Wynn wasn't sure how to answer. All she had were Domin Tilswith's brief descriptions, and his assurance that dwarven trams were the fastest way from one settlement to another.

"You'll see," she said. "It would take longer to stand in the cold and explain."

An exaggeration, but she'd never actually seen the trams for herself.

Shade fidgeted in the street, ducking sideways whenever someone passed too near or cast a suspicious glance at a tall black wolf standing with two humans.

"Come on," Wynn said. "I'm guessing scheduled departures will be fewer after dusk."

Chane sighed, casting a sour glance at the cargo lift. Now full of fishmongers and others with late cargo, it rolled over the landing's lip, out of sight, and down the mountain. Wynn grabbed his sleeve and tugged him onward. But when they rounded the great frame stones of the mountain's mouth, Wynn's jaw went slack at the spectacle.

A thinned forest of sculpted columns the size of small keep towers rose to the high domed roof of this smooth, chiseled cavern. The chaos of vendors, hawkers, peddlers, and travelers filled the open spaces. All forms of goods were being traded at carts and stalls and even makeshift tents. Everything from meat pies and tea to small casks of dwarven ale and honey-coated nuts were bartered for by dwarves on their way home for the night.

In the avenues between the columns, more large glowing crystals steamed atop stone pylons, as in the streets outside. Smoke from portable braziers and steam escaping around crystals filled the great cavern with a hazy orange-yellow glow.

"Oh . . . my," Wynn whispered.

Chane turned a full circle as Wynn recovered from shock. She cast about, trying to figure out which way to go.

Standing near the entrance's side, she couldn't see clearly through so many people, columns, and pylons. She did spot the tops of four large tunnel archways around the cavern's back, heading deeper into the mountain. But which one did they need?

The back of her right knee buckled as something shoved hard against it.

Wynn found Shade cowering behind her and put a hand on the dog's head, passing memories of their quiet times in privacy, but she still felt Shade's panicked rumbling.

"This is madness," Chane rasped. "Which way do we go?"

Wynn followed his gaze into the cavern's heights and was immediately daunted again.

More tunnel openings filled the dome walls above, though these were smaller than those at floor level. And there were more people as well. Stone walkways the size of narrow roads passed between arch-supported platforms surrounding any column's upper reaches. Those paths eventually ended in more tunnel mouths at varied levels up the cavern's walls. Carters and peddlers as well as others hurried along the high paths amid large steaming crystals mounted in iron brackets upon the columns.

So many voices, footfalls, and hawkers' calls amplified off the cavern's stone. In the rumbling din, Wynn's head felt like a beehive had been dropped into her skull.

The whole place was like every open market in Calm Seatt packed into one giant hole in the mountain. There were too many choices, far more than she'd imagined.

"Not above," she finally got out. "The trams have to be easily reached by cargo coming up the mountain."

Wynn looked about for loaded wagons or carts that might point the way, but she saw none. Then she glanced back toward the way station outside. That was due east, and Sea-Side was roughly west by southwest. She rose on tiptoes, scanning about. One major tunnel seemed headed in the right direction. Shrugging her pack higher, she gripped her staff and Shade's scruff and pushed through the crowd.

"*Prunnaghviâh!*" a gruff voice called above the noise. "*Prunnaghviâh chûnré!*"

Someone was offering venison sausage for barter, and Wynn thought of Chap's taste for greasy foods. Shade suddenly lurched, pulling Wynn off course.

"Whoa!" she cried. "Shade, stop . . . Shade!"

Wynn stumbled in a rush as Shade's nose bobbed through the crowd. They broke into an open space with a cart-rack of smoke-cured meats and dangling sausages. Behind it stood an old male dwarf in a lopsided leather cap, and Wynn jerked Shade back with a groan.

Shade's anxiety was overcome by her nose and stomach, just like her father. But it brought Wynn to her senses and the obvious remedy to their predicament.

"Stay here," she told Chane.

"Why?"

"I'll ask directions." And she passed her hand over Shade's head.

Wynn sent a quick memory of when she'd made Shade sit and wait while loading baggage during their bayshore journey. Then she hurried for the meat vendor.

"Which way to the tram . . . to Sea-Side?" she asked in a rush.

The dwarf started. He pushed back the leather cap on his half-balding head and frowned just a little. Wynn regained her manners. Information was bartered just like goods among the dwarves, but there were ways around the complication.

"How much for a small sausage link?" she asked.

"What you trade?" he returned in broken Numanese.

Wynn hesitated. Dwarves didn't use coins like humans. They gauged them by the metal's bulk value, preferring more useful ones like copper and iron, or even steel. None of these were used for coins in human cultures, but dwarves sometimes took such from nearby cultures, especially Malourné, to be used in commerce with humans.

Wynn had nothing to trade and fished out her coin pouch, offering up a silver penny.

The vendor groaned as if it were a burden.

"I just arrived," she explained. "It's all I have . . . and I offer it in whole."

At that the dwarf chuckled.

"Too much," he replied, and bent over.

Hefting a loop of braided lanyard strung with punched disks of steel, copper, and a few of brass, he untied it. He sorted out two larger copper disks and traded these for the penny.

Wynn had no idea what they were worth.

The vendor handed over a sausage couched in a brown oak leaf made supple with some kind of oil. He pointed to the very tunnel she'd headed for.

"All ways to all seatt places," he said. "Stay right when branch come."

"*Vuoyseag!*" she uttered in thanks, and rushed back to Chane. "Come on; I know the way."

While she wasn't looking, Shade snapped the sausage out of her hand, leaf and all.

"My fingers!" she yelped. "You little . . . You will not turn into some pig like your father, I warn you."

The sausage was gone. Shade lolled her tongue, trying to spit out the shredded leaf.

Chane pulled the pack off Wynn's shoulder before she could stop him. He bundled it under his arm, slinging his own pair over one shoulder.

"Lead," he said, "and take us out of here."

Wynn grabbed Shade's scruff and pushed toward the second tunnel from the left.

Sau'ilahk rose from dormancy, his slowly returning awareness filling with one clear memory.

He could "awaken" to any place distinctly remembered, and he fixed upon the shadowed space with the fir tree beyond the temple of Bedzâ'kenge. He was instantly startled by sight of Wynn and her companions heading across the street and down wide steps. But he clearly heard her use the words "way station."

Sau'ilahk sank briefly into dormancy, focusing upon another clear memory.

This time he materialized inside a poorly lit alcove of one access tunnel into Cheku'ûn's great market cavern. He had been here before in his searches. Other quarry had passed this way, ones he had followed over the years, decades . . . centuries. . . .

Others far more noteworthy than Wynn Hygeorht.

Throngs of dwarves and scattered humans passed by the small tunnel's opening, but his height let him clearly watch the cavern's wide entrance. Waiting was something Sau'ilahk had turned into an art. Soon enough, Wynn appeared, along with Shade and the man who was there and not there.

Sau'ilahk watched Chane's mouth move and then Wynn's. He seethed, not near enough to even read their lips. His black burial attire blended well with shadows, but he would not pass unnoticed in the open. Even if he did, the majay-hi would sense him if he came too close. For now, the masses of the living clouded the animal's awareness.

His quarry pushed through the crowds, stopping only once at a meat vendor.

Sau'ilahk did not have to follow to know where Wynn headed. It was unlikely, in leaving the temple, that she was going into the underlevels of this settlement. He let himself dissipate again.

His presence faded as he sank once more toward dormancy—but not all the way into its pure darkness. He clung to the image of another well-memorized place. In a blink, he awoke some fifty yards down a tunnel beyond the tram station, standing between deep and wide ruts in its floor lined with scarred steel. Again, it was not long before Wynn arrived.

Where was she going and why? Had she found some clue at the temple that might lead her to the texts—to the writings of Li'kän and Häs'saun and Volyno, three of Beloved's "Children"? A small wave of relief overtook him. This night, she might bring him to his desire. But spite followed quickly.

Hkàbêv—"Beloved"—whom lowly Sumanese soldiers of old had called il'Samar, the Night Voice, had entrusted its treasures to the Children—vampires—rather than to Sau'ilahk's own caste of the Reverent.

Beloved was as treacherous as glorious, as Sau'ilahk had learned an age ago. But even treachery could be turned to advantage, given patience and time. Sau'ilahk had learned patience in prolonged torment. In this moment, he was closer than he had ever been to what he wanted.

Wynn Hygeorht believed she could find those texts and unveil secrets from what her sages called the Forgotten, a history so long lost that its fragments were bread crumbs scattered across a desert plain. When he had taken all she gained for him, he would feed on her little life, a morsel tasted before a lavish feast.

But first he must learn where she was going and why.

Wynn struggled to lead the way down the tunnel. The throng thinned as people finished their passing barters, but more were coming out than going in. She tried to hug the tunnel's high wall as she waded against the flow. When the way branched off in a gradual curve, she glanced back, making certain she hadn't lost Chane. Then Wynn stumbled out into another wide cavern.

It wasn't nearly as large as the market's, but she still pulled up short.

In place of columns and crowds, two tunnels the width of three roads took off into the mountain's depths. One bore nearly southward, its destination likely Chekiuní, "Point-Side." The other aimed more west by southwest, and that had to be to Sea-Side.

Two wide and long platforms in the cavern were made of stout wood planks and timbers like the docks of a harbor. Each aimed toward one tunnel, and triple sets of twined, steel-lined ruts in the granite floor ran from each platform into a tunnel's mouth. One of each trio was wider than the others, likely for a cargo-only tram.

At the Point-Side platform, a few dwarves and a single human in gentleman's attire waited to board.

Shade tried to back up, pulling on Wynn's grip as her grumble rose into a whine.

"*Odsúdýnjè!*" Chane cursed in his native Belaskian as he scowled at a string of open-sided cars.

"Would you two rather walk *over* the mountain?" Wynn returned.

She was getting fed up with their reluctance for dwarven travel, though she was a little doubtful herself. The trams were basically a long string of connected cars constructed of solid wood. Painted in tawny and jade tones, they rode upon steel-and-iron undercarriages, their thick iron wheels shod with steel. Rows of benches faced ahead inside each car, separated by a narrow walkway down the center length. Passengers were protected on the outside by waist-high rail walls. Each car was roofed, but only their fronts contained a full wall and a door, probably to break rushing winds once the tram gained speed.

A wide and paunched dwarf in a plain leather hauberk stood with his feet spread slightly on the platform. He cupped his mouth with gnarled hands, shouting, "*Maksag Chekiuní-da!*" and then repeated in Numanese—"Leaving for Point-Side!" He then trundled along the platform, shooing scant passengers into the cars.

Wynn didn't watch him long. No sooner had the last passenger settled when a cloud of steam billowed around the tram's lead car, making it impossible to see clearly. She barely made out its front, which seemed to end in a point. She saw that much only because it glowed.

Within the steam cloud, its front point burned like one of the massive pylon crystals. But it seemed larger still, more cleanly lined, and it pulsed in a slow rise and fall of light. A sharp explosion of steam belched from the lead car's undercarriage, and the glow brightened to a steady, hot yellow that hurt Wynn's eyes.

The tram's whole chain of cars inched forward with a metallic scrape of wheels along the ruts. In moments, it picked up the speed of a trotting horse. As it bore into the tunnel, the sharp glow at its lead end lit the way, and Wynn heard its wheels' rhythm building steadily. As it vanished from sight, her mouth went dry.

Chane stood staring after it as well.

"Some arcane engine," he whispered. "And the pylon lights in the street and cavern. Do dwarves engage in thaumaturgy through artificing?"

Wynn struggled for an answer. "Something like it. Domin Tilswith explained it more in terms of the dwarves' innate connection to the element of Earth. But he was rather evasive. I don't think he fully understood it himself."

Watching after the vanished tram, Wynn felt Shade grow silent in quivering, as if too frightened to even whine. She stroked the dog's back, suddenly realizing what an ordeal this journey would be for Shade—underground, away from natural day and night, surrounded by masses of people, and traveling in such unnatural ways.

"We need that one," Wynn said, pointing and heading off toward the other platform. "Shirvêsh Mallet believes High-Tower's family resides below Sea-

Side. If we can find them, we might find his brother . . . and then the Stone-walkers and the texts."

Again, there was only a passenger tram waiting among its three tracks.

Chane quickly outdistanced Wynn. As he climbed the ramp ahead of her and gained the platform, he craned his head, trying to see the tram's lead car. It was already obscured in rising steam.

Another stationmaster walked back along the platform, herding passengers into the cars. The Sea-Side tram was only slightly more full than the one to Point-Side.

"Hurry," Wynn said, taking the lead, and she ducked into the nearest car.

A young female dwarf was directing passengers to seats. She gave Shade a long stare but didn't object to the animal's presence.

"How long to Chemarré?" Wynn asked in Dwarvish.

The stocky girl put her hands on her hips and answered in a shockingly deep voice, "No stops on this run, so by Night-Summer's end."

Then she was off through the forward door to the next car.

Wynn understood why so many vendors sold food and drink in the great market cavern. It was well past dusk, even past mid-Night-Spring and the second bell of night. The trip would take over a quarter-night. She settled on a bench at the car's midpoint.

Shade flattened, trying to crawl under the seat, but only managed to get half her bulk out of sight.

Wynn reached down, scratching Shade's back. "It's all right."

Chane piled their packs next to her and climbed into the next empty bench.

"Did you pay for passage?" he asked.

"Transport inside the mountain is a public service," Wynn answered. "The tribes and clans take pride in the upkeep of streets and access that serve their settlements."

Chane barely nodded, watching the last travelers board—all dwarves. She and he were the only humans. Then he leaned over the rail wall, peering forward along the tram.

Wynn knew he was trying to see the lead car—the "engine," as he'd called it. But he wouldn't from their current vantage point.

"Are you acquiring a taste for dwarven culture?" she asked.

He leaned back, and any wonder had already faded from his eyes. Perhaps someone like Chane couldn't allow himself to enjoy anything too much.

"It is orderly," he answered, "even in its occasional chaos. I can appreciate this." Then he paused as if thinking. "Do they have a constabulary . . . or a city—settlement—guard?"

Wynn frowned suspiciously.

"Not precisely," she answered. "Each tribe has a warrior caste, somewhat like human armies, but they haven't known outright war since . . . I don't know when. Some clans man local constabularies in their areas, but there's little to no crime. Justice is handled by a clan conclave."

"Conclave?" he echoed. "A council?"

"Not exactly," she countered. "Council members are usually elected or appointed. It's more complicated with a dwarven conclave, from what little I know. And it always meets behind closed doors."

"So, politics persist in all cultures."

"It's complicated," she repeated, "in who sits on a clan or tribe conclave. Disputes between clans, and families of differing clans, or more complex issues are settled up at Seattâsh—Old-Seatt. That's where representatives meet for the conclave of five tribes. Why do you ask?"

Chane glanced away.

Wynn grew anxious to press him for answers, but then the tram car lurched. She grabbed the seat's edge as Shade let out a pitiful moan beneath it. The tram picked up speed, and Chane settled with his back to her.

The journey through dark and stone began.

Still in the tram tunnel's darkness, Sau'ilahk had to know where Wynn was headed. In the end, he had little choice but to expend preciously consumed life. Pulling back against the tunnel wall, he focused inward.

In his mind's eye, in midair, he shaped a glowing circle for Spirit the size of a splayed hand. Within this, he formed the square of Air. And in the spaces between these nested shapes, he stroked the lines of sigils with his thoughts.

Sau'ilahk fixated upon the glowing grand seal, and a part of his own energies bled away in a brief wave of weariness.

A silent breeze built inside the tunnel.

He ignored this side effect and called the air inward, into the seal that only he could see. There was no change of temperature in the tunnel, but the pattern's center space warped like the horizon across a hot desert. That nearly invisible distortion held its place within the seal's center—a servitor of Air.

The most base of elementals, no more than a mindless automaton, awaited his implanted instructions.

The effort of its creation left him lethargic, but he was not yet finished. He focused his will upon a tiny fragment of Spirit infused within the construction of Air and embedded five simplified commands in proper order.

Target the being in gray robes.

Record all sound.

If target leaves this area, return to origin point.

Reiterate all sound.

Banish!

Sau'ilahk released the glowing lines in his mind's eye.

They faded to nothing—but not the small twist of Air. Freed of restraint, the faint warp of the servitor shot down the tunnel into the station's cavern to fulfill its purpose. Not even a breeze was raised in its passing.

Sau'ilahk drifted toward the tunnel's mouth.

No one noticed the fist-size warp. All were far too busy, including Wynn, as she led her companions to the nearer platform. This at least told him where she was headed, but he waited as the trio boarded and took their seats, and yellow-orange light erupted with steam at the tram's head.

It gained speed and hurtled toward him in the tunnel.

It could do him no harm, but he backed to the side before its glow bore through him. As the second-to-the-last car passed, he glimpsed Chane sitting before Wynn.

Sau'ilahk still sensed nothing from this man. Chane seemed no more than an illusion of light and sound that somehow had gained physical presence.

Who—*what*—was he?

In Calm Seatt, Sau'ilahk had tried to drain that one's life with a touch and found only emptiness where life should have existed. Chane was indeed undead, but not like any that Sau'ilahk had ever encountered. Were he a vampire, his presence would immediately be sensed, and the dark majay-hì with Wynn would have attack him.

The last car dwindled in the tunnel's distant darkness.

The servitor's warp reappeared before Sau'ilahk.

He tensed in anticipation, waiting for the tunnel's Air to shiver with its recorded sounds. Wynn's voice echoed lightly and he listened.

Most of the sparse conversation was useless, but one utterance brought him some revelation.

Shirvêsh Mallet believes High-Tower's family resides below Sea-Side. If we can find them, we might find his brother . . . and then the Stonewalkers and the texts.

The servitor vanished with a *pop* as normal air rushed in to take its place. Its last command completed, it returned to nothingness.

Sau'ilahk's thoughts filled with fragile hope amid puzzlement.

So the little sage's reason for traveling to the mountain's ocean side was to search for the kin of Domin High-Tower, for his brother . . . and for the Hassäg'kreigi. What could she possibly know of Stonewalkers? That dwarven sect was all but a mystery, even to its own people. Yet, she now seemed to believe they were connected to the ancient texts. She had sounded resolute in her deductions. She must have learned something critical.

Sau'ilahk's mild fatigue from conjuring left him with no regret. He was on the correct path, and Wynn would lead him the rest of the way. He let himself slip down toward dormancy.

This time, he did not recall a memorized place. He focused instead upon the tram's distant glow and held it within his consciousness.

Sau'ilahk vanished from the tunnel, swallowed in an instant of dormancy. He immediately struggled to reawaken.

The tram's clatter erupted around him in the tunnel, startling him for an instant. Its last car was so close he could touch it, as if in one blind step he had crossed the long distance to catch up. Then it quickly rushed onward.

Blink by blink, to dormancy's edge and out again, Sau'ilahk followed Wynn's night journey through the mountain.

CHAPTER 4

Wynn gripped the bench's edge—not from panic but from growing nausea. Poor Shade had long since gone silent.

The tram constantly shuddered, rocking slightly whenever rounding a gradual curve. It didn't agree with Wynn's stomach, and worse, Chane appeared annoyingly immune. He glanced back at her now and then in concern.

"On our return, we will take a forward car," he said. "Being closer to the engine may minimize the rocking."

Wynn bit down on her lower lip. Such ideas were all well and good, but they didn't help her now. Rationalizing every problem was always his way of helping, but she wondered if he possessed any true empathy. She was also beginning to feel trapped.

Even with a welcome breeze from the tram's rush, there was little to see along the way. The absolute blurred *sameness* throughout the night made her feel as though the tunnel were closing in.

"The uneven motion may partly be the tracks' construction," Chane went on. "Did you notice them?"

Wynn glowered at the back of his head. Normally he was so quiet. Why all the prattle now? Perhaps he was trying to distract her from suffering.

"Simple and easily maintained," he added. "They need only forge new steel to reline the ruts, likely guiding the tram without need for a steering mechanism."

Wynn swallowed hard. "Chane, please . . . stop . . . *talking*!"

He pivoted and raised his eyebrows, as if surprised at her tone, and the tram took a hard left turn.

Wynn closed her eyes with a groan. Her fingernails bit into the bench as a strange metal screech built around their car.

"We are slowing," Chane said. "There is light ahead, more than from the engine's crystal."

At least that was a welcome comment.

Wynn opened her eyes in fragile hope and leaned over the tram's rail wall. She saw some light ahead, enough to make out the tram car's side . . . and the tunnel's stone wall rushing by in a blur.

Her stomach lurched.

Light grew quickly, building to a warm glow. The tunnel wall's rush began to slow, and to Wynn's relief, the tram rolled into another constructed cavern. In a screech of steel, it finally stopped, lurching her forward in her seat.

Shade groaned somewhere below amid a scratch of claws on the car's floor.

Wynn saw a station platform on the car's far side. Dwarves aboard immediately got up and began disembarking. She sagged forward, bracing against the back of Chane's bench, and reached down for Shade's head.

"We're here . . . it's over," she whispered with effort, but she couldn't find Shade by touch.

A moaning growl rose from somewhere behind her. Without a breeze from the tram's rush, so did a thin, foul smell.

"Shade?" Wynn whispered.

She stood up, wobbling as she stepped into the aisle, and bent over, looking for the dog.

Shade lay under the next bench back. Her rib cage bulged with each heaving breath, and spittle dripped freely from her half-open jaws. Below Wynn's own bench was a pool of saliva surrounding undigested sausage lumps.

Wynn covered her mouth against a gag.

"It wasn't any better for me," she muttered.

Shade exposed still-dripping teeth, and Wynn regretted her words, even if Shade couldn't understand them.

"Come," Chane interrupted, and hoisted his packs and hers as well.

Wynn took up the staff, checking the sun crystal under its leather cover. Then she crouched, patting the side of her leg as she peered at Shade.

Shade crawled out, rising on shaky legs, and Wynn felt even worse at having put Shade through this ordeal. It couldn't be helped. They had to find High-

Tower's family as soon as possible. She stroked Shade's head, passing memories of quiet inn rooms, and then pulled Shade along as she followed Chane onto the platform.

Sea-Side's tram station wasn't set deep into the mountain, as in Bay-Side. It was couched directly behind the settlement's main market cavern, smaller than Bay-Side's but still filled with the hazy glow of steaming crystals upon pylons. Beyond scarce vendors and others, only four great columns with few upper walkways supported the high ceiling. Scant passengers already gathered on the platform for the tram's return trip. As the stout female dwarf came along to usher them aboard, Wynn caught the young woman's attention.

"How late is it?" she asked.

"Barely Night-Summer's end," the girl answered. "About your midnight."

She stepped back on to the tram with the last of her passengers.

"And now?" Chane asked.

Wynn looked about. Some arriving passengers headed for the archway leading outside into the cold night, but most of them disappeared into the widest of three other tunnels leading deeper inside the mountain.

"That way," Wynn said, nodding toward the latter.

With Chane on one side and Shade on the other, she stepped off the platform to search for Sea-Side's "underside." Motion sickness passed as curiosity took its place.

After a short walk down a vast columned tunnel, she spotted side paths through archways the size of normal roads. These were placed at intervals akin to a city block. Squat pylons with engravings stood at each intersection, but only every other one held a steaming orange crystal, smaller than the ones of Bay-Side.

"This settlement is not as developed as the other," Chane commented, stepping ahead.

"Wait," Wynn called, circling the nearest pylon.

She studied dwarven engravings on all four sides. It took a moment to figure them out, and then she peered down the left-side path. The way broadened farther on, and she spotted signs, flags, and banners in front of varied doors and openings.

"The pylon says this is Chamid Bâyir," she said, pointing down the main tunnel. "Oblique Mainway—wherever that goes."

A few dwarves and fewer humans milled past them.

Chane looked warily at a thickly bearded human in a shimmering head wrap and short umber robe. Dark skinned, with a sheathless curved sword slid into his fabric wrap belt, he returned Chane's stare with haughty disdain before moving on.

"Do not get out of my sight," Chane warned.

Wynn shot him a glare. She was as well traveled as he was, and far more accustomed to this culture.

Shade growled.

The tone was different from her pained suffering on the tram, and Wynn forgot Chane's irritating manner. She spun about and found Shade watching a dwarf in a leather hauberk striding toward them along the mainway. Two matched, overmuscled, and short-haired hounds padded beside him.

Both animals were barrel-chested, their raised heads easily higher than the dwarf's belt. In contrast, Shade looked even more like a slender, long-legged wolf. Her hackles rose as she pulled back her jowls.

One dog slowed and began growling back.

Wynn crouched, quickly laying down her staff and grabbing Shade's neck. She'd tried to warn Shade about growling at strangers, but doing so with memories hadn't been easy. She hadn't mentioned—shown—Shade anything about other dogs.

"Apologies," she said in Dwarvish. "My dog is a bit protective."

"Dog?" the dwarf replied.

His bushy brows rumpled as he eyed Shade, who obviously looked like a wolf. But he didn't appear offended and nudged his own animal with his knee, growling, "Quit!" With a polite smile to Wynn, he continued on his way.

Wynn watched the houndmaster and then saw Chane's hand on his sword's hilt. The dwarf either hadn't noticed or hadn't cared. Holding Shade fast, Wynn called out in Numanese so that Chane could follow.

"Sir?"

The dwarf paused and half turned.

"Do you know of the Yêarclág . . . the Iron-Braids?" she asked. "And where they reside?"

"No, miss," the dwarf answered, this time glancing at Chane's tensed hand.

"But you are in the upper trade district. You may need to head beyond it, possibly down, to find dwelling districts. Maybe someone there can help you."

His Numanese was perfect, but most dwarves spoke it well enough, along with a smattering of other tongues. Dwarves, who valued good trade with other cultures, were so oral that language came easily to them.

"Thank you," Wynn called.

The dwarf returned a shallow bow and headed off with his hounds. Shade was still leering after them, and Wynn grabbed her gently by the snout.

"No!" she whispered firmly.

Shade rumbled, glaring back with blue crystalline eyes. She shook herself free of the grip.

Wynn sighed in frustration. Sometimes she forgot that Shade didn't understand language—not like her father. Trying to use memories and present them in clear and meaningful strings was daunting. Wynn stood up and turned on Chane.

"And you!" she said. "Keep your hand off that sword, unless you have no choice! Most dwarves are quick to laugh and slow to anger, but once aroused, they don't calm easily. Even *you* would have trouble facing one of them."

Chane's eyes widened and his jaw muscles bulged. Clearly offended, he opened his mouth to respond.

"I'm not questioning your skill," she went on, but lowered her voice to a whisper. "And keep your sword in plain sight. To them, only a villain carries concealed weapons. Magiere and Chap both saw visions of the past . . . through the memories of others. Dwarves are a match—or better—for an undead's strength."

Chane's expression relaxed. Perhaps he took her at her word—or he was patronizing her. The barest slyness surfaced in his expression—almost a thin smile—and he lunged sideways.

By the time Wynn twisted to catch sight of him, he was behind her.

"They would have to get a hold on me first," he rasped.

She just stared at him. Was he joking? Did Chane know how to joke?

Wynn almost smiled—and then scoffed. He might be faster than a dwarf, but that wasn't the point. The last thing she needed was his overprotective gallantry getting them into trouble.

Chane gestured down Oblique Mainway, then cocked his head toward the side tunnel.

"Onward or outward?"

Wynn had no idea. If the Iron-Braids lived in the poorest district, then they would have to head below sooner or later. How and where was another matter, and she would rather have the answers before they tried navigating unknown regions. She should've asked more from the polite houndmaster.

"The main tunnel," she finally answered. "Maybe it will lead to some way down."

At that wild guess, they were off once more.

A single row of sculpted-based columns stretched along the avenue's center. The structure of Oblique Mainway was plain but astonishing, not only for size and supports but for the chaotic structures that lined it.

Shops and stalls were carved into or built out of the side walls, but their spacing, shape, and size had no discernible pattern. Between one with wide double doors and another with an archway blocked by a garnish of braided drape was a third with a vertical set of three windows—triangle, square, and hexagon. Even those were obscured with curtains. Occasionally, vendors' stalls of wood or canvas surrounded a column, but nearly all along the way were closed for the night.

There was no one who appeared to be a resident to ask for directions. The farther they went, the fewer passersby scurried off their own way. More than half of those kept to the other side of the center columns once they spotted Shade.

Wynn was thankful that Shade kept quiet, but she couldn't help noticing the near absence of humans. Even without Shade, that alone made her and Chane stand out.

"If we cannot find guidance," Chane said, "then we should secure lodging. Tomorrow, more people will be about. We cannot visit these Iron-Braids in the middle of the night, if manners are valued here."

"I want to at least find where they live, and you can't be out during . . ." She paused when he glanced sidelong at her. "Oh . . . I suppose you can down here."

The thought hadn't occurred to her before. Underground, shielded from the sun, Chane wasn't limited by daylight.

"Let's look a little longer," she added.

They finally reached the end of the shops. Farther on, the tunnel emptied into a tall, domed chamber somewhat wider than the mainway. Four slimmer columns supported its ceiling, and narrow passages spidered outward around it. Thick steps on both sides climbed upward into stone. On the cavern's far side, one broad tunnel continued onward in a gentle downward slope that arced left.

Wynn heard someone walking toward them.

It took a long time for the figure to enter the mainway's light. An ancient dwarf in a faded gown hobbled into Oblique Mainway, leaning upon a walking rod. Her hair was so thin that her age-speckled scalp showed through it all around. Gnarled wrinkles over her features all but obscured her small eyes. In her stoop, she might have been shorter than Wynn, but was twice as wide, with a large mole on her wrinkled cheek.

"Old mother," Wynn said, a respectful phrase learned from Domin Tilswith, "we are looking for the Iron-Braids. Could you help us?"

The elderly dwarf raised her milky eyes, but her voice was clear as she shook her head.

"I only recently came to live down below . . . with distant relations. . . ."

She trailed off somberly. Perhaps she'd lost her immediate family and been reduced in circumstances enough to fall back on relatives in the underside.

"Could I ask," Wynn began, reluctant to press, "where do you and yours reside? It might be near where I can find those I seek."

The old woman took a slow, haggard breath, answering in Numanese. "Go all the way down to Âyillichreg Bâyir . . . Limestone Mainway. Look for the cheag'anâkst called Kìnnébuây. It stays open all the time."

"Cheag'anâkst?" Wynn repeated, trying to decipher the term. "A greeting house?"

The old woman nodded. "The locals there may have heard of your friends."

"Thank you," Wynn replied.

She wanted to say more, or offer trade for welcome advice, but the old woman had already hobbled onward.

"What is this . . . greeting house?" Chane asked. "A tavern?"

"Not exactly," Wynn replied. "I've never been in one. It's closer to an eatery, lodge, and gathering place all in one."

"Then a common house."

She shook her head. "Dwarves have another word for that. And such places are for family or clan only, not outsiders."

She looked across the wide end chamber to where the tunnel began its downward curve. She'd hoped for more specific directions before going into the depths. Without a word, Wynn trudged onward, and Chane and Shade paced her on separate sides.

A few small crystals were set in the walls along the gradual downward spiral. In a while, another wide tunnel with a single row of columns shot off in what she assumed was the same direction as Oblique Mainway. She stepped through the end chamber to the first crystal-mounted pylon. The new tunnel wasn't Limestone Mainway.

Here, the look of the shops and structures were much the same as above. She peered back to where the curving tunnel joined the right side of the end chamber. On the left, its gradual spiral continued downward. And they were off again. . . .

Down to the next level, and the next, and yet again, but none of the names upon the first pylons depicted the symbols for Limestone Mainway. The lower they descended, the fewer crystals lit the spiraling tunnel, until there were none at all. Wynn took out her small cold lamp crystal and rubbed it briskly to provide light.

She stepped out through yet another end chamber, but this time, the curving tunnel didn't continue on its far side. It was the last place to look. Sure enough, the first column was marked for Limestone Mainway. It was nothing like Oblique Mainway far above.

Perhaps it had been named for the shots of limestone that ran through the wide tunnel's walls. There was an ocher dinginess to the whole place. It was brightly lit, as were all the main tunnels, but none of the excavated shops here were smoothly finished. All looked hastily cut for their space, with no thought for appearance. Some fronts were even made of old timber and piled stone. Dust and grime had built up in the crevices around column bases and where the mainway's walls met the floor.

And the only place with any signs of life was hard to miss.

A dingy banner too dull to read from a distance hung above a wide, plain arch with no door or curtain. Yellow light spilled out across the mainway's stone, as did a loud, raucous noise of deep voices that echoed in the tunnel.

Wynn took a step, eager to find someone to direct her. Chane's hand settled on her shoulder, and she looked up. He studied the greeting house's entrance, and a twist of distaste spread his thin-lipped mouth.

"I do not like the sound. You do not belong anywhere so . . . common."

Wynn shrugged off his hand. "Don't be a snob."

She reached the doorway and stepped inside before he could catch her. There she paused as Chane and Shade pushed through. At first she couldn't see clearly through all the pipe smoke swirling in the air and the numerous bodies packed around the tables. Wynn coughed and her stinging eyes began to adjust.

The room was large and dauntingly crowded. Dwarves of all shapes and walks of life sat drinking from large mugs of wood or clay rather than pewter or tin. Some tugged on short and squat clay pipes, sending rolling ribbons or great blasts of gray smoke up to the arch-supported ceiling. At the room's center, the only open and clear space, a large dwarf paced around a wide circular stone platform one step in height.

Some of crowd called out, cheered, or banged their mugs, but all eyes remained fixed on the one pacing dramatically before them.

He was quite stout but also tall for his kind, with steel-streaked ruddy hair and a curly cropped beard a slightly darker hue. A well-crafted chain vest covered him over a quilted leather hauberk. Steel pauldrons and couters protected his shoulders and elbows. Two war daggers were sheathed at his hips, and a double-sided war ax was sheathed upside down on his back, so he could draw it instantly over either shoulder.

"And then?" someone called out in Dwarvish. "What then, Fiáh'our? Finish already!"

Wynn glanced toward the voice, but couldn't spot the speaker. When she looked back at the warrior upon the platform, her breath stopped at one final detail of his attire.

A slivery thôrhk hung around the dwarven warrior's thick neck.

Its ornate loop, looking as if made of braids, was thicker than two of Wynn's fingers. Traditional flanged knobs, each as big as a sword's pommel, were mounted on its ends resting below his collarbone. But in place of round domes, those ends protruded like butt spikes on the hafts of war axes.

Not just a warrior—this was a thänæ, marked in honor with a thôrhk. What was he doing drinking and telling tales in an underside greeting house?

His voice was low and loud, like rolling thunder.

"After the goblin raid on the village of Shentángize, no one dared step beyond the stockade at night. I had no choice but to set out . . . with only my ax for company."

The audience roared, banged mugs, and slapped the tables in anticipation.

"What is happening here?" Chane whispered.

Wynn remembered he didn't speak Dwarvish. She tried to explain but stumbled over the storyteller's name. Its components were simplified truncations of dwarven root words.

"Uhm . . . Stag . . . Battering. . . . no, Hammer-Stag. He's a thänæ, a paragon among his people for virtuous accomplishments."

"Paragon?" Chane rasped in disbelief. "That bellower?"

Someone snorted, and Wynn flinched around to meet pellet black eyes. A dwarf seated an arm's length away tilted his head with an angry glare. He slowly set down his mug.

"Apologies!" Wynn spit out quickly in Dwarvish. "My friend is an uncouth foreigner . . . out of his element." She turned on Chane, switching to Belaskian in a sharp whisper. "Keep quiet, before you start something! Dwarven virtue differs from human cultures. He is telling them a story of his exploits."

"That is not virtue," Chane hissed, "only bluster."

"I found no tracks," Hammer-Stag continued, and his low conspiratorial tone brought the room to attentive silence. "But I could smell their passing."

He paused near one table. The room remained silent as he stepped off the platform.

Hammer-Stag reached across the nearest table. He dragged the mug of one patron slowly toward himself, as if waiting for its owner to object. But that dwarf and all others remained quietly still. Hammer-Stag hefted the mug, took a long gulp, and slammed it back down.

Wynn had no idea what this meant, but his audience roared as he returned to the platform.

"So, I tracked them," Hammer-Stag went on, tapping the side of his broad nose.

Chuckles and snickers rose briefly, likely at some jest concerning the stench of goblins.

Wynn stopped listening. Solving the mystery of the thänæ's presence here wouldn't help her find the Iron-Braids, and Chane's elitist contempt was only going to get them in trouble.

Standing close, Chane looked down and gave her a short, sharp shake of his head.

"Some of these people must live nearby," she whispered, ignoring his suggestion that they leave.

Quietly, Wynn slipped forward, trying not to interrupt the thänæ's story.

"Excuse me," she whispered between a pair seated on the outskirts. "Could you tell me where the Iron-Braids live?"

Dwarves were usually willing enough to help a lost stranger. If one of them knew anything, perhaps a quiet response would be enough.

The male to her right dropped his jaw in shock, and then gritted his teeth as if she'd committed some terrible offense. He spun back toward the platform, crossing his arms and pretending not to see her. Others at the table grumbled and followed suit.

The thänæ glanced over but didn't break stride in his tale.

"When the first three came, I took two heads at once!" he called loudly. With one hand, Hammer-Stag whipped the ax off his back into a level arc. It passed swiftly before those nearest, as if severing heads right before their eyes.

A cry of triumph rose in the crowd, and Wynn sighed. Clearly she'd chosen the wrong table, and she moved farther toward the back wall near the entrance.

"Pardon me," she whispered to a small group in the leathers of laborers. "Could you please—"

She was cut off in a gasp as someone grabbed the back of her robe and cloak.

Wynn was up on her toes as she headed unwillingly toward the exit. Shade burst into a loud snarl, and Chane began pushing toward Wynn, his expression darkening. Her heart sank as she flailed her hands before her, trying to wave them both off before this all ended badly.

Chane still had his hand on his sword hilt as Wynn's heels hit the floor. She spun about, wobbling a bit under her pack's weight, and came eye-to-eye with a wide-faced woman.

"If you want to act like a rude little turnip," the female warned in a baritone voice, "then at least be silent like one!"

The dwarven woman straightened and brushed off her muslin apron.

Chane looked about uneasily as a dozen irritated patrons turned in their seats. Shade stayed put and ceased snarling as the woman proceeded back through the tables. Although the thänæ never paused in his telling, his squinting eyes turned once in Wynn's direction.

"Then the pack was upon me!" Hammer-Stag shouted. "I thought to face fifteen or twenty of the half beasts, but they poured from the forest's dark spaces by the scores. . . ."

Wynn rolled her eyes.

Scores? Hardly! A rare pack of goblins had been known to raid far settlements beyond Malourné's eastern reaches. No more than a dozen had ever been seen at one time. Her frustration grew.

Someone here had to assist her, for where else could she go asking at this time of night? But no one seemed willing to speak during the thänæ's tale. By his overly dramatic manner, he might go on until dawn.

Chane jerked his head toward the door.

Wynn sighed and nodded, fighting down annoyance at the open relief on his face. For a homeless wanderer, he was such an elitist.

"I swung over and over," Hammer-Stag called, "cleaving the first ten who reached me. But in my brazen courage, choosing to face them alone, I was outnumbered by the beasts. I knew I would die there . . . but I would take many with me on my way to our ancestors."

He paused again, and as Wynn turned to leave, she heard him gulp from another mug.

"Then a white-skinned woman with wild black hair came at me out of the dark."

Wynn stopped and shivered as if dropped in a frigid river.

White-skinned . . . black hair . . . wild . . .

An image of Li'kän's pale, naked form rose in her mind. Magiere had locked that ancient undead in the orb's cavern below the ice-bound castle . . . the place from which Wynn, with Chap's aid, had gathered the same texts she now sought.

Li'kän was one of the thirteen "Children" of the Ancient Enemy of many names . . . perhaps one of the first vampires to walk the world in the time of the Forgotten. Had she escaped? Was that monster loose, somehow crossing the world to this continent?

"She shouted at me in the Numans' tongue to 'give room,'" the thänæ exclaimed.

Wynn spun in confusion.

Li'kän had been fascinated by the power of speech, but she'd been alone for so many centuries that she'd lost her own voice.

"Her blade was long and broad," Hammer-Stag went on. "Single-edged, and too weighty for her stature, but she wielded it as if it were light as a scribbler's quill. Sparks of bloodred ran in her tresses."

Wynn teetered on her feet. The thänæ was speaking of Magiere!

"Before I knew where the pale one came from or why, she charged in at my side. . . ."

Wynn shoved Chane aside, rushing back between the tables.

"Then came a silver wolf, taller than its kind, rending its way to give me aid. . . ."

Wynn's mouth opened, but she couldn't get a word out. Now, he spoke of Chap and tears welled in her eyes.

"And last, an elf with blunted ears dropped from the treetops and bolted in faster than I could—"

"Where?" Wynn cried, shoving forward toward the platform. "Where did you see them?"

Sudden silence filled the greeting house.

Hammer-Stag stopped midsentence, looking at her, and then gasps and curses exploded all around.

Wynn froze in place. She'd just committed some terrible breach, but she didn't care.

"Where?" she shouted more firmly.

"You broke my tale!" he barked, but his haughty tone was as overly dramatic as his telling. "Have you no manners . . . puppy?"

Then his gaze shifted aside and down. Wynn heard Shade's rumble as the dog pushed in beside her. Hammer-Stag straightened. As he stared, his broad face filled with stunned puzzlement. The crowd's hostile grumbles grew again into loud, derisive shouts.

Wynn cringed. But Hammer-Stag had spoken of Magiere, Leesil, and Chap. She was desperate to hear more, no matter what else she'd come here for. And she had just offended the locals, who might have helped in either pursuit.

"I . . . beg your pardon," she said quickly.

She couldn't be sure anyone heard amid all the noise. Chane's hand closed on her arm from behind, but she jerked free, trying to think of some way to serve all her desires.

"I came seeking the whereabouts of the Iron-Braids," she shouted. "But your tale was so engrossing that I spoke out of turn. Please go on. What happened next?"

Hammer-Stag blinked again. His astonishment at Shade vanished.

"Too late!" he shouted, and then snorted like a bull, swinging his arm to silence the crowd. "The tale is broken, the mood gone! So *you* must have a better one to take its place . . . if you wish to barter."

"What is he saying?" Chane demanded.

Confusion overtook Wynn, and she waved him off. Too much was happening, and she kept her eyes on the thänæ.

"Barter?" she asked. "Barter for what?"

"This is the way you seek my aid . . . our aid?" he challenged, smoothly changing to Numanese as he gestured to the gathering. "Do you think me some servant to fulfill your demands? Fair trade is our way, and rightly so, here and now. If you find my tale wanting, enough to cut it off, then tell me—us—a better one!" He smiled with a knowing wink to the crowd, spreading his massive arms wide. "Perhaps one of your own worthy exploits."

Wynn choked on smoky air and swallowed very hard.

"If your tale is as grand as your nerve," he added, "someone here might point your way."

Mixed reactions broke out in the greeting house. Someone laughed aloud, and that laughter spread, laced with grunts of disdain. Others shook their heads in disagreement, shouting in outrage at some young girl taking the thänæ's place.

Wynn felt small compared to Hammer-Stag's hulking stature as her mind raced for some way out of all this. Hammer-Stag raised his large hands in a gesture to quell the crowd.

"Of course, you must win the audience along the way," he continued, pointing to a large tankard resting before one soot-covered listener. "At any need, take your fill, if you dare . . . if the mug's owner finds your tale worthy so far. That is the way of a *telling*."

Wynn's stomach tightened, and a bit of the tram ride's nausea returned.

Even a stout human male would find dwarven spirits hard to bear. Would she give more offense if she didn't stop to drink? What if she accidentally sipped wood alcohol? Playing this game—this unknown custom—without knowing all the rules grew more daunting by the moment.

"Oh, dead deities!" she whimpered—another crass phrase picked up from Leesil.

But she was sick of all the hoops she'd been forced to jump through in the past year. Her guild superiors had looked at her with Hammer-Stag's same arrogant expression every time they dangled a carrot before her. Always one more proof of loyalty, obedience, propriety, always one more requirement, one more game.

Amid panic came anger.

She wasn't leaving here without learning of the Iron-Braids—and of the friends she'd lost in returning home.

"Wynn?" Chane whispered. "Do something."

"I am! I'm trying to think!"

"No more low-life nonsense!" Chane hissed, reaching for Wynn. "We find directions elsewhere."

She grabbed his wrist before he got a grip, but her attention remained fixed on the blustering dwarf.

"I can do a tale justice only in my own language," she stated clearly.

Hammer-Stag frowned as Chane's eyes widened. The dwarf scratched his beard thoughtfully and then called out to the crowd, "S*kíal trânid âns Numanaks*?"

More grumbling rose among the listeners. Chane heard "*chourdál*" uttered more than once.

"Done!" barked Hammer-Stag, and nodded assent to Wynn.

"No!" Chane whispered, but Wynn pushed him off.

"If my tale is enough," she went on, "will you also tell me more of the white woman, the silver dog, and the elf who isn't an elf?"

Surprise spread across Hammer-Stag's broad face. Then it was gone. A wry smile took its place, and Chane shook his head. Wynn had just upped the stakes before her tale had even begun.

Rumblings sharpened around the room, but she stood her ground.

Chane was at a loss. Would pulling her out of here start an outright brawl?

Hammer-Stag slowly began to laugh. His guffaws grew until it seemed tears welled in his eyes. Others began to chuckle as well.

"By the Eternals," he barely got out. "This must be some tale. Agreed, O mighty little one!"

Hammer-Stag stepped down and, with a wide sweep of his hand, ushered Wynn to take the platform. Shoving his way onto a bench at the nearest table, he dropped down, grabbed a mug, and clacked it once on the table with a shout.

"To the telling!"

Chane saw too many eyes locked on Wynn amid stony, disgruntled expressions filled with doubt. At more chuckling around the room, Hammer-Stag slapped his table.

"Silence!" he shouted. "And respect!"

The room went instantly quiet.

Wynn stepped up amid the crowd and turned slowly about. Shade trotted closer as well, perhaps unwilling to let her get too far away. All Chane could do was fight the wild urge to throw Wynn over his shoulder and haul her out of this detestable place.

Why had they ever come in here? What was she thinking? He could not believe she would succeed at what amounted to street-level theater. Wynn was a guild sage, the highest of scholars, yet she had made a bargain upon her word. He could not break that any more than she would herself.

Chane crossed his arms, waiting. Within moments, she would be jeered out of this commoners' arena, and he could finally take her away.

Wynn raised one hand and pointed to Hammer-Stag. Her voice low and not quite steady, it still carried.

"This honored thänæ spoke of a pale woman, a silver dog, and an elf," she began. "These were *my* companions of old. In company, we faced horrors not imagined, things to make goblins into bed tales for children."

Hammer-Stag raised his eyebrows, and Chane groaned softly. Why did she have to begin with an insult?

Wynn held both hands out toward her audience.

"Five seasons past, we traveled to the top of the world, to a place of year-round ice on the eastern continent known there as the Pock Peaks. We searched for a treasure lost beyond history—but not for our own gain. We sought to keep it from the hands of a murdering villain and worse . . . one of the undead."

Chane's mouth went slack. Did dwarves even know about the undead? From what he had learned of the Numan Lands, such creatures were only fables and folklore here. Several dwarves fidgeted like children suffering in boredom, but all remained quiet. Wynn's low voice carried throughout the smoky room.

"He was what the people there called a Noble Dead, the highest and most feared of the undead . . . an *upér*, *upír* . . . a vampire, a drinker of the blood of the living. We struggled on in those white mountains, trying to find the treasure before he did."

Wynn's exaggerated accounts of trials and hardships built as she circled the platform, fixing upon the whole audience and perhaps purposefully ignoring Hammer-Stag. After a while she paused, and silence filled the room. She met the steady gaze of one female dwarf sitting at the back side of Hammer-Stag's table.

Wynn stepped down from the platform and reached past Hammer-Stag for the woman's mug.

Though she faltered, no one tried to stop her. She took a fast and deep drink, and slammed the mug back down like Hammer-Stag—or tried to. Compared to his pounding, it sounded like she had dropped the mug.

Ale sloshed out on the table.

Its owner frowned, shaking bits of foam off her stout fingers. Wynn quickly retreated to the platform while others at the table tried to stifle their amusement.

"One night in our search," Wynn began again, "I became lost in a blizzard. But Chap, the silver sire of my own companion"—and she gestured toward Shade—"found me. Together, we took refuge inside a stone chute to wait out the storm." Her voice rose slightly. "But we were fools to think a storm our worst enemy. We heard a sound at the chute's bottom. . . . We peered downward to see two of the Anmaglâhk, the Thieves of Lives, a caste of elven assassins, crawling up to murder us!"

Chane grew still and attentive. He had heard only scant bits of Wynn's journey, and little to nothing of her time up in the Pock Peaks. He knew what had become of those two elves, for he had seen the bodies. But he had not known they had come so close to Wynn.

A low rumble passed briefly through the crowd. Chane's ire rose for an instant, until he looked at their faces.

The mention of elves as assassins seemed to startle them into disbelief. But distaste came quickly, as if they accepted Wynn's accounting. Even the fanciful notion that such a caste might exist did not sit well with the dwarves. Chane remembered Wynn's earlier warning to keep all weapons in plain sight as an issue of honor and virtue.

"Until then, we didn't know these eastern elves sought the treasure as well. Chap is fierce, as Hammer-Stag has said, but he would be hard-pressed against such trained assassins. They moved like a sudden night breeze, wielding stilettos as if born with them. I'm ashamed to say I faltered in fear."

She paused once more at Hammer-Stag's table, this time reaching for a closer mug, but Hammer-Stag quickly covered the mug with his hand.

Wynn's face drained of all color at his denial, but Chane was relieved. She had finally failed in her challenge.

"Perhaps another mug would be better," Hammer-Stag said quietly, and then his face flushed with anger as he glared at the mug's bleary-eyed owner.

That ragged-looking male with ruddy features blinked in confusion. Horrified realization took him, and he quickly pulled his mug away.

Chane was baffled. For such stout and hardy people, he wondered at any dwarf being so drunk.

Wynn recovered. Exchanging respectful nods with Hammer-Stag, she grabbed another mug and took a drink. And Chane realized what had happened.

That one drunken dwarf had been swilling wood alcohol—which would have killed Wynn if Hammer-Stag had not intervened. Chane's discomfort grew, not only for Wynn's safely, but because she was doing better than he expected.

"But as those murdering elves began their ascent," Wynn continued, "a black shadow passed overhead." She raised one arm, draping her robe's sleeve below her eyes. "When I looked up, I barely made out the transparent ghost of a raven as it dived down through the chute."

She jabbed her other hand through the sleeve, the fabric whipping aside as her fingers shot out at a nearby table. One young male stiffened sharply in startlement, almost dropping his tankard.

"That black ghost rammed straight through the first Anmaglâhk!"

More dwarves sat upright in their seats.

"He grabbed his chest in pain, but something more pulled my eyes skyward. A hint of white flashed by, running down the chute's wall. It went straight at the elves, and the second one vanished from the chute's mouth as it came. That white form was gone, and the first elf slumped against the stone wall.

"Chap raced after them, for in protecting me, his heart would never turn him from a fight. I rushed after him but stopped at the chute's bottom when I saw the one fallen Anmaglâhk. The elf's ribs protruded around a gaping hole in his chest . . . where his heart had been torn from his body."

Wynn raised her hand, closed in a partial fist like a claw, as if gripping that heart. She turned, walking slowly around the platform. All the dwarves watched in silence.

"Then I heard the snarls and screaming," she whispered. "I rushed on after Chap to a sight I still cannot push from memory. The other elf lay dead in the snow, his head torn from the gushing stump of his neck . . . and standing over him was a naked white woman.

"She was so deceptively frail in build, but with fangs and clear crystal eyes. Her hair shimmered black as night, its tendrils writhing in the snow-laced breeze. She was undead, a vampire, but centuries old. And she had torn apart two of the Anmaglâhk like gutted fish."

Wynn paused near another table and locked eyes on a young wide-eyed dwarven couple.

"I could barely breathe," she whispered, "as I stared at her."

This time she did not hesitate and took another long drink. Her brown eyes glittered as she twirled back around to the platform's center.

"To my despair, Chap charged. So fierce was he that he held the white woman in combat for a while. But finally she threw him against the cliff side, and he fell limp in the snow. She turned her eyes on me . . . and I ran!

"I barely made the chute's mouth before she was on me. She grabbed my throat and slammed me against the sheer stone as I cried out."

Wynn paused so long that Chane thought someone might speak.

"She released me . . . and cringed away against the chute's far wall."

Hammer-Stag leaned forward, neither smiling nor scowling, his eyes locked on Wynn.

"She stared at me with those colorless eyes. Even through terror that froze my body more than cold, my thoughts were racing. I had cried out for her to stop . . . and the sound of my words, not my voice, had caused this. I spoke again."

Wynn glanced toward Chane.

"She had been locked away in those white mountains, alone for hundreds upon hundreds of years . . . so long that she'd forgotten the very sound of speech. Upon hearing *words* once more, so vaguely remembered, like a home lost so long she had forgotten even the hope of it . . . she did not kill me.

"Instead, she grabbed me and raced through the mountains. She carried me to a six-towered castle trapped upon a great snow plain, the very place my companions and I had been searching for. *She* was the guardian of the treasure we sought.

"Even wounded, Chap came for me, and finally closed upon us once we reached the castle doors. I spoke to the white woman again. She did not understand me but held off from tearing me apart as she had the elves . . . only because of the sound of my words and that *I* spoke to *her*.

"She was mad, driven insane by isolation. She led Chap and me inside her castle, the first to enter it in . . . well, who knows how long. All because I kept speaking to her, and she listened."

Wynn turned a full circle, her hands held open.

"She was destined to destroy all who came near the treasure, but I alone gained her secrets. Though helpless, *I* was strong enough of heart and wise enough to best her. Not by ax or sword or feats of might, but by my voice, my words . . . my *telling* . . . given in charity to her."

Wynn fell silent, pulled her robe and cloak closed around herself, and bowed her head.

Chane stood rooted to the floor.

He had never seen this side of Wynn. Her sense of drama, of the moment, was surprising if not perfect. It took several breaths for others to realize she had finished, and then the rumble began. One dwarf shouted out in Numanese, "No, that cannot be the end! What happened after? Did you find the treasure?"

Wynn raised her head with the hint of a smile.

"That is another story . . . another *telling* . . . for another time." She turned her large brown eyes upon Hammer-Stag, adding, "And for some other fair trade."

At first, Hammer-Stag simply gazed at her, his expression unreadable. Then he slowly shook his head. He began rumbling with laughter, and suddenly he slapped the table, making the nearest mugs jump and shudder.

"By the Eternals, fair trade indeed! You will sit with me, little one!"

Wynn's gaze wandered to Chane.

He could not help wondering if the dwarves believed a single word of her tale. Elven assassins and ancient white undeads? But it did not seem to matter. Several raised their mugs high as she joined Hammer-Stag and took a seat. Shade trotted after her, and Chane reluctantly followed, settling beside her at the table.

Another dwarf remained sitting with Hammer-Stag, younger and wearing a cleanly oiled leather hauberk. His mass of brown hair was pulled back with a leather thong, and his slightly darker beard was trimmed and groomed. He observed Wynn, but did not speak.

Hammer-Stag gestured to his companion.

"My kinsman, Carrow," he said simply. He gathered a pitcher and mugs from the table, shoving one down to Chane.

Chane did not touch it. Then Hammer-Stag slapped a hand over his heart.

"I am Fiáh'our," he claimed, as if only the sound of his name was needed for anyone to recognize him.

"Hammer-Stag?" Wynn interjected.

He pondered her translation. "Yes!" he agreed. "Hammer-Stag of the family of Loam, Meerschaum clan of the Tumbling-Ridge tribe. And who are you, girl, and your young man?"

"He is *not* my . . ." Wynn began through clenched teeth, and then fidgeted. "My name is Wynn Hygeorht, of the Calm Seatt branch of the Guild of Sagecraft. This is Chane Andraso, a scholar I met in the Farlands, a region of the eastern continent."

Chane frowned. Her words were now slurring, and her eyes appeared overly bright. Amid the tale, he had lost track of how much ale she had sampled.

"I see," said Hammer-Stag, raising thick eyebrows. He glanced down at Shade, who flattened her ears but did not growl. "A fine tale," he went on. "And well told."

"So, why is a thänæ telling tales in this poor neighborhood, in the middle of the night?" Wynn blurted out.

Chane's eyes widened, as did Carrow's, but Hammer-Stag did not appear insulted.

"Tales must be told . . . a *telling* is the way . . . most especially if one is honored among the *living*," he said. "How else will they be *re*told, molded over years by the many, and hopefully stand the test of time? That is the only way to become one of the honored dead, to be reborn among the people. So was it with all of the Eternals, whose tales belong to all of the people, no matter where they live."

Chane frowned. Wynn had mentioned that the dwarves believed their "saints" lived on in this world, watching over them. To claim that their Eternals—their patron saints—still lived seemed strange.

Hammer-Stag waved his hand, brushing off Wynn's question. "Now, what is it you wish to learn from me?"

Wynn had made that clear from the start, and Chane said, "The location of the Iron-Braid family."

Carrow winced visibly at that family name.

"Ah, yes." Hammer-Stag's expression turned thoughtful, almost sad. "Continue down Limestone Mainway, and turn in at the fifth tunnel to the north. You'll find a smithy a short way down; you cannot miss it. But only two Iron-Braids remain among us—Skirra Yêarclág Jäyne a'Duwânláh, the daughter, and her mother, Meránge."

The long dwarven title jumbled in Chane's head, but he knew from Wynn that Yêarcläg meant "Iron-Braid," based on some respected ancestor in their direct family line.

Wynn tettered on the bench. "Why are . . . you . . . sad . . . when you speak of them?"

Her speech slurred and faltered more and more.

"The fifth side street on the right," Hammer-Stag repeated softly, glancing at Carrow in apparent concern.

"And what of my . . . com . . . panions?" Wynn said, struggling to pronounce the words, and her eyes turned glassy with threatening tears. "Magiere and Leesil . . . Chap. . . . where are they?"

Hammer-Stag shook his head. "I do not know, Wynn of the Hygeorhts. After they aided me in my own audacity, I asked about their journey. But they preferred to keep to themselves. They headed north, perhaps to one of the Northlander coastal towns."

Chane watched a tear roll down Wynn's cheek as she closed her eyes. She looked broken, as if something she sought, desperately needed, had turned into only a figment. She was drunk, and he feared she might crumple onto the table.

Wynn looked up at Hammer-Stag, and Chane saw desperation in her face.

"But they are alive?" she whispered.

Hammer-Stag leaned in upon her with a toothy grin. "There is slyness in those three. And yes, O mighty little one, I would barter my honor that they are still alive!"

Chane rose up. "We thank you for your assistance."

"A little thing," Hammer-Stag said absently, and then laughed, poking Wynn in the shoulder. "And I had the better of the barter!"

Under that one-fingered push, Wynn nearly toppled over. Hammer-Stag quickly grabbed her before Chane could, and studied Wynn with something akin to affection.

"The ale could not be helped—it is part of the telling," he said. "You gave us much enjoyment tonight. A dark tale it was, but a fresh one we have never heard!"

"Dark?" she whispered. "Not compared to others I know."

That was enough for Chane. He grabbed Wynn under the arms and hoisted her up. She struggled until he breathed in her ear, "Let us go . . . and find the Iron-Braids."

What he intended was to take her straight to find lodging, but first he had to get her out the door.

"Yes, to the Iron-Braids!" she said loudly, struggling to stand on her own. She looked down at Hammer-Stag. "Good-bye, thänæ . . . and thank you."

Before the parting dragged on, Chane turned her toward the exit, and Shade followed after. But as he steered Wynn between the tables, her story would not leave his thoughts. . . .

Or rather, Chane could not stop picturing her upon the platform, pretending to clutch the heart of an Anmaglâhk.

CHAPTER 5

Wynn sucked air, trying to clear her head of pipe smoke as she stumbled from the greeting house. That was why she felt dizzy and nauseous. She wasn't drunk—not on a few gulps of ale.

Limestone Mainway was a dim and hazy umber in her sight. Chane still gripped her arm, and she pulled away, instantly unsteady under her feet.

"Five tunnels down . . . on the right," she mumbled.

Shade pricked up her ears with a whine.

"No, we go to an inn," Chane stated flatly.

"I'm fine . . . now come on."

"You need to sleep this off."

Wynn flushed indignantly. "Sleep what off?"

Who did he think he was? He wouldn't even be here if not for her, and now he was acting like . . . like High-Tower—sanctimonious, overbearing, and stuffy.

"I'm *fine*," she repeated. "I just need some fresh air."

"Where would we find that, this far underground?" he rasped back. "I grew up among nobles who started drinking as soon as the sun set. I know someone drunk when I hear them!"

A pair of dwarves in laborers' attire stepped from the greeting house and glanced at the two humans arguing in the empty mainway.

"We are going to an inn," Chane whispered.

"No! To the Iron-Braids . . . now!"

Wynn spun about—and all the tunnel's columns suddenly leaned hard to the right. Great crystals steaming on pylons blurred before her eyes. But no one was ever again going to order her about. Not even Chane . . . especially not Chane.

"It is late," he said behind her, and then paused. "But we will locate their smithy, so we know where it is. Then return tomorrow evening at an appropriate time."

Even through Wynn's haze—from smoke and glaring crystals, not ale—this made sense. So how could she argue if he was right? She hated that. Rational counters were another ploy her superiors had used to manipulate her.

Wynn found herself leaning with the columns, until she accidentally sidled into one. She braced a hand on its gritty stone until the columns straightened.

"Very well," she finally agreed.

Shade huffed, and Wynn found the dog peering around her side.

"Don't you start," she warned, and headed off.

Her boot toe snagged in her robe.

She teetered for an instant and righted herself in a few tangled steps. She wasn't going to give Chane's accusation any credence. She wasn't drunk, damn him. It was just the greeting house's stinky air.

Shade padded beside her, intermittently whining and huffing. Chane caught up on her other side. Why was he so tall? He towered over everyone here among the dwarves. That too annoyed her.

They passed varied closed shops so worn and nondescript she couldn't even tell what they were.

"You never told me that story," Chane said, catching her off guard.

"What . . . what story?"

"About the white woman—the one you call Li'kän. I did not know that you had kept her from killing you by the power of words."

Wynn peered up at him and almost tripped again. His pale features were drawn and pensive.

"Oh . . . that." She hesitated. "I didn't figure everything out by myself."

"I assumed as much," he answered.

"What's that supposed to mean?"

"Nothing," he returned quickly. "It seemed too brief and simple—but necessary for a tale. I see that."

"Chap figured it out," she admitted. "I helped once he understood what we should do . . . embellishment is part of dwarven 'telling.' The teller *has* to be the hero. Facts wouldn't have gained fair trade."

"You did well," he said. "Very well. I had no idea you could give such a performance."

Wynn flushed, surprised by the effect of his praise.

"I thought they would jeer you off the floor in three or four phrases," he went on.

She stopped in her tracks. "You thought what?"

Chane's expression went blank. "I only meant—"

Wynn hissed at him, mocking his voice, and trudged onward. Jeered off the floor? Indeed! Was that what he thought of her? She lost count of the tunnels, and spun about to check again.

"Five!" she said tartly, and turned back to the last one they'd passed. "Let's find the smithy."

Then her stomach rolled. Or the stone beneath her seemed to do so. An acrid taste coated her tongue.

Chane's mouth tightened, as if he were still puzzled by her offense—the dolt.

Just as Hammer-Stag had said, they couldn't have missed the smithy. Of the few establishments or residences cut into the dark path's stone, it was the only one still aglow. With its old door shoved inward, warm red-orange light flickered upon the tunnel's floor and opposite wall.

"It's still open?" Wynn said in surprise.

"Not likely," Chane answered. "It is well past the mid of night . . . unless . . ."

Wynn didn't need him to finish. How long had they lingered in the greeting house? Was dawn already near?

Shade sniffed—and then sneezed—as she crept toward the door.

The scent of char and metal increased around Wynn, sharpening her dizziness, but she spotted no smoke. That seemed impossible at this depth. She stepped in beside Shade, peeking through the smithy's open door.

Inside, a young dwarven woman pounded on a red-hot mule shoe gripped in iron tongs. Sparks flew at the hammer's dull clanks. Although wide like her people, she looked slight for a dwarf. A mass of sweaty red hair was tied back at the nape of her neck.

Her simple shirt was of some coarse, heavy fabric and rolled up at the sleeves. She wore leather pants with a matching apron darkened from labor. Strangest was her glistening, soot-marred face.

All dwarves had small, pure black irises, but hers seemed a bit larger than High-Tower's. Her nose was a touch smaller, and she didn't have his blockish wide jaw. Hers was smoothly curved. Severe-looking, she still didn't bear much resemblance to her older brother.

Was she an Iron-Braid or a hired craftswoman in the family's smithy?

Glancing into the red-lit space, Wynn took in the long, open stone forge, its hot coals so bright they stung her eyes. Thick-planked tables lined the walls, laden with tools as well as rough collections of goods either finished or needing more work. A pile of mule shoes rested on the table nearest the door. A way back was another table burdened with ax, pick, and sledge heads, and other implements for miners.

There was so much for such a small, out-of-the way place that Wynn realized other workers must be employed here. But on this late night, the young woman labored alone. That didn't seem right for hired help.

Then, upon the rearmost table, Wynn caught a soft glint—two glints, actually.

A pair of swords lay beside one heavy buckler shield. One was shorter and broader, with a thickened hilt obviously made for a dwarf. The second was a single-handed longsword suitable for a human. Both had the distinctive dark, mottled gray sheen of dwarven steel.

Not all smiths were weaponers. It was a specialty of great skill, though Wynn knew little about the craft either way. But those weapons, simple and unadorned, as preferred by the dwarves, looked finer than all she remembered from her travels.

Someone here had higher skills than the making of mule shoes.

A strange sound filled the smithy, like a rhythmic puffing of breath, as a gray mass slowly descended beyond the open forge. Two cask-size iron counterweights, one rising as the other fell, hung on a chain over a cart-wheel-size gear mounted to the ceiling. At each jolting descent, a smaller gear did a full turn, driving an iron arm connected to a bellows pump. But the coals did not pulse with the bellows.

A wide tin flue above the forge caught rising smoke and seemed to suck it up like a mouth. Each "breath" came in time with the bellows' pumps. The counterweights halted, and the tin mouth went silent.

Wynn saw thin smoke spill upward over the flue's lip.

The woman jammed the mule shoe into the coals in a burst of sparks and stepped around to grab a chain dangling from the higher counterweight. She hauled upon it, thick muscles bulging in her arms as it changed places with its counterpart. When she released her grip, the clicking of chains and gears resumed, along with the flue's pulsing breaths. The woman rounded the forge and picked up her iron tongs.

Though dizzy, Wynn clearly remembered Hammer-Stag's accounting of names. High-Tower's sister was named Skirra, which roughly meant "Sliver" in Numanese. As the smith jerked the mule shoe from the coals and set its red-hot metal upon the anvil, Wynn stepped in and dropped her pack inside the doorway.

"Is this the Iron-Braid smithy?" she called out. "Run by Sliver?"

The woman's hammer hung poised in the air. Her dark eyes rested briefly on Wynn, shifted to Chane, and finally dropped to Shade.

"We are closed," she said in a deep voice.

The hammer fell with a sharp clank, sparks spitting from struck metal.

Wynn hesitated. "Are you . . . Sliver Iron-Braid?"

"Come back tomorrow," the woman said.

That wasn't a denial. Wynn's stomach rolled again as she took two steps, trying not to trip on her robe.

"We're not seeking s-s-services," she said, and then stopped, trying to swallow away the cottony sensation in her mouth.

The woman lowered her hammer until its head barely clicked upon the anvil.

"I am Wynn Hye . . Hyj . . . orth . . . of the Guild of Sagecraft," Wynn added. "I . . . we stay at the temple of Bezu . . . Bedaka . . ." She gave up on Dwarvish. "We stay at the temple of Feather-Tongue. We traveled a long way for news of your brother."

Sliver's expression hardened. Even her cheekbones appeared to bulge above a clenched mouth.

"The smithy is closed!" she snarled. "And maybe you would know more of my brother than I!"

Shade paused in sniffing about the nearest table legs, and Chane stepped in quickly, placing a warning hand on Wynn's shoulder. Wynn didn't know how she'd given offense.

"No . . . not High-Tower," she corrected. "Your other brother."

Sliver straightened slowly, not blinking once as she stared back. She sucked air through reclenched teeth and took a fast step toward Wynn, the hammer still in her fist.

"Get out!" she roared.

Before Wynn finished a cringe, Chane stood partially in front of her. Sliver sneered at him, not the least bit intimidated.

"I said leave," she repeated, full of warning. "I have no other brother!"

Wynn's brief fright faded. Perhaps it was how dwarves respected strength and forthrightness, or maybe just pride at her successful "telling" in the greeting house. Something emboldened Wynn, but it certainly wasn't the ale. She stepped directly into Sliver's face.

"Don't lie to me!" she shouted back. "I saw him when he came to the guild to visit High-Tower. He's one of your people's Stonewalkers."

Sliver's mouth gaped, and she backed one step. "Meâkesa . . . went to Chlâyard?"

Then her voice failed, and so did Wynn's.

Why did a meeting between brothers shock their sister so much? Then Wynn realized through her haze that Sliver had just given her the name of a stonewalker.

Meâkesa . . . Ore-Locks.

"We need to speak with Ore-Locks," Wynn insisted. "It's critical. Where do I find him?"

Sliver shuddered as her face twisted in revulsion . . . or was it fear, perhaps pain?

When Wynn had eavesdropped outside of High-Tower's study, she got the sense that he hadn't seen his brother in years. They were both so bitter, with no connection other than blood. Shirvêsh Mallet hadn't heard from High-Tower for a decade or more, and the mention of Ore-Locks visiting High-Tower had struck Sliver even harder.

How long had it been since either brother had looked in upon their younger sister?

Sliver snatched the front of Wynn's robe.

Wynn sucked in a breath in fright. Before she shouted a warning, Chane latched onto the smith's thick wrist, and Wynn never got out a word. Sliver released her hammer and rammed her flat palm into Chane's lower chest.

Chane was gone before Wynn heard the hammer clank onto the floor.

She heard Chane hit the outer passage's far wall in a clatter of packs as Shade let out a savage rolling snarl. Sliver's face twisted in an echo of the dog's noise as she hoisted Wynn higher.

Wynn's feet left the floor, and ale welled up in her throat.

She couldn't even gasp as Sliver threw her out of the smithy after Chane. She slammed against something yielding but firm, and the staff clattered from her grip as she flailed. Then Chane's arms wrapped around her as they both fell back against the passage's far wall.

The tunnel's dimness, welling ale, and the haze in Wynn's head mounted one upon another. She slid down Chane's legs to the floor, struggling to get untangled from her twisted cloak. She heard and saw Shade poised and snapping in the doorway before the maddened smith.

"Shade . . . no!" she gagged out.

Foam built in the back of Wynn's throat, filling her whole mouth with a bitter, acrid taste. She tumbled forward onto all fours as Chane crab-stepped aside to get his footing.

"Shade!" Wynn choked out. "No!"

The dog finally backed into the passage, still growling.

Sliver spun away into the smithy and slammed the door shut.

Wynn's last glimpse of High-Tower's sister was of a face warped by outrage and fright. She tried to get up, but the floor seemed to roll beneath her hands like a ship's deck.

Her stomach clenched so hard she squeaked in pain.

Chane watched helplessly as Wynn vomited all over the tunnel floor. When she retched again, he dropped to his knees and pulled back her hair. He had to grab her when she almost collapsed in the pool of slightly foaming ale.

She felt so small in his arms as her body clenched and heaved, and she finally collapsed against him. Her eyes closed as she went limp with a shuddering inhale.

"Wynn?" he whispered, afraid to even shake her a little.

Shade rushed over, whining in open alarm, and began pawing at Wynn's robe.

"Back," Chane rasped, but the dog either did not understand or would not listen.

"Witless . . ." Wynn mumbled. "Witless . . . Wynn . . . me and my stupid—"

Another heave cut off her babble, and she curled over Chane's folded knees, trying to hold it back.

Chane looked frantically up and down the tunnel.

Lost in an underground city of foreign people, with only an antagonistic elven dog and a half-conscious sage, what could he possibly do? If not for Shade's presence, he would have hunted down some lone resident and forced answers to his need.

Down the way, a bulky figure stepped out of a draped doorway.

Chane glanced at Shade and gritted his teeth.

"Pardon," he rasped in Numanese, hoping his maimed voice did not startle the person.

The figure paused and turned and then came thumping down the way. As the man entered the bit of red light seeping through the smithy door's cracks, Chane looked into the face of a young male dwarf. Beardless and dressed in burlap breeches and jerkin under a rabbit fur vest, he wore a sloppy hat of lime-striped canvas slouched upon his head of wiry brown hair.

"I need to find the nearest inn . . . common house . . . lodge," Chane said in frustration.

The young dwarf crouched, frowned at the pool foaming ale, and then peered at Wynn's huddled form.

"*A'ye, dené beghân thuag-na yune rugh'gire!*" he said, and shook his head with a sympathetic sigh.

Chane sagged. His first lone encounter was with a dwarf who did not speak Numanese. Even intimidation would gain him nothing. He slid Wynn's staff into the lashing on his own pack, mounting the whole of it onto his back, and then grabbed for his other pack, preparing to head out in search of an inn.

"*Cheâ, âha a-chadléag silédí?*" said the dwarf, jutting his broad chin at Wynn, and then glanced expectantly at Chane.

Chane shook his head in confusion.

The young dwarf huffed his own frustration. He slapped his hands together, fingers flush, then tilted them and laid his cheek against them. All through this, Shade quietly crept closer, staring fixedly at the dwarf. With his eyes closed, the young dwarf made a show of snoring. Then he opened his eyes, pointed at Wynn, and repeated insistently, "*Chadléag!*"

Shade bolted off up the tunnel, but Chane had no time for her nonsense.

"Yes . . . sleep!" he replied. "She needs sleep! Where . . . where do I go?"

"*Kre?*" said the dwarf.

Chane set down his second pack. He walked two fingers across the floor, mimicking someone on their way, and then pointed in every direction. Finally, he held up his hands in mock futility.

"Chad-lay-ag?" he tried to repeat.

The young dwarf chuckled. He slapped the floor, held up four fingers, and pointed to the tunnel roof.

Chane stared back in confusion. To make matters worse, somewhere behind him up the tunnel, Shade began barking.

The dwarf shook his head again. He walked his own fingers across the floor, and then up and up into the air in a steady rise. He slapped the floor, held up four fingers, and pointed upward again.

Chane finally understood, but it was not the best news. A place for Wynn to sleep was at least four levels up, possibly all the way to the tram level, if he had correctly counted the levels down.

Shade kept on with her noise.

"Be quiet!" Chane rasped, turning on one knee.

Shade snarled at him, pacing near the intersection. She then lunged partway down the tunnel, wheeled about, and rushed back to its end. She stood there rumbling before the side way's exit.

"You are an idiot," Chane whispered to himself, remembering how the dog had stared at the dwarf.

Shade already knew where to go. She had caught the young man's memories as he tried to make his instructions understood.

Chane hooked Wynn's legs and shoulders in his arms. The dwarf scooted forward, as if to help. Chane shook his head and rose up, towering over his happenstance guide. The young dwarf's expression blanked in surprise at how easily he bore all that he carried.

"Thank you," Chane said flatly with a nod.

The young dwarf acknowledged him silently in turn, and Chane hurried off, carrying Wynn.

Shade ducked into the mainway ahead of him, trotting too quickly. Then she suddenly stopped.

The instant Chane caught up, a twinge halted him as well—so quick it was but a feathery touch. Or rather it felt as if something should be there but was not, like stepping into an empty room that did not *feel* empty. Then it was gone.

Shade rumbled. Her sound broke and stuttered. The charcoal fur on her neck stood on end.

Chane held Wynn tighter against his chest. That presence, or lack of it . . . had it been there at all?

Shade fell silent and inched forward, swinging her lowered head side to side, and watching all ways with each step. Chane knew he was not the only one who had felt it. Something had been there, was not there but should have been, or . . .

He turned a full circle but felt nothing—truly nothing at all.

Chane had worn Welstiel's ring of nothing for moons. As much as it hid his nature and inner self from all unnatural detection, it also dulled his awareness as a Noble Dead. Taking it off in Shade's presence was not an option; she would instantly sense what he was. But was something near, something even Shade could not pinpoint?

Shade quieted and raised her head as if listening.

Wynn moaned in discomfort, and Chane took off down the mainway. Shade finally darted ahead to lead.

He had a long way to go, and hunger was beginning to weaken him. As they followed the wide turns to the upper levels, he walked as fast as he dared without breaking into a run. He was nearly to the top, or so he thought, when Wynn stirred in his arms and open her glazed eyes.

"Be still," he said. "Shade is leading us to a place where you can rest."

"I'm so sick," she whispered.

"I know."

She groaned when he shifted his arms; then her eyes widened. "My pack . . . where . . . do you have it?"

Chane halted on the sloping turn. He had not even thought about it; he had thought only of the staff. And now, he could not remember her pack in the passage when he had knelt next to her.

Then he did remember. Wynn had dropped her pack inside the smithy.

She struggled in his arms. "Put me down. Everything . . . my notes . . . elven quill . . . translations . . . someone will find them!"

Chane cursed under his breath—another oblivious stupidity on his part. For an instant, he considered abandoning the pack, but he could not. Wynn was right on every count. Her journals held recent notes of folklore research on undead, of their encounters with the wraith and pieces from the ancient texts . . . and the partial translation from his scroll.

It was all in her pack.

He had to get to it quickly before anyone stumbled upon it, digging inside to figure out where it had come from or to whom it belonged. Or worse, walked off with it, not even knowing what they had.

Chane trotted past Shade around the turn, entering one of the end caverns of a mainway tunnel. He spotted the first shop down the way with a thick stone archway, and he caught a hint of sea salt in the air. They had reached the uppermost level, though he had not noticed. Chane hurried over and set Wynn inside the door's shadowed archway.

"Shade will stay with you. I can go faster alone. Rest here and stay out of sight."

Wynn bit her lower lip, her sallow face scrunched in a grimace.

"I ruined our only real lead!" she whispered.

There was plenty of blame to share for this fouled exploit, but Chane had no time to console her. Wynn's head rolled back, and he feared she would be sick again, but she just leaned against the archway's cold stone.

"Shade!" Chane rasped, and pointed to Wynn. "Stay."

Shade wrinkled a jowl at him. The order was unnecessary, as the dog had never willingly left Wynn's side. Halfway to the end cavern and downward passage, Chane stopped one last time, gazing at Wynn's pretty face—so miserable.

As Chane backed away, Shade drew in next to Wynn. He turned and jogged back into the depths, his own emotions a puzzle to him.

For so long, he had tortured himself with visions of Wynn the sage, the perfect and pure scholar—the one he could never have. In his mind, she was always in clean gray robes, her brown hair tucked back, a parchment before her, a glowing cold lamp and a mug of mint tea nearby. Always studious, intellectual, inquisitive, she was so far above the human cattle of the world.

Yet this night, she had entertained a mass of common dwarves, performing for them—something he could not possibly have imagined. Now drunk, her own vomit staining her hands, she slumped in a doorway, bemoaning her mistakes.

This Wynn was nothing like the one in Chane's mind. Yet, he was driven to care for her, to protect her, even more than the one of his fantasies. He hated leaving her alone, but he kept hearing her words concerning all that was in her pack.

Someone will find them.

Chane rushed into a cavern where the downward-curving tunnel ended. He ran past the greeting house, counting off northbound passages until the fifth. He slowed near its mouth, looking inward. A full red glow spilled into the passage where the smithy was positioned.

Sliver must have waited until her unwanted guests departed and then reopened the door.

Chane did not have time to ponder why. The open door could be lucky or unlucky, depending upon the exact spot where Wynn had dropped her pack. Slipping along the wall, he drew as close as he dared without being seen by anyone inside. He leaned around the door frame enough to peek at the floor inside—and spotted no sign of the pack.

Ducking low, he shot across to the door's other side and peered in again.

To Chane's relief, there was the pack, just inside the door's left atop a stack of folded canvas. It blended so well in the low red light that anyone might have overlooked it. Dropping to his hands and knees, he reached in and then spotted Sliver.

Chane pulled back quickly.

Sliver stood leaning against a table with one hand covering her mouth.

Embers in the open forge were waning, and it was hard to make out her face. Another movement at the workshop's rear caught Chane's attention.

A door opened in the workshop's back wall.

Sliver looked up, turning her back to Chane. An old dwarven woman with wild white hair and a long, dull blue woolen robe stepped out of some well-lit back room. Sliver hunched her shoulders as she spit out a curt string of Dwarvish.

The old woman stepped closer, and her wrinkled face twisted into desperation. She gripped a table's edge and uttered a reply so pained that Chane was riveted, wishing he understood the words.

Sliver scoffed and turned away from the old woman. Perhaps it was to hide the sudden doubt that crossed her face.

A domestic dispute was clearly in play. Chane wondered, considering it came so close behind their visit, if the two events were connected.

The old woman's next utterance was sharp if not loud, and Sliver straightened. So did Chane at the sound of one word—*say-gee.*

Could that word have been "sage," garbled by the old one's accent?

Sliver turned angrily to face her elder, her back to the outer door.

Chane took the opportunity and reached in for Wynn's pack.

Sau'ilahk hung motionless at the intersection as Chane scurried across the smithy's doorway. He had tried to follow all three of his quarry, but the cursed dog had picked up his presence. On some level, Chane had seemed to "feel" him as well. Sau'ilahk had been forced to slip into dormancy, vanishing quickly from either's awareness.

He waited in that pure darkness as long as he dared, then awakened once more in the same dark spot inside Limestone Mainway's end chamber. At the sound of footsteps in the upward-bound tunnel, he followed and watched as Chane hid Wynn in a doorway and turned back.

Sau'ilahk was pleased, even as he blinked away once more to let Chane pass by. He now had the chance to pull closer, to see and hear what Chane sought in this dingy, forgotten smithy. He focused on a point farther down the side tunnel, slipped into dormancy, and reappeared at that place.

Beyond the smith shop, Sau'ilahk listened to two female voices arguing within. Dwarvish was one of many tongues he had picked up over the centuries. He ignored Chane and focused on their words.

"Go back inside the house, Mother," said the first, low and bitter.

The other cried out in an age-broken voice. "If the shirvêsh of Bedzâ'kenge assisted the sage, there is good reason she seeks Meâkesa . . . and you sent her away! Why did you not help her to find your brother?"

Sau'ilahk knew from his servitor eavesdropping on Wynn that these people must be High-Tower's family. "Meâkesa" translated as "Ore-colored Hair." Wynn sought the Stonewalkers through a link between them and a son of the Iron-Braid family—High-Tower's brother.

"Why should I help her?" the first voice returned. "He abandoned us long ago . . . as did Chlâyard! Neither of them even returned when Father fell ill. Tell me, Mother, how should I have helped? We do not even know where he is!"

"It is a sign," the creaking voice wailed. "The coming of a human sage is a sign. Do you not see? We are to be rejoined with Meâkesa. Help her!"

The smithy fell silent, and Sau'ilahk saw Chane stealthily reach inside the open door. An instant later, he pulled back, holding a faded canvas pack.

This was what he came for—a forgotten pack?

Sau'ilahk mulled over the conversation.

Wynn had come all the way down here and been sent away. She had been seeking a connection to the Stonewalkers, but it seemed she had gained no lead. But that connection was here, waiting, and only an old woman seemed to care that it was fulfilled.

Sau'ilahk had little knowledge of these Stonewalkers—little more than rumors of the sect from centuries ago. At the least, they were hidden guardians of the dwarven dead. He had never had a reason to learn more.

In Calm Seatt, he had searched the guild grounds for many nights. Rumors passed on by his informants had called him to the king's city of Malourné after Wynn's return. But other than translation folios sent to scribe shops, he found neither trace nor hint of where the original texts were hidden. If the Stonewalkers knew their location, as Wynn seemed to suspect . . .

Then why had some cult of the dead become involved with the texts?

Sau'ilahk grew impatient with the inept sage. Wynn should be gaining information much faster! All the trouble she had caused him so far left him seething and indignant in even allowing her to live.

Chane rose, his attention no longer absorbed by his task, and then he froze. He turned about, staring deeper down the side passage. His hand dropped to his sword's hilt.

Sau'ilahk could have hissed in rage—he had been sensed! Anger turned to alarm as Chane stepped slowly in his direction. He had no fear of this man who was there and not there, but this one had survived his touch, an anomaly not to be taken lightly.

Sau'ilahk backed into—through—the tunnel's stone wall.

He lost sight of everything and twisted about—what he thought was about—hoping there was no other space behind him. He remained immersed, blinded and deafened by solid stone. But how long should he wait before Chane gave up?

Yes, Wynn was waiting, and Sau'ilahk ticked off in his mind what Chane might do.

Perhaps traverse no more than a few doorways down the tunnel. Then urgency would take him back the other way. Sau'ilahk waited even longer, and then slipped forward through stone.

As pure black broke before him into the faint red light in the passage, Sau'ilahk peered up the tunnel toward the mainway.

There was Chane, rushing away as fast as silence allowed.

Sau'ilahk stewed in envy.

Tall, pale, and handsome, yet some strange form of undead, Chane would look that way forever. Waves of jealousy grew into spite at Beloved's betrayal. Once, Chane would have been a meaningless shadow compared to Sau'ilahk's great beauty . . . so long ago.

Sau'ilahk hung there in self-pity.

If Wynn did not locate the Stonewalkers or draw them out, perhaps he would have to do it for her. There was only one way. But for this, he needed strength—he needed life to feed upon. Not a local, a dwarf, but a foreigner, some visiting human not quickly missed.

Sau'ilahk drifted along the twisting back ways of the dwarven underlevels.

The light of crystals grew sparse and excavation was not so smooth or painstaking. Places where the walls were jagged with small hollows and depressions offered shadows for him to meld into without arcane effort. He calmed, letting his presence sink into sensual awareness, searching for human life.

And he sensed one, not far off.

Sau'ilahk turned into a southbound tunnel that might even hook back toward the far-off mainway. The distance between smaller crystals in wall brackets decreased. He prepared to wink out into dormancy if needed. He could not be seen, not clearly noticed, or word of a strange dark figure might accidentally reach Wynn.

To his delight, footfalls drifted toward him from around another turn.

Sau'ilahk peered around the gradual corner and saw a lone human—a bearded man of dark skin with a curved sword in a fabric wrap belt. It was one of his own kind, or at least a descendant of such people from his lost living days. He pulled back, waiting until the man took the turn in the tunnel.

Even the approach of a victim—living in flesh—taunted him.

Long ago, he had been first among the Reverent, favorite of Beloved—before the Children came. His mere visage among the hordes and followers had inspired awe. Now he was nothing but a shadow of black robe, cloak, and hood. Not true flesh, and only by the act of feeding could he gain enough strength to take physical action. He did not even have the grace of a true ghost, to pass unseen if he wished.

All because of the bargain he had struck, once the Children first appeared.

All because of Beloved's coy consent, twisting Sau'ilahk's plea.

The bearded Suman rounded the corner. Jarred from misery, Sau'ilahk lashed out.

His black cloth-wrapped fingers passed down through the man's face.

The Suman's skin paled slightly along those fingers' path. And quick as the stroke was, the man never cried out. He shuddered, his breath caught, and his hand reaching for the sword only convulsed in spasms, until . . .

Sau'ilahk's hand slid down through the man's throat and sank into his chest near his heart, draining his life away.

The Suman dropped hard onto his knees and toppled over. He lay there, face frozen in shock, with mouth agape, and Sau'ilahk's immaterial hand embedded in his chest.

Shots of gray spread through the Suman's dark curls and beard, until cloth-wrapped fingers withdrew, leaving no physical wound.

Sau'ilahk's weakness faded beneath the consumed life, and he could not afford to waste any of it in destroying the corpse. He might require even more life for what he needed to accomplish. He threaded a mere fragment of his gained energies into one hand, turning it corporeal, and dragged the body along the passage to a nearby shadowed depression.

Then he sank into dormancy to fully absorb his meal.

But as he dissipated into darkness, his last thoughts were of Wynn. If the bungling sage could not find the Hassäg'kreigi, the Stonewalkers, then he would have to draw them into plain sight. And the Stonewalkers emerged for only one reason.

Sau'ilahk had to kill a thänæ.

CHAPTER 6

Misery dragged Wynn toward consciousness. Grudgingly, she cracked open her eyes.

She lay on a rock-hard bed in a strange room, still fully dressed, but she had no strength to wonder why or where she was. Rolling over was torture, and she came face-to-face with Shade's snoring muzzle.

"Oh," she moaned, slapping a hand over her mouth and nose.

Dog's breath wasn't good for a sick stomach.

Cream-colored shimmers from Shade's undercoat peeked through her charcoal fur every time her rib cage rose in a slow breath. Fragments of the previous night returned to Wynn: the greeting house, a barter with a thänæ, and a telling before a crowd, then the smithy . . . and Sliver. She had enraged High-Tower's sister, alienating the one possible lead to finding the Stonewalkers.

"Oh, seven hells," she said, groaning as her stomach clenched.

Shade's left ear twitched, her crystal blue irises peeking through slitted eyelids.

Wynn rolled away to hang over the bed's side, desperately looking for anything to throw up in. Another convulsion came, and she hung there to vomit on the floor. But nothing came up.

When her dry heaves passed, they left a skull-splitting headache and a feverish flush. Something cold and wet snuffled Wynn's cheek, and a slathering warmth dragged over her face.

"Oh, don't do that!"

Wynn shoved Shade's muzzle away, but at that touch, flashes of last night poured into her head.

She remembered—Shade remembered—Wynn sitting in a doorway as

Chane headed off after the forgotten pack. Clear images showed him returning to carry her down the mainway near where they'd first entered Sea-Side. He had all three packs and her staff.

"All right, I see," Wynn grumbled, looking around the unfamiliar room.

Where was Chane?

Shade growled, and Wynn rolled back. The dog sat behind her, gazing steadily beyond the bed's foot. Wynn crawled around Shade and went to look.

Chane lay prone on the floor with a pack for a pillow and his cloak as a bedroll. His jagged red-brown hair was a mess, and his white shirt was wrinkled. With his eyes closed, his long features were smooth and relaxed.

He wasn't breathing and lay still as—was—a corpse upon the floor.

Self-pity and a throbbing head made Wynn almost envy such a state.

The tiny room had no window, of course, and was sparsely furnished with the one hard bed, a lidded brazier of dwarven crystals, and a small door-side table bearing a tin cup and clay pitcher. She desperately needed to wash the horrid taste from her mouth.

Scooting back, Wynn climbed off the bedside, not wanting to step over Chane's body, and staggered to the table. She hoisted the pitcher and gulped from it.

Her stomach felt as if it had been turned inside out. How could three or four—or was it more—sips of ale affect her like this? What was in those tankards that had worked so slowly, creeping up on her, until the night had gotten completely out of hand?

She sipped again and then grabbed the cup, pouring water for Shade. As Shade hopped off the bed to lap at the cup, Wynn plopped down on the floor, sick and miserable. She remembered Sliver's raging and pained expression.

She couldn't go back to the smithy again. She had closed that door more soundly than Sliver had. So what now? They couldn't give up. They had to locate the texts and uncover what the wraith had been seeking. She had to learn more about the orb, its purpose, and the Ancient Enemy of many names. She had to find out if it was returning . . . and if it could be stopped.

Something—anything—that might connect even one disjointed piece to another.

All of this made her dizzy and sick again.

She rose with effort, barely able to stand with her head pounding even more, and then slapped a hand over her mouth. For an intant, she feared she might lose the water she had just swallowed. Then she heard soft voices somewhere outside the wide oak door.

Where was she? There were only two things she could reason out: Chane had procured a room in some inn, and it must be daytime, since he was still dormant. She pulled back the slide bolt and cracked the door open.

Two doors down, the corridor emptied into an open space. There stood a somewhat flabby dwarven woman in an apron, gripping a straw broom. She was chatting with a young male behind a stout desk.

"Pardon," Wynn called, and her own vile breath made her want to cover her mouth again. "Can you tell me the time of day?"

The male leaned sideways, peeking around his companion, and both dwarves' eyes widened.

Wynn winced—she must look worse than she imagined. But the one behind the desk corrected his expression to polite disinterest.

"Yes, miss, it is just past Day-Winter's start."

"My thanks."

Wynn pulled back and shut the door. How could she have slept until midafternoon?

She had only one friendly contact in all of Dhredze Seatt. That was Shirvêsh Mallet, back in Bay-Side—all the way on the mountain's other side. Perhaps if pressed more subtly, the old shirvêsh might give her another lead, some other way to find the Stonewalkers. Or failing that, he might provide some custom to help make amends with Sliver.

The dwarves were a people of long tradition, couched in clan and tribal rules and rituals. Yes, for now Shirvêsh Mallet was her best and only choice—in a retreat from her mistakes.

Wynn slid down the door and patted the floor for Shade's attention. The dog just stared at her, so she held out her hands. Shade padded over, and Wynn took the dog's face in her hands, calling up memories of the temple. Before she even raised an image of the tram, Shade backpedaled out of reach, growling at her.

"I know it was awful," Wynn whispered, "but we have to go."

Chane still hadn't moved. Back at the guild, he'd slept in a bed in Domin il'Sänke's chambers, but she'd peeked in there only occasionally. So far in this journey, they'd arranged for separate rooms, and Wynn had never seen him in full dormancy before. The sight was unnerving, but at least the sun didn't matter inside the mountain.

If they started back now, the tram would arrive at Bay-Side by early night. They would reach the temple not long past supper—a good time to speak with Shirvêsh Mallet.

Trying to ignore her pounding head, Wynn crawled toward Chane.

She stopped near his shoulder and looked down at him, almost feeling as if she invaded his privacy. He might not like for her to study him like this—so dead and still upon the floor.

He was proud, but secretly this was one of the things she admired about him. She could not help thinking back to those distant nights in Bela, at the newly founded branch for the Guild of Sagecraft, when he visited and drank mint tea with her as they pored over historical parchments. A handsome young nobleman seeking out her company, of all people.

Then she'd learned the truth about him.

He was a vampire who drank blood to continue existing, and of course she'd shut him out of her life. But nearly every time her life was in danger, he'd appeared from nowhere to throw himself in front of her, to protect her at any cost. Once, when she'd been locked away by a brutish warlord, Chane had broken into the keep, killed several soldiers, and carried her out through an underwater tunnel.

Wynn didn't fully understand Chane's feelings for her. She knew they were strong, and she wasn't the sort of woman who normally inspired such in men. There had been only one other.

Osha, a young elf and an'Cróan had been in training to be an Anmaglâhk—an assassin—though he'd been ill-suited to such a pursuit. He was not handsome, even compared to a human, with a long, horselike face. Nor was he as brooding or intellectual as Chane. Osha's emotions were always so plain to see, but this made his wonder and kindness show as well, even when tainted by his people's hate and fear of other races. He was unflinching and steady, and had befriended Wynn when she'd needed one. And perhaps he had felt even more than friendship for her.

If Wynn had wanted to, she could have pulled him further toward her—

but she hadn't. He'd had to return to his people, and she'd been told to return home as well. What could've been, couldn't be between them.

Sometimes, she missed him, thought of him. But when his face rose in her thoughts, somehow, Chane's always did so as well—even when she didn't want it to.

Wynn sat there on the floor, looking down at Chane's smooth, pale features and red-brown hair, wishing. . . .

Things could be different, if he weren't undead. But he was, and nothing could change that.

She finally reached out and touched his shoulder, stiff under her fingers.

"Chane," she said softly. "Wake up."

He didn't move. The sun's rhythm shouldn't affect him down here. Was something wrong? She grasped the side of his shirt, trying to shake him, and the effort made her stomach worse.

"Chane!"

His head lolled. That limp movement was almost frightening, as if he were truly dead . . . or no longer undead . . . dormant . . . whatever.

Chane's eyelids snapped wide.

Wynn jerked upright, but not before his hand shot out and grabbed her wrist.

"Oww! Stop!"

Before she pulled against his grip, he whirled over and pinned her to the floor.

"Chane, stop it!"

He sat halfway up, staring down at her, and then recognition spread across his twisted features. He rolled off of her in sudden shock and closed his eyes as he flattened onto his back again, as if exhausted.

Wynn sat up, watching him cautiously as she rubbed her wrist.

"Don't go back to sleep," she urged. "We need to catch the tram and return to Bay-Side."

This time, Chane opened his eyes and truly looked at her. "Wynn?"

"Of course," she answered, but the question left her worried about his state. "You have to get up. We've lost too much time already."

She felt as if they'd lost whole days because of her blundering.

"Tonight . . ." Chane slurred. "We can . . . go . . . tonight."

If they waited until dusk, it would be the middle of the night before they reached the temple. Mallet would be asleep, and she didn't know if anyone else would be up to let them in. Who could say when she might catch the shirvêsh at another opportune moment?

Wynn took hold of Chane's arm. "Get up! You can sleep on the tram."

"I do not . . . sleep!" he snarled. "That is for the living."

Wynn froze, but she didn't have time to ponder his strange comment. With a mix of coaxing and bullying, she got him on his feet, and they gathered their belongings.

Without Shade, Wynn didn't know how they would've managed. The dog's perfect memory led them back to the tram station, though in the end, Wynn had to wrestle a groggy Chane and a stubborn Shade on board. At least it distracted her from her own reluctance for the ride.

Chane collapsed on a bench, and Shade growled as Wynn shoved the dog's rump to get her into the tram. Wynn settled on the bench's end near the aisle.

The long ride back began, and soon, the sickness she'd felt upon waking became nothing compared to the return to Sea-Side. Somewhere along the way, she forgot everything but her misery.

The car was sparsely populated, and she leaned forward, bracing against the back of the next bench. She tried hard not to retch, but Shade lay under her bench making enough pathetic noises for both of them. Only Chane remained still and silent.

Time passed too slowly in the tram's endless rush. Trying to think of anything besides her suffering, Wynn found herself wondering . . .

Was there something more Chane had meant about sleep being "for the living"?

"Chane," she whispered with effort. "Do you . . . do Noble Dead dream . . . when they sleep . . . I mean, go dormant?"

At first he didn't answer. He finally twitched, straightened, and then fell back against the rail wall before catching himself.

"Wynn?" he rasped, his eyes half open in confusion. "Where are we? Are you all right?"

He seemed himself again, and in part, she was relieved to have him back. The sun must have set outside the mountain, though it was always dark as night in the tram tunnel. He frowned and reached for her, trying to help her sit back.

"No," she managed to say. "I'm not all right. Just let me lean here."

They returned to silence beneath the chatter of the tram's wheels in the tunnel's steel-lined ruts. Wynn was barely aware when those wheels began to screech and finally slowed.

Bright lights from huge crystals in the walls illuminated the Bay-Side station platforms.

Chane tried to help her up. She pulled away, grabbing her pack and staff.

"I can walk."

When they reached the market cavern, Wynn balked at the noise of lingering vendors and customers hammering at her aching head. She couldn't remember ever feeling this ill before, not even the morning after Magiere and Leesil's wedding feast. Chane led them out through the cavern's enormous mouth.

Wynn later remembered stepping into the cold night air and seeing the back side of the way station's crank house. She remembered Shade trotting up the street of great steaming orange crystals, and Chane taking hold of her to follow. But the rest remained a blur.

She forgot about speaking with Shirvêsh Mallet and barely recalled passing through the temple's tall brass arch bell and the wide marble doors. Even these details didn't come back until she found herself in a small room, dimly lit in red-orange, and she crumpled upon the hard bed. Chane pulled a blanket up around her chin.

He held a cup of water to her lips, but she could take only a sip.

"I will check on you before dawn," he whispered.

The little world of that room grew dark, but not before Wynn again wondered . . . *Do the dead dream?*

It wasn't the best thought with which to fall asleep.

Chane slipped from Wynn's room under Shade's cold stare and quietly closed the door. He was hungry and dazed. Rarely had his dormancy been interrupted, and he felt something like what he remembered of going without sleep in his living days.

It made him feel even weaker . . . and hungrier.

Worse, when he turned about, Shirvêsh Mallet came bustling down the corridor. Chane was not up to polite conversation.

"I was told young Wynn is ill," Mallet blurted out. "Does she need care?"

Chane tried to stand straight. The blunt question was welcome, as all he could do for Wynn was give her water and let her rest.

"She drank dwarven ale . . . too much, in a Sea-Side greeting house," he rasped. "It has affected her badly."

"Oh, good grace!" the shirvêsh exclaimed. "What was she thinking? And you moved her? What were *you* thinking?"

Chane bit his lip in restraint. "She insisted on coming back," he answered politely. "I could not refuse."

Mallet's wrinkled face softened. "I will fetch purifying herbs for tea to clean out her blood. She will be shaky for a few days." He shook his head, white hair swishing over his shoulders. "Dwarven ale is not for such a tiny Numan . . . *someone* should have stopped her!"

Indeed, Chane thought.

"Get some rest yourself, lad," Mallet added.

Nodding, and surprised at his own gratitude, Chane stepped into his own room across the way, but only closed the door to a crack. He waited long enough for the shirvêsh to trundle off and then slipped along the passages and through the roundabout circling the chamber of the dwarven Eternal. No one seemed to notice him, even as he exited out into the night. He paced the mountainside's winding streets, his thoughts twisting inward.

Wynn's ignorant gift of goat's blood made him wonder about feeding on livestock. Mules used at the crank house's turnstile had to be stabled nearby. Or could he solve the mystery of Welstiel's arcane feeding cup?

The beast with hands, chained down within him, lunged at its bonds, howling to be fed.

Neither cup nor livestock appealed to him. Yet he had to find a way to survive, while keeping his feeding to a minimum. He wandered down the mountain's street, poignantly aware that he was alone and unrestrained. To protect Wynn, he needed the strength of life—and she need never know how.

Chane slowed.

Directly ahead lay the lift's way station, crank house, and the huge glowing maw of the market cavern's entrance. He had not even thought about where he was going, yet here he was. Or had that other part of him known? Had the beast pushed him here, already hunting while he was distracted in thought?

Chane looked from the way station to the cavern's entrance. People were still about. A few even passed him on the street, giving him little notice. He could not risk feeding upon someone who lived here—someone with a clan and a tribe, as well as family, who would notice one of their own gone missing. His brief encounter with Sliver emphasized Wynn's warning against matching strength with a dwarf.

He needed a visitor, a traveler . . . a human.

Chane stepped away from the pylons' crystals and slipped into a darker path between buildings at the settlement's cliff side. He took little notice of the structures' back sides as he moved quietly down the short-walled cobbled walkway along the cliff. When he neared the row's end, close enough to see the way station, neither a cargo nor a passenger lift was currently docked. He peered over the retaining wall and along the sheer mountainside, but did not see any lift crawling up the steep stone road.

Chane leaned against the wall and looked upward. He had to shift along the path to see between the buildings. It was the same above, where the empty stone road continued toward the mountain's top, perhaps all the way to what Wynn had called Old-Seatt.

Sudden voices made him duck away from the wall and against the last building's back side.

Chane peered around the corner toward the night chatter's source. Four humans in the attire of the well-to-do rounded the crank house. One sounded as if he were chuckling at his own wit. The others merely smiled or nodded, and only the last responded, too low to hear. But the first boisterous one . . .

Chane knew what to look for.

The small group separated as three headed off toward the lift. But the talkative one, so amused with himself, waved a hand in parting and turned up the street along the pylons.

A lone merchant in a foreign settlement.

Chane sped along the cliff-side path behind the buildings. When he reached the next alley back to the main street, he crept out near its end to watch. Searching the street's far side, he could not find the man—not until he looked along the frontage of the cliff-side structures.

There was his quarry, strolling along, but Chane held back, remaining still in the shadows. Beyond the merchant, a pair of dwarves in matched attire trudged the street's far side. Both appeared armored in hauberks of hardened leather scales. Each carried a long oak staff, used like a walking stick, not that they needed such. They glanced about with no serious interest, yet they were clearly some kind of night watch.

Chane ran his tongue over his teeth and backed deeper into the alley until the two dwarves moved on, out of sight. Then he flattened, still and quiet at the sound of approaching footfalls.

The merchant strolled right past the alley's mouth.

Chane stepped out and dropped his coin pouch.

It landed on the street with a clinking thud. An old but simple trick, used many times before—because it always worked.

"Sir," he called in Numanese. "You dropped your purse."

The merchant started at the sound of Chane's maimed voice and spun too quickly, stumbling for an instant. When he spotted Chane in his long brown cloak and well-made boots, he calmed, and then quickly checked the small bulging pouch tucked into his belt. He was more stout and solid than Chane had first noticed, with a large brown mustache hiding his upper lip.

"Thank you," he said, "but I have mine."

"Are you certain?" Chane asked. "I thought I saw it fall in your passing."

The man clearly had his purse, but he walked back toward Chane with an expectant expression. Either he too wondered who had lost it, or he thought it was just a lucky find that he might share in. He never had the chance to express either notion.

Chane lashed out.

His right hand closed over the man's mouth and jaw, and he spun back into the alley. The merchant flailed in surprise, his feet twisting under him. Before he could set his heels, Chane jerked him further into the darkness and slammed him hard against one building's stone wall.

On impact, the merchant shuddered and slumped.

Chane held his unconscious prey pinned as his senses widened.

He smelled warm flesh, heard a quickened heartbeat. His jaws ached under shifting teeth as his canines elongated. Somewhere within him, that beast clawed the floor of a dark cell, trying to break its chains and reach for the promise of blood. Its snarls mixed with screeches of hunger that shook its whole body.

Chane began to shake as he stared at the merchant's throat.

A thunder crack jarred him into sharp awareness, and he whipped his head around.

Far beyond the alley's end, across the wide main street, the two dwarves had turned back on their patrol. Their wooden staves rose and fell with every other step, cracking out the rhythm that had seemed so near in Chane's heightened hearing.

Chane rushed down the alley, dragging his prey along the wall. When he reached the end, he pinned the man against the short wall above the cliff, and clamped his other hand around the merchant's throat. He glanced back for an instant.

The night watch passed up the main street beyond sight.

Chane wrenched the merchant's head back. His jaws widened at the sight of a distended throat. The beast within him went still, panting in anticipation—until Chane paused, frozen as well.

Reason crept in—he had to think.

This moment promised ecstasy . . . and consequences. Among Numans, the humans of these lands, and perhaps dwarves as well, undead were nearly unknown. If Wynn heard of a corpse with its throat torn, who else would she think of but him?

Could he cut the man's throat, not even kill him, and make it look like a common assault? He could still drink, and the blood as a conduit would carry a bit of life into him—just enough to sustain him for a while.

The beast snarled, howling denial.

Chane wanted . . . needed this moment . . . this kill. He could do this and simply heave the body over the precipice. Days, or even a moon, would pass before it was found, if at all. No other hope of bliss was his in this existence. . . .

Except a small place in Wynn's world.

A howl vibrated deep inside Chane.

He released the merchant's throat, still gripping the man's jaw, and reached for his sword. It would take a deep but careful slice, enough to be life-threatening but not fatal.

The merchant awoke, and his hands latched onto Chane's wrist.

Even muffled beneath Chane's palm, the man's shriek rang in his ears.

Panic—or a rush of delight—smothered all reason.

Chane jerked the merchant's head aside and clamped his jaws onto the man's throat. Fatted flesh tore in his teeth and he swallowed blood as starvation took over. Life filled him, coppery and salt-laden and vibrant with a prey's horror. It had been so long since he had given in. Even in feeding in Calm Seatt, he kept himself distanced from the pleasure.

There was no beast. There was no Chane. There was only painful hunger to smother and drown. He remained fastened to his prey's throat until the man's thrashing weakened beneath him. He heard—felt—the final heartbeat.

Chane raised his head, swallowing blood that welled back up his throat into his mouth. He languished, wavering slightly in regained strength and release from hunger. When he finally opened his eyes, he gazed up at one string of stars barely shining through a cloud-coated sky.

To him, those points of light were as brilliant as full moons. The stars, like a writhing path in the blackness, reminded him of . . .

Something he thought he had glimpsed once in dark dormancy . . . and a question.

Do Noble Dead dream?

Memory of Wynn's voice made every muscle tighten, and Chane heard a muffled crackle.

Bone shifted beneath the flesh clenched in his left hand. His gaze dropped instantly from the night sky.

The merchant's jaw had shifted sideways in his grip, broken and disfigured. Even then, the beast settled in glutted contentment, and Chane dared not close his eyes or he might see Wynn staring at him.

Do Noble Dead dream when they sleep . . . I mean, go dormant?

Chane shuddered, suddenly cold inside.

Perhaps they did—or he did—but not always. When had that first started? At times, as his limbs and eyelids grew heavy and he slipped into that vacant darkness, he had been thinking of her.

He would remember her in the library of the old converted barracks in Bela. Or he imagined her in a castle far away, searching through a great library of books, tomes, and scrolls that stretched beyond sight's reach. In this last day's dormancy, he had been remembering her small room back in the guild at Calm Seatt—a place he had seen only once.

Wherever he imagined, always at night while he lay dormant for the day, she was there with him. But there was someone . . . something . . . else?

Now and then, something had moved in a dark corner or under a table beyond the reach of a dreamtime Wynn's cold lamp. Something like stars—or glints upon a black reflective surface—that coiled and rolled. But whenever he looked, nothing was there.

Always just before he rose at dusk, or when he roused too early for the tram back to Bay-Side. Wynn had been pulling at him and . . .

The beast's eager rumble made Chane convulse and then turn rigid.

Had he lunged at her? Pinned her beneath himself? No, that could never happen.

Chane jerked his hand from the corpse's dislocated jaw and let it drop. None of this mattered. It was just the power of his desire, like that of the hunt. He needed her so much that it breached the vacant time of his dormancy. That was all.

He remembered the sight of her standing in his doorway, an urn of goat's blood in her arms. What she must have endured to get it for him. He would never let her suffer that again. Now he was strong, his thoughts clear and sharp, and she need never know how.

Chane crouched to seize the body, pausing long enough to wipe his face off on the man's cloak. He heaved the corpse up and out. It cleared the wall and fell down the mountainside.

One prey among many meant nothing.

But vampires each developed different and differing degrees of abilities. In the past year, he had started to *feel* the difference between truth and deceit. Not often, and only when he was not expecting it. The beast inside of him snarled in warning, as if sensing a threat.

If Wynn found him gone, later asking where he had been . . .

Would Chane hear—feel—his own lie to her?

Sau'ilahk waited in a Sea-Side side tunnel just beyond a common dwarven tavern called Maksûin Bití—the Baited Bear. He had risen from dormancy feeling strong and alert, vital with the life of three victims. On this second night beneath the mountain, he was beginning to appreciate its many shadowy places.

Wynn had gone back to the temple at Bay-Side, but this did not matter for now. Within moments of awakening, he had conjured two servitors of Air and sent them in search of a word: "thänæ." Any such mention would trigger his elemental constructs to record all utterances until conversation ended. And one had proven useful, returning to echoing dwarven voices chattering in excitement.

". . . thänæ will come tonight!"
"Where did you hear this? No one's seen him in nearly a season."
"Well's Bottom and Gatherer were at the People's Place last—"
"Oh, mirth of the Eternals! Do not believe what you hear in that place!"
"He is back—Hammer-Stag has returned! And tonight he comes to the Baited Bear!"
"Why? That is no greeting house, and even so—"

Sau'ilahk banished his servitors, not needing to hear more. It took time to find this basic house of ale and an opportune place to lie in wait. He knew a dwarven "telling" could last late into the night. It was not necessary to see the thänæ's arrival, only his departure.

The thänæ in question, like all such, had already achieved a place among the dwarves' honored dead. Ultimately, all such hoped one day to become Bäynæ, one of the Eternals, the spiritual immortals and ancestral patrons of their people. To do so, one had to accomplish great feats that exalted their virtues or served the people—and in the "telling" to be judged worthy by all. Only when the people began to demand the marking of a new thänæ would a tribe's leaders sit in conclave. A unanimous vote was required before shirvêsh of the appropriate temple were called to bless a new thôrhk for the recipient. Only the Thänæ had their names engraved upon the temple's walls, but even then, decades or centuries would pass before even one of them, one day, might be ranked among the Eternals . . . if any ever did.

Sau'ilahk knew these general details, and that the process was more complex in subtle ways—and that dwarves were fools.

To spend one's life, even one as long as a dwarf's, in such a pursuit was insipid. He had no interest in their superstitions or false divinities—compared to his Beloved. Only the final detail of the process mattered, the one thing that would make the Stonewalkers come.

A thänæ had to die.

And after all, was not this what they all wanted . . . if they wished to become false saints?

Sau'ilahk waited within sight of the alehouse, a place usually not sought for a "telling." As night dragged on, he memorized other passages along the tunnel, as well as the far end of his own leading back to this level's mainway. He had to be able to blink to the mouth of any one of them at will without line of sight. But not until dormancy threatened, warning that dawn was near, did he hear voices growing in the mainway.

People poured from the alehouse, their noise quickly overriding the indistinct murmur from inside.

"What a night!"

"I will be dead on my feet for the day, but it was worth it!"

"And I will relive that last tale unto my death!"

Exclamations and adoring claims mounted one upon another, as patrons headed off both ways along the mainway of closed shops. Finally, Sau'ilahk heard one voice that overrode all others . . . deep, sure, and arrogant.

"No, no, brothers and sisters, you've paid me enough drink for the next two tellings! Time for all to sleep. But I promise to share your hospitality again before I venture afar once more."

Sau'ilahk remained as still as a shadow, listening to Hammer-Stag. This one preferred wallowing with riffraff, those too ignorant to see through him. All to procure a name he hoped might last into eternity. How pitiful.

There was only one true divinity who could grant eternal life. Such as Sau'ilahk had prayed and begged for—and been given by his Beloved. But he had no time to mourn the bane hidden within that boon.

The thänæ turned the other direction down the mainway, and Sau'ilahk was forced to blink ahead of the bulky loudmouth by three intersecting passages. There, he focused on the life presence of his quarry, feeling Hammer-Stag's spirit like a breeze or running stream one touched but could not hold on to. He no longer needed to listen to the braggart's bluster.

Twice more he blinked down the mainway, staying well ahead, then again down a side passage the thänæ turned into. He watched Hammer-Stag's every turn, until the last of the well-wishers and sycophants went their own way.

Hammer-Stag was alone in the deep sleeping back ways under Sea-Side. He was still far down a passage as Sau'ilahk retreated from its other end.

Sau'ilahk hurried along the wider intersecting tunnel, and then stopped, quickly preparing. He would not take a dwarf directly. It had been a long time, but he remembered how difficult they could be. He had to put this one down before noise attracted attention. Sound carried far in these underground ways.

Sau'ilahk manifested one hand, making it solid long enough to snuff the closest lantern. He quickly began the first conjury, calling up its shapes not in the air but upon the tunnel's wall. He needed a powerful banishing.

Within his mind's eye, a glowing crimson circle appeared upon the rough stone, large enough to encompass him if stepped up to it. Another of pulsing amber rose within that one, followed by an inverted triangle. Sau'ilahk raised one incorporeal finger wrapped in frayed black cloth. He traced signs, symbols, and sigils between the shapes, his fingertip racing over the stone. Though no else could have seen, every mark burned phosphorescent.

Soon, all light reaching from down the tunnel toward him began to dim—not everywhere, but only within the great seal that only he could see. Lantern light from up or down the way faded within an expanding space bulging outward from the wall.

Sau'ilahk drifted in against the stone, poised at the center of his banishing circle.

To conjure the Elements, or construct the lowest of elemental servitors, took years of dangerous practice. Banishing was often no more than releasing them, if one did not make them last longer than willful attention. Dealing with the natural world was another matter. Banishing anything natural to the world was nearly impossible, always temporary, and not for dabblers.

Though the next and previous lanterns still burned in the tunnel, clear to see, their light touched nothing within the outward bounds of his pattern. Sau'ilahk stood unseen within a pocket of pure darkness that ate all light.

It was costing him, weakening him. Yet he had one more conjury to accomplish, as he heard the thänæ's heavy footfalls closing on the passage's exit.

As a spirit, Sau'ilahk did not posses a true "voice." Even in the brief moments he willed himself corporeal, as an undead he did not draw breath. When and if he spoke, it was by conjury, faintly manipulating any noise made by the air's natural movement. He now needed a true voice—one urgently familiar to Hammer-Stag.

Sau'ilahk put the heels of his palms together, one hand below and the other above, with fingers outstretched. As he sank halfway into the tunnel wall amid his pool of darkness, he forced his hands solid. Envisioned glowing glyphs swirled in a tiny whirlwind. He arched his hands, fingertips still touching, and those bright symbols rushed into the space between, as if inhaled by a mouth.

Sau'ilahk felt air shudder between his hands, until it became a dull, vibrating thrum.

Hammer-Stag stepped out of the passage into the tunnel, turning the other way without pause.

Sau'ilahk curled his fingers inward like claws. He opened his hands like a clamshell, fingers tearing at thrumming air as if prying open a mouth.

A woman's agonized shriek echoed along the passage.

Hammer-Stag halted and spun about.

He looked down the passage, eyes wide, and then the other way. When he turned back, apparently seeing nothing, he reached over his right shoulder. His wide callused hand gripped the battle-ax handle behind his head, but he did not pull it out.

Sau'ilahk rotated his grip, twisting the air between his hands.

A whimper rolled out of his pool of darkness, followed by a familiar terror-choked voice.

"Please . . . help . . . *me*!"

Hammer-Stag pulled the ax and gripped the haft with both hands. He lunged two steps and then paused with his brows furrowed.

"Who is there?" he growled.

Sau'ilahk's satisfaction grew. This was so predictable. He twisted his hands again, feigning the familiar voice.

"Fiáh'our . . . Hammer-Stag? It's me, Wynn . . . Wynn Hygeorht!"

The thänæ craned his neck, trying to see where she was.

"Little mighty one?" he breathed, then shouted, "Where are you?"

"Please help me! It's coming!"

"No!" he snarled. "I am! Call to me . . . I will find you!"

Hammer-Stag charged down the passage, straight toward Sau'ilahk. As he passed the place where no light reached, Sau'ilahk opened his hands. The patch of darkness died under the light as Sau'ilahk slipped out behind the thänæ.

CHAPTER 7

Wynn awoke the next morning feeling weak and rubbed her eyes. She found herself in the familiar trappings of her room at the temple. Vague, broken memories returned.

She recalled Chane helping her to bed, and Shirvêsh Mallet gently feeding her a bitter liquid. Her ill-used stomach still hurt, but her headache had dulled. She sat up and, to her surprise, felt hungry, not remembering the last time she'd eaten.

Shade lay at the bed's foot and lifted her head to whine.

"Yes . . . you're hungry too," Wynn acknowledged, "but after we make ourselves presentable."

Getting to her pack was a wobbly exploit. She fumbled inside it for a brush and fresh kerchief, and teetered to the door-side table. She poured water from the pitcher into a basin, though she desperately wanted a full bath. All she could do was scrub her face, arms, and neck with the dampened kerchief. Finally, she tried pulling her hair back into a tail and out of her face, but without a mirror, she ended up with the usual wisps floating around her cheeks. She gave up and filled a clay mug, trying to clean her teeth with a finger.

Shade reared, forepaws jostling the little table, and began lapping the basin's water.

"Shade!" she warned. "That's dirty."

Try as Wynn might, Shade wouldn't listen, but at least the water wasn't soapy.

"We need a launderer," she mumbled. "I stink . . . and my clothes are no better."

She'd brought only one change of clothing, gifted to her during her time in the an'Croan's Elven Territories. Disrobing, she started to shiver, and quickly lifted the brazier's lid off the glowing crystals. She dipped into her pack and pulled out the yellow tunic of raw-spun cotton and the russet pants. Sewn for a youth of the tall Farlands elves, the sleeves and legs were too long. She had to roll them up before dressing.

Cleanly attired, Wynn felt relieved to wear pants again. She'd grown accustomed to not wrestling with a long, bulky robe, or even her shorter travel robe, during her journeys with Magiere, Leesil, and Chap. But as she turned to leave, she grew light-headed and hung on to the door handle until it passed.

Such was the price of bartering in a greeting house. If she hadn't been so foolish and botched her first meeting with Sliver, all the suffering might have been worth it. Now she could only press blindly onward.

"Come, Shade."

Wynn stepped out, waiting as Shade followed. But when she closed the door, she paused, studying Chane's door across the passage.

Hopefully he suffered no ill effects of missing a half day's dormancy. She still knew so little about the daily—nightly—existence of the Noble Dead. Chane seemed less affected by the sun than by the time of day where dormancy was concerned. Did his body sense the sun's rhythm, even when he was underground?

She wanted to check on him. Knowing her knock might not be heard, she gripped the handle of his door. The latch wouldn't budge.

"Locked?" she whispered.

Wynn couldn't remember if he'd ever done this in their stops along the bay road, but she'd never looked in on him during that time. Shade pricked her ears and huffed as she backed down the corridor.

"I know," she whispered. "Really, you're as bad as your father . . . thinking with your stomach!"

But Wynn strolled off after Shade, leaving Chane in privacy. She headed straight for the meal hall, and three shirvêsh looked up as she entered.

She couldn't tell whether they were acolytes or otherwise; all shirvêsh dressed the same, in simple orange vestments. Others must have finished breakfast already, and only this trio remained at the table with pots and plates of food. The dark-haired woman who'd first helped her locate this place looked up and smiled.

"Feeling better?" she called. "We heard of your adventure."

Wynn blushed, and the two others at the table chuckled. It was all good-natured, and the woman waved her over.

"I am Downpour," she said. "Anything here look appetizing . . . as yet?"

"Best she stick to oats and bread for a day," warned a younger male across the table.

His high, flat brow was capped by frizzy brown hair and only the barest matching beard showed on his blunt chin. He filled a bowl from a cast-iron pot while the third, an older male with creased features, nodded in silent agreement.

"Thank you," Wynn said.

In truth, something plain sounded best, but she felt uncomfortable under all this attention. She took the bowl and settled next to Downpour.

"This is Held-All, and that is Scoria," Downpour said, pointing first to the younger male and then to the rough-featured one.

Shade pushed her head in under Wynn's arm, nearly knocking the bowl over, and snuffled at its contents. Then she backed out with a grumble, craning her head to peer over the table.

"Ah, your wolf," Downpour said.

Before Wynn even asked, all three dwarves were scrounging about the table, lifting lids and peeking into pots.

"Salt-fish!" exclaimed Held-All. "Would she like that?"

Scoria snatched a stiff piece of dried fish from the pot. Wynn tensed as he rose and leaned across the table toward Shade.

"She's very shy of strangers," Wynn warned.

Scoria grunted in seriousness. "Very wise," he said, then rumbled down at Shade, "Mind your manners . . . you hear?"

He reached out, lowering the fish with two fingers.

Shade reared and clacked her jaws on the morsel, and Scoria snatched back his empty hand with a start.

"Shade!" Wynn scolded.

Held-All snickered, trying to stifle himself.

"Not funny!" Scoria growled at him.

"That depends," Held-All forced out with a faked cough. "Did she get any meat with that fish?"

Scoria frowned, slowly opening his hand as if counting fingers.

"*A'ye!*" Downpour sighed. "Stop being a bother—both of you!"

After having dealt with the greeting house and Sliver, Wynn sat silent at their quick and friendly acceptance. Dwarves took harsh offense when insulted with intent, but otherwise, nothing rattled their good nature, not even Shade's poor table manners.

Shade licked her jaws, all signs of the fish gone, and Wynn scooped a spoonful of oats.

She listened to her companions' chatter, and even answered a question or two about what it was like to be a sage. She took no offense at their perplexed glances over the human obsession with writing everything down. Finally, she paused at one more spoonful of boiled oats.

"Where is Shirvêsh Mallet this morning?" she asked. "I need to speak with him as soon as possible."

Downpour shook her head. "He is in private conference. Two elder shirvêsh from the temple of Stálghlên—um, you might say Pure-Steel—came at dawn. He has not come out since."

Wynn slumped. Something serious held Mallet's attention if he was occupied this long.

"We hate to leave you to eat alone," Downpour added. "But we have duties to attend."

Wynn put her spoon down, for she'd had enough.

"One more thing," she asked. "Do you have anything here like a records room? I mean, for whatever is worthy of being written down. May I be permitted to do some research?"

She knew this was an outside chance.

Scoria blinked twice, probably uncertain how to answer without insulting a "scribbler of words."

"Something . . . like it," Downpour answered. "But there may be a better place to start. We call it . . . well, you might say the Hall of Stone-Words. Come, I will take you there."

Wynn quickly gathered her bowl and spoon to carry them off to the kitchen.

"No, no, leave those," Downpour instructed, rising to stop her. "Others will attend the cleanup."

Downpour stood no taller than Wynn, but of course twice as wide. Shade whined, and Wynn glanced down.

The dog sat with her muzzle resting on the table's edge, gazing hopefully at the lidded pot of dried fish.

"Should I give her more?" Scoria asked, though he didn't sound too eager.

"No, she's had enough for now," Wynn replied.

Shade grumbled in clear disagreement, but Scoria nodded and ushered Held-All on his way. Wynn was more curious about this Hall of Stone-Words, so with Shade in tow, she followed Downpour out of the meal hall.

Instead of rounding the far side of the temple proper toward the passages to quarters, they slipped into the near side, traipsing the curving corridor all the way to the back. There, a wide passage lined with glyph-marked archways and doors shot deeper into the mountain.

Downpour's brisk pace offered Wynn no time to peer about. She glimpsed little of the other rooms or halls through any opening, at least not until the wide passage ended in a final grand arch of framestones. The opening spilled into a room so tall that Wynn couldn't see its ceiling from the outside. All she did see were three large emblems on a bare wall straight ahead, no more than three paces into the room.

Downpour paused outside the archway. "Anyone can come here whenever the temple is open."

Wynn stared at the inside wall. The Hall of Stone-Words couldn't be this small, even for dwarven brevity in writing.

"Hopefully something here will fulfill your needs," Downpour added. "Now I must get to my duties."

Downpour headed up the passage, and Wynn moved closer to the archway. Dwarves might not care for writing everything down, but certainly they had more records than this. There had to be more than three platter-size engraved symbols of complex strokes . . . or *vubrí*.

Certain Dwarvish words weren't always written in separate letters. Just as the sages' Begaine syllabary used symbols for whole syllables and word parts, the harsh strokes of dwarven letters could be combined into a *vubrí*. These emblems were used only for important concepts or the noteworthy among people, places, or things. They were also how the families, clans, and tribes emblazoned or embroidered their identity on some personal attire. It took Wynn a moment to untangle the three engraved upon the wall.

The two to either side—Virtue and Tradition—connected by a straight line to an engraved circle holding the central emblem of Wisdom.

Wynn stepped fully through the arch, and a sudden sense of space made her look up.

The engraved wall went only halfway to the space's height, but it was still tall enough that she would've barely reached its top with her upstretched staff. Far above, amid stone arches supporting a high ceiling, metal mirrors reflected light down into the hall from three shafts in the ceiling.

Wynn stepped back and saw that the ceiling's arch supports went well beyond the partition.

She was baffled until she noticed that neither partition's end joined the hall's side walls. She headed left, finding the wall as thick as she was from shoulder to shoulder, and she peeked around its end. Wynn's mouth and eyes opened wide.

Multiple stone partitions cut across the hall at regular intervals, like the casements of a library. Each was clear of the side walls, allowing anyone to walk around them and up and down the hall's length. The only furnishings were thick stone benches, worn by use. But there were no massive *vubrí* on the next partition's front side.

Engraved Dwarvish letters filled five columns, each as wide as her spread arms. The same covered the back side of the first partition. Even the hall's side walls had columns written in twin sets, positioned to face the spaces between the partitions. Those paired side columns stretched nearly all the way to the ceiling's high arches.

Wynn had never seen anything like this among the dwarves, not even in her visit with Domin Tilswith. But it seemed most fitting in the temple of their poet Eternal.

"Stone-words," she whispered, "words engraved in stone."

Dwarves recorded only what they considered worth such permanence, such as the teachings of Feather-Tongue. Even to say "written in stone" meant that what was said must never be forgotten.

Shade pushed past, sniffing halfway down the partition's back side before Wynn regained her wits. She followed the dog, running her fingers over the engravings' sharp edges. Not only could she see these words, she could *feel* them. She flushed with unfamiliar awe as her fingers slipped from one column of crisp carved characters to the next.

"Stories," she whispered.

She'd never even seen some of the characters before. Perhaps they were older than the written form of Dwarvish she'd learned. As she reached the third partition's back side, she lingered on one obscure *vubrí*. Wynn knew she'd seen it before, somewhere upon these walls, and she tried again to decipher it.

Lhärgnæ?

She frowned, trying to remember her lessons with Domin High-Tower.

The old Dwarvish root word "yarghaks" meant "a descent," as in a falling place or a downslope. In the vocative, it was pronounced "lhargagh," but such a formal declination implied a label or title. And the ancient, rare suffix of "-næ" or "-æ" was for a proper noun, both plural and singular.

She knew the letters and *vubrí* for the Bäynæ, the Eternals. That reference had appeared often in passages she had scanned. Strangely, she didn't remember ever spotting "Lhärgnæ" written out in plain letters. But its *vubrí* seemed akin to the one for the Bäynæ.

"Lhärgnæ" . . . the Fallen Ones?

She scanned several more lines, and the obscure *vubrí* appeared again, this time in a sentence that also mentioned the Eternals. She traced back along engraved letters, reading more slowly.

Our Eternal ancestors exalt our virtues over our vices, and shield us against the . . . Lhärgnæ.

Wynn paused in thought. She knew some dwarven "virtues," such as integrity, courage, pragmatism, and achievement. There were also thrift, charity for those in need, and championship of the innocent and defenseless. The possible vices might be counterpoints to these, at least in part.

Dwarves believed that their Eternals were part of the spiritual side of this world. They were not removed from it, to be called upon in another realm, as with the elves, nor sent to an afterlife, like most human religions taught. The Bäynæ were the revered ancestors of their race as a whole. Their presence was thought strongest wherever dwarves gathered in great numbers. They were believed to be always with their people, wherever they went.

So what place did these Lhärgnæ—these Fallen Ones—hold in the dwarves' spiritual worldview?

She sidestepped along the wall, scanning for more occurrences of the rare *vubrí*. Near the wall's bottom, it was couched in a phrase with the terms "aghlédaks" and "brahderaks"—cowardice and treachery. The rest of the sentence held too many older characters she didn't know.

Wynn straightened up, sighing in frustration.

She'd expected this to be easier. She was a sage, after all, and spoke a half dozen languages or dialects fluently and others in part. She could read even more. When she turned about, Shade lay at the wall's far end, her head on her paws, silently watching Wynn.

This was all quite boring to Shade.

For an instant, Wynn wished she had Chap here instead. His counsel had helped her choose the texts to bring home from Li'kän's ice-bound castle.

Her gaze drifted to an oddity on the next partition's front. These columns of text were framed in engraved scrollwork. Curiosity pulled her to them.

She read a few random lines with little effort, for it was written in contemporary Dwarvish characters. The text appeared to be a story. A way down the column, she found one familiar *vubrí*—Bedzâ'kenge, the poet Eternal. Another *vubrí* was mixed in the text closer to the first column's top.

Wynn settled on the bench, working out its patterned strokes.

"Sundaks"—avarice.

But the context implied more. It should be in the vocative case as well, like a title or a name pronounced in formal fashion—Shundagh.

Wynn lifted her eyes to the story's beginning.

A fine family of renowned masons lived in a small but proud seatt of only one clan and one tribe among the Rughìr.

She faltered before remembering something Domin High-Tower had mentioned. "Rughìr" was a common truncation for "Rughìr'thai'âch"—the Earth-Born—how the dwarves referred to their own kind.

Anxious to serve their people, the family's sons and daughters sought to become merchants as well. They hoped to have more to offer—and to gain—by way of trade as well as skills plied. But over many years, all members passed into earth or went away, until only one son remained.

Wynn came to the new *vubrí* formed like a title: *Shundagh . . .*

Avarice . . . as the last of his line, inherited all that his family had acquired—but he had lost his love of masonry or the way of honorable barter.

At first, he grudgingly plied his skills, but not in fair exchange for returned services or goods. Nor did he trade in worthy metals, such as iron, copper, forged steel, or even brass. He took payment only in foreign coin of silver and gold or in pristine gemstones. Soon he abandoned service altogether, selling off what remained of family wares and tools.

Avarice no longer bartered.

He purchased all he desired, always in gold, silver, and gems, but offered only meager amounts to those in dire need who must accept his set price. Through trickery and profiteering, he amassed a fortune from his fellows. The people became gray and grim.

Avarice's wealth grew as steadily as his skills dwindled.

He forgot all that his forebears had handed down through generations. When his false wealth was greater than that of all the seatt, he demanded the clan elders title him "Thänæ." They agreed, for even the elders had been made destitute. They saw that only Avarice possessed the way to fortune and renown.

The shirvêsh were told to sanctify a thôrhk. Avarice demanded that it be made of gold and studded in jewels of his choosing, to remind all how great he had become and why. But the shirvêsh refused.

Avarice called in debts to have a thôrhk made to his own liking, though it was never blessed under the sight of the Eternals. It is said that the day he donned it, since no servant of the Eternals would place it upon him, all shirvêsh of the seatt left, never to return.

With a false thänæ as the example of excellence, envy spread like plague.

Such was Avarice's reputation that even the flow of trading foreigners dwindled, until none from the outside world came to trade and barter at that seatt. The people were left to prey only upon one another's misfortune.

Until one dawn, a lone traveler did come.

At first the people gave him little notice. Though he was Rughìr, he possessed nothing of worth. He carried only a pack that sagged half-empty and a stout but tarnished iron staff. His boots and garish orange tunic were overweathered and travel-worn. When he stopped at the lone greeting house, no one gave note to this shoddy traveler, not even when he stepped upon the dais without invitation.

Wynn came to the first occurrence of the *vubrí* for Bedzâ'kenge.

Feather-Tongue began his first tale.

Offered in charity, and in the proper place for a telling, when he finished the story of Pure-Steel and the Night Blight, silence filled the greeting house. Even servers stood petrified, like dead wood poured upon for centuries until it turned rigid as stone. But the silence would be broken.

Avarice had heard word of a telling in the greeting house.

At first he could not believe it, but any brief diversion was rare. He came to see for himself and stood just inside the doorway. Arriving late, he had caught only the story's last half. Though it cost him nothing, it left him frustrated, as if he had paid even one precious coin but received only a portion of his purchase.

Avarice could not help himself.

He entreated the pauper poet for another tale—by story, song, or poem—but in private, only for himself. For the service, he offered one quarter wedge of the smallest silver piece found among the Churvâdìné.

Wynn paused, and frowned. The old word sounded so familiar. Dené was now the common dwarven word for any "human"—Numan, Suman, or otherwise. But once they had been called the Churvâdìné. . . .

The Confused or Mixed-Up People.

No one else said a word at Avarice's offer; no one else had the coin to spare. They all waited expectantly for the poet's reply.

With a slow shake of his head, Feather-Tongue refused.

He would tell a tale in good charity—a story or two, a song, or a poem to break the heart—but only to those too poor to even barter a sip of ale. He would not sell his tales for coin, like possessions to be hoarded.

Avarice became angry.

He believed this pauper poet was either too conceited or too stupid to part with simple tales for good profit. Instead, the wanderer squandered his skills on the unworthy and beggarly. Still, the false thänæ would not turn away.

Avarice doubled his price—and Feather-Tongue refused again.

Avarice offered more—and more—but each time the poet declined. He offered yet again, cringing at the amount, this time for a telling before himself and the clan elders as well. At the least, he would have the credit for providing a meager treat, and the elders would owe him for it.

Feather-Tongue refused again—then he countered.

He would accept only if all the people were allowed to listen. The telling would take place atop the mountain in the seatt's central amphitheater, where any council was held before the people.

Avarice would not be outbartered by some wandering street performer.

He nearly snarled refusal, but he bit it back in the last instant. If the clan elders would have been indebted to him for a private telling, how much greater his gain would be in what the poet proposed. Though it would be hard to account and collect on such widespread debt, all in the seatt would know to whom it was owed.

Avarice agreed.

Feather-Tongue bowed graciously to the false thänæ, and Avarice escorted him to the mountain's top. They did not wait long.

Word spread upon shouting voices and running feet. Soon, all came to listen. The crowd settled in, restless and noisy, until the poet raised his iron staff and let it slide down upon the amphitheater's floor. He hammered it three times upon the flagstones, and all became quiet.

Feather-Tongue began his second tale.

There was no silence when he finished three episodes in classic chain link. Cheers and stamps and slaps of approval upon stone were somewhat hesitant, but not for lack of heart. Many eyes turned on the poet's counterpart, seated front and center among the clan's elders.

Avarice's aged eyes were glassy.

The false thänæ was still caught in the tale's dreamtime, and the pauper poet waited in polite silence. Eventually a low rumble spread through the crowd, until someone finally called out for another tale.

Avarice started to awareness.

He leaned forward, glaring at the poet as the demand spread throughout the stands. Finally, he tossed a scant pinch of silver coins upon the flagstones in payment. But then he too demanded another tale, claiming he was not satisfied with the worth of his purchase.

The poet nodded acceptance, never stooping to touch one coin.

Feather-Tongue began a third tale.

He broke into song and then slid into an epic poem, which ended upon three quintets of limericks that raised so much laughter, even Avarice smirked twice.

Feather-Tongue fell silent and waited.

Avarice shook off the disquieting touch of long-forgotten mirth. He leaned forward, ready to claim that he was not yet satisfied. But the way the crowd cheered, stamped, and slapped stone made him hesitate. A few even tossed out a coin or two they could hardly have spared.

Being seen as an ingrate would not work for Avarice, but he had no leverage as yet, seeing that this vagabond was still indifferent to proper wealth. And he too wanted more tales—and more debts to collect. He held up the smallest of his purses with a sum slightly more than the last payment. When the poet nodded acceptance, he tossed it out.

Feather-Tongue began his fourth tale.

Throughout the morning and afternoon, the ritual of purchase repeated. With each song, history, poem, or legend, the poet grew tired a bit earlier than the last, saying he could tell no more this day.

The crowd's adoration had grown, as had Avarice's frustration.

Each time the poet paused, Avarice increased his offers, bit by grudging bit, until the next telling commenced. The false thänæ's servants, indentured for debts, were sent under mercenary guard to fetch more coin and even gems from his hoard. The people were puzzled, but Avarice knew that they were too ignorant and poor to calculate what he could.

By custom and tradition, only the recipient could first touch any payment.

Without servants, companions, or pack animals, the poet would be forced to leave the bulk of his gained wealth behind. The amount had already grown too large and heavy to handle alone. And once Avarice had exhausted all tales, he would rejoice in how little the poet could carry away. Any remainder not retrieved first by the poet himself would be forfeit.

When dusk came, Feather-Tongue halted midtale.

A rumble of discontent rose in the amphitheater, but he shook his head, claiming he was too tired, famished, and parched. Before Avarice cried foul, Feather-Tongue reassured all. He would return the following day to finish—but not before.

At that, the false thänæ relented, but he made sure of his purchase. Mercenary guards were posted outside the greeting house where the poet was lodged for the night.

In the morning, Feather-Tongue began again—and for seven days more.

Along the way, he often told of faraway places, events unheard-of, and ancestors long forgotten in this seatt, all glorious in wonder and some fearfully dark, so that awe filled the people's expressions, and sometimes mixed with longing.

Each dusk, he ended midstory, midsong, or in a jarring stop at the most poi-

gnant beat in a poem. Each dawn, all hurried to the amphitheater, only to find Avarice already waiting as the poet arrived under guard.

Not once did the poet touch coin or gem heaped upon the old stone floor. Not by a toe, let alone a finger. He could have, for any smaller part had been fairly gained in barter for what he had given so far. The piles had grown so large that even one would be unmanageable to carry off.

On the ninth day, Feather-Tongue finished his last tale.

When the crowd cried for more, amid shouts of praise, he only shook his head, and they slowly grew silent. He announced that he had told all that he possessed and there was nothing more he could offer.

Avarice began to laugh.

It was a rude, disquieting noise that carried everywhere in the silence. He claimed again that he was not satisfied for his last purchase. A wave of resentful leers spread through the crowd. Some even braved curses under their breath.

Feather-Tongue bowed politely, offering to gladly return the last and final payment.

Avarice smiled at this.

He sent out a servant to gather three pouches' worth of gold and gems. It was only what he had paid the final time. He need not try to take anything more. A hundred–fold still remained that could never be carried away by the poet.

Shouts rose from the crowd, some in pleas that the poet might have just one more telling in him. But others shouted at Avarice that the barter was complete, now that the one final payment had been returned.

Avarice grew nervous. He had no choice by law and custom, and he waved off his guards. He had finally gotten everything this vagabond possessed, and the poet was free to go.

Feather-Tongue returned a final bow—but not to Avarice.

He faced each of the eight directions, offering his humble thanks to the people, and then turned to leave. He was halfway to the northern tunnel running under the stands when a crackling voice called out.

Avarice alone stood up among the elders.

All stared dumbfounded at the great treasure littering the amphitheater's floor. Avarice asked why the poet had not taken his payment.

Feather-Tongue only shook his head.

Avarice grew gleeful. This fool now would not carry away even a meager part of the payment. Not only had Avarice gained all the tales of this idiot, but his wealth was left for him to reclaim.

Feather-Tongue turned about.

"I do accept your payment, and so it is mine," he said. "But I will touch none of it . . . and until I do, neither shall any other. That is the law of barter . . . even for purchases."

Avarice went cold with uncertainty.

Feather-Tongue's gaze passed over the elders and then around the masses gathered upon the amphitheater's stone steps and stands.

"But I offer this, by my oath, and witnessed by all," he added, and then pointed to Avarice. "Whoever gains any true barter with that one . . . may take an equal measure of what I leave here."

Avarice's old heart hammered in panic. His gaze raced feverishly over the wealth he had paid, mixed with the paltry offers of others.

"But only in honorable barter," Feather-Tongue repeated, still pointing to Avarice. "For those who give or take only coin with that one . . . shall have none of mine by fair trade."

Avarice looked about, and all eyes were on him.

He had no skills left, nor goods to spare, with which to barter in the old ways. Even trickery could not regain his payment, for he could not barter with himself in order to share in what the poet offered to all others. He could not even risk thievery, for his wealth was laid out before the eyes of the whole seatt.

Feather-Tongue retrieved his staff and pack from one astonished guard staring at the glittering mounds. He walked away from that unhappy, fallen place. It is said that no one of that forgotten seatt ever touched a single coin or gem of the poet's wealth.

Bartering with Avarice was impossible. He had nothing to offer by way of goods or services.

Perhaps the false thänæ visited his lost wealth each day, gazing at it piled up in plain sight. Certainly someone else would always come, watching him, and he dared not steal a single coin.

Perhaps in time, the taunt of the poet's wealth became too much. Its constant reminder of the shame that Avarice brought upon the seatt, and the shame of all who had made no attempt to stop him, were too much to bear. One can only guess that all left that place, slipping away with their families. Perhaps some few went in search of what they heard in Feather-Tongue's tales.

But not Avarice, that is certain.

Awaking one day to find himself alone, he would have seized upon his lost fortune—and then wept. No one remained from which to purchase anything. He had no servants, pack animals, or companions to help carry it away. But Avarice would never leave it behind.

Somewhere in a forgotten place rest the bones of a . . .

Wynn straightened, staring at the strange *vubrí* once more.

. . . rest the bones of a Lhärgnæ . . . a Fallen One . . . upon a great cairn of silver and gold and bright gems of all hues. But do not seek that place.

Avarice waits to purchase all who come.

Wynn sat still upon the bench, her thoughts tangled and racing.

Bedzâ'kenge—Feather-Tongue—had pulled down a Fallen One. He had freed an entire seatt from the miser's greed, and done so with nothing but wit and a telling. But the story raised more questions than it answered. The final line implied something about dwarven beliefs and their form of ancestor worship.

Bedzâ'kenge was revered as one of the Bäynæ, an ancestral spirit still *among* his people even now. But then what of Shundagh . . . what of Avarice? Did the dwarves believe that Lhärgnæ had presence and influence in this world as well? This would certainly explain the earlier account of how their Eternals not only exalted virtue but remained on guard against vice . . . against the Fallen Ones. Such enemies would be seen as still vital in this world, ready to lay siege and assault upon dwarven virtue.

Wynn's thoughts turned quickly to a name—no, a title—overheard in Domin High-Tower's study on the day Ore-Locks had come in secret.

Thallûhearag.

This hall held accounts of Feather-Tongue's life and exploits, and it mentioned one—or perhaps more—of the Fallen Ones for any to read. Yet Mallet had been severely upset when she'd asked about Thallûhearag. And why did the Lhärgnæ have titles in place of true names?

Though the Bäynæ she knew of had no mention of their heritage in life, such as family, clan, or tribe, apparently they retained their true names. Not the Lhärgnæ—or not the ones she had read of, like Shundagh—Avarice. If Thallûhearag was one of them, then she couldn't tell who or what he was or had been. She couldn't decipher that ancient title of a dwarf forgotten by all but the few who knew it, and who wouldn't speak openly of mythical Bäalâle Seatt.

What had Thallûhearag done in that place? Had he been involved in its fall during the great forgotten war? Anything regarding such events might be critical, and Wynn wanted to discuss her findings with . . . someone. A nostalgic pang made her long to read the story to Chap, to hear what he made of it.

Something wet, warm, and fuzzy burrowed in under her hand.

Shade pushed her muzzle under Wynn's fingers and rested it upon her thigh.

"If only you could understand words," she whispered, "I wonder what you would think of this." Then she half smiled. "Just more people nonsense."

Shade pricked her ears and then suddenly jerked up her head. She trotted off to peer around the partition's end.

"What is it?" Wynn asked.

A distant cry of grief echoed faintly into the Hall of Stone-Words.

Wynn rushed to join Shade, but when she reached the entrance, Shade was already trotting down the outer passage.

"Shade, wait! Stop . . . come!" she called, but the dog kept on.

Shade slowed only when she reached the passage's end, where it connected to the curved hallway running around the temple proper. Wynn hurried to catch up, but Shade trotted out, approaching the near-side arch into the chamber of Feather-Tongue. Wynn followed to peer in.

A group of orange-vested shirvêsh had gathered inside. There was Downpour, her large hands over her face, apparently weeping. Even Held-All had lost his grin, as everyone present listened closely to Shirvêsh Mallet, though at first his words were too low for Wynn to hear. He looked exhausted and lost.

Scoria heaved a sigh and folded his arms.

"I do not believe it!" he growled. "Only three nights past, I ate with him, and he would not keep quiet all night! This cannot be true."

Shirvêsh Mallet nodded slowly. "It is certain. Hammer-Stag passed over last night."

Wynn clutched the archway's edge. Hammer-Stag was dead?

"Once his body has been prepared by family or clan," Mallet continued, "and tribal mourning is observed, he will be carried up to Chemarré . . . and we will see if the Hassäg'kreigi find him worthy to pass into stone."

Wynn's breath caught. The Stonewalkers were coming—or *might* come?

She didn't understand why there was doubt. Weren't all thänæ who passed over to be taken? What more was—could be—required, other than a thôrhk and the title that came with it? But if the Stonewalkers did come . . .

Would Ore-Locks be there? Could she find a way to see him or the others, to speak with them?

And what did Mallet mean by "pass into stone"?

Wynn shivered with self-loathing. Hammer-Stag had helped her, treated her as a friend. He had fought beside Magiere, aided by Leesil and Chap. Now he was gone, and all she thought of was what it might gain her.

She stepped in behind the gathering, wanting to ask how one such as he had died. But she halted at the sight of Downpour weeping and Held-All's young face devoid of mirth. Of all present, Mallet's demeanor silenced her most of all.

Struck with grief, the old shirvêsh glanced up at the immense statue of Feather-Tongue, with hand outstretched and palm upward to the sky above the temple. When Mallet lowered his eyes, his brows wrinkled, darkening the lines on his old features.

Mallet glared at nothing, lost in a troubled thought that shadowed his face.

CHAPTER 8

Two long nights passed, and Wynn entered the great amphitheater atop the mountain at Chemarré—Old-Seatt. In her freshly laundered gray robe, she was dressed as a sage of the guild. Shirvêsh Mallet and Chane stood with her, while Shade pressed against the backs of her legs amid a throng of dwarves milling about upon the flagstones. The size of the place made her feel so very small, even more than the great council clearing of the Farland's elves.

On their way through the streets of Old-Seatt, she had seen ancient fortifications and tiered walls built to withstand any assault, and twice as thick as those of Calm Seatt. The amphitheater itself was more daunting.

As the traditional meeting place of Dhredze Seatt and its last-stand fallback fortification, the amphitheater's round outer wall was at least twenty feet thick and as high as any castle's first battlements. Two dozen stone tiers for seating rose all around to the broad promenade running along the wall's inner circumference. Entrances made of great iron doors were flung wide between framed obelisk columns, opening above the steps of the aisles. The stands were already half-filled, and still people poured in. Constabularies from various clans walked the aisle steps with their tall staves, assisting attendees and overseeing proper order.

Hammer-Stag, boisterous and loud, had been well-known to his people.

And this was his final appearance among them.

Wynn was aware of the favor bestowed upon herself and Chane. They stood with Mallet on the floor's far right, just within sight of the nearer steps leading up to the raised stone stage. Only family, close friends and comrades, as well as clan elders and thänæ, were allowed on the floor among the shirvêsh in attendance. One elder shirvêsh from each Eternal's temple, such as Mallet, was present, along with more from a temple appropriate to Hammer-Stag's calling.

Wynn should've felt grateful at being included, and that thought made her feel all the worse. When she'd first asked Shirvêsh Mallet if she and Chane might attend—on the pretense of learning more about dwarven customs—she'd been stunned when he'd agreed.

"Of course," he had said. "You will stand with me."

Mallet had explained that the Hassäg'kreigi did not come for all departed thänæ. Only those deemed worth preserving for the people would "pass into stone." When she'd asked what that meant, he shook his head. Answering seemed difficult for him.

Stone was revered for permanence, like the bones of the world. Even when broken, it was still stone, and its parts one day were reborn anew. To be part of such was to become part of what held up the world and kept it sound. Even among the Thänæ, only those strongest in the virtue they exemplified would bring the Stonewalkers. The bones of earth deserved nothing less. Mallet said that in all his years, he had seen the Stonewalkers only twice before.

Wynn had then asked if something else was wrong. The old monk's intense expression within the temple proper was still stuck in her mind. Mallet didn't answer, but the suspicious glare returned briefly beneath his grief, as if his mind wandered into darker thoughts. Wynn's own thoughts kept turning back upon the Stonewalkers. The guilt made her shrivel inside.

Hammer-Stag, so strong and alive, had died the night after she'd met him. Death followed too often in her wake. And now, how did she honor this loss? With sacrilege, using him as bait. She could barely lift her gaze to the stage.

Beneath a shimmering gray cloth draped over a litter upon a waist-high stone block, the body of Hammer-Stag rested, hidden from sight.

On one side of him stood an aging, white-haired thänæ in a bright girdle of steel splints, with two war daggers lashed to his chest. On the other stood three shirvêsh in white vestments from the temples devoted to three Bäynæ called Stálghlên, Skâpagi, and Mukvadân—Pure-Steel the champion, Shielder the guardian, and Wild-Boar the warrior.

Funerary ceremonies had been going on for several days. First the body was carefully prepared, though Wynn didn't know what that entailed. Then came a series of wakes overseen by immediate family, clan, and then tribe. This night was the culmination. If the Stonewalkers didn't come, Hammer-Stag might be cremated or interred, according to his relatives' wishes. Either his corpse or ashes would be carried away to a prepared family barrow.

"Will he be uncovered or taken as is?" Chane asked softly.

Wynn glanced up. He appeared to suffer none of her guilt or anything besides fascination with the spectacle.

"If they come to take him into stone," Mallet answered, "he will be uncovered . . . presented to the people one last time. For now, we wait."

Wynn pondered those words again—"into stone." Earlier, as they'd rode the lift up to Old-Seatt, Mallet had also mentioned the "underworld" when speaking of the Stonewalkers. Did the two terms mean the same thing, or was the latter something separate? But she believed the Stonewalkers would come.

Hammer-Stag had been special. Judging by all who gathered here, he'd achieved greatness in a world where others sought it only in self-service—if they sought it at all in more than wishes and fantasies.

She noticed Chane looking down at her, studying her. Perhaps he saw her shame or sadness. He looked much better since they'd returned to the temple. Although he was still pale, a hint of color showed in his narrow face. The goat's blood must have helped.

The three shirvêsh upon the stage held up their hands, and the crowd's buzz quickly died.

Wynn saw movement everywhere around her.

All the shirvêsh on the amphitheater's floor slowly formed a line. Mallet followed with a quick gesture for her and Chane to wait. One by one, they filed up the steps to the stage as the trio of shirvêsh in white stepped back, bowing their heads with closed eyes. Each passing shirvêsh paused, laying a hand upon Hammer-Stag's draped form, and their lips moved in some unheard whisper to the dead thänæ.

Wynn remembered the an'Cróan's elders that she'd encountered in the Farlands. Compared to their tall, cloaked forms and reserved expressions, these wide, stout dwarven monks in breeches and bright vestments were a stark contrast.

One white-haired woman in a deep azure vestment stopped beside the cloth-draped body. Unlike those before her, she lifted her eyes to the people.

"I will miss your fine voice and the just swing of Burskâp," she said aloud to all.

Wynn grew confused, wondering if that final word were some nickname for Hammer-Stag.

"Joy be with you . . . always," that woman said, then leaned over and kissed Hammer-Stag's covered head. "May Arhniká favor you."

Tears welled in Wynn's eyes.

Arhniká—Gilt-Repast—was one of the oldest Bäynæ she knew, revered for the virtue of charity. Her shirvêsh were known for helping the destitute to find placement for learning new trades and skills to rebuild lives of honor. Wynn wondered how a warrior like Hammer-Stag had gained such affection from a monk of Arhniká.

One by one, the shirvêsh offered silent blessings, acting as avatars of their respective Eternals. Wynn watched as Mallet approached near the line's end. His eyes closed in a moment of stillness, and he too whispered something to Hammer-Stag. With his hand still upon the thänæ's covered form, he raised his head.

"You were our strong arm, a champion of those in need," he said simply. "You will live among us in our tellings. May Bedzâ'kenge sing to you."

Wynn looked away, anywhere else. She peered among those upon the floor who watched the blessing of the dead, and then raised her eyes to the crowded stone stands. Her gaze caught on a familiar face.

Sliver sat in the lowest stand nearest the stage's far side still dressed in blacksmith's attire, as if she'd come straight from her forge. Her expression was tightly set in distaste.

Wynn tugged lightly on Chane's sleeve, whispering, "Look."

Chane followed where she pointed, spotting High-Tower's sister, and his eyes narrowed in a flicker of hostility. Then he frowned in the same puzzlement Wynn felt.

Sliver would've had to close the smithy for several days, traveling by tram to attend the ceremony. There was no direct lift from far Sea-Side to the mountain's top. Had she known Hammer-Stag personally, or was she just here like all the others, paying her respects? Her expression said otherwise. She didn't appear to notice Wynn and only glared at the stage—or at one of two square entrances in its back wall.

Before Wynn pondered further, a rolling resonance grew in the amphitheater. All the shirvêsh began to sing in deep baritone voices as they filed back down the stairs. Their chant vibrated between the high stone walls.

Their song was too difficult for Wynn to follow, perhaps uttered in some ancient dialect reserved for such ceremonies. All she picked out were the names of Eternals, but to her, their thundering tones mattered more than their words. Mallet finally stepped down to the amphitheater floor, but any new questions Wynn had were cut short.

Three armored and armed dwarves, two graced with thôrhks of spiked ends, stood at the floor's far side. The third warrior looked somehow familiar to Wynn. With them was a young shirvêsh in the white vestment of one of the three warrior Bäynæ. All four spoke close together until the younger warrior cocked his head at Mallet's passing.

Wynn suddenly recognized him. It was Carrow, Hammer-Stag's kinsman from the greeting house.

The monk among them quickly reached out, and Mallet turned to join them.

They stood talking below where Sliver sat, but the dwarven smith never looked down. As the last of the filing shirvêsh exited onto the floor, their chant died away. Wynn saw the dark, uncertain expression return to Mallet's old face. Carrow made some sharp exclamation, and one warrior thänæ gritted his teeth. The youthful shirvêsh in white frowned as well.

Wynn craned her head, wishing she could hear them. Something troubling passed among those five. She took one step, peering about to see if she might sneak closer.

Chane's grip closed on her arm.

Wynn tried to pull away but couldn't break his hold. "I'm just trying—"

"Quiet!" he rasped.

Chane was also staring at Mallet and his four companions.

Wynn had known a few Noble Dead since first meeting Magiere, Leesil, and Chap. Like their skin, their disquieting eyes lost some color in death. Still, there was always some tint that remained.

Any hint of brown drained from Chane's irises, and Wynn shivered as his eyes turned as colorless as ice.

The instant Chane gripped Wynn, halting her, he heard Shade snarl. Wynn tried to pull free, but he was not going to let her try to sneak up on Mallet. He fixed upon the far gathering around the old shirvêsh. As the chant died away, and the amphitheater remained quiet for the moment, Chane quickly widened his senses, listening.

Unlike the others in the small group, Carrow looked more outraged than forlorn.

"*Heârva!*" he snapped.

Whatever that meant, the closest thänæ clenched his jaw as the white-clad monk frowned in silence. Chane was uncertain if they disagreed with whatever Carrow had uttered, or if they just disapproved that he had said it aloud. No one verbally denied the young one.

Chane heard Wynn suck in a sharp breath, but kept his gaze locked on Mallet and the other four.

"Your eyes . . . what's wrong with . . ." she began, but never finished. "What are you doing?"

"I am trying to listen."

"Why?" she asked. "You don't understand Dwarvish."

True—especially if she kept interrupting—as it was hard enough to pick up on the conversation. But he might catch something she could translate.

"You would hear nothing," he answered, "if caught sneaking up on them . . . in plain sight!"

"You can't possibly hear them from here," she argued in hushed voice. "Can you?"

"Not if you keep talking!"

Wynn's intelligence and education were never in doubt, but not so for her wisdom at times. She did not always make wise choices in the moment. Her rashness had already lost them one potential source of information.

Mallet leaned close to the monk in white, and Chane could not pick up their whispers. In frustration, he glanced down at Wynn.

"He-air-va," he said, trying to pronounce the one word he had caught clearly. "What does it mean?"

"You mean . . . *heârva*?" she asked, and he nodded. "Umm . . . a past-tense verb from the root *heâr*, referring to 'slaughter' . . . so 'slaughtered.' "

"In other words, killed . . . or slain?"

"No, *marû* is the root for a killing or execution. Dwarvish and Elvish, akin in structures, have more specific terms for—"

"This is no time for language lessons!"

Wynn's brow furrowed in anger. "*Heâr* is the concept of 'slaughter' . . . the killing of that which cannot defend itself or does so to no effect!"

Some of her ire faded when she glanced across the amphitheater floor.

"What is going on over there?" she whispered.

Chane wanted to know as well.

Only Mallet and the other monk still spoke in close whispers. The three warriors listened in silence. Wynn's question stuck in Chane's head as he looked to the stage and the body covered in gray cloth.

Hammer-Stag, braggart that he was, seemed more than able to defend himself. So what made Carrow so angry at a time of mourning? And by Wynn's accounting, why had he used such a specific term for his kinsman's demise?

Wynn watched that quiet gathering with intensity, until Shade suddenly inched out ahead of her. About to grab the dog, she realized Shade was standing at full attention, ears raised, staring at Mallet and his companions. Carrow turned away from the others in sudden disgust—and Shade's head moved.

Shade wasn't watching the gathering, just Carrow. Then she looked up at Wynn and whined softly. Her face almost expressed frustration, as if she didn't know what to do next.

Wynn reached down. The instant her hand lighted between Shade's shoulders . . .

. . . a memory erupted in Wynn's mind.

She was looking down a long passage lit by braziers spaced far apart. Then she was moving, walking along it. Hunks of stone lay on the floor among scattered chips of pulverized rock. She looked aside, running her hand across stone, feeling and seeing the deep gouges and pitted marks. All along the way, the walls were beaten and broken by something swung with great force.

One pit was so deep that her thick fingers slid in to the last knuckle.

Wynn went cold inside. That hand was broad and heavy, callused of palm, its wrist nearly three times as thick as it should be.

This wasn't her memory.

Wynn glanced down at Shade, now watching Mallet weaving his way back among others on the amphitheater floor. Another image rose in Wynn's mind, and it flickered with a third.

She saw Hammer-Stag's face, seemingly pale and shocked but with hints of frozen rage at the instant of death. The dead visage quickly vanished, replaced by one of two shirvêsh from the temple of the three warrior Bäynæ.

She saw them speaking to her, their expressions strained, but their voices were muted and garbled, as if not remembered clearly. Then it dawned on Wynn that these weren't Shade's memories either.

Wynn snatched her hand off Shade's head, sucking in a breath so fast she heard it.

"What?" Chane asked. "What is wrong?"

Shade cocked her head and one ear twitched in a hint of puzzlement.

Wynn shuddered. Those memories couldn't have been Shade's. They had come from someone else—perhaps someone here in this place. But that wasn't possible.

Chap couldn't pass the memories he'd dipped from others, and Wynn had been among other true majay-hì. They didn't have even his ability to read people's memories from a distance. He'd once told her they could memory-speak only by touch with one of their own. They couldn't even pass on a "heard" memory not their own unless it was given to them by another. This accounted for how Shade had received a few hazy memories through Lily long after Chap had left his chosen mate behind.

And Wynn . . . she was the only exception.

Chap's dual nature—Fay-born within a Fay-descended body—combined with how he'd tried to suppress the taint of awry magic left in Wynn, somehow ended up allowing her to hear him inside her head. This also had to be how Shade was able to memory-speak with her alone.

But not with stolen memories.

"How could you?" Wynn whispered.

Shade's blue eyes widened until their yellow flecks showed clearly. She crept closer, sniffing wildly at Wynn—then lunged suddenly.

"No!" Wynn squeaked.

Shade slammed her forepaws into Wynn's chest.

Wynn toppled flat on her back. Before she could fend off the dog, Shade shoved her face hard against Wynn's cheek. A cascading flood of images followed.

A shattered passage . . .

Hammer-Stag's dead, pallid features, his hair streaked with gray . . .

Two elder shirvêsh in white vestments, faces lined with fearful worry . . .

"Get off of her!" Chane hissed.

Wynn's head was still spinning as Shade wheeled away. Her sight had barely cleared when she heard Shade's jaws snap. When Wynn sat up, all the hackles on Shade's neck and upper back stood on end.

Shade faced the other way, growling as her whole body shook in rage. And Chane . . .

He stood a pace off, holding one hand with his other as he glared at the dog.

Chane must have tried to pull Shade off, and she'd bitten him!

"Both of you, stop it," Wynn whispered, and looked to Chane. "She wasn't trying to hurt me."

Chane acknowledged with a quick glance toward Wynn, but Shade wouldn't budge.

"Shade," Wynn whispered. "No . . . no more."

Shade pivoted about, growing quiet. Inching closer, she lowered her head, though she was still so tall she looked Wynn straight in the eyes.

Wynn stared into those sky blue crystalline irises and hesitantly reached out, running her fingers down Shade's neck. She felt the persistent shudder in Shade's whole body.

Shade whined, a pitiful sound, full of uncertainty.

"You didn't know," Wynn whispered. "You didn't know you could do that . . . with me, did you?"

"What is going on here?" someone demanded.

The sharp tone made Wynn jerk upright where she sat.

Shirvêsh Mallet stood over her, his hands on his hips.

"This solemn occasion is not the place for such behavior!" he growled, and his outrage turned on Chane. "Your presence is a privileged consideration. Do not take it lightly!"

Wynn cringed, searching for a plausible lie to explain all this away, but Chane cut in.

"What about *he-air-va*?" he asked Mallet. "What 'slaughter' were you talking about?"

Mallet went slack-jawed and backed up a step.

"Chane, watch your manners!" Wynn warned. She'd been so overwhelmed by Shade that she'd forgotten what Chane had somehow overheard.

"My apology," Chane said, though his civility sounded forced.

Mallet was still stunned speechless, but the shock in his expression quickly vanished.

"I see no need to answer to a thief!" he snarled, "who steals words not given to him."

Wynn quickly got up. Mallet's choice of words implied something worse than eavesdropping, considering he was an elder monk of a poet Eternal in a culture of oral tradition.

"Please, shirvêsh," she pleaded. "There's no time for formality. What happened in the shattered passage? How did Hammer-Stag die?"

Mallet turned renewed astonishment on Wynn. The obvious unspoken question was how did she know that? But there was no time to cover up her blunder.

"It could be very important," she said. "We need to know."

The old shirvêsh eyed her as if he had indeed caught a thief in his temple.

"Nothing is certain," he finally answered, "only that a vicious battle took place. Passersby found him and alerted the local clan guard. No one knew what to make of what they found. His ax lay just beyond his hand and . . . and as you said, the passage was shattered all around him. Yet no blood . . . as if not one of his blows had struck true on his opponent, and there were no wounds on him. He was just . . . pale, eyes still open . . . as if his heart gave out in an instant and all blood drained from his face."

Wynn grew colder with every word that Mallet uttered. Hammer-Stag was renowned as a warrior. In that narrow tunnel that Shade had shown her, how could he not have struck his attacker even once?

A thunderous beat echoed about the amphitheater. Any low sounds among those present died instantly. Four more beats of an unseen drum echoed around the high curved walls, and Mallet spun about.

His eyes roamed the stage and then fixed as she heard him inhale. Wynn forgot everything as her gaze followed his.

From out of the far square opening upon the platform came six dwarves, all dressed in black and dark gray. The drum kept on, its thunder matched to their steps. Wynn barely caught that two of them were women, dressed exactly like the men, before she focused entirely on their leader.

Black, steel-streaked hair framed an old face with a broad nose over a mouth rimmed by a cropped and bristling steely beard. Like all the others, he wore char-gray breeches and a shirt beneath a hauberk of oily black leather scales that glinted strangely. In the low light, it took a moment to make out those sparks. Polished steel fixtures covered the tips of each scale upon his armor.

Wynn had seen him once before in the doorway of Domin High-Tower's study. As much as his attire, she remembered that face, that bearing. If Death personified stepped into the path of this one, the grim dwarf would walk right through him without acknowledgment. Or Death would scurry out of the way.

Wynn stared at the Stonewalkers as their elder paced straight to the litter upon the stone block. The amphitheater's silence was so complete that she heard every grind of his heavy boots upon stone. He stopped directly behind the head of Hammer-Stag's draped corpse. The five remaining Stonewalkers took places around the litter, two to either side and one at his feet. The last caught Wynn's full attention.

His red hair was unmistakable . . . the one she'd overheard High-Tower call "brother."

It was Ore-Locks.

Wynn took one furtive glance toward Sliver in the stands.

The smith was on her feet. She leaned hard upon the stone rail, but without eagerness in her face. Her expression twisted over and over, as if she might weep in pain, but then instantly hardened in resentment at the sight of Ore-Locks.

Wynn understood why Sliver had come tonight—to hopefully catch a glimpse of one long-lost brother. But Wynn didn't know why hate rather than love shone upon Sliver's face.

A roaring voice like cracking stone jerked Wynn's gaze to the stage.

"Who brings this one to wait upon us?" called the eldest of the Stonewalkers.

"Stálghlên—Pure-Steel—brings him," answered a white-clad shirvêsh.

There was hesitation in his voice, as if Hammer-Stag's fate remained uncertain.

"Then he comes by virtue of championship?" asked the eldest stonewalker.

"Most certainly Fiáh'our—Hammer-Stag—was this and more," the monk answered.

Another long silence left Wynn fearful that something had gone wrong. A shout rose from the silver-streaked elder of the Stonewalkers.

"An honored thänæ!"

The entire amphitheater erupted in shouts and cries, and the crowd's noise pounded in Wynn's ears. It was so loud she could almost feel it upon her skin. Warriors upon the floor before the stage unsheathed weapons, raising them in the air. Every dwarf in the place was on his or her feet, chanting that Hammer-Stag was to be taken "into stone."

Chane's hissing voice rose close to Wynn's ear.

"We should slip out amid the distraction," he insisted. "We must find out how they got in before they take the corpse. This may be our only chance to catch them."

Wynn came to her senses. She was here for a reason, but how could she just slip away? What would Mallet say when he discovered his guests were gone? She hadn't thought through her hopes for this night, but High-Tower's brother was right *here*. She couldn't miss the chance of getting to him.

The elder stonewalker abruptly jerked off the gray cloth, and his comrades instantly tilted the litter up. Shouts for Hammer-Stag's acceptance turned into an incomprehensible roar.

Wynn's gasp was drowned in the cacophony.

Hammer-Stag's body stood carefully dressed and groomed, his armor oiled and polished. The sides of his hair were braided, the two tendrils bound at the ends by tight rings of dark metal. His arms were folded and bound across, clutching his great ax against his chest. But Wynn stared only at his face and hands.

They were ashen—almost gray beyond the mottled undertones of his people.

His features weren't twisted as in the memory Shade had passed. But whatever attempt had been made to relax them in final repose hadn't fully succeeded.

Hammer-Stag was as sallow as the victim of a Noble Dead.

Wynn looked up at Chane. He too stared at the dead thänæ.

A few others on the floor nearest the stage exchanged disturbed glances. Those in the stands were too far off to notice. The roar in the amphitheater continued as Wynn struggled to get hold of herself.

She grasped Chane's sleeve.

"Say nothing!" he insisted, but his eyes flickered in rapid thought.

The Stonewalkers lowered the litter and re-covered Hammer-Stag with the shimmering cloth. They jointly hoisted the litter upon their shoulders as their elder turned toward the stage's far exit.

"We must catch up with them," Chane whispered, and grasped Wynn's hand.

She half turned, following him, and then spotted a small group entering the amphitheater.

Duchess Reine Faunier-Âreskynna swept out of the dark tunnel onto the flagstones. A trio of the weardas surrounded her, followed by the white-robed elf so often seen at her side. Everyone standing near the tunnel's mouth quickly stepped aside for the entourage.

"*Valhachkasej'â!*" Wynn cursed, and pulled out of Chane's hold.

She grabbed the back of his cloak, jerking him halfway around as she ducked in behind him. Then she had to grab him again to keep him from turning around on her.

"Don't move!" she whispered, and peeked cautiously around his side.

Dressed in high riding boots and a dark sea green cloak, Duchess Reine had thrown back her hood. Thick chestnut hair was pinned up with twin combs of mother-of-pearl, shaped like foaming ocean waves. Neither she nor any of her companions broke stride as they drove straight through the crowd.

What was a member of Malourné's royal family doing here?

"Master Cinder-Shard," the duchess called out. "Please wait."

And the leader of the Stonewalkers paused.

Wynn's mixed fears faded for an instant. The duchess had called the dark elder by a given name.

Duchess Reine had done everything possible to turn aside investigation into the murders surrounding the guild's translation project. In acting for the royal family, as well the domins and premins of the sages, she'd also tried within the law to keep the texts out of Wynn's reach. She could very well do so again, if she saw Wynn here.

Wynn leaned out a little farther, trying to see without being noticed behind Chane's tall form. The duchess had never seen Chane or Shade, and Wynn didn't wish to be spotted, not until she understood what was happening.

As the duchess's entourage reached the nearest steps, Reine walked lightly up onto the stage. The other Stonewalkers lowered the litter at her approach. She paused briefly before Cinder-Shard with a respectful bow of her head.

Duchess Reine peeled back the shimmering cloth and looked down upon Hammer-Stag's face.

Wynn couldn't see her expression, but it seemed the duchess froze for a long moment. Then she pulled off one glove and placed her bare hand upon the thänæ's—gripping the ax. She didn't look up as Cinder-Shard drew near, though she nodded.

Reine's hand slipped off of Hammer-Stag's. As she pulled the cloth back over his body, the stonewalkers hoisted Hammer-Stag again. The duchess, the white-clad elf, and all three Weardas followed as the Stonewalkers carried the litter toward the far exit at the stage's rear.

Shade's whine startled Wynn in the silence.

The dog watched her with questioning blue eyes, as if sensing Wynn's uncertainty. Wynn dropped to her knees. Touching heads with Shade, Wynn passed every memory she could summon of the duchess back in Calm Seatt. Hopefully Shade would understand some part of why Wynn had to keep out of sight. As she finished, Chane lowered his head, glancing down at her.

"We have to go . . . now!" he whispered.

"I can't," she whispered back, rising behind him.

What could she do? The Stonewalkers were leaving, and Ore-Locks with them, but Duchess Reine was in their company. Until she parted ways with the Stonewalkers, Wynn couldn't risk being seen.

One of the white-vested shirvêsh on the stage held up both hands.

"Hammer-Stag is taken into stone," he called. "The bones of our world will be strengthened by him."

Everyone in the amphitheater became still. Many bowed their heads with closed eyes.

Chane mimicked this, yet looked at Wynn in obvious urgency.

"I can't be seen by the duchess," she whispered.

"Then we keep back until she leaves," he answered. "But we will lose all of them if we do not go now!"

It was a terrible option, but for as little as Wynn had uncovered so far, she could see no other choice. She finally nodded, ready to send Shade ahead of them. Shade would be far better at sensing whether they got too close, yet still be able to track the Stonewalkers.

Wynn turned carefully about, her fingers still cinched tightly into Chane's cloak. But when she reached down with her other hand . . .

Shade was gone.

CHAPTER 9

Duchess Reine Faunier-Âreskynna followed Master Cinder-Shard out of the stage's far exit. The passage widened enough for three, and Chuillyon and Captain Tristan stepped in beside her. Her other two Weardas guards, Danyel and Saln, came last, followed by five Stonewalkers bearing Hammer-Stag's remains.

No one spoke, and Reine kept her eyes on Cinder-Shard's large boots.

The official claim was that Hammer-Stag's heart had failed from strain, but other rumors had reached Reine at her inn in Sea-Side. Few details were forthcoming, and gossip and speculation varied too much. She inquired at a local clan's constabulary post but learned no more—other than that three more unexplained deaths—a Suman, and later two Northlanders—had been discovered less than a day before the thänæ's body was found.

This, as much as paying respects to an old savior, drove Reine to the final public ceremony. Now she dared not look back at the litter. Even so, she couldn't stop seeing Hammer-Stag's face in her mind—as he was now and when they'd last met, years ago.

Her husband had gone missing in a small sailing craft.

Hammer-Stag and two of his clan had brought Freädherich safely home. At that time, the thänæ's face had the mottled gray undertones of his people. Though venerable by human standards, he was of good age for a dwarf. He had strength and a spark of presence that could goad anyone out of worry and fear. When he sat with her and the royal family, assuring them that all was well with the young prince, his exaggeration still brought them momentary respite.

As the procession took another turn, Reine spotted a deep and broad arch halfway down the next passage's left wall. When they approached, she found wide double doors of iron set more than a yard deep. There was no latch or lock, no visible way to open them. Only a smooth seam showed where they separated. She looked about the archway for any mechanisms, and her attention caught briefly on the surrounding framing stones.

The *vubrí* of the five tribes and twenty-seven clans were engraved there. When she came to that of the Meerschaum clan, she turned to stare at Hammer-Stag's cloth-draped corpse.

When she'd stopped upon the stage, he'd looked ashen in death, and much too old. She couldn't be certain what it meant, not even after the deaths of the sages so recent in memory. A chill crept up her spine.

"Are you cold, my lady?" Chuillyon asked.

Reine looked up at his feathery eyebrows drawn together beneath his lined forehead.

"No," she whispered and closed her eyes.

She slipped back to one night, farther back than Hammer-Stag's kindness or even the first of her husband's disappearances, back to a happier time. It was a place in memory she often went that still connected her to a life of pretense and a reason for bearing loss.

The first time Reine met Freädherich—Frey—had been on her first visit to Calm Seatt, some seven years past. . . .

King Jacqui Amornon Faunier—or rather Uncle Jac—had been invited for another royal visit to Malourné. He was told to bring whomever he pleased among his family.

Reine's own parents had passed on long ago, and she'd inherited the duchy. It had never sat well with her. The weight of her station frustrated her, as did nobles sniffing about, circling in upon the unwed niece of a king. Uncle Jac hadn't once pressured her about this.

He politely dealt with all suitors, for any engagement to her had to be approved by him, and he would never consent unless she did. He handled Faunier's noble houses with great care whenever one sent a son, brother, or nephew seeking a royal alliance by marriage. Some were not so bad, but Reine had grown tired of being a desired acquisition.

And so, Uncle Jac insisted that his favorite niece—his only niece—join him on this visit with their nation's staunch ally. His wife, Evonné, would remain to oversee affairs of state, so he needed good feminine company, someone only half as wild as his two sons.

Reine didn't mind, nor was she fooled by his excuse. Uncle always had her happiness at heart, and she did love the freedom to be abroad at will. It was the way of the Faunier, horse people by ancestry.

She loved her homeland, especially the eastern granite steppes, where she could stand upon high stone ledges and look back across her native land. But a more distant excursion would take her beyond the reach of suitors, if only for a short while. She readily agreed to accompany her uncle for a chance to visit Calm Seatt.

The splendid city didn't disappoint her, and she couldn't help finding the third castle of the Âreskynna a marvel. However, upon meeting the royals of Malourné, Reine felt distinctly out of place.

They were too tall, too pale, too blond, seeming to float in a detached somber serenity rather than walk naturally upon the earth. They made her welcome enough, but even in their reserved hospitality, there was something not quite right in their aquamarine eyes.

Reine especially noted this on the first night.

A grand banquet was held in her uncle's honor. Along with him and her two cousins, Edelard and Felisien, Reine entered a lavish hall on one upper floor of the third castle. Three Weardas in red tabards stood to either side of the open white doors. And within the long and tall chamber, scores of people in evening regalia gathered in clusters.

They sipped from crystal goblets and polished pewter tankards while waiting to go down to dinner. The place was filled with the humming buzz of their low chatter—and a strange light.

Reine looked up to high iron chandeliers, three in all, along the domed roof. Each bore a host of oil-fed lanterns, their flames caged inside perfect glass balls in varied tints. They reminded her of fishermen's floats she'd seen on a brief pass near the city's northern piers.

King Leofwin of Malourné and his wife Queen Muriel Witon, disengaged from two serious-faced men Reine would later know as Baron Âdweard Twynam and his son, Jason. The monarchs came straight for her uncle, ushering him off after friendly greetings passed between the families.

"There he is!" Edelard declared, pointing, and Felisien leaned over to look along his brother's arm. "Come on . . . I'll introduce you."

Both were off, forgetting their elder cousin. Only Felisien stopped halfway and glanced back. With surprise on his lean, rather pretty face, he swung his head with a smile, urging her to follow.

Reine just shook her head.

Felisien rolled his eyes. Prim as a peacock in his glistening long coat, he went after his brother, and Reine glanced about the room.

Not one other lady present was dressed in a split riding skirt over breeches and high polished boots. Oh, yes, her attire was made of satins and elven sheot'a, as fine and proper as any royal among her people. But it wasn't like theirs. Among the men, she saw a number of officers, some bearing arms, a sword or dagger—but not the women.

Not one wore a horse saber on her hip, like Reine, regardless that it hung from a belt gilded with silver rosettes. All these ladies in their floor-length gowns and robes left Reine feeling . . . *foreign.*

She would never let it show, but she didn't care to ride into this kind of wilderness. She tried tucking her saber a little farther behind her and then stopped. Why should she be embarrassed by who and what she was? She let the blade hang in plain sight.

Cousin Edelard had set in renewing his acquaintance with Prince Leäfrich Âreskynna, each dressed in their fine uniforms. They'd met before on exchanges between the nations' militaries. Felisien was pestering a young officer with his raffish banter. The younger dazzle-eyed sublieutenant looked almost as uncomfortable under such attention as Reine felt in the hall. Amid the men were three ladies. Reine had met the tallest briefly that morning.

Princess Âthelthryth Âreskynna, heir to Malourné's throne, stood close to her brother.

Reine knew the ways of court and how to deal with its society and ploys. But as much as the Âreskynna were hospitable in their aloof way, there had to be better and more interesting places to wait until dinner. She backed one step toward the doors and . . .

Âthelthryth turned her head on her long neck and stared straight at Reine with her family's deep aquamarine eyes. The princess's lithe form turned, sending a gentle sway through a white gauze overskirt atop her pastel sea green gown. She moved—flowed—around her brother toward the chamber hall's doors.

Reine quickly smiled, but under her breath she exhaled. "Oh, give me a horse!"

"Pardon, Highness?" a deep voice asked.

Startled, she glanced aside—then up—into the hard eyes of a Weardas by the doors.

Triple braids on his vestment marked him as an officer, though she didn't know enough to discern his rank. A tuft of dark beard stuck out upon his square jaw.

"Nothing," she answered, then cleared her throat, repeating with disinterest, "It is nothing."

He bowed with only his head.

Reine looked away—straight into the bodice of that sea green gown. She quickly raised her eyes, more and more, until they met the studying gaze of Âthelthryth.

"I've meant to ask," said the princess in an emotionless lilt, "do you know how to use that?"

Confusion stifled Reine until Âthelthryth's focus slowly lowered, and her attention fixed briefly on the saber's protruding hilt.

"Of course," Reine answered softly, on guard for some implied slight.

"Hopefully not on anyone here," returned Âthelthryth, "much as you might wish to cut yourself free of this event."

The barest empathetic smile broke Âthelthryth's tepid serenity.

"You would not be alone in such desire," she added, letting a brief but tired sigh escape. "Regardless of what station requires of us."

With that, Âthelthryth gently took Reine's arm and steered her into the crowded hall.

Lost in confusion and growing discomfort, Reine maintained dignified composure as many an eye turned their way, along with respectful nods at the passing of two ladies of royal blood.

"At least we might keep you from being hunted," Âthelthryth whispered. "Though I've heard you handle predators well enough."

Reine wasn't certain what to make of this. As direct heir to a throne, the princess would have had her share of suitors to fend off. Then they passed Prince Leäfrich's group.

He paused midsentence, though his companions didn't notice in their chatter. Leäfrich glanced at his sister, offering a slight nod of some covert agreement. Then he looked once toward the back of the long chamber.

A shadow of concern raced quickly across the tall prince's face.

Reine tried to follow his gaze. Wherever or whoever he had sought, there were too many people to pick out his target.

Around a cluster of self-amused debutantes, Reine spotted Uncle Jac with the king and queen of Malourné. He smiled at her, though it looked forced, veiling some unspoken worry. King Leofwin, hand-in-hand with Queen Muriel, looked to his daughter.

"Keeping our cousin well cared for?" he asked.

"Always, Father," Âthelthryth answered. "Like my very own."

Familial references were common respect for royalty of allied nations, but it left Reine unsettled—more so when King Leofwin glanced in the same direction that the prince had only moments before. Reine tried again to find their source of concern.

Queen Muriel whispered something in her husband's ear, too soft and low to catch. Leofwin slumped, hanging his head. His eyes clenched shut, and Muriel grasped her husband's hand in both of hers.

"Come," Âthelthryth urged. "Let us find a defensible spot with more room to breathe."

Reine was swept onward before she heard anything more.

What was happening here? And why had her uncle looked as concerned as the Âreskynna?

At the hall's rear, before a tall window of crystal clear panes, stood a fragile-looking young man, his back turned to everyone. He was dressed plainly but elegantly in a white shirt of billowing sleeves beneath a sea green brocade vest. All alone, he faced the outside world, and dangling locks of sandy blond hair hid any glimpse of his face. His shoulders bent forward under some unseen weight, his hands braced upon the sill.

Was this where all wayward glances had turned?

"Freädherich?" whispered Âthelthryth. "Could you keep our cousin company?"

Again that familial term.

It bothered Reine even more—especially as she stared at the younger prince's back. She wouldn't have recognized him as he was now, though she had met him earlier that day. He'd been silent then as well.

"I must see to late arrivals," Âthelthryth said, and still her youngest brother didn't turn.

Reine began to heat up with barely suppressed anger.

For all Uncle Jac's supposed understanding, was he now trying to make *her* suitor to some foreign prince? Or had the Âreskynna coerced him into this, so quickly executed by Âthelthryth?

Reine turned on her royal "cousin," ready to remove herself, even at the cost of insult—but she held her tongue.

The princess watched her brother with the same wounded concern as had the king and queen and Prince Leäfrich. Then her gaze wandered.

Âthelthryth stared intently out the window beyond Freädherich. Her fixed eyes turned glassy until she blinked suddenly. With a shudder, she pulled Reine back a step.

"Please," she whispered, "decorum's pressure might force him to speak with you."

With a final pained glance at Freädherich, Âthelthryth turned away, gliding back through the crowded room.

Reine was left alone with the young prince, but it only made her ire grow.

She wasn't about to be played, especially under her uncle's betrayal. No wonder he'd fended off suitors in their own land. He'd kept her like a prized purebred to barter for political gain. Why not just throw one of his sons at Âthelthryth and aim directly for the crown of Malourné?

No, that would be pointless. Edelard was already heir of Faunier, and Felisien . . . well, his numerous indiscretions leaned entirely in another direction.

Reine turned like a cornered fox and cast her spite across the room at Uncle Jac. But King Jacqui only lowered his head with firmly pressed lips, and then cocked it slightly toward Freädherich. All Reine saw in her uncle's face was more concern, and Queen Muriel watched her with frightful expectation.

Reine slowly turned about, frustrated as she gazed at Freädherich's back.

Something more was happening here, aside from an attempt to throw her at the young prince. Much as she wouldn't allow the latter, she stepped closer, coming around two paces off so as not to startle him.

Prince Freädherich was young, certainly a few years younger than she was. Shoulder-length sandy hair framed a long, pale face. His narrow nose looked slightly hooked, but nothing too severe or unappealing. The thin lips of his small mouth were parted, as if his jaw hung slack, and his eyes . . .

Those eerie aquamarine irises were locked unblinking into the distance outside.

His face was barely a hand's length from the window, and quick, shallow breaths briefly fogged the chilled panes.

"My apologies for the invasion," she said quietly. "This seems the quietest corner of the hall."

He didn't respond or turn from the window.

"I am Duchess Reine Faunier, if you remember," she added. "Except for my uncle and cousins, I'm . . . unacquainted with anyone here."

Freädherich blinked once. His head turned just a little toward her. His eyes turned last, so reluctant to relinquish the view.

"I don't know anyone but my family," he whispered.

Unlikely for a prince of the realm, Reine thought, unless he had purposely cloistered himself for many years.

His gaze touched hers for an instant before he turned back to the window. It was enough to fill her with a sudden shiver. Over the outer castle wall, she made out the full moon hanging high above the dwarves' distant mountain peninsula. It cast a shimmering road of light across the wide bay and out into the open ocean.

Reine stood rigid, watching Freädherich stare again out the window. She knew that desperate look, or thought she did.

There were times when demands of station, even in her remote duchy, grew too smothering. She would grab her horse bow, perhaps go hunting covey in the scrub, or just ride until exhausted. Her escapes always ended in the high eastern granite steppes. She would stand where the sky was large enough that she no longer felt trapped.

Freädherich gazed the other way, to the west. The desperation on his face wouldn't let Reine back away.

"Then we'll wait here," she said, "and pretend a deep conversation. No one will bother us until dinner is announced."

It was all she could think to say.

Freädherich's eyes shifted her way but not to her face. He glanced over her foreign attire, ending not upon her sword but rather on her calf-high boots. It gave her a notion, something, anything to say.

"Have you chosen a mount for the ride?"

His thin lips parted suddenly, as if her words startled him.

"The tour of the local province?" she urged. "Your father arranged a ride. I have my horses but was wondering about the stock of your stables. I assumed that . . . you . . ."

Her voice failed as he shrank upon himself, as if no one had ever tried to force him into conversation like this.

"I don't know how to ride," he said.

"And I do not know how to swim," she answered—then regretted it instantly.

Freädherich slid away along the sill, grown wary at some implied expectation. Reine was suddenly smothered in guilt for her quip. She'd thought only about his longing to escape. Stupidly, mistakenly, she'd frightened him more in turn.

"I can teach you," she added. "With a gentle mount, it wouldn't be difficult."

Freädherich remained silent—then he nodded slightly, just once.

Another stillness hung between them for so long that Reine became self-conscious. This was something she'd seldom felt before coming to this coast among these seafaring people. When she finally grew too uncomfortable, she turned her back to the window and its disturbing view.

That seemingly endless ocean, dark yet with no firm ground to race across, could swallow her into its depths in the first step. Perhaps her ways of horse and plains and steppes were as unsettling to him.

She half sat upon the sill, and to her surprise, he turned and did the same.

But when Freädherich faced the crowd of drinking nobles, panic filled his eyes at the sight of so many people. Not like a child. More like a wild horse spotting roving winter wolves that hadn't yet noticed it. On instinct, Reine slid her hand along the sill to cover his.

Not everyone was watching them—only Uncle Jac and the royals of Malourné. Or at least these were the only ones Reine noticed. The relief in Queen Muriel's face was almost disturbing. King Leofwin took a deep breath, hand on his chest.

Reine was baffled by all of this.

When a finely suited servant rang a silver bell, announcing that dinner would be served, Freädherich's hand tightened upon the sill's edge beneath Reine's. She watched his frantic eyes race about as everyone flowed toward the doors. Then he fixed upon someone across the chamber.

Reine's cousin, Prince Edelard, offered his arm to one lady in their group. Prince Leäfrich did the same for his sister, Âthelthryth.

Freädherich looked down at Reine.

At first, she thought he might spin around, fleeing to the safety of his window view—but he did not. She kept her eyes on his until he calmed and lifted his arm for her. And she took it. They sat together at dinner, talking little throughout the meal—which consisted of more courses than Reine cared for. Afterward, Freädherich grew agitated and nervous again.

"Take me on a tour of the castle," she said.

Without a word, he got up, gripping her chair to slide it out. Reine quickly covered for him, making their excuses. Neither the king nor the queen questioned this and were more than obliging. Uncle Jac appeared pleased, and Reine shot him a cold glare before she took Freädherich's arm and they left. As they wandered through the maze of the castle, coming upon a gallery of family portraits, she had to finally ask.

"Freädherich . . . is something wrong?"

"You should call me Frey," he said, ignoring the question. "That's what Âthel and Lee call me."

Such nicknames were a little amusing compared to how formal the Âreskynna were with outsiders, but she wouldn't be put off so easily.

"I meant, you seem somewhat beside yourself . . . elsewhere," she insisted.

Again, her quiet directness startled him. This time he recovered more quickly.

"The ride," he whispered. "Father insists that I go."

That wasn't what was really on his mind, though it obviously bothered him as well. At another evasion, Reine chose not to press him into whatever more uncomfortable thoughts he wouldn't share.

"You don't wish to go?" she asked.

Freädherich—Frey—looked at the floor.

"I don't like horses," he said flatly. "I prefer to sail."

Reine was a bit stunned. Coming from a nation of horse people, she'd never met anyone who feared those proud animals. Then again, perhaps he'd never met anyone afraid of the sea . . . the endless ocean. Why was she so drawn to protect this strange young man?

On the edge of the next dawn, Reine secretly slipped out to meet him at the stables.

Frey was waiting outside and wouldn't enter until she pulled him in. She showed him the tall mounts her uncle brought in their entourage, but he wouldn't step near even one. When she came to her own three—Cinnamon, Nettle, and Peony—she made him stay put as she led out the latter gentle and dappled mare.

By the time Felisien came searching for her, Reine had already gotten Frey to mount. To her surprise, he learned quickly. And she later learned that he'd been forced onto a soldier's stallion by his elder brother at too early an age. But he'd never been taught in proper fashion to work *with* a horse. Peony took to him well.

By afternoon, the Weardas and a contingent of cavalry prepared to escort all the royals out for their tour. Reine was mounted atop Cinnamon, her muscular stallion. Frey, still atop Peony, remained at ease so long as he had Reine in his sight.

He worked easily with the calm mare, or rather she with him, even cantering past his father twice, much to everyone's shock. But Frey seldom left Reine's side. If he did, she kept watch on him. When Felisien tried to goad her into a round of tag-arrows on horseback, wheeling his mount in her way, she booted him in the rump. She wasn't about to panic Frey with the sight of such a wild game.

By the time the tour ended, and they'd returned to the castle, Reine decided that she would put off leaving when her family headed home. Something inside her didn't wish to abandon Frey—or that was how she viewed it. Three days later, she went to see off her cousins . . . her uncle. She hadn't spoken to him since the night of the first banquet.

Uncle Jac, mounted on his plains-bred stallion, looked sternly down at Reine.

"This was only for hope of your happiness," he said, and then added with emphasis, "nothing more. The rest is up to you . . . and him."

Was all of this truly only seven years ago?

Metal grating upon stone wrenched Reine into the present. She turned about as the iron doors split down their center seam. They slowly parted, sliding into the walls. A second pair began to separate as well, and then a third.

There was Cinder-Shard, on the doors' other side, standing dead center in the widening portal. Reine hadn't even seen him enter.

At his brief wave, the remaining Stonewalkers passed by, bearing Hammer-Stag's body into the chamber. Cinder-Shard turned away out of sight to the portal's left.

"Time to go," Chuillyon said from behind her.

All Reine saw between the chamber's inner rounded walls was an opening in the center of its stone floor. It looked like a shaft as wide as a bailey gate.

Filled with blackness in the low light, that hole seemed to drop straight into the mountain's bowels. She could swear she caught the scent of seawater filling the chamber, perhaps rising from the shaft. It wasn't possible, though she shivered again.

"My lady," Chuillyon said, "did you hear me?"

Reine looked up into his triangular, tan elven faced lined softly with age.

"Pardon?" she said.

"It is time," he answered softly. But as he took a step to lead her on, he paused and became still.

"What?" she asked.

Chuillyon blinked, pivoting his head quickly, and gazed down the outer passage. Reine turned, wondering if they'd been followed. Chuillyon's feathery eyebrows twisted, one cocking higher than the other. With pursed lips, he suddenly smiled and shook his head.

"I'm just getting too old," he muttered. "The mind wanders, I suppose."

Yes, old Chuillyon was becoming a bit odd at times.

Reine forced down all feeling, hardening herself. She stepped through with him, not glancing back as the triple iron doors closed behind her.

"We can't follow yet!" Wynn whispered. "Not without Shade."

Chane scowled down at her.

It was difficult to speak without being overheard. The stands were emptying as the public filed up and out of the amphitheater, but handfuls of dwarves were now carrying tables and benches onto the floor for the impending wake. Wynn tried to keep out of their way as she looked about for Shade.

She couldn't stop thinking of Hammer-Stag's pale face. It hinted too much about how he had died. Unless some other Noble Dead, another vampire other than Chane, were here among the dwarves . . .

"Who was that woman?" Chane asked.

"A royal of Malourné!" Wynn took a breath and tried to calm herself. "The duchess—I mean, Princess Reine, widow of Prince Freädherich. She did everything possible to hinder Captain Rodian's investigation—and to keep Premin Sykion in control of the texts. If she sees me here . . ."

Wynn trailed off at Chane's frown.

This was difficult to explain. He hadn't been in the middle of the murder investigation, as she had. More than once she'd run into the blockades set by the duchess for her family, keeping Wynn from getting anywhere near the texts.

What was the duchess doing here? And where had Shade gone?

"Coming through!" a young dwarf called, holding one end of a heavy table over his head.

Wynn hopped aside, tugging Chane out of the way. Had Shade picked up something in her thoughts, some rising memory? Had she gone looking for the Stonewalkers on her own? If so, which way had she gone?

Wynn didn't know—didn't believe—the dog was accustomed enough to civilization to seek anything but a direct path after her quarry. She looked about, trying to spot other openings in the side walls below the stands, and then her attention caught on Mallet.

The old shirvêsh was busy with monks from other temples, and Wynn wasn't certain about protocol. The banquet was intended for family, close friends, and any other thänæ appropriate. They would eat and drink amid a telling to celebrate Hammer-Stag's final honor in death. But from scant bits she could overhear, Mallet was making his farewells.

"He'll be leaving soon," she whispered. "And we'll have to leave with him!"

Chane straightened to his full height, looking all around.

"There," he said, jutting his chin over his shoulder. "Follow me, slowly."

He backed toward the floor's side and another opening near the tunnel where they'd first come in. Wynn followed him.

Together, they drifted along the wall amid busy preparations. When they reached the opening, Wynn ducked in ahead of Chane. She found herself in a dim chamber without internal light. She could barely make out the shadowy outlines of square openings in its other three walls.

"Oh, seven hells!" she swore.

Which way would Shade have gone, if she'd come this way at all? Wynn dug her cold lamp crystal out of her robe's pocket and rubbed it once to get light.

"Keep that covered," Chane said. "We do not want to attract attention."

Wynn bit her tongue at his needless reprimand. With the crystal couched between her palms, she stepped farther into the chamber.

Stout wooden doors were set deep in the openings ahead and to the right. Both had iron bar handles but no locks. Even so, could Shade know how to open them, let alone close either? Impossible. But the arch on the left was doorless.

Wynn headed through it, finding herself at the bottom of a short flight of stairs. At the top, a narrow passage turned right. Overall, this path headed toward the stage, not away from it. She squeezed the crystal in one hand and spun away, slumping against the dark chamber's side wall.

"This is pointless," she said. "We should wait for Shade to reappear."

Chane hung by the room's entrance, watching outside. "What if Mallet misses us?"

"We'll tell him we were looking around and got lost."

Chane glanced at her in frustration. "This could be our only chance. How often does a thänæ die?"

How often indeed?

"I can't let the duchess see me!"

Losing track of Shade was her fault. Bit by bit, her continual failures were destroying their chances of ever getting a lead on the texts.

Chane returned to watching out of the chamber's entrance, leaving Wynn alone in turmoil. Then he snapped his fingers once. She straightened as he gestured outside. Shoving the crystal in her pocket, she drew closer.

"There," he whispered, "at the tunnel where we first came in."

Wynn leaned slightly against the arch's other side.

Shade's head peeked out of the tunnel as she swiveled it, looking around the amphitheater floor.

"Shade!" Wynn called as softly as she could. "Here!"

But the dog didn't seem to hear. All the bustle of setting up the wake made too much background noise.

A sharp, piercing tone made Wynn jump and turn.

Chane uttered another brief whistle. Wynn turned back in time to see Shade's ears stand up. As Shade looked over, Wynn crouched, waving to the dog around the entrance's side. Shade slunk along the side wall, all the way to the chamber's entrance, and Wynn dropped to her knees in relief.

"Where have you been?" she demanded, grasping the dog's face.

Shade's pink tongue flipped quickly out over her nose.

A barrage of images hit Wynn so suddenly she wavered on her knees. She saw clearly through Shade's eyes.

At first, she saw the Stonewalkers carrying Hammer-Stag's body through the exit off the stage. Then she saw herself standing on the amphitheater floor, talking to Chane. It was unsettling, as if she'd become disembodied, a spirit of herself watching herself. Then she was moving away, weaving through a forest of stout dwarven legs.

When she reached the wall, she began examining low drainage openings, but they were too small to crawl into. Even stranger than this experience through Shade's eyes was the strong feeling that accompanied these memories. She could *feel* Shade's desperation, her need to search.

Then the floor began to rush past beneath her charcoal-colored paws.

She headed back for the tunnel through which they'd first entered. Instead of continuing to the outside street, she turned at the first side passage. She trotted in the same direction that the Stonewalkers had traveled upon leaving the stage and suddenly slowed to listen.

Distant footfalls on stone echoed faintly from down the passage. She quickened her pace to track them.

She padded down corridors, turning at intersections and creeping down stairs, always listening for heavy booted feet, until finally, she peered around a corner. Wynn could smell earthy, musky sweat and leather, as if her nose were shoved right into it. But the closest people she saw were . . .

Halfway down the passage, on the left side, the duchess and her entourage stood near a wide arch in the side wall. Stonewalkers stood beside them, bearing Hammer-Stag's litter.

Wynn couldn't tell what they waited for, but then she heard metal grinding on stone. When it stopped, the Stonewalkers carried the litter through the arch, vanishing from sight. The duchess and her companions remained.

Wynn found herself watching the back of a tall, white-robed elf. When he turned around with a frown, his slanted almond-shaped eyes searching, she quickly backed around the corner and lost sight of everyone.

The grinding came again, echoing softly down the passage, but she remained in hiding. Suddenly everything blurred for an instant as she—as Shade—rushed around the corner and down the passage.

A pair of iron doors were closing deep inside the arch as they slid out from the sides. She caught only a glimpse of Cinder-Shard before the portal clanged shut.

A blur followed, as if the memory skipped quickly forward in time.

Wynn felt cold metal against her ear as she leaned her head, her muzzle flattened against the doors. From inside came another sound like metal on stone, but different—rhythmic, and softly pounding, like quick, even steps. It grew louder, closer, and then stopped altogether.

She heard voices beyond the doors.

One was higher in pitch than the others. It had to be the duchess. But why had she gone in with the Stonewalkers? She'd paid her respects and left with them, but Wynn assumed that was only to avoid being caught in the crowd. Hadn't she gone her own way?

Everything went dark.

The memory ended so quickly that Wynn tottered on her knees. She wrapped her arms around Shade's neck, her thoughts reeling with all that she'd seen and heard.

News of Hammer-Stag's death couldn't have reached the duchess so quickly in Calm Seatt. So why was a member of the royal family here among the dwarves? How had she known the thänæ, and had she gone with the Stonewalkers, or passed beyond those iron doors along some other route?

Wynn leaned back, holding Shade's face, and whispered, "Clever girl!"

"What?" Chane asked.

"She saw where they went," Wynn answered. "At least the doors they passed through somewhere beyond the stage. If we can get through them, perhaps we can follow their trail."

She hadn't seen how the iron doors functioned, but maybe Shade had missed something.

Chane was studying both of them.

"Can she lead us there?" he asked.

"Right now? Tonight?"

Though eager, Wynn wavered with doubt. The amphitheater's floor was filling with dwarves who would feast and drink late into the night.

"Wynn?" a deep voice called out.

She leaned around Shade's tall form and looked out of the chamber's entrance. Shirvêsh Mallet wandered among the tables, searching, and he didn't look happy about doing so.

"Do not call to him," Chane whispered. "We cannot pass up this opportunity."

Wynn was tempted to agree, but she couldn't.

"We can't alienate him anymore. We may need his aid. If we can't find a way to follow, he's our only link to learn what happened to Hammer-Stag . . . and maybe why the duchess is here. She seems favored among the religious castes of the seatt."

Wynn stood, about to leave. Chane opened his mouth to argue, but she shook her head. He closed his eyes in resignation, and she stepped out into plain sight.

"We're here," she called.

Chane stepped out as well as Mallet closed on them, his bushy white eyebrows raised.

"What are you doing in there?" he asked.

Wynn searched for a quick answer. "Giving you a little time with the others. I know Hammer-Stag was dear to you as well, and we didn't want to intrude."

Mallet's expression softened. "Never mind such things. I have said my farewells, and we should leave the family and friends to their feasting and telling."

"Of course," Wynn agreed, glancing at Chane.

Mouth tightly set, he followed as they headed out.

CHAPTER 10

Sau'ilahk waited in the night, sunken halfway into the wall near an alley's mouth. The amphitheater was too crowded to approach or enter, even by slipping through its stone. He did not know the place; certainly not enough to wander its back ways, seeking some hidden vantage point. But he longed to see the Stonewalkers for himself—and if the meddlesome little sage had uncovered anything of use.

Killing the thänæ had cost him more than he could have guessed, nearly draining him of all the life he had consumed. He had taken dwarves before, and as difficult as it was, it had never been this costly. In two days of recuperation, he could barely conjure a few servitors of Air to monitor the amphitheater's exits.

How many times had he thrust his hand through Hammer-Stag's chest? He could not even count, and still the blustering dwarf would not die. In the end, what vital life Sau'ilahk consumed, touch by touch, was a fraction of what he lost in effort. Now he stood exhausted, waiting for any sight of Wynn.

Evening passed into deep night. Finally, dwarves began emerging from the amphitheater's settlement-level tunnels and higher arches, descending stone stairs and out into the streets. They spread and scattered, talking amongst themselves, or marched on in somber silence.

Sau'ilahk watched for Chane, who would tower over these short, stocky people. Dwarves kept coming, but there was no sign of the tall undead. Panic began to set in, which only made Sau'ilahk angry.

Wynn *must* have been witness to the final rites, but what if she did not come out? And he had not seen any Stonewalkers enter. Had he made a mistake? If they had come and gone another way, had she gone after them? Could he risk slipping inside to look for her?

Sau'ilahk hung in indecision. Then the air rippled before him as one servitor appeared.

It emitted three soft tones like a reed whistle and then vanished with a pop of air.

Sau'ilahk flowed up the building's side, drifting from one rooftop to the next. Before he reached the third entrance on the amphitheater's near side, he spotted a dark form on the street below.

Shade padded ahead, hurrying out of a crowded intersection. Wynn jogged after the dog and then paused for Chane and a white-haired dwarf in an orange vestment to catch up.

Sau'ilahk held his place on the rooftop. Even here, the dog might sense him, but would not likely look upward. He let Wynn and her companions pass on.

Two other dwarves in orange vestments came down the steps from the amphitheater's next high entrance. They fell in beside the white-haired one, and Wynn slowed, dropping back a few paces with Shade and Chane. She hung close to Chane, and her lips moved, as if she were engaged in quiet conversation beyond the hearing of their dwarven companions.

Sau'ilahk desperately wanted to hear what she said.

He stilled his mind, calling to his remaining servitors. The air around his head warped and swirled as they joined him. Banishing all but one, he focused his reserves to recommand it and fixed the image of Wynn in his mind.

Target the gray-clad one. Remain above the target. Absorb all sound. If the target reaches the temple . . .

He faltered, so tired that he was not being concise. His mindless creation would not comprehend such references.

If the target passes inside stone, then return to me. Reiterate all sound and banish.

The ball of distorted air sped over the roof's edge and up the night street.

Once Wynn was well on her way, Sau'ilahk followed along the rooftops. At every alley or side street, he watched for her passing along the main avenue. When she slipped beyond sight again, he sped onward, staying ahead of her. He kept changing his position and orientation, in case the dog became aware of his presence.

When Wynn reached the way station, the old dwarf stepped into the crank house building, walking through it to the lift's landing. Wynn followed through the opening in a wall . . . made of stone.

Sau'ilahk could have shrieked in rage as his servitor came rushing back. Wynn passed out of the building's other side, boarding the waiting lift with the others. But she was no longer talking with Chane while in the close company of the three dwarves.

The servitor began to replay what it had gathered, gruff dwarven voices low and dull behind Wynn's and Chane's whispers.

"No, it's too crowded!" Wynn said. "We'll go back tomorrow night."

"The trail will be cold," Chane rasped.

"Shade may have found a door to their underworld. It has to be where they went . . . where they would take Hammer-Stag. We don't need to track them. Shade can lead us there."

"Come along, young Wynn," a deep voice called. "No lagging on such a cold night."

The servitor popped and vanished.

It had recorded so little, but enough. The dog had found a way to this "underworld." Whatever it was, Wynn believed the Stonewalkers had gone there. Tomorrow night she would return to follow them.

But how had the animal gathered or relayed such information?

The answer could wait. Wynn had finally learned something useful! The cost of killing one dwarf had played out to some small satisfaction. As Sau'ilahk mulled over the best strategy for the following night, his form wavered in the darkness. Or rather the world began to dim as dormancy threatened to take him.

Sau'ilahk had exhausted his energies more than he realized. He cursed his useless excuse for a form. But if—when—Wynn located the texts, he might finally learn the secrets of Beloved's Children. Somewhere in the world, one of the Anchors of Creation waited in hiding. Once he found it, he would have flesh again after an age of searching.

Sau'ilahk faded, and his last conscious thoughts tumbled back through centuries past. . . .

Sau'ilahk, master conjuror, first of the Reverent and high priest of Beloved, trekked up the mountain's craggy base to a place far above the desert. The day's heat lingered into night but never bothered him, even in his black robe.

As he passed, minions bowed their heads, from scattered packs of goblins with yellow eyes and repulsive speckled canine faces to the rare hulking locatha, reptilian abominations half again the height of man. Even his own people, from their desert tribes, showed him obeisance.

But not as much as they once had—not since the night the Children had walked out of Beloved's sanctuary, naked and pale under the full moon.

Later, their victims in battle rose from the corpse-strewn sands, at least the few still whole enough to do so. The bows to Sau'ilahk from even Beloved's lowest among the horde were no longer as deep as they had once been.

He ignored them all as he climbed upward through the darkness. Beloved had called amid his dreams. His reward was finally at hand.

At the cavernous entrance, pairs of locatha stood to either side beneath burning braziers upon pike-high poles. Covered in thick scales of muted olive green, except for their ocher underbellies of banded plates, they rose from all fours to full height on their hind legs. Each gripped a spear with a haft thick as a man's wrist and a head like a Numan broadsword. Their clear eyelids slowly nictitated over black orb eyes. They lowered their long heads with jaws of serrated teeth.

Sau'ilahk did not crane his neck to look up at them. That they stood in his presence was another reminder of how things had changed since the Children's appearance. Those pale, blood-gorging, *undying* ones took his glory and had replaced him in Beloved's prime affection.

That would change this night, as he stepped into the mountain.

He paced through seemingly endless tunnels, always downward. He wandered into the deep, where even sparse braziers along the rough walls thinned and were soon gone altogether. There was only darkness as he stepped purposefully through the sanctuary of his god.

To be called here, after so long since his plea, was a good sign. Though others had come here over the years, some called and some not, only he had ever returned. . . .

Except for the Children.

Finally he reached a chasm, guessing the distance of its near edge by the changing sound of his footfalls' echoes. Uncertain whether he should raise a light, defiling this sacred place, he could not see how else to go on.

Sau'ilahk raised his hand and filled his mind's eye with scintillating glyphs and sigils. A spark ignited in the air, and he quickly dulled its sharp white to amber, hoping this would be less offensive.

He stood upon the chasm's lip, but its depth was beyond the reach of his conjured light. It did not go straight down but twisted with broken sides, as if torn open ages ago by something immense that ripped wide the bowels of the earth. Above was the same, a great gash that rose into the peak somewhere high above. Across the chasm on the other side, he saw another wound in the mountain's stone.

It was so large a dozen pachyderms could have fit through it.

But there was no bridge to that other side, and that far hollow was so deep his sparse light could not penetrate its pitch-black. Then he heard the grating sound.

Soft at first, it grew, until he feared the great gash beyond his boot's toe might widen.

Something moved in the far cavern, shifting on broken stone. He thought he saw the darkness within it glitter, perhaps conjured light catching upon something smooth and writhing.

Sau'ilahk dropped to his knees, bowing until his forehead touched the chasm's edge.

"My Beloved," he whispered. "I come as you bade me."

A grating hiss rolled from the far gash, echoing off raw stone.

Are you worthy?

He heard the words only within his thoughts, but they were as breathy as the noise surrounding him. He lifted his head but kept his eyes down.

Worthy of what? Of his hope, his desire?

"Yes, my divine sovereign," he whispered, but doubt made him tremble. "Always, I serve. Do you have . . . Have I given . . . cause to doubt it?"

He could not help but raise his eyes a little more. He saw only a still and silent darkness across the chasm.

Not as yet.

Sau'ilahk quickly lowered his gaze. It fell upon his own slender, tan fingers, so perfectly shaped like his face, but vanity meant nothing to his patron. Such a small deviance could not be judged a transgression. At times, he could not help reveling in his own beauty. Along with the fear he inspired, all looked upon him with awe. But he quaked, knowing that beauty would fade—unlike the Children, eternal and undying.

I am pleased . . . perhaps enough to answer your prayers.

Sau'ilahk wanted one thing—to never end, to forever see awe in the eyes of all who looked upon him.

"Eternal life, my Beloved?" he dared ask again.

Are you so certain of your heart's desire?

Sau'ilahk faltered.

The Children were mere tools of bloodshed, powerful, useful, but only because Beloved had made them so. They had not labored as Sau'ilahk had in service and devotion, given with no expectation, until now. Yet they were treasured and favored—gifted by his god. Was it so much to ask that he be allowed to continue, devoted as he was?

Then just as you have wished . . . so it is.

Sau'ilahk grew anxious, and barely lifted his head, waiting . . . for something.

Perhaps he expected to feel . . . anything . . . different. But he felt the same as he had an instant before. Yet his god had spoken, granting him the one and only boon he had ever asked for.

Was it that simple now, after waiting so long, suffocating in want?

Joy crept in like a hesitant child wondering if its parent were truly pleased. Just a little, and then it filled him fully. To think he would be alive and beautiful forever, and he dared to raise his head ever higher. He straightened fully upon his knees as he whispered.

"My love is eternal as well . . . my Beloved."

He meant those words, even as utter relief made him suddenly weary—even as he stiffened when he saw the eyes.

On the chasm's far side, two pinpricks of light appeared. From a distance, they were no larger than latent sparks in a dying fire. The pair drifted downward like eyes lodged in the head of some figure walking toward the far cavern's edge.

Sau'ilahk was awestruck.

He looked upon the barest hint of his god's presence. Such blessing had never been given to any that he knew. He began weeping, not realizing it until the salt of tears seeped between his lips.

Sau'ilahk had been granted eternal life.

His beauty would never fade.

Sau'ilahk recoiled from the memory as he sank toward true dormancy. On the edge of his fading awareness, the familiar hiss rose again in his mind.

I watch . . . as you draw nearer . . . the answer almost within your grasp.

Despite centuries that had melded love to hate within his devotion, whenever Beloved called, Sau'ilahk could not help but answer. As he vanished into dormancy, to a place between life and death in the dreamland of his god, he whispered . . .

"Yes . . . my Beloved."

Wynn followed Chane into the temple's entryway, planning to drag him away into privacy as soon as it seemed polite. She knew she'd better force him to promise not to go back to the amphitheater tonight—or he'd just get himself caught. But she made it only a few steps inside when a young shirvêsh trundled up the hallway.

"Journeyor Hygeorht," he said quickly, "a visitor is asking for you."

Wynn stalled in confusion. She couldn't guess who'd come looking for her here.

"Who is it?" she asked.

The young one shook his head. "She will speak only to you."

"She?" Chane asked, but the acolyte just shrugged.

"How long has *she* been waiting?" Wynn added.

"Not long," he answered. "She is in the meal hall, when you are ready."

With a curt bow, he left. Wynn exchanged puzzled glances with Chane and then turned to Mallet.

"Thank you for letting us join you this evening. Please excuse us, so I can see who has come."

"Yes, of course," he said. "Off with you."

The old dwarf looked exhausted, the wrinkles of his face deepening. In part, that was best. Wynn didn't want to counter any more questions about how she and Chane had overheard him in the amphitheater.

Wynn hurried on with Shade and Chane. Had someone come from the guild, perhaps Premin Sykion or another as equally opposed to her pursuits? She couldn't imagine the duchess had tracked her down. But when she reached the meal hall's entrance, she stopped, hand still on the framing stones. The woman waiting was the last *she* whom Wynn could've expected.

Sliver sat at one long table.

Grim and dark as the last time, she had her arms folded tightly. She barely turned her head at Wynn's appearance and glared in silence. Wynn wasn't even sure what to say, though Shade growled softly as she inched into the hall.

Wynn grabbed the dog's tail, halting her, though Chane stepped in as well and stood there, tense and watchful. Wynn brushed him back as she approached her visitor.

"My apology for the other night," she blurted out. "To learn your home's location, I had to trade stories in a cheag'anâkst. And . . . with all the ale, I wasn't myself."

"Save your excuses," Sliver growled, and looked away, staring at the tabletop. "I am here at my mother's insistence. I will have words with you . . . alone!"

"Your mother sent you?"

Sliver said nothing more, but she cast a challenging glare at Chane.

"I have some fine mint tea in my room," Wynn told him. "Would you please get it for us? And send for hot water."

Chane's jaw twitched. "No."

"Please," she whispered. "I'll be all right."

"Then Shade stays," he said loudly enough for Sliver to hear.

"I care nothing about a wolf," Sliver returned disdainfully.

Wynn glanced back. There were moments when she kept forgetting the way other people saw Shade, rather than as the intelligent creature she was.

Chane pursed his lips and left.

Wynn sighed once in relief before returning to Sliver. Shade immediately inched in behind her, watching them both.

"He'll be back with some tea," Wynn said.

"I will not be here that long. My mother wishes to know why you seek my brother."

Wynn settled on the bench across from the smith. Looking into Sliver's angry, pain-filled face, she gave up on any further polite conversation.

"That is a guild matter. But it is important."

"Have you learned anything for your *guild*?" Sliver snarled.

"I mean him no harm. But you would know a good deal more about him than I."

"I do not."

Wynn fell silent at that. It raised questions she wasn't sure were safe to ask.

"No one does," Sliver finally said, her voice turning weak and tired. "The Hassäg'kreigi are little known to anyone. When one of our people joins them . . . is called to their service . . . all other ties are broken."

Wynn shook her head. "I don't understand. Heritage is everything here. Even your Eternals are considered 'ancestors' to your people as a whole."

"And that is where their devotion lies! Nothing else means more to them. Do you not know that the honored dead, such as Hammer-Stag, are where we get our . . . *Bäynæ*?"

The last word made her mouth twist like a vile taste.

"I've heard this," Wynn answered, "but I don't fully understand how it comes to pass."

"Then you are not alone, Numan," Sliver spit. "No one does."

She looked about the meal hall, and the skin around her eyes crinkled. The smith almost fidgeted and shuddered, as if this temple—any temple—were a vile place. And Wynn began to understand just a little.

Sliver had lost one of two wayward brothers to a secret order little known to her own kind, one entrenched in dwarven mysteries. To Sliver, Ore-Locks had chosen their spiritual patrons over devotion to his own flesh and blood.

"My father passed over," Sliver continued. "For a while, Ore-Locks felt duty-bound to visit my mother . . . to do what he might. Even that fell beneath his devotions. He stopped coming at all, years ago. And . . . as *you* know . . . High-Tower left his own, his people, to live with your kind."

Wynn struggled to listen beneath Sliver's bitter words, to see the pictures Sliver painted.

Her mother would be elderly if her father had already died, yet Sliver was young for her kind; strange, since dwarves didn't usually bear children late in life. Both her brothers had abandoned the family to seek their own paths, leaving her to support their aging mother in the poorest depths of Sea-Side.

More reason for bitterness.

"What do you want from me?" Wynn asked bluntly. It seemed the only way to get anywhere with the daughter of the Iron-Braids.

Sliver's mouth twisted several times, until she spit out the words.

"My mother clings to foolish hope! She goes to temple, any she can reach, and prays for word of her eldest son. Then she heard *you*, the night you came!"

Wynn flinched, already fearful of where this was headed.

"She thinks the Eternals have answered her by sending you," Sliver accused. "You know one of her sons . . . and now you come seeking the other. She requests that you share anything you learn, for pity's sake."

One word Sliver had spoken stuck in Wynn's head.

"Eldest?" she repeated in surprise. "But Ore-Locks looks much younger than High-Tower."

Sliver was silent for a few breaths. She planted her wide hands upon the table, leaning forward.

"You will share all you learn of my brother . . . with me," Sliver whispered. "That is not a *request*!"

Wynn couldn't help leaning back under Sliver's glare. Shade began to rumble, the sound increasing to a growl, but the smith never glanced away. Wynn reached down to wave Shade closer.

None of this was helpful and only complicated finding the texts. But if managed carefully, Sliver's reluctant need might still be useful.

"Of course," Wynn answered as calmly and coldly as she could. "Tell your mother I would be honored to help her."

Sliver didn't even acknowledge the words. She rose instantly and headed for the meal hall's main entrance. She was gone before Shade finally quieted. Wynn's hand shook as she settled it upon Shade's back.

Sliver clearly clung to the last of her pride, as the last of her remaining family was coming apart. Asking, demanding help from some interloper—and a noisy scribbler of words, no less—was a final humiliation.

Wynn could barely imagine what Sliver's life must be like.

Dwarven marriages were often arranged by the families and clans, based on benefits either the bride or groom might provide. Yes, there was love, and it was considered, but if at odds with what was best, it was sacrificed. If the Iron-Braids were part of a clan, its leaders had clearly forgotten Sliver.

She had no one to speak for her, no family name of honor to offer, and no father or siblings with skills or community influence her clan might value. She possessed only a small smithy in a depressed underside and an elderly mother clinging to faith.

The more Wynn thought on this, the more depression overwhelmed fear and frustration. But she had to push aside sympathy.

Chane returned, carrying a pot of hot water, two mugs, and her small tin of mint tea leaves. He hesitated in the entrance and scanned the room once.

"Where is she?" he asked.

"Gone."

"What did she want?"

"Information—about her brother."

"Information . . . from us?" he scoffed.

Wynn didn't find the irony humorous.

"Should I fix you some tea?" Chane asked.

Wynn sighed. "No . . . no, thank you."

Something terrible was coming. She was certain of this from all she had seen and learned in company with Magiere, Leesil, and Chap—and afterward with Shade and Chane. There were larger issues at stake—the world might well be at stake. If she had to manipulate Sliver, she would.

It was an ugly thought.

Uglier still was a ploy forming in her mind.

CHAPTER 11

The following night, Chane led the way into the amphitheater and waited as Wynn warmed up her cold lamp crystal. The empty stands surrounded them as they faced the stage.

The cavernous amphitheater looked different tonight—ancient, stark, and silent. Not one brazier burned beside any of the upper great doors. It was startling to see the vast place so quiet and deserted compared to the crowd at Hammer-Stag's final wake.

"We should hurry," Chane said, glancing down at Shade.

Wynn crouched, cupping Shade's muzzle in her free hand. A blink of stillness passed before Shade wheeled and headed back into the tunnel. Wynn rose, holding out her glowing crystal, and took off after the dog.

Chane followed, watching Wynn's hair, bound back in a tail, swish gently across her slender back as she trotted.

They turned into a side passage midway down the tunnel, following twists and turns, stairs and ramps of stone, almost too many to remember. But Shade never faltered. As another corridor veered slightly right, ending at a corner, Wynn slowed as the dog pressed on.

"I saw this in the Shade's memories," she said. "We'll come to a sharp left, and then another slighter one." Her oval face was filled with anticipation. "Do you have the scroll?"

"Of course," he answered.

She scurried after Shade, and Chane kept up easily on his longer legs. Desire for the missing texts pushed Wynn, perhaps too much. But this was the first true, if tenuous, lead they had gained in getting anywhere near these Stonewalkers.

"From what you described," he said, "I do not know if we can get through the doors."

"We'll get through," she answered flatly. "Leesil never let a door stop him. Neither will I."

Mention of her old companion raised quick resentment in Chane. Whenever she spoke of either Magiere or Leesil, he wondered if she would have preferred them here in his place.

Shade took a left, picked up the pace, and then veered down a slant. As she reached another corner, she slowed and huffed softly. Wynn bolted down the slope to the dog.

"Here!" she called.

Chane jogged around them, his hand dropping to his sword as he looked down the next passage. There in the side wall was an archway with deep-set iron doors surrounded by frame stones. He saw no other opening along the corridor, up to where it ended in a left turn a ways down.

Wynn rushed blindly on, skidding to a halt before the arch. She leaned her staff against the frame stones and ran her hand over the metal as Shade sniffed the portal's base.

"Here's the separation," she whispered.

Shade backed up and sat at the passage's other side as Wynn traced the seam with her index finger.

Chane came up behind her, studying the flat panels. He saw no handles or latches, not even a lock or empty brackets for a bar. Wynn fingered her way around the left door's outer edge, inch by inch along the groove where it disappeared into stone.

"What are you looking for?" he asked.

"Trip mechanisms, catches . . . anything," she answered. "I can't reach the top, so you start there. Feel every spot carefully for anything abnormal."

Frowning, Chane stepped in beside her. He probed slowly along the top but found only smooth iron all the way to where the door slipped deep into a groove in the stone. He worked toward the other side, but Wynn finished more quickly.

Chane wished there were something to be found, but he had doubted it from the start. When he finished, he saw no resignation in Wynn's expression. She continued to study the doors, undaunted.

"All right, we start on the walls," she said. "Last night, Shade heard a grinding sound from beyond the doors. Someone opened them from inside, and Cinder-Shard wasn't in the passage. So there has to be a way through, some hidden access he used."

Chane shook his head. "Why not take the others the same way? Why bother opening the doors at all?"

"Maybe the other access was too small for the litter, and these main doors aren't used unless necessary."

"Then would not the *access* be blocked as well?" he countered.

Wynn ignored him and sidestepped left along the passage, inspecting the stone wall beyond the arch.

Chane found her stubborn certainty unsettling. He finally turned to inspect the wall on the arch's other side. Together, they went over every speck of stone, going farther down the passage than Chane thought reasonable. Only then did Wynn's certainty begin fracturing.

"It has to be here!" she insisted, her words rolling along the stone passage. "How else could Cinder-Shard get inside?"

At Wynn's too-loud voice, Shade lifted her head where she lay. Wynn did not even notice as she stared at the seam between the doors.

"Get out your sword."

Chane shook his head in disbelief. "You cannot be ser—"

"I'm not walking away. Not when we're this close. Seven hells, Chane! You're undead. Put your strength to use."

Wynn's recent penchant for cursing was another sign that much had changed in her.

"This doorway was built by dwarves," he argued. "Rationally, it can withstand them. So why do you think I would fare any better?"

"Try to pry it open," she urged, "at least enough to peek inside. I know I heard grinding in Shade's memory *after* the doors were closed. We need to know what caused it."

Chane looked at the narrow seam. He wanted to agree with her, especially for as little as they had uncovered. But as he drew his long sword and set its point to the seam, he had no confidence in the effort.

"This will leave marks on the doors," he said.

"I don't care."

Chane gripped the hilt with one hand, keeping the blade in place, and stepped back as far as his reach allowed. He lunged sharply forward with all his mass, slamming his free hand's palm against the cross guard.

The sword's tip pierced the seam with a metallic shriek that echoed along the passage.

He peered closer. The point had sunk two fingers' width, more than expected, but the seam had widened only to the blade's thickness. It was not enough to peek through.

"Step back," he ordered. "Have your crystal ready. If the doors part, I do not know how long I can hold them."

Wynn backed up, joining Shade, and Chane shifted to the right of his embedded sword. He pulled up his cloak's hem and wrapped the fabric around the blade. With one hand gripping near the hilt, and the other nearer the tip, he began to push.

The blade flexed slightly, but the doors did not budge.

Chane released his pressure and turned sideways, facing the doors. He reached out his right foot, braced it against the arch's inner stones, and pushed again. This time, he let hunger come.

It flooded his dead flesh, and all his senses came alive as they opened fully. The crystal's light upon the iron was brighter to his eyes, almost uncomfortable. A faint sound rose from somewhere inside the walls.

Like a pinch of sand spilled upon stone.

He would not have heard it without his senses heightened. Then he felt a slight vibration through his sword. He redoubled his efforts.

"Keep going," Wynn urged.

Chane began trying to shift the sword's point deeper as he levered it, and the seam began to part.

"Now!" he rasped.

Wynn rushed in beneath the blade.

Before she even raised the crystal to the seam, Chane saw it was futile, and he heard Wynn sigh in frustration. Through the space parted by the sword, they both saw another set of iron doors tightly shut behind the first.

Chane closed his eyes in resignation. He could not possibly keep the first pair open and lever the second. The instant he released any pressure to move the sword's point to the inner doors' seam, the first set would slam closed around the blade. And he could not lever both sets at once.

Wynn slumped, leaning her forehead upon the iron.

A soft clank reached Chane's heightened hearing. He felt a dull and muted vibration shiver through the doors and into his sword.

"Get back!" he ordered.

Wynn shoved off, retreating with a stumble, as Chane pulled his foot off the arch's side. A thunderous crack shuddered through the whole passage, as if coming from inside its walls.

The doors snapped closed.

A ping of steel pierced Chane's ears. All resistance in his sword failed.

His blade tore free as something sharp and cold grazed his neck, but he was already tumbling along the doors. He hit the archway's far side, spun off, and fell into the passage as a clatter of steel rang in his ears. Wynn came to him before he could sit up.

"Chane?" she asked in alarm, touching his shoulder. "Are you all right?"

He sat up, staring at the soundly shut doors. Something had forced them closed again.

"What happened?" she asked, following his gaze.

Chane shook his head, uncertain. "Some latent countermeasure," he answered.

"You're . . . cut."

Only then did he feel a trickle of wetness at the side of his shirt collar. He reached up, touching his throat just above the old scar around his neck, and his fingertips came away stained.

Not red with the blood of the living but viscous black.

"It is nothing," he said. "The wound will shortly close on its own. The sword must have grazed me when forced out."

The sword was still in his hands, still wrapped in the cloak, though the fabric had slid down across its tip. Chane got up, frustrated by that one moment of false hope when the doors had parted. He swept back his cloak, lifting the blade to sheathe it.

A hand's length of the tip was gone.

Chane just stared at it.

Shade huffed once, and he saw the dog nosing the missing piece on the passage's floor.

"*Odsúdýnjè!*" he swore, slipping into his native Belaskian.

Wynn sighed. "We'll get it fixed or replace it."

"How?" he snarled. "A sword is not some idle purchase of a pittance. I do not have that much coin. Do you?"

"No."

Wynn dropped to her haunches, hands over her face, and began muttering, "Think, think, think," over and over. Chane closed his eyes, willing himself to remain calm.

He sheathed the broken sword and gathered up its severed end. The blade was still usable, in part, and he had little choice. It was the only worthwhile weapon he possessed. Their efforts were pointless, and now costly.

Still, Wynn would not relent. If she did not do so, and soon, he would force her, no matter any complications with Shade.

"Perhaps Cinder-Shard had another method," he suggested. "Some tool needed for the doors that Shade could not see."

He meant to imply that they had no more options and should give up for now. When Wynn lowered her hands, he could almost *see* her mind turning in a different direction.

"What about my mantic sight?" she asked.

He opened his mouth to protest, but she rushed on.

"Perhaps I could find traces of where someone's spiritual presence has passed through? If I find the exact spot, we may see something we've missed."

She took a few breaths, slowly rose, and focused on the iron doors.

Chane stood watching her, about to drag her off.

"I've never seen trails . . . residue of passing," she whispered, speculating aloud. "Only strength or weakness of Spirit in what is present. But it's worth a try."

Renewed hope in her eyes made Chane weary.

"It's worth a try," she repeated adamantly. "But I can't turn it off once it comes."

That was the part he did not like. Her gift was a taint, not true art, the result of a dangerous mistake when she had once tampered with a mantic form of thaumaturgy.

"Back at the guild," Wynn went on, "it took half a day or more to fade on its own. You'll need to get me back home to the temple."

Chane sighed, that leftover habit of living days. "I will always get you home," he answered.

Wynn tried to maintain her facade of confidence. Even a failed attempt to summon the sight by will could be overwhelming. Chane had seen this once, and he'd politely called her methods "undisciplined."

She knelt before the doors, afraid she might fall once mantic sight came. All Chane did—could do—was stand over her, watching. Extending her index finger, she traced a sign for Spirit on the floor and encircled it.

At each gesture, she focused hard to keep the lines alive in her mind's eye, as if they were actually drawn upon the stone. She scooted forward, settling inside the circle, and traced a wider circumference around herself and the first pattern.

It was a simple construct, but it helped shut out the world for a moment, and she closed her eyes. She focused upon letting the world's essence, rather than its presence, fill her. She tried to feel for the trace of elemental Spirit in all things. Starting first with herself, as a living thing in which Spirit was always strongest. She imagined breathing it in from the air.

In the darkness behind Wynn's eyelids, she held on to the simple pattern stroked upon the floor as she called up another image. She saw Shade's father—Chap—in her mind's eye and held on to him as well.

Shade huffed somewhere nearby.

Wynn's concentration faltered. She pulled both pattern and Chap back into focus. Just as she'd once seen him in her mantic sight, his fur shimmered like a million silk threads caught under blue-white light. His whole form was encased in white vapors that rose like flame.

Moments stretched on. Mantic sight still wouldn't come.

The ache in her knees threatened her focus. She clung to Chap—to memories of him burning bright behind her envisioned circle around the symbol of Spirit. She held on to him like some mage's familiar that lived only in her memory.

Vertigo came suddenly in the darkness behind her eyelids.

"Wynn?" Chane whispered.

She felt as if she were falling.

Wynn threw out her hands. Instead of toppling onto the gritty floor, she felt her palms slap against cold, smooth iron. Startled, she opened her eyes—and nausea lurched upward as her stomach clenched.

Wynn stared at—through—the iron doors.

They seemed even thicker than the glimpse she'd had of both layers. Somewhere nearby, Shade's whimper twisted into a low growl.

A translucent white, just shy of blue, dimly permeated the iron. The doors' physical presence still dominated her sight, but there was more, something beyond them. Pale shadows of a large chamber became visible.

Shade whined so close that the noise was too loud in Wynn's ears. She glanced aside, straight into the dog's dark face—and gasped.

For an instant, Shade was as black as a void.

Wynn quickly realized this was only the darkness of her coat beneath the powerful glimmer of blue-white permeating her body—more so than anything else in sight. Traces of Spirit ran in every strand of Shade's charcoal fur. She was aglow with her father's Fay ancestry, and Wynn had to look away.

"Are you all right?" Chane asked.

She looked at him, using him as an anchor.

He appeared exactly the same, unchanged, but only because of the ring he wore. So long as he wore Welstiel's ring of nothing, he was impervious to anything that might sense or see him as undead.

"Yes," Wynn choked out, and quickly turned back to the doors.

The chamber beyond was no more than inverse shadows, like looking into a dark room, its walls outlined by some inner glow. She scanned about before nausea crippled her and searched for a hint of entrances from other passages.

There were none.

Shade had seen the duchess and the Stonewalkers here. But when the white-clad elf turned, Shade had ducked into hiding. She hadn't seen who had gone in or not. At first, Wynn assumed the duchess and her people had merely gone off another way. But if Duchess Reine had gone in . . .

The only other fixture Wynn made out within the chamber was a huge circle of darkness upon the floor. The harder she focused, the more she saw the dim residue of Spirit in the stone where the floor ended around a large hole, about four yards wide.

She turned her focus downward to penetrate the floor by whatever blue-white shadows lay beyond it. But stone and iron were dense. In them, Spirit was perhaps the weakest of the Elements. Either that, or perhaps looking through so many pale layers of Spirit outlines was just not possible. She couldn't make out the shaft's depths.

Wynn pondered the rhythmic grinding in Shade's memory. The only thing that could've made that sound was a mechanism—like a dwarven lift and tram. Without other fixtures in the chamber, even chains and gears, Wynn had doubts. Whatever the sound had been, the Stonewalkers were gone. If the duchess had entered, then she must have gone with them.

Why?

"What do you see?" Chane asked.

"A dim chamber . . . a dark hole on the floor."

Saying even this made her gag against nausea. About to turn away, she noticed something strange to the left.

At first it looked like a stack of rods, perhaps resting on a ledge beside the chamber door. When Wynn stared longer, focusing beyond the framestones' physical shapes, she counted a three-by-four grid of what might be squared iron rods. Behind them were several small round shapes, possibly metal, and vertical struts inside the wall.

This had to be some mechanism for opening the portal, but the wall's outer side was at least a yard thick. Not even Chane could batter a hole to get at the switches. Whoever opened the portal had done so from the inside, but how had they gotten in?

Wynn's strength of will faltered and vertigo overwhelmed her. She shut her eyes and crumpled as strong arms wrapped around her. Shade began to growl.

"Get back!" Chane hissed.

At a clack of jaws, Wynn jerked sideways in Chane's hold. She lifted her head, just barely opening her eyes.

There was Shade, a glistening dark form haloed in blue-white. Her irises burned with so much light they made Wynn's head spin even worse. But the dog ceased snarling.

Shade wasn't looking at Chane; she looked straight into Wynn's eyes.

A sudden memory rose in Wynn's head—not an image, but a sensation. A warm, wet tongue dragging repeatedly over her face, as if her eyes were still closed. They had been closed—at another time—when she'd used mantic sight to track Chap in the elven forest of the an'Cróan.

"Put me down," she whispered.

She tried sinking to her knees, and Chane lowered her.

Shade lunged in so quickly that Wynn grabbed the dog's neck in panic. Shade lashed her tongue over Wynn's face, and Wynn shut her eyes tight, feeling a wet warmth drag over her lids.

Nausea faded as she clutched Shade's neck.

She didn't know how Shade had learned Chap's trick for smothering mantic sight, but when the vertigo finally subsided, despair remained.

"Are you well?" Chane asked. "What was she doing?"

Wynn quietly hugged Shade.

"Wynn?" Chane urged. "Your sight?"

"It's gone," she whispered.

But the iron doors were still closed. There was no other way into that chamber.

"After all this," she went on, "going to Sea-Side, Hammer-Stag's death, seeing the Stonewalkers . . . we've lost again."

She had hoped Shade's lead might play out and keep her from a crueler plan. Wynn slumped against Shade.

Chane crouched beside her.

"It is not over," he whispered. "I wager Welstiel and I breached as many doors as . . . Leesil. But we used a mix of intimidation and manipulation. You and I simply have to find another. . . ."

He never finished, and Wynn sat up, still holding Shade. "What?"

"Ore-Locks!" he rasped. "What a fool I am!"

"What about him?"

His eyes narrowed like those of a predator that had finally cornered its prey. Wynn didn't care for the expression at all.

"You said Sliver told you her brother used to come to the smithy," he went on. "The smithy is on the mountain's other side."

"Yes . . . and?"

"Stonewalkers came to the amphitheater in Old-Seatt . . . supposedly without being called. Yet as you pointed out, there is no lift up from Sea-Side to Old Seatt."

Wynn felt some connection emerging but wasn't certain to what. "The settlements are far apart," she returned in confusion. "Mallet says no one ever sees Stonewalkers."

"Do you not see it?" Chane urged. "How do they appear at such distant places without being spotted or using the trams? If they used an access point here, behind these doors, then how did Ore-Locks visit his family? There has to be—"

And they finished together—"another portal at Sea-Side."

"Perhaps one at each settlement," Chane added.

Wynn blinked slowly in self-spite. "I should've reasoned that myself."

"This is not our usual scholarly pursuit." Then he shook his head. "Even if we find another portal, it might be no different from what we have here. No guards, no visible locks or bars . . . and no way through."

Why did he always do that, make helpful suggestions and then cut them apart? Before Wynn said as much, he rocked back on his heels.

"There is nothing for us here," he said. "But Sliver's visitation gives us an invitation."

"I've already considered that."

She stood up under Chane's suspicious attention. Another failure tonight, and at another cost—this time Chane's sword. It might not be the last price to pay.

"To Seaside?" he asked.

"We'll need our gear from the temple first."

When she turned about, Shade was already waiting at the passage's first turn. Wynn was too obsessed to give this any thought.

Again, Sau'ilahk waited outside the amphitheater. He had followed Wynn from the temple and watched as the trio entered, but he went no farther. He did not know the interior's layout and feared being seen if he simply appeared in the open floor to get his bearings.

Conjuring even one servitor would cost him too much. His energies were so low that the effort might drive him straight into dormancy. He feared losing Wynn, if she found a way through the doors, but keeping his continued existence secret outweighed all other concerns.

If she did not emerge, he would have to wait until the late hours before dawn and attempt to search on his own. He might still track where she had gone. He also needed to feed, to eat life, and doing so here upon the open mountaintop was risky.

Waiting gnawed at him, but being so close to the end of suffering made it impossible to alter his state of mind. As the moon reached its zenith, muted voices grew inside the closest tunnel, and he pulled back between the buildings.

Wynn stepped out of the amphitheater with her companions.

What had she learned? Had she found a path to this "underworld," whatever or wherever it might be? If so, had she already taken the way and returned? It seemed unlikely.

Sau'ilahk saw no great defeat in Wynn's face as she paced purposefully down the street. He saw no triumph either. With no one else about this late, he easily shadowed the trio along parallel paths. Again, they took the lift back down, but when they reached Sea-Side's station, they paused before the mouth of the great market cavern.

Where was Wynn leading them?

After a brief exchange, Chane left, trotting up the street out of sight. Wynn remained with Shade at the far side of the cavern's entrance.

Sau'ilahk kept his distance beyond the way station. In a short while, Chane returned, bearing three packs. Sau'ilahk suffered a moment of panic.

She was leaving. Had she given up, after all of his efforts to steer her onward?

Wynn turned into the cavern with her companions, and Sau'ilahk's thoughts went blank for an instant. He drifted closer in a staggered glide between side streets. At this time of night, few people milled about the multitiered market. When he reached the edge of the cavern's mouth, Wynn was heading for the tunnel to the tram station.

But why?

He blinked through dormancy as he focused upon a memory of the dark tunnel beyond the tram. Awaking there, he waited nerve-racking moments before she reappeared. The trio headed directly for the platform to Sea-Side.

Sau'ilahk backed halfway into the tunnel wall, watching.

It was a while before a tram arrived. The dog held back, curling its lips, as Wynn attempted to drag it on board. Chane tried to assist, and did, if only because the dog wheeled away from him and, by doing so, ended up inside the car. All three were seated, and the lead car's massive crystal ignited amid belching clouds of steam.

Wynn was going back to Sea-Side.

All this sudden change filled Sau'ilahk with uncertainty. With no time to replenish himself, and too little energy to conjure a servitor to eavesdrop, he had but one choice.

Sau'ilahk followed blindly after the tram as it raced beyond him.

CHAPTER 12

Near dusk the following day, Wynn stood clinging to the sun-crystal staff before the passage to the Iron-Braids' smithy. Shade sat expectantly nearby while Chane leaned against the wall with his eyes barely open.

They'd arrived in Sea-Side before dawn and procured two rooms at the same inn as their last visit. A decent place close to the station, it was the only one with which they were familiar. They'd slept much of the day, but before retiring, Chane had insisted that Wynn wake him by late afternoon. He believed Sliver would be less trouble if they approached during business hours, and with possible patrons about, she might be less confrontational.

Wynn was dubious about this—and about trying to rouse Chane. He seemed determined to master being awake during daylight while safe beneath the mountain. She'd reluctantly agreed, instructing the innkeeper to knock at Day-Winter in late afternoon.

As she'd anticipated, waking Chane hadn't been easy. He'd been disoriented from the moment she'd finally dragged him to his feet. Now the three of them stood outside the fifth northbound passage off of Limestone Mainway, and Wynn hesitated.

She couldn't botch this again, yet her plan might—would—anger Sliver even more in the end. Of course, she could always walk in and say, "Hello, we're looking for a door to the underworld. Care to show us how your brother gets out?"

Wynn scoffed under breath, and Chane raised his bleary eyes.

"I should've let you rest," she said. "Shade and I can handle this."

"No. I am . . . better than last time."

That was a lie, but Wynn couldn't think of another excuse. So she stepped into the passage.

The smell of fumes and heated metal grew strong before they even neared the smithy. Peering through the open door, Wynn blinked in surprise. Sliver wasn't alone.

Two male dwarves in char-stained leather aprons pounded upon mule shoes near the open furnace. Each hammer's clang rose above the bellows' hoarse breaths and sent scant sparks showering to the floor.

Sliver stood at a rear worktable examining the shorter and wider of two finished blades, both the mottled gray of fine dwarven steel. She looked impressive with her determined expression, thick red braid, and leather apron—a master crafter engrossed in her trade. She scraped her thick thumb across the sword's edge, testing its keening, and then set it down to inspect its human-proportioned companion.

Wynn cleared her throat. "Umm, hello."

All three occupants looked over, and Sliver's eyes widened.

"Could we have a word?" Wynn asked more nervously than she intended.

Sliver appeared both puzzled and stunned. Perhaps she hadn't expected Wynn to come with news so soon. The smith glanced at the workers before fixing her gaze on Wynn again. Her wide mouth parted.

The workshop's back door slammed open and banged and shuddered off Sliver's worktable.

A wrinkled dwarven woman stood in the opening. Wild white hair hung over the shoulders of a long sashless robe and a shift of faded blue. Shuffling out, she grabbed a worktable to steady herself. Both workers froze, casting wary glances at Sliver.

"Here!" the old woman called, and caught her breath from the effort. "Come, sage . . . you are welcome in my home!"

That crackling, manic voice made Wynn flush with shame. But Sliver's expression turned vicious. She set down the long sword and moved toward her visitors at a threatening pace.

Wynn tightened her grip on the staff.

Chane and Shade pushed through the door, rounding either side of her. Sliver halted beyond arm's reach, and with one derisive snort fixed her glare on Chane.

"Spare me your display!" she growled, then turned on Wynn. "Move!"

Sliver backstepped toward the old woman.

Wynn advanced, passing the smith as steadily as she could. Shade and Chane followed closely. The old woman wobbled through the rear door and everyone but the workers followed. As soon as they were all in, Sliver slammed the door shut.

Standing in a small room carved from the mountain's stone, Wynn spotted openings on either side near its back. Both were curtained with much-mended wool that had once been blue. Years and too many washings had rendered the fabric a pale slate color. A small hearth with a battered iron screen was set in the north wall, and an old maple table filled the room's center.

Unglazed urns and old iron pots filled scant shelves pegged into the walls. There was no sign of meat or fish, bread or vegetables. Sliver most likely had been too busy to visit a market, and the old woman looked too infirm to do so.

Wynn ceased looking about. Could she possibly feel any worse for how she would use these poor people?

"Here, sage, come and sit," the old woman urged, pulling out the only chair before she settled on one of three plain stools.

"Mother!" Sliver snapped. "Stop acting like these people are—"

"I'm honored, Mother Iron-Braid," Wynn cut in, nodding politely as she sat.

Shade circled away from Sliver to settle beside Wynn. The old woman barely glanced at the "wolf."

Chane cracked the door open, leaving it slightly inward and ajar. Perhaps he thought a lack of privacy would keep Sliver in check.

The old woman took a long breath, and when it rushed back out, her voice shook. "You have news of my son, of Ore-Locks?"

"Why else would she come?" Sliver crossed her arms, watching Wynn. "So, out with it . . . and leave!"

Chane tensed visibly at her tone, locking his nearly colorless eyes on hers.

Wynn was too confused to worry about their mutual hostility.

Sliver had visited the temple demanding that Wynn share all she learned, yet now seemed surprised that she'd come. Obviously the smith didn't want her here—unlike the mother. But Wynn's determination faltered at the manic hope in Mother Iron-Braid's eyes.

She sat there, suddenly uncertain of her scheme.

Chane kept watch on Sliver as much as Wynn, but he did not follow the verbal exchange closely. The smith's gaze often twitched his way. Sliver seemed less than pleased that he had cracked the door, but anything that kept her off balance was good enough for him.

Through the opening, something more had caught his eye. Something he had already seen once before, but now had all the more reason to notice. Widening his power of sight, Chane peered through the crack.

By the forge's reddened light, he saw two swords lying on the rear workbench. Both were as plain and unadorned as his own, but these were whole. Beneath their crisp sheen and strange mottling, he spotted not one imperfection—not even a polish-hidden dimple.

The long sword's end rounded to a point, though the tip was broader than normal. With no fuller or ridge down the blade, it was slightly thin for its kind. He wondered at its weight compared to his own sword. The balance would be different, likely turning closer to the guard. By estimation, an agile fit in the hand, but it looked almost fragile.

If Wynn's claims held true concerning dwarven steel, Chane would not see its like anywhere but in a seatt. In this particular smithy, it seemed out of place.

Impoverished Sliver had somehow afforded whatever rare materials and processes were needed for that strangely mottled steel. How odd that anyone with such skill had not risen from this low life.

Chane had never coveted a weapon. All his resources, when he had any, went into his intellectual pursuits. But from the instant he had seen that sword in Sliver's hand, he had wanted it. Even if he had coin, most dwarves did not value precious metals, and how could he barter when he could not estimate its worth? In truth, he had little to trade by way of goods or services. Was the blade even available for purchase, let alone barter?

He worried about what lay ahead, especially for Wynn. Her search for the texts had already put them in dangerous positions, some of which were not overcome by combat. That might not hold for the future. Even if—when—the texts were found, wherever their secrets led would likely be more hazardous, not less.

Keeping Wynn safe meant acquiring every advantage. A broken sword was a still sword—but not like the one he now fixated upon.

"I have no news," Wynn finally said, steeling herself for the next tactic. "But if you help me, I might get a message to Ore-Locks . . . something to make him come."

"More lies!" Sliver snarled. "Peddling false hopes for your own gain!"

"Mind your ways, daughter," the mother warned. "She is a sage, likely sent by your brother High-Tower."

"Mother, please," Sliver returned. "High-Tower could have come himself after so many years. But he did not. This conniving scribbler is not here because of him . . . or your prayers to the Eternals. Your sons are gone . . . Ore-Locks will never return!"

Startled, Wynn caught the strange twitch of Sliver's eye. The smith's final declaration seemed to have escaped on its own. Perhaps she now regretted it.

Sliver's denouncement of High-Tower clearly pained her, as if she wished at least one brother might come home. But not the other. Did Sliver believe Ore-Locks would never return—or did she wish it so?

Mother Iron-Braid didn't even look up.

"Your daughter is correct in one thing," Wynn said. "Domin High-Tower didn't send me."

The old woman's features sagged. If faith could've crumbled in a wrinkled old face, it began to crack right before Wynn's eyes. Guilt left a bitter taste in her mouth.

She was so lost regarding what drove Sliver. And by truth or ploy, she was doing damage here in that ignorance. Her only choice was to fumble along the middle ground between the two.

"In Ore-Locks's past visits," Wynn began, "did either of you see by what path—or where he went when he left?"

"If I knew that," Sliver grumbled, "I would have gone my—"

"At the Off-Breach Market," Mother Iron-Braid cut in, "on the second level, down the Breach Mainway."

Sliver choked.

Chane shuddered, nearly convulsed.

The beast with hands inside of him suddenly rose in wary agitation. Chane pulled his gaze from the sword to look upon Sliver's stunned face.

The smith's eyes were so wide that the whites showed all around her black pupils. Sliver's claim still hung in Chane's mind.

If I knew that . . .

It was a lie—or half of one. She knew something concerning her brother's whereabouts. Again, the warning of deceit had hit Chane when he was not paying attention.

"I believe he came from there," the old woman went on. "I followed my son when he left but lost him near a clothier's booth . . . and a cobbler's stall, if they are still in the same place. I could not keep up, and he was gone."

"When was this?" Sliver demanded, and then swallowed hard, faking composure though her eye twitched.

"Years back, before he stopped coming at all," the mother answered. "You were busy . . . always busy."

"I was seeing to our needs," the daughter returned, "unlike your sons."

Mother Iron-Braid raised her eyes. "Then see to them now!"

Sliver jabbed a finger at Wynn, and shouted, "She is using you—you are nothing but bait to her! Ore-Locks's *calling* keeps him now!"

Chane cocked his head. At mention of Ore-Locks's status among the Stonewalkers, a flicker of revulsion rolled across the smith's face. It was revealing but puzzling.

"Why would he come to this sage, if not to us?" Sliver asked disdainfully.

Why indeed? Chane wondered. Why had Ore-Locks stopped visiting his family?

Chane fixed on the smith, trying to sense the truth—or the lack of it.

Wynn wished she understood.

Sliver stood shocked at her mother's claim of following Ore-Locks, yet

Sliver had come to the temple demanding that Wynn share all she learned. Perhaps Sliver had never intended anything to reach her mother's ears. Was it Sliver, and not Mother Iron-Braid, who wanted to know all that Wynn found out? And again, why?

"Do not spit in the face of the Eternals!" Mother Iron-Braid chided her daughter. "They answered my prayers, regardless of your fallen faith! Never speak of Ore-Locks in that way again."

"Mother, stop—"

"Your brother . . . both your brothers, sacrificed all to serve a high calling, each to his own. You will take this sage to the market. She will find Ore-Locks . . . because the Eternals wish it so!"

The old woman's large, bony hand fell on Wynn's tiny one, clasping it tightly.

"Tell Ore-Locks to come home," she whispered, her voice quavering as tears welled. "Tell him I . . . we need to see his face once more. Tell him. It is so little to ask."

Wynn wanted to pull away, and not because her hand hurt under that grip. The very ploy she planned to use to lure Ore-Locks had just spilled from Mother Iron-Braid's lips. What better way to drive a son home than with the heartbroken desperation of a mother?

"I will," Wynn answered. "No matter if it gains me . . . or not."

"Show them, daughter!" the mother ordered, like a matriarch rather than a frantic old woman.

Sliver spun in angry silence. She jerked the door wide, forcing Chane to step aside, and strode out into the workshop. Chane held back, waiting upon Wynn.

Amid confusion and shame, Wynn carefully pulled free of Mother Iron-Braid's grip.

"I'll reach Ore-Locks," she promised, "or tell him . . . somehow."

A good distance down Breach Mainway, on Sea-Side's second level, Wynn followed Sliver into the strangest open market she had ever seen. Deep inside the mountain, Off-Breach Market was set up in a huge space carved from the granite innards, rather like the interior of a great cathedral. Voluminous, it was lit in orange by massive crystals steaming upon stone pylons the circumference of oak tree trunks. Even thicker columns supported the ceiling all the way to the tile-ringed opening at the dome's apex. Vapors and smoke from various coal pots and food vendors' carts wafted up to escape through the central air shaft.

The columns here were brightly painted in purples, greens, and yellows, from their sculpted base rings to their flanged tops. All were embellished with dwarven characters and *vubrí* surrounding wedge-arrow symbols pointing the way to sectors for produce, clothing, housewares, leatherwork, and even livestock.

A goat's bleating carried over the market's noise, and Wynn craned her head, looking for the source. She spotted a makeshift pen at the far left side. Inside a stick corral for goats and chickens, two young dwarves shoveled animal refuse into a wooden wheelbarrow.

Stalls, carts, and tents of all shapes, colors, and materials filled the spaces around the columns, defining paths between for all patrons. None of it seemed odd to Wynn, for she'd visited many open markets on two continents. No, it was the looming ceiling that struck her the most.

She understood the transport of goods, but this was the first time the underground settlement felt so artificial. Some merchandise was likely made here beneath the surface, but others, such as fresh fish, vegetables, and grain, had to be transported from outside and a long way off. Like Bay-Side, Sea-Side's outer slope was a sheer drop down to its small port.

Chane turned a full circle. "The noise is getting worse."

He looked more alert, so dusk must be close. Then Wynn noticed other tunnel mouths around the cathedral market. As the day's end neared, more people were drifting in. Dwarves swarmed the vendors, haggling over fair trade of goods. The mounting din bounced off of stone, the walls magnifying the sound downward, and wrapped Wynn in its cacophony.

Soon, hundreds of dwarves were engrossed in loud verbal bartering as they tromped about. There weren't as many humans among them as in Bay-Side. Dozens of conflicting scents filled the air, all trapped and mingling, even with the central air shaft above.

Wynn barely heard Shade's whine and settled her free hand on the dog's neck. Shade kept swiveling her head, trying to track the constantly shifting masses.

Sliver grew impatient with their gawking. "This way," she barked, shoving through the crowd.

Chane waved Wynn and Shade on ahead.

Perhaps he wanted to cover the rear or just keep her in his sight. Wynn hurried on, murmuring, "Pardon me, excuse me," over and over as she struggled to keep up with Sliver. Then Chane's hand fell on her shoulder from behind.

Wynn slowed, but he pushed her onward. His whisper came close to her ear.

"Sliver is lying . . . she knows more than her mother of Ore-Locks's coming and going."

"What?"

"Keep walking. Do not look back."

"How could you know this?" she asked.

"Trust me," Chane whispered. "Can you get Shade to read Sliver's memories . . . on command?"

"I don't know. Maybe—"

"Then try," he insisted. "But only after I ask Sliver, 'Where to next?' Shade must wait for these words . . . or at least be watching for Sliver's memories when I say them."

Wynn finally grasped what he was up to.

At such a question, memories might rise in Sliver concerning the path—assuming she did know more than her mother. But how did Chane know Sliver was lying? Worse yet, how was Wynn going to explain all this to Shade with just memories—before they reached the end of Mother Iron-Braid's instructions?

Wynn curled her fingers deep into Shade's neck fur.

"Ah, Shade." She sighed, and the dog's pace slowed. "I wish you understood language, like your father. Even a few words, like 'dip' and 'memory.' "

She concentrated on the simplest, most ordered memories she could recall. First of Sliver, and then the sound of Chane's voice a moment ago.

. . . Where to next?

She followed with another glimpse of Sliver and then quick ones of any stolen memories Shade passed on from others. And again, Sliver, and again, *Where to next?*

Wynn repeated the sequence over and over, until her head began to ache.

She glanced down and found Shade's ears upright, as if she were listening. An echo of sight and sound filled Wynn's head.

First of Sliver, then a dizzying series of memories from others, and finally a sound like a breathy, broken voice but too garbled to understand.

Wynn hadn't actually heard words at the end. Another image rose in her mind.

Chane stood in the small back room of the Iron-Braids' smithy. Though his lips didn't move, as he'd said nothing while there, the image mingled with the sound of his rasping voice.

. . . *Where to next?*

Wynn flushed with relief, though she was still uncertain Shade truly understood. Was the dog merely echoing everything back, asking for explanation? Memory-speak was so frustrating!

They passed booths selling potatoes, turnips, and dried fruits, and then a section of glazed pots, urns, and bowls. Ahead, another tunnel led out of the market's rear, but Sliver veered away from it. The vast cavern grew more and more packed.

Wynn glanced behind but couldn't see where they'd come in. Or was she even looking in the right direction? Hopefully Chane's height gave him a better view if they had to turn back. As Shade pressed against her thigh, Wynn worried that the distressing throng had hampered the dog's understanding.

Then a flash of red caught Wynn's eye.

Sliver pulled up short, pointing. "There," she said.

A stall near the market's back wall sported numerous folds of cloth hung upon wooden racks. Many bolts were dyed in a wide array of colors, though one was pure apple red. A wide dwarven woman with extra-wide hips, dressed in a myriad of colors like her wares, was straightening a cloth bolt left askew by some browser. She spotted the onlookers in turn.

"Need something for a new shirt?" she called out. "Have a look at this weave. Stout and light, it is."

"No, thank you," Wynn replied politely.

At the next stall hung leather vests and shirts, and pairs of premade boots were piled on a makeshift plank counter. Between the two merchants, Wynn saw a narrow tunnel leading off beyond the market.

"I have shown you," Sliver muttered, turning around. "For all the good it will do."

She didn't even look at Wynn as she started shoving her way back through the crowds. Wynn waited for Chane to speak, but at his silence, she called after Sliver, "And that's all?"

"That is all I was told to do," the smith retorted. "This is as far as my mother got."

Wynn pivoted, watching Chane and waiting.

He dropped his hand onto Sliver's shoulder.

She instantly slapped it away and turned on him, outrage flushing her face.

"But not as far as you went," Chane said. "*Where . . . to . . . next?*"

Sliver froze, and Wynn's fingers cinched in Shade's neck fur.

The smith's eyes widened with anger—or perhaps a flicker of panic? She lingered, as Chane waited in silence, and then her brow furrowed.

"Do not make that mistake again," she warned. "The only deceiver here is your puppy of a sage!"

With that, Sliver strode off.

Chane whirled about, glancing once at Shade before turning expectant eyes on Wynn.

"Well?" he whispered.

Wynn tried raising a memory of Sliver, hoping Shade would pick up her intent.

A cascade of images answered.

Stone corridors . . . branching paths . . . fewer people at every turn . . .

Wynn was following a wide, short figure concealed in a full cloak and hood. It tromped ahead along the path, and she ducked into hiding whenever the figure slowed or paused.

Wynn raised her face to Chane, as he watched her hopefully.

Then Shade lunged.

"Oh—wait—Shade!" Wynn squeaked, nearly jerked off her feet. "Chane, come on . . . she's got it!"

Chane was already on her heels.

Shade took off through the crowd, dragging Wynn by her grip on the dog's scruff. But Shade didn't bolt between the cobbler and clothier. She veered along the stalls at the market's rear wall.

Wynn stumbled after, fearful of letting go, and not everyone saw the overly tall wolf in time. Twice Shade snarled at someone in her way. Twice Wynn got a startled or nasty look from whoever twisted aside. Too many times she bumped rudely into someone as she tried to hold on to Shade.

"Slow her down, before I lose you!" Chane called, and his maimed voice seemed a bit far behind.

"I can't!" Wynn shouted. "Shade, stop!"

But Shade didn't, and then Wynn did, very suddenly. She slammed into something like rock beneath leather.

Her hold on Shade broke as she recoiled, careening backward. Wynn toppled as her footing failed, and she tensed, waiting for her back to hit the flagstones. She tried to hold out the staff to keep its crystal from striking.

Strong hands hooked her under the arms.

Chane hoisted Wynn up from behind, and she came face-to-face with the solid wall of padded rock . . . or rather an armored dwarf with a perplexed expression.

A fringe of beard ran around his jawline beneath his steel pot helmet. His leather hauberk was overlaid with an orange diagonal chest sash embroidered with a yellow *vubrí*. He also carried a tall iron staff.

"Oh, no," Wynn moaned. "I'm so sorry."

She had just slammed headlong into a member of a local clan's constabulary. The dwarf glowered as if she were some rambunctious child run amok.

"Mind your pace, missy," he warned. "There's too many people to go rushing about."

"Pardon us," Chane said. "Our dog got away."

"Then get a leash." With a final frown, the constable turned off through the crowd.

"A leash," Wynn muttered, but right then it was an appealing notion. "Shade, where are you . . . Shade!"

One bark carried over the market's ruckus.

Wynn couldn't see Shade, but at the dog's noise, a few people turned to look.

"There . . . go," Chane urged.

They wove through shoppers, vendors, and stalls, until Wynn spotted the top of a large tunnel. One brief break in the crowd exposed Shade hunkering in that opening.

Wynn pushed on. "Shade . . . come here!"

The dog backed another step into the tunnel, glowering at the crowd. She openly snarled at anyone who got too close, gaining far too much attention. Wynn rushed into the tunnel opening and clamped her hand over Shade's muzzle.

"She *must* learn not to growl at these people," Chane admonished, jogging up behind. "Can you not get that much through to her?"

Wynn only heard Shade's answering snarl and felt the vibration beneath her small hand.

"It's not her fault."

Apparently, whatever Shade had learned from Sliver's memories had immediately become an excuse to bolt out of the market.

"If she is as intelligent as her father," Chane returned, "then she should understand simple commands."

"Not now, Chane."

Shade seemed uninterested in communicating in any way other than memory-speak, which was understandable. But Wynn wished Shade might've picked up a few spoken words by now.

Shade shook her nose free and snapped her jaws closed on Wynn's sleeve. She jerked on it as she backed down the tunnel. Her intent here was clear enough.

Wynn pulled her sleeve free and stood, but as she turned to Chane, a passing white figure appeared briefly amid the crowd. Wynn froze, peering around Chane's side, and there it was again.

A stark-white-robed and cowled figure towered above the dwarves in the market.

"Oh, no . . . no . . . no!" she breathed, and grabbed Chane, wrenching him in against the tunnel wall.

"What are you doing?" he demanded.

"Shush. Don't move!"

She reached back, urging Shade in behind herself, and then peeked around Chane. There in the crowd was the white-clad elf she'd seen at Hammer-Stag's funeral. Beyond him, she quickly spotted the Weardas. And last . . .

Duchess Reine stood a little ways beyond the tunnel mouth, bartering with a clothier. She inspected a pair of folded pants and a heavy wool shirt. Both were simple—quite plain, in fact—and certainly not what a royal of Malourné would wear. And they were obviously too large for her.

Wynn frowned at this. The duchess was out shopping? That hardly seemed likely, since she would have anything she needed.

"It's the duchess," Wynn whispered.

She grabbed Chane's belt, pulling him as she backed down the tunnel. Shade kept huffing impatiently behind her. Once they were far enough along a curve and lost sight of the market, Wynn let go of Chane—only to find him scowling at her.

"She would not be coming our way," he said, and spun her around to push her onward.

Shade wheeled and took off, and they followed the trail she held in her mind.

Along twists and turns, they passed people in the crystal-lit tunnels, most heading back toward the market. But at each divergence, they encountered fewer passersby, until Shade made two turns in which they saw no one for a long while. Orange crystals mounted in the iron fixtures upon the walls grew scarce, until Wynn had to pull out her cold lamp crystal.

Then Shade halted.

By the crystal's light, they saw that the narrowing passage ahead split in two directions. Both branches sloped downward, arcing away from each other into the dark distance, for neither had any crystals mounted upon the walls.

Shade stood at the split, looking down one branch and then the other.

"What is wrong?" Chane asked.

Wynn crouched, touching Shade's back, and the dog looked at her with a whine. Wynn tried remembering the cloaked figure Shade had shown her from Sliver's memory. It was difficult, since it wasn't truly her memory. But in turn, Shade just whined.

"She doesn't know which way," Wynn said. "Maybe Sliver lost Ore-Locks here, or Shade didn't catch the whole memory of the way Sliver went. We've already come quite a ways and—"

"Then we must guess," Chane said, "and continue with . . ."

He never finished. Chane lowered his head, turning it to one side as his eyes half closed.

"What is it?" she asked.

He hesitated and then answered, "Just footsteps, some group headed off to the . . ." He trailed off again.

Chane spun around, staring back the way they had come. Shade paced past Wynn, following his gaze as she sniffed the air. Even stranger, Wynn saw Chane's nostrils flare.

"They are coming!" he whispered.

"Who?"

Then she heard the footsteps—more than one pair—and Shade's jaws snagged in her robe and jerked.

"Douse the crystal!" Chane whispered.

Wynn shoved the crystal in her pocket as they fled down the right-side passage. Chane got ahead and veered in against the wall. He pulled her in beside himself, and they flattened there.

"Be ready to hurry on if they come our way," he whispered.

Wynn peered up, still wondering why they hid. She just made out the branch head around the wall's gradual curve—and light was growing there. Chane pulled his cloak's hood forward, and Wynn did the same with her robe's cowl.

Over the rise at the passage's head, a sharp point of light appeared. It glowed from the hand of a tall and slender figure in a white robe.

"The elf," Chane whispered.

Wynn glanced up. Was that what he'd smelled? She tensed as the tall elf paused and looked back. Behind him came a much shorter figure in a deep sea green cloak, followed by three Weardas.

Duchess Reine was carrying a folded stack of clothing.

Chane gripped Wynn's hand, flattening his other against the wall. She knew he was preparing to bolt, and his hand in hers felt as cold as the stone. Shade stood poised at her hip, unblinking eyes watching up the passage.

The duchess approached the elf holding up a bright cold lamp crystal.

Yes, that was what it was, and Wynn's eyes widened. There were no orders of the guild that wore white, so where had the elf acquired a guild crystal?

The duchess passed the elf and disappeared down the other passage branch, the left one. The tall white-clad elf followed her, as did her bodyguards, and they all vanished from sight.

Chane's grip slackened on Wynn's hand. "Let us continue down this direction for now."

"No, wait," she whispered.

Wynn wondered why the duchess was wandering these lonely backways under Sea-Side, the same in which Sliver had followed her brother. Wynn took a step upslope.

"What are you doing?" Chane hissed.

"You saw her," she whispered. "At the funeral, she and the others were the only ones allowed to leave the same way as the Stonewalkers."

It was too dark to clearly see Chane's face, but she heard the incensed tone of his breathy voice.

"You told me at the amphitheater's iron door that you did not know if she went with them."

"Just the same," Wynn countered, "she's the best lead we have."

She strode up the passage in soft steps, ignoring Shade's sudden huffing and growling. When she reached the top and peered around the sharp corner into the left branch, light receded below, beyond the passage's gradual curve.

Wynn stepped out to follow, until Chane grabbed the back of her robe. She glared up at him, but he held fast, and Shade quickly slunk by down the passage branch. Only then did Chane let go, and he slipped in ahead. Wynn followed them both in silence.

It wasn't long before Shade slowed her creeping advance, and Wynn saw that the surface of the walls had changed.

She hadn't even noticed until she spotted thin seams next to her shoulder. Finely masoned mortarless blocks fit tightly together in place of smoothly chiseled mountain stone. Why were masoned walls needed in place of native rock?

Shade stopped, and Chane swept back a hand in warning.

Wynn slipped up behind him, peering around his side.

The passage had straightened, but she could see a spot of light spreading on the walls ahead. There stood the elf with his stolen crystal, its light revealing the duchess and her guards.

Duchess Reine looked worn. Strands of chestnut hair had loosened from her sea-wave combs. She merely stared at the passage's stone-block wall as her companions waited in silence. Then she took a deep breath, releasing it slowly.

She handed her burdens to a Weardas and flattened her hands upon the wall's stone—but not together. Separated beyond shoulder width, her left landed distinctly higher than her right. She held them there, and none of the others made a sound, as if this act was familiar.

Wynn couldn't tell if the duchess applied any pressure, but it didn't seem so. Then she heard the sound of stone grating.

The block beneath the duchess's left hand shifted slowly inward. She lifted her hand, but the stone continued to sink. In another moment the grating grew louder as the block under her right hand sank as well. Wynn watched as the duchess repeated the process over painfully long moments, until prolonged touch sent five scattered wall blocks sliding inward, and all without any pressure applied.

The grating amplified even more, echoing down the passage.

Wynn had leaned so close to Chane that she felt him flinch with her.

All of the blocks before the duchess slipped and twisted, spreading away into a hidden space beyond the wall. As the opening formed, so did a risky notion in Wynn's mind.

Perhaps there was a reason Sliver and her mother had lost track of Ore-Locks.

No one with the duchess appeared surprised at what they saw. Yet none had opened the strange portal for her. Even if Wynn remembered which stones to touch, would the wall later respond for her or Chane? Did it even lead anywhere she wanted to go?

Duchess Reine stepped through the opening, and her entourage began to follow.

Wynn dodged around Chane.

"She will see you!" he hissed.

"And that's our only chance."

She scurried down the passage before he could stop her.

One Weardas saw her coming and jerked out his sword.

"Captain!" he shouted.

The only other one still in the passage was the tall elf in white. He twisted about, revealing a lined face of advanced age. Wynn hadn't covered half the distance when the duchess's voice carried from the opening.

"Wait here!"

All three Weardas encircled the duchess as she stepped out. The white-robed elf shifted closer, and everyone was watching Wynn. All of the duchess's people stood in the passage, so whom had she told to wait inside that hidden place?

"Wynn . . . Journeyor Hygeorht," the duchess began.

In those three words, her tone slipped from surprise to disdain. Wynn knew the duchess had gained more than a passing familiarity with the young sage who'd caused so much trouble.

"Ah, the curious one," added the elder elf.

When Wynn glanced at the crystal in his hand, the barest smile spread upon his lips, crinkling the corners of his mouth. He nodded slightly to her, but his eyes held no malice—unlike Reine's.

"Duchess," Wynn said, bowing respectfully.

Reine's gaze shifted slightly, and Shade and Chane stepped into plain sight.

"What are you doing here?" she demanded. "How did you find this place?"

"Domin High-Tower sent me . . . on a family matter," Wynn answered. Lying was getting far too easy for her. "I must speak with his brother among the Stonewalkers immediately. The domin said you would be at Dhredze Seatt, and if I located you, you could help."

"Answer my question!" the duchess ordered.

Wynn flinched, and then again for visibly flinching the first time.

"We've been looking for you for several days. The Off-Breach Market was one place Domin High-Tower suggested. This man was sent as my guard."

Wynn stepped slightly aside, gesturing to Chane.

Reine's lips parted, but the elf spoke first. "And *you* are far out of place."

Wynn wondered how this elf of no known guild order knew that Chane was a foreigner. But his gaze was low and to her other side. He was looking at Shade.

A quick laugh rolled out of him, and Shade answered with a rumble. Puzzled as Wynn was that the elf seemed to recognize Shade, she couldn't afford the distraction. Not if she were to gain more from the duchess.

Reine remained quiet and swept a hand downward before her bodyguards.

"My lady?" the chin-bearded one returned sharply.

"It's all right, Tristan," she said.

Unlike the other two, he only lowered his sword rather than sheathing it, and with visible reluctance.

"Very well, journeyor," the duchess continued. "Since our honored domin is in need, I would never refuse. Give me whatever letter you bear for him. I will see that Ore-Locks receives it."

Wynn caught Reine's slip. Not only did the duchess know the Stonewalkers, she knew High-Tower's brother by name. Duchess Reine advanced half the distance and held out her hand.

"Do not get any closer to her," Chane whispered.

He spoke in Belaskian, so only Wynn understood, but the captain, the one called Tristan, inched forward with his gaze fixed on Chane.

"I have no letter," Wynn replied.

"And I have no patience for more of your meddling!"

Wynn shook her head. "Forgive me, but as I said, this is a family matter . . . a private matter . . . difficult for the domin to speak of."

"Then tell me. I will pass it to his brother privately."

"Domin High-Tower's instructions were explicit. I must deliver it personally. Please take me to Ore-Locks."

The duchess dropped her hand. Suspicion mounted in her expression.

If the Stonewalkers truly guarded the texts, had Wynn just hinted too much concerning her true goal?

Chane slipped a hand beneath his cloak to his sword's hilt. He did not dare step in front of Wynn and cause this whole standoff to suddenly crumble. Beneath the duchess's suspicion, he saw discomfort and uncertainty surface. It was not hard to guess what troubled her.

If the duchess believed Wynn at all but did nothing to help, there could be repercussions with the guild. But if the duchess even suspected Wynn was lying . . .

Chane's gaze slipped to the saber's hilt protruding from the duchess's cloak.

It was not the weapon that troubled him but rather the way it hung, not high near the belt, dangling like the ornament of a royal. It was slung low, raked back, loose on its suspension strap.

Duchess Reine knew how to use it—or at least how to set it for a smooth draw. If something went wrong, she could be on Wynn as the guards came at him. Even if he broke Wynn free, they would be running with no hope of ever getting near the texts.

The captain watched him, never seeming to blink, but Chane ignored the man. He shut out everything, even Wynn, waiting for the duchess to speak again.

"Surely, even for a family crisis," the duchess began, "High-Tower would have faith in the royal family. He would trust my discretion, as we have always trusted his."

Chane caught no deception beneath those words—he felt nothing at all. Why could he not tell truth from lies when it mattered? Why did such warnings only come when he was not focused on trying to listen for deception?

The duchess shifted weight between her feet. She was obviously disturbed by Wynn's sudden appearance. But that was all Chane could discern.

"I can't break my word," Wynn insisted. "I'm allowed to speak only with Ore-Locks."

"And I cannot take you to him," Reine answered flatly.

Again, Chane could not tell if that was a lie. Wynn took a step forward, and he tensed.

"This is urgent, Highness," she pleaded. "Domin High-Tower assured me you would help."

"Of course I will," Reine answered sharply, and then sighed. "There may be a way."

All amusement washed from the tall elf's lined face. "My lady," he warned.

"I know, Chuillyon," she answered, and then studied Wynn. "Come with me."

As the duchess turned away, Wynn advanced, but Shade did not. Chane found the dog standing tense, eyes locked on the duchess's back. Was Shade trying to catch the woman's memories?

"Shade?"

The dog shook herself, peered up at him, and then padded after Wynn. Chane hurried onward, still dumbfounded at the risks Wynn took.

The duchess could detain them and send an inquiry to High-Tower, uncovering Wynn's deception. Wynn had already related that Duchess Reine, acting for Malourné's royals, had used her influence to keep the texts in the hands of guild premins. The Stonewalkers' involvement was still only an educated guess, but Chane was certain of two things.

First, Duchess Reine was hiding something, and second, she was only playing Wynn's polite game for now.

Wynn inhaled a sharp breath an instant before he stepped through the opening. His attention immediately fixed on what he saw there, even as he heard the bodyguards enter behind him.

At the back of a hidden stone room was another pair of iron doors, just like the ones at the amphitheater of Old-Seatt. But these doors were guarded.

A dwarf in plated leather armor stood to either side, and both held iron staves. Both wore sashes, one of russet with green lines and the other of pure plum. Embroidered emblems on each were different, so their clans were not the same. But both were obviously constabulary.

Chane's frustration grew.

A hidden door behind a hidden opening in a deep lonely passage—and guarded as well. The only other difference was a recessed iron panel behind the guard with the plum-colored sash.

"Now, please," the duchess said.

The dwarf turned, grasping the panel's handle, and then paused and glanced back. Duchess Reine turned to face Wynn.

"You and yours will turn around, until told otherwise."

Wynn pivoted, and Chane saw her dejected frown before he turned as well.

He heard the panel slide open.

A series of steady scrapes followed, like honed metal sliding on smooth stone. He could only guess at some set of rods being pressed or pulled, like the ones Wynn had described beyond the amphitheater's iron doors. It made him wonder why that other door's lock had been on the inside.

A louder grinding began—once, twice, and three times.

Chane shook his head. He knew this portal had the same triple-layered doors as the last.

Every new sound reaffirmed how impossible it would be to come this way again if Wynn's gamble did not get them to the Stonewalkers. Despite his claim to her about using mixed intimidation and manipulation, that ploy had worked only on humans who had viewed Welstiel as a powerful noble. It would not work here.

Whatever lay beyond the doors was of such importance that the dwarves took no chance of anyone finding—let alone gaining—the entrance.

"This way," said the elf.

Chane turned around to find the iron portal fully open. But he was not looking into another chamber, rather at the head of a wide passage that turned sharply left. The duchess and her elven advisor stepped through, disappearing around the portal's left.

As Chane followed Wynn and Shade, he entered the passage's head and saw that it curved away, gradually downward. The Weardas came last, and the captain still had his sword out. Chane quickened his step, closing behind Wynn. Strategically set orange crystals lit their path.

He remained silent, hearing only an indiscernible whisper or two pass between the duchess and the elf walking ahead. This was too easy, and going far too well from Chane's perspective.

The journey continued along the tunnel's gradual spiral down—and down. Soon, Chane lost all sense of which direction they headed through the mountain. They had been walking for something less than an eighth-night when the tunnel finally ended in a small round chamber.

Another door waited between two more armored constables, though it was normal wood and overly broad. Both guards clearly knew the duchess. One began unlocking the door as the second studied Wynn and Shade—and Chane. The elf said something in Dwarvish. Other than his higher-pitched voice, it sounded as if he was fluent. The guard studying Wynn shook his head, perhaps not liking surprise guests, and then motioned everyone forward.

Chane stepped through the door into a wide domed chamber of smooth stone. His gaze immediately locked upon the floor's center.

Embedded there was a perfectly round mirror big enough to hold a wagon. Light from the elf's crystal bounced off its surface, sending flickers across the domed walls. But the closer Chane stepped, the less certain he became.

The mirror was not glass.

Milky, perhaps a gray nearly white, it appeared made of some kind of metal. Chane spotted a hair-thin seam dividing the great disk. Another portal, this time in the floor, but again, no bars, locks, latches, or handles of any kind. What was it made of, and where had he seen such metal before?

Wynn whispered, "Chein'âs . . . the Burning Ones!"

Wynn stared at the glistening portal in astonishment. She wasn't even aware she'd spoken until her own whisper filled her ears. She clamped her mouth shut, hoping no one had heard her clearly, but there was no mistaking that metal.

It was the same as the head of the elven quill given to her by Sgäile's uncle, Gleann, while she'd been in the Elven Territories. It was the same metal as the weapons gifted to Leesil and Magiere by . . .

The Chein'âs—the Burning Ones.

They were one of the five races of the mythical Úirishg, though only dwarves and elves were commonly known to exist. At least until Sgäile had taken Magiere, Leesil, and Chap on a secret side trip during the journey to Pock Peaks in search of the orb.

Were the Chein'âs here as well, hidden somewhere below the seatt?

It didn't seem possible they had been so close all these centuries and remained unknown to the world. Then again, First Glade, at the center of the Lhoin'na's lands, had been hiding in plain sight since the great war and beyond. Or had the dwarves learned to mine this metal themselves from somewhere deep in the earth? That was unlikely.

From what little Wynn had learned, the Chein'âs lived in the depths amid severe heat. Only they seemed to know the working of this white metal.

Shade's quick huff startled Wynn to awareness.

Four dwarves stood post around the domed chamber at equidistant points, but they weren't constabulary. Though they carried tall iron staves, their armor was more layered bands of steel than leather, and their iron-banded helms would've been too heavy for a human male. Two were armed with double-bladed axes, harnessed head-down on their backs. Another held a long hafted mace, its butt resting on the floor, while the last had a wide sword in a scabbard on his waist. All carried paired war daggers sheathed on their belts.

And the one beyond the Chein'âs portal rounded toward the duchess and her attendant.

Wynn spotted a thôrhk wrapped around the raised steel collar of his armor. Its ends were spiked like Hammer-Stag's, and she quickly saw all four wore the same. All four guardians were warrior thänæ.

The one paused before the duchess, offering a curt nod, as if that were all she were due, and then he glanced slowly between Wynn and Chane.

Wynn couldn't clearly see his face between the helm's brow and cheek wings, but his posture seemed challenging enough. He looked back at the duchess.

"Why have you done this?" he demanded.

Duchess Reine returned her own slower nod. "A family matter for one of the guardians of the honored dead."

"No *matter* is enough to breach the secrecy of this place!"

"It involves other kin as well, one who is a member of *her* guild," the duchess added, and she looked toward Wynn, as she continued speaking to the thänæ. "I would never do this lightly. They will go no farther, and I will vouch for their sealed lips . . . at any cost."

The duchess's wintry gaze explained it all.

One slip, one hint of ever having been here, would get Wynn—and Chane—killed. There would be no court or tribunal, no charges at all for them to defend against. Wynn could only nod her understanding as she grew sick to her stomach. But it didn't matter how deep she'd mired herself, so long as she had any chance to find the texts.

"So . . . is everyone now clear on the matter?" Chuillyon interjected, his tone a little too mockingly bored. "Very good then."

He went straight to the far wall and grasped a rope Wynn hadn't noticed. Unwinding it from an iron tie mount, he heaved with all his weight.

The chamber rang with a deep tone, and Wynn clamped hands over her ears. She felt the floor stones vibrate beneath her and looked up. In the dome's height hung a great brass bell. It was mounted to one side, out of the way of a wide shaft running upward from the ceiling's center. The opening's circumference appeared to match that of the floor's white metal portal. Then the elf rang the bell again.

Wynn cringed through six tones vibrating her whole body before the duchess's companion released the rope.

"What's happening?" she finally asked.

"We wait," Reine answered.

"Aren't we going on to meet Ore-Locks?" Wynn asked, growing worried.

Duchess Reine's eyes widened just barely, as if she'd heard something of keen interest—and Wynn knew she'd said too much.

"Your promise to Domin High-Tower will be kept," the duchess answered. "You will pass your message directly to his brother."

An awkward silence followed. Wynn used every ounce of self-control to keep her expression relaxed. Her seemingly successful bluff was vaporizing with each long moment.

A familiar grinding began to grow in the chamber. Wynn had heard it only in Shade's memories.

She glanced upward to the ceiling's large opening but saw nothing. When she lowered her gaze, Shade had crept to the edge of the white metal floor portal. With her ears flattened, the dog then backed away.

The portal's center hairline split.

Its two halves began sliding smoothly away beneath the floor. A stone platform slowly rose, filling the opening as it came level with the chamber. It held only one occupant.

Ore-Locks stepped off, looking annoyed.

His thôrhk hung around his neck, but otherwise, he wore only dusty chargray breeches and an untucked shirt. Red hair hung loose to his shoulders, as if he'd been engaged in something that required little attention to appearance.

"My lady?" he said. "Is something wrong? Why did you not just come down?"

His tone suggested resentment for the summons.

"Forgive us, but . . . something else required that we wait here." The duchess half turned toward Wynn. "This young sage says she has a message from your brother, and she was entrusted to tell no one but you. I could not ignore this and I brought her here."

Ore-Locks looked Wynn up and down.

"From High-Tower?" he asked.

Wynn swallowed hard. This wasn't how she expected things to play out. She'd hoped upon spotting the duchess that she might make it all the way to the Stonewalkers. Now she was stuck with nothing more than another lie.

"In . . . in private," she stammered.

Ore-Locks's brow wrinkled. He closed on her, taking her firmly by one arm.

Chane took a step, but Wynn shook her head, warning him off. Shade trotted after as Ore-Locks pulled Wynn out through the chamber's entrance. No one stopped the dog, though Wynn thought she saw Chuillyon watching with too much interest.

"Please wait inside," Ore-Locks told the outer guards, and once they'd stepped in and closed the door, he faced her. "What message is so urgent that my brother sends a little sage all the way from Calm Seatt?"

He was so close that she smelled his breath—dusty, yet dank at the same time. Most male dwarves wore beards, but he was clean shaven. His mouth was a wide slash like Sliver's, but his black eyes reminded her of High-Tower by shape rather than the common dwarven color. Somehow Ore-Locks was more intimidating than either of them, and that was no easy feat.

But Wynn stood face-to-face with one of the elusive Stonewalkers.

A hundred questions filled her head. Foremost was whether he knew anything of the texts. He would never answer that, so she straightened and said the only thing she could.

"A crisis in your family." She paused, considering her words. "Your brother asks that you take leave and visit your mother."

Resentment faded from Ore-Locks's expression, but his forehead wrinkled again.

"Crisis? And how would High-Tower . . ." He broke off and took a heavy breath. "Has my brother come back? That is not possible." He shook his head. "What has happened with my mother and . . . ?"

Wynn never heard him speak the obvious final word—"sister."

"Why would my mother," he continued, "if not my *sister*, send word all the way to the guild? Why not to me?"

He faltered, as if knowing the answer.

"Because no one could contact you here, until now," Wynn confirmed. "It's not that easy, is it?"

"What else? What crisis?"

She shook her head. "I don't know. He begs that you take leave to see them."

"And that is all to your message? Nothing more specific?"

Wynn realized how flimsy this sounded, but she couldn't risk expanding the lie. She could think only about four words he'd spoken—*if not my sister.*

Sliver had vehemently opposed any attempt to bring her elder brother home. Ore-Locks seemed to imply that she never would've sent for him. He now paced the entrance chamber, lost in his own thoughts, and finally turned to face Wynn. His features hardened as if he resented the messenger because of the message.

Ore-Locks wheeled and shoved the door open, leaving his hand extended, commanding her to return to the inner chamber. When she and Shade stepped inside, the duchess was waiting, blocking their way.

"Your task is complete?" Reine demanded.

"It is," Ore-Locks answered before Wynn could.

"Tristan!" Reine called out.

The captain quickly joined her. "Yes, my lady?"

"Escort them back to the market," the duchess instructed, and when he nodded, she turned to Wynn. "You have well served your domin. You may now return home."

Wynn couldn't mistake that as anything but an order. The other two bodyguards closed on Chane, and he was ushered out as the outer guards regained their stations. Wynn was about to follow at the captain's silent urging, but Duchess Reine never moved.

"Are you not returning to the market as well?" Wynn asked.

The duchess looked her up and down, then turned away to join her elven advisor and Ore-Locks.

Chane looked down questioningly at Wynn as she exited with Shade, but he kept silent.

Captain Tristan pointed up the passage for the long walk back.

Wynn was seething by the time the escort unceremoniously showed her, Chane, and Shade into the market. It was late, and the place was nearly empty. Many of the stalls were closed or gone. But only when the Weardas turned back into the tunnel were they free to speak.

"What is the duchess doing here?" Chane immediately asked.

"Clearly more than paying respects," Wynn answered. "There are too many implied connections between the royals and the Stonewalkers . . . not to mention Ore-Locks's previous visit to High-Tower."

"Yes, the guild is involved as well," Chane agreed. "That is a trio of powerful factions in our way."

"And the duchess has gone to the Stonewalkers. I suppose we could hide here, wait until she comes out, and try to follow her."

"If she comes out," Chane countered. "Likely she did go with them after the funeral. She may be staying with them."

Wynn wasn't so sure. "Why shop in the market for clothes she wouldn't need and didn't fit her? She may be welcome among them, but I hardly think a royal would take quarters in the underworld. No, she's here for something else."

Shade whined loudly, and Wynn looked down.

The dog scratched the flagstones with one paw and barked.

"Shush," Wynn said, but knelt to grip Shade's face with both hands.

Everything blurred in Wynn's vision as a dark image overtook her mind.

She was walking down a damp tunnel. Mineral-glazed walls of natural rock glistened, faintly phosphorescent, though the floor beneath her feet felt level and smooth. She could smell . . . seawater.

The tunnel was narrow, barely wide enough for two to walk abreast, or one dwarf. The rough walls were calcified, as if the path had been created long ago. For some reason, no one had seen fit to finish them smoothly.

Near the path's end was an iron door, slightly mottled by rust.

The memory wavered.

Wynn suddenly stood before the door, looking down. She glimpsed the long hem of a deep green cloak around high riding boots—those of the memory's owner. Then her attention caught on a palm-size shining oval on the door where a lock's keyhole should've been.

There was no mistaking that silvery white—more Chein'âs metal.

Wynn felt herself reach up into her hair, pulling something out. When her hand lowered, she held a pearly sea-wave comb in her palm, and she knew the memory's owner.

Duchess Reine took the comb and pressed its concave side to the door's oval.

Wynn heard the scrape of metal sliding.

She passed the comb to someone behind her and pushed the door open. Its hinges squeaked lightly. As she stepped through, no other footsteps followed, though someone shut the door. She stood in a dark chamber of natural stone where the smell of the sea permeated the air.

Just beyond a near ledge, Wynn spotted a pool filling most of the chamber's floor. An iron grate in the back wall was half-submerged in its water. Beyond that was a dark tunnel half-filled as well, though she couldn't see more than a few yards down it. She suddenly turned left.

A rough opening led to another chamber, but it was too dark to see what lay there, and she didn't even approach. Dim light came from somewhere, but Wynn wasn't certain of its source. The sight of the opening became misty, blurred. . . and her eyes began to sting.

There were tears running down her cheeks.

Something wet slapped stone, the sound echoing from that next chamber.

Something moved in there.

She began to feel dizzy, trapped between her own fears and the grief welling from within the duchess's memory. And then everything winked black.

Wynn was shaking as she looked into Shade's crystal blue, yellow-flecked irises. She crumpled on the market's flagstones.

"Wynn?" Chane said in alarm, crouching beside her.

While she'd been tangled in a failing scheme inside the white portal's domed chamber, Shade had been quite busy. Wynn took a long, shaky breath and pressed her cheek against Shade's as she closed her eyes. The dog was clearly trying to tell her something, but she wanted—needed—more than what she'd seen.

"Wynn?" Chane insisted. "Say something!"

"An underground room . . . a pool in its floor . . . and an iron grated tunnel," Wynn whispered, still trying to make sense of it.

"Whose memory?"

"The duchess . . . she started crying."

"Why would Shade show you this?"

"I don't know."

Without warning, another flash surged upon her.

She sat at the table in the Iron-Braids' back room. At first, she thought it was her own memory of just a short while ago. But Chane and Shade weren't present.

The table was laden with roasted venison, fresh sliced bread, and baked apples, all served in plain clay bowls. Mother Iron-Braid hobbled about, setting out bleached wooden plates and tin forks and knives as she babbled away with shining joy on her face. But Wynn was staring across the table at Sliver, who sat glaring back. Unlike her mother, the smith didn't care for . . .

Whom did this memory belong to?

Mother Iron-Braid rounded the table, reaching out a gnarled hand to lay it on Wynn's cheek.

"It is so good to see you again, my son," she whispered.

Wynn shivered, her fingers closing in Shade's neck fur. The spoken words were much clearer this time than anything Shade had shared with her before.

It was Ore-Locks's memory.

Everything winked black for an instant.

Wynn stood in a dark passage where orange crystals were few. It looked familiar, like someplace she'd walked herself at some recent time. At the sound of heavy footfalls behind, she paused and turned.

There was Sliver again, following her.

"No more," the smith hissed in Dwarvish. "No more of you . . . and your twisted *calling*! No more of your shame and hidden sin upon us. Mother does not know what you are, what really took you—and I will keep it that way."

"I was called," Wynn answered—in Ore-Locks's deep voice. "Called by one that so few remember . . . and none know for the truth. But I hold that truth."

"You hold a lie!" Sliver nearly screamed back. "And if it calls you, then faith itself is a plague—and you are nothing but its carrier. Is it not enough that we've fallen so low that you try to infect us with its horror? Follow it alone and keep away! Do not come again!"

Sliver backed up the passage as she began to shake—as she had upon Wynn's visit when the smith first uttered Ore-Locks's name.

"Stay away from us!" she shouted. "Go to your *fall* . . . alone!"

The memory faded, and again Wynn looked into Shade's eyes.

Whatever called Ore-Locks to service among the Stonewalkers horrified Sliver, and perhaps High-Tower as well. Was that why the domin had nearly denounced his brother in that one secret visit to the guild?

Shade had been very . . . very busy, indeed. Wynn sat astonished, now realizing just how intelligent the majay-hì were as a whole—or Shade for her youth.

"Did you see more?" Chane asked. "Did she show you anything that would help us locate the texts?"

Wynn shook her head. "No, it was Ore-Locks's this time. I'm not certain, but I may have gotten to him. I'll tell you more later. Right now, I need you to stay and watch for the duchess, while I go back to the Iron-Braids'."

Chane frowned. "I do not like that plan."

Wynn stroked Shade's head. "I can't miss a chance to catch Ore-Locks if he goes home. And someone has to watch for the duchess. Shade will come with me, and I'll be fine."

Chane paced, and Wynn waited for him to accept the only option.

"If the duchess comes out, I will follow her," he finally agreed. "But once you leave the smithy, go directly to the inn, so I can find you."

Wynn nodded and stood, picking up her staff. She still wished Shade could grasp language more than just remembering sounds, but at least in that she understood it was meaningful. And there was no denying certain advantages of memory-speak. She reached for her pack hooked over Chane's shoulder. When she saw his face, she stopped with her hand gripping the strap.

He looked expectantly down at her, perhaps a hint of hope glittering in his eyes, which now had a touch of their original brown.

"We made contact with a Stonewalker," he whispered. "We are getting closer."

"Yes," she agreed. "So no matter what else, don't you get caught."

He touched the back of her hand, still high upon his shoulder. "I will find you later."

Wynn took the pack and started off with Shade pressed against her leg.

CHAPTER 13

Wynn headed for the Iron-Braids' smithy, her arms loaded full of bread, potatoes, and a burlap-wrapped halibut. She'd stopped in the market long enough to procure goods from what few vendors remained. Hopefully Mother Iron-Braid wouldn't take it as an insult, though Sliver likely would. Shade traipsed beside her, snuffling hopefully at the scent of fish.

"You'll wait—and behave yourself," Wynn said, not that Shade would understand. "We'll have dinner soon . . . I hope."

As she neared the smithy's open door, she paused at the sound of raised voices within.

"You refuse me . . . again?" a male voice boomed in Dwarvish.

"I will not repeat the reasons . . . again!" Sliver shouted back.

Wynn crept closer, peering inside as Shade stuck her snout around the door frame.

A stout male dwarf in fine dark pants and a cleanly oiled hauberk stood face-to-face with the smith. His mass of brown hair was pulled back in a leather thong, and his slightly darker beard was trimmed and crisply groomed. It was Carrow, Hammer-Stag's clan-kin.

"You protect nothing," he said, and then anger softened into pleading. "There is nothing left to protect. Your family name has faded. It will be lost one way or another."

"To even say so shows you know nothing of me," Sliver answered, "let alone my heart. So how could I accept you?"

Wynn swallowed hard. Hammer-Stag's clan-kin had proposed marriage—and not for the first time.

"Your brothers are long gone," he said, stepping closer and holding out his hand. "They have abandoned you—I have not—and I *do* know your heart. Take my family's name. Our children will be so honored to have you at our table's head."

For an instant, Wynn thought Sliver might reach for his hand, but the smith backed away.

"I cannot, Carrow . . . you know I cannot."

His expression turned cold. "Then marry into some lesser family, and keep your name . . . for what it is worth!"

He strode for the door.

Wynn scrambled down the passage, fumbling with her burdens. She quickly spun, pretending to stroll idly the other way. Carrow stomped past without a glance, and Wynn slowed, watching him fade down the passage.

Poor Sliver. A clan-kin of the great Hammer-Stag was in love with her. Maybe she had feelings for him, but she valued her lost heritage more.

Dwarven matrimony was complicated, leaning heavily on notoriety, honor, and status. If Sliver married into a family lesser than her own, her husband would've taken the Iron-Braid name. But she hadn't done this, and from her state, living in the depths of underside, how could there be a lesser family? Sliver was proud to a fault.

Wynn turned back. With her arms full, she tapped her foot on the door frame.

Sliver raised her head where she stood slumped over the forge. At sight of Wynn, the smith's surprise quickly vanished under ire.

"What now?" she growled.

"Might we share a meal?" Wynn asked, trying to hold up the food.

"Unless you have something to tell me alone . . . be gone!"

"Is that your mother's wish?" Wynn returned. "Or are you now the matriarch of the Iron-Braids?"

Sliver straightened instantly but faltered in answering.

"Then your mother's welcome stands," Wynn claimed, and stepped in without invitation. "Shall we cook?"

She headed straight for the rear door, not looking at Sliver.

As she passed, the smith snarled, "Where is your tall friend?"

"He had business at the market," Wynn answered.

"My mother is resting."

"Then we'll prepare the food first and wake her when it's ready."

Wynn tried to grip the door latch but couldn't get a hold with all her burdens and her staff.

"Are you going to help?" she asked. "Or should I just kick it until your mother answers?"

Sliver appeared too weary for more argument. "You are persistent . . . little scribbler."

Wynn shrugged. "I've been called worse."

The smith's gaze slipped to the goods in Wynn's arms. Exhausted by labor or other pressures, or not having gone to the market herself, Sliver grabbed the latch and gave it a wrench. Wynn shouldered the door open, entering the hearth room with Shade.

Preparations proceeded silently as Wynn nosed about. Sliver often had to retrieve or point out whatever Wynn needed. Otherwise, they didn't speak. Sliver prepped the hearth with lumps of raw coal from a battered pail. But while peeling potatoes, Wynn couldn't stand the silence anymore.

"I understand your reasons," she began, "for not accepting Carrow."

Sliver half turned. "You were listening!" she accused.

"You were loud."

The smith turned back to the hearth. "At least this time my mother did not hear."

Soon the coals gave birth to small flames, and Wynn waited, even until the last potato was peeled and cut.

"If one of my brothers married," Sliver whispered, "our lives would have been different . . . maybe."

Wynn stopped cutting bread. Sliver's tone betrayed how deeply her brothers' chosen paths had affected her. It was surprising that she spoke of this at all. Perhaps Sliver hadn't had anyone to talk to in a long while. This tentative truce wasn't something Wynn wished to shatter.

"How did . . . Why did High-Tower leave to join the guild?" she asked.

Sliver glanced up in suspicion, but Wynn simply waited.

"He was always strange," Sliver said. "Both of them were. Running off the moment work was done or sometimes before. Father would go looking for them. After the first few times, he always went straight to the temples. In the latter days, it was always the temple of Bedzâ'kenge."

Sliver shook her head with a breathy scoff.

Wynn took up the bread to cut once more. So Ore-Locks must have spent time at that temple as well. But why? Intuition told her it wasn't the right moment yet to speak of him—not until Sliver actually spoke his name.

"And it remained so," Sliver continued, "at least for High-Tower. The shirvêsh told Father that my brothers would not stop asking about our family's history, trying to learn more than what we had from our own ancestors. And High-Tower wrote everything down . . . like a human." Her voice turned cold. "Then Ore-Locks started leaving for days at a time, showing up at every temple in every settlement of the seatt. Until the day he disappeared altogether . . ."

Wynn paused with the knife halfway through the loaf. Before she asked about Ore-Locks, she hesitated again. The smith's voice grew quiet.

"Not long after, High-Tower told us he would join the order of Bedzâ'kenge. My father tried to show pride, but he was broken, his second son gone. When High-Tower left for your guild, we stopped speaking of him at all. Father passed over soon after, and I was left to tend the smithy."

"How long ago did High-Tower leave?" Wynn asked.

Sliver paused, considering. "Thirty-seven summers."

Wynn accidentally tore the next slice of bread.

She had no idea of the domin's age, but dwarves often lived to two hundred years or a bit more. High-Tower was at least middle-aged, and yet Ore-Locks appeared in his prime.

"My girl?" a thin voice called.

It came from beyond the left curtained doorway at the room's rear, and Sliver rose from tending the fire.

"Here, Mother," she called. "Come have some bread. Supper will follow soon."

The curtain pulled back, and Mother Iron-Braid shuffled out. Upon spotting someone else present, she squinted her old milky eyes.

"Young sage?" she asked, and then her voice turned manic. "Have you reached Ore-Locks?"

Wynn wasn't certain how to answer. Should she admit that she'd spoken with him? Was Sliver ready to hear of a banished brother who might appear this night?

The hearth room's door swung inward, and for an instant, Wynn was relieved by the interruption.

Ore-Locks stood in the doorway.

He still wore only char-gray breeches and a shirt in place of his traditional attire. But the thôrhk of a Stonewalker hung around his neck.

"Mother?" he asked. "Are you all right?"

Then he spotted Wynn.

Time crawled as Chane stood behind a weaver's booth, a quarter of the way around the market from the tunnel to the Stonewalkers' hidden passage. Half of the vendors had closed or packed up their stalls. Once the rest were finished, how long before a constabulary passed by on rounds and spotted him lurking about?

Chane tensed as a flash of white caught his eye.

Around the cavern's back, Duchess Reine and her elf and guards came out of the tunnel. They headed directly across the nearly empty market for the passage to Breach Mainway.

Chane bent down and rounded the market's back wall, keeping out of sight behind scant booths and the tall, painted columns. Once he had obtained a position behind the duchess's group, he pulled up his hood and quietly closed in.

The elf spoke in hushed tones as the group neared the exit, and the duchess paused and turned.

Chane ducked behind a column and peered carefully along its side.

She looked up at her elven companion, her features stiff and unreadable. Some lingering shock or long fatigue had left her numb. But her arms were empty, the breeches and shirt gone, and no one else carried them. Barely a stone's toss behind them, Chane fully widened his senses.

A thin scent began to fill his nose.

The duchess's hair was a bit out of place. One loose tendril hung against her left temple and cheek. The sea-wave comb on that side was askew, as if removed and replaced without a mirror's aid. And her boots and cloak's hem were dark, perhaps soaked.

Chane sniffed cautiously. The scent of seawater lingered from the duchess's passing.

She never replied to the elf, and Chane never caught what the advisor said. The duchess turned and resumed her journey without any change in her withdrawn expression.

Chane crept onward, keeping Reine in his sight.

Ore-Locks's intense gaze pierced Wynn as he whispered, "You!"

Sliver stared at her brother, perhaps too shocked for outrage.

But Mother Iron-Braid nearly toppled her stool in a rush across the room.

"My son!" she wailed, grabbing Ore-Locks's shirtfront. "My son, oh, Eternals, thank you."

Ore-Locks took her shoulders, steadying her. He stood in tense discomfort, watching Wynn over the top of his stooped mother.

"You said my brother sent you," he said, "that my family was in crisis."

"What?" Sliver gasped.

Wynn stiffened. She was in it now, up to her neck in her own lies.

"Do they look well to you?" she challenged Ore-Locks.

"You already spoke to him?" Sliver demanded. "You brought him here and told me nothing?"

Ore-Locks ignored his sister, glaring only at Wynn. "Did High-Tower send you . . . or not?"

She had no lies left to cover her others. "No, I came on my own. I needed to speak with you. It's vital."

"Then you lied to the princess as well," he returned.

Willful deceit was notable among dwarven vices; doing so to Princess—Duchess—Reine was just that much worse. And there was little she could do to amend it.

"Only about High-Tower," she answered. "Look around. I brought the food. Sliver works too hard and long to go to market, and your mother is too—"

"No, no," Mother Iron-Braid cut in, petting her son's chest. "We are well enough, and you have come back." She turned her head a little toward Wynn. "Do not speak so, or you will drive him away!"

Ore-Locks winced at this. He carefully took his mother's hands and cast a not-so-gentle glance at Sliver. Hers in turn was even less kind for him.

Wynn knew nothing of the Stonewalkers' ways or their lives apart from their people. But she had some notion of what it had cost Ore-Locks to come home.

"Sit and rest," he said, guiding his mother toward the table.

As yet, Sliver hadn't greeted him. Instead, she intercepted him and gripped her mother's shoulders.

"Get your hands off her!" she hissed.

Ore-Locks backstepped, and Sliver settled her mother in the only chair.

The sight of his family clearly pained Ore-Locks, as if this were the last place in the world he wished to be. He glanced once at the door. Sliver crossed her arms, daring him to leave. Ore-Locks remained. Even as Mother Iron-Braid reached for his hand, he fixed his gaze on Wynn again. She couldn't help fidgeting under his scrutiny.

"I never introduced my . . ." she began. "I am—"

"I know who you are," he answered.

A chill sank straight through Wynn. The duchess had told him—perhaps all the Stonewalkers—about her. They knew exactly who she was and had been warned against her.

"Yes, I'm the one who . . . brought those texts back," she confirmed. "I'm responsible for the translation project, the one you and Master Cinder-Shard warned High-Tower to stop."

Ore-Locks carefully pulled from his mother's clinging grip and backed toward the door.

"Forgive me, Mother," he said. "There is great treachery here, and I cannot stay."

"Treachery?" Sliver echoed, glancing at Wynn. "From her?"

Mother Iron-Braid frantically turned from one to the next. "What is this . . . ? What are you all talking—"

"No!" Wynn snapped at Ore-Locks. "I simply need to see the texts, for all our sakes. Just listen—"

"Enough from you!" Sliver shouted, then lunged one step at her brother.

"You speak of treachery? Look to yourself! We have suffered enough without you bringing your false ancestor among us!"

Ore-Locks didn't wince this time, but he didn't quite meet his sister's eyes.

"We want no part of you . . . or *it*," she went on. "I will not let you taint us further. Get out!"

Wynn was confused by this exchange.

"I never imagined High-Tower would leave," Ore-Locks whispered. "But deny our past all you want. It changes nothing. One of ours, long gone before us, called me to serve . . . and I am no longer part of this world."

Ore-Locks stepped out into the dim workshop, and his mother let out a mournful wail.

Wynn panicked, rushing for the doorway. "Ore-Locks, stop!"

He'd already reached the outer door and didn't turn. Wynn tried desperately to think of something to halt him. He wouldn't speak of the texts, but there must be something to give him pause, even for an instant.

"Who is Thallûhearag?" she called.

Ore-Locks paused.

"No, daughter!" Mother Iron-Braid shouted.

Shade's deafening snarl came quickly, but Wynn never had a chance to turn.

Something struck her back, and her head whiplashed as she shot out of the hearth room. Tumbling and scraping across the smithy's floor, she heard Shade barking and snapping. She tried to push up and roll over, but her hands stung sharply when she pressed against the floor.

Sliver shrieked, and Shade yelped, and Wynn flopped over on her back.

Shade stood between her and the hearth room's door, all her fur on end and her ears flattened as she lowered her head in menace. Sliver stood in the doorway with mixed shock and revulsion on her broad features. She was gripping one forearm. A bit of blood seeped between her thick fingers.

"Oh, no!" Wynn breathed. "Shade was only—"

In one fluid motion, Sliver chucked out Wynn's pack and staff.

"Don't!" Wynn cried, reaching out where she lay.

To her shock, Shade lunged sideways and under the falling staff. Its sheathed crystal's end struck near Shade's shoulders, and the haft rolled off her rump to the floor. Wynn's surprise at Shade's action was short-lived, and she caught one last glimpse of the smith.

Sliver slammed the door shut, and its crack echoed through the workshop.

Wynn sat up as Shade wheeled and padded over. Then the dog let out another warning rumble, baring her teeth as she glared beyond Wynn.

"Where did you hear that title?"

Wynn jerked around.

Ore-Locks's massive form stood above her. The light of the forge's dying embers cast his face in orange-red and glimmered faintly on his thôrhk. He looked like a hulking statue of heated rock ready to fall upon her.

"From you," she answered, "when you came to see your brother."

"So you are spying on me?" he accused. "Hunting me?"

"No . . . I mean, yes," she fumbled. "It was an accident. I'd gone to see the domin but heard voices. I didn't want to interrupt, so I waited."

Ore-Locks crouched, and Wynn's hand stung sharply as he took it. At another warning from Shade, Wynn waved off the dog. Ore-Locks let out a sigh.

"My sister should not have assaulted you, but the scrapes are not bad and should heal soon enough."

"I agreed with you," Wynn said, though it brought a puzzled wrinkle to his brow. "In what you said to High-Tower. The translation project isn't being handled well. That's part of why I came. Four sages dead, as well as city guards in Calm Seatt, and next to nothing has come from all the work on those texts . . . from the Forgotten . . . in the time of Bäalâle Seatt."

Wynn caught the unmistakable spark in his eyes at that last mention. She saw hunger there, and maybe some strange thirst for relief. For the first time, she wondered if he'd given her something to bargain with.

"I can read some of the languages in those texts," she rushed on. "Take me to them . . . and perhaps I can learn what really happened. I *know* Bäalâle is not a myth."

Another bluff, for she didn't *know* any such thing. All she had was Magiere's account of a single mention of a fallen seatt in the memories of Most Aged Father. That, and a cryptic reference found within the obscured verse of Chane's stolen scroll.

What she truly needed was to learn where Beloved's thirteen Children had gone and why.

The wraith had selectively murdered for this knowledge. More important was how the Night Voice . . . Beloved . . . il'Samar was connected to it all, past, present, and future.

Wynn sat in the forge's dim light, looking into the black eyes of a Stonewalker, the one and only who might help her.

Ore-Locks dropped her hand and stood up. As he straightened, his eyes seemed too dark for even a dwarf.

"You know no such thing," he said. "It is only myth . . . unless proven otherwise."

Wynn's hope withered. She'd had him for an instant and then lost him.

"Regardless of what you *think* you heard from my lips," he added, "my sect has sacred oaths. Fragile trusts and faiths you do not understand, even among your guild. I will not be the one to shatter them . . . not for the misguided guesses of one wayward sage."

Ore-Locks looked at the hearth room's door. His lips parted, but he never said a word. Instead, he turned and strode out of the smithy.

"You won't shatter them," Wynn insisted, scrambling to her knees. "You might even serve them all the better if—"

"I serve the honored dead," he returned without looking back. "Go home, Wynn Hygeorht. I pray to the Eternals that no more harm comes to you . . . nor that you bring further to my own."

Ore-Locks vanished, leaving Wynn kneeling on the floor with a silent Shade.

Once the duchess reached Breach Mainway, Chane worried about trailing her farther in the open. But she turned down the very next southward-side passage. He rushed to the tunnel's mouth, pausing a moment before peering around the corner.

Several large frontages carved from the passage's stone looked much like other shops and businesses. Perhaps even an inn in one case, since both dwarves and humans lingered out front, coming and going from that third establishment down the way. This made sense. At least some inns or common houses would be near a major market.

The duchess stopped before that third frontage, with its wide, heavy doors propped open. Captain Tristan was the first up the two steps, glancing inside before ushering her in. The rest followed, ducking their heads to clear the low doorway.

Chane leaned back against the mainway's wall. Wynn had been correct. Duchess Reine was not lodging with the Stonewalkers but in a place very near where she could reach them. How and why was another matter. Why had the Stonewalkers allowed her to accompany them at Hammer-Stag's funeral?

Surely she did not need to check on the texts, if some arrangement existed for the Stonewalkers to look after their safety. So what had she been doing in the time between now and when Wynn and he had been escorted out?

At least he now knew one place to pick up the duchess's trail.

Chane headed off along Breach Mainway. It was a long way down to the Iron-Braid smithy. His own task complete, he broke into a trot, hurrying to see how Wynn had fared with hers—the far more difficult one.

Wynn gathered her things and numbly headed out of the smithy. When she stepped into the narrow passage, Ore-Locks was nowhere in sight. A part of her couldn't believe what she'd just done to the Iron-Braids. Another part knew she'd had no better choice. Too much was at stake.

But Ore-Locks had spurned her just the same.

Wynn shuffled back toward Limestone Mainway, remembering the look in Ore-Locks's eyes at the mention of Thallûhearag—and then Bäalâle Seatt. He wanted to know more of the latter; that much was clear. But she couldn't mistake the conviction in his voice. He would never break the oaths of his sect, even for his own desires. She had played an all-or-nothing game . . . and she had lost.

She felt sick inside, and then Shade barked.

Wynn was too tired for whatever the dog wanted, but Shade wouldn't stop.

She barked twice more and halted, pawing the passage's stone floor. Her crystal blue eyes sparked in the limited light. The mainway lay just ahead, and it was early enough that other people would still be about.

"What now?" Wynn asked.

Shade dropped to her haunches and rubbed the side of her head with a paw.

Wynn sighed and crouched down. Obviously Shade had another memory she insisted on sharing.

Touching the dog's neck, Wynn whispered tiredly, "Show me."

The passage vanished.

She saw Ore-Locks rising upon the platform through the domed chamber's white metal portal. The image faded instantly, and Wynn guessed that Shade was simply identifying Ore-Locks. Just as quickly, she found herself staring through the smithy's workroom, and Ore-Locks stood in its outer doorway.

Wynn heard her own voice say, *Who is Thallûhearag?*

The smithy vanished.

That brief memory had been one of Wynn's own, but the rapid changes were making her dizzy. Still uncertain what Shade was trying to tell her, Wynn found herself standing in a dark cavern.

A greenish phosphorescence tinged the rough, glistening walls. Stalactites and stalagmites joined together in concave, lumpy columns. Odd twisted shadows played over and between them. In a few steps, Wynn realized the walls' own glimmer caused everything to throw multiple shadows every which way.

She understood the purpose behind Shade's chain of memory-speak. Her own question in the smithy's hearth room had triggered a memory in Ore-Locks.

Wynn—or rather Ore-Locks—walked through the cavern's dim glimmer. Now and then, natural openings appeared, leading off to other places, but he never glanced aside enough for Wynn to get a peek into any of them.

Everything flickered to black—then returned.

The surroundings had changed. A rough stone path still wove in and out of adjoining caves and pockets. Two more flickers, and Wynn guessed that Ore-Locks's scattered memory had raced onward in skips rather than tracing a complete path. Something caught her attention for an instant.

In one place, out of the corner of her eye—Ore-Locks's eye—she thought she saw standing figures. They hid in the cavern's dim recesses among the lumpy, bulging columns and half-formed mineral-laden cones protruding from the ceiling. But those mute figures remained still as statues. The only sounds were the scattered patter of drips and the echoes of Ore-Locks's heavy footfalls. Then he stepped upslope toward a ragged opening ahead.

Half-hidden behind a rising stalagmite, something passed on the left as she stepped out of the cavern.

Wynn stiffened for real. Had that been a face shaped in glistening wet stone?

The memory shifted and altered. Wynn stood before an arch filled with age-darkened iron. It looked just like the triple-layered portal in the amphitheater at Old-Seatt, but smaller. Again, the memory wavered, as if Shade hadn't been able to follow or comprehend what Ore-Locks was doing.

The archway was now open.

The space beyond was so dark that Wynn couldn't see anything except a flight of stairs arcing downward along a curved wall. She took only four steps and stopped—or Ore-Locks stopped—going no farther into the depths.

She couldn't see how far down the stairs went, but far enough that any floor below wasn't visible over the stairs' outer edge. The curved wall to her other side was smooth and perfect. This wide space wasn't natural and had been carved out. But what was down there?

"Enough," she whispered—but in Ore-Locks's deep voice. "Please leave me be."

Wynn shivered, locked inside his memory. She was in the Stonewalkers' underworld.

"You called me," Ore-Locks whispered. "I came to that calling . . . to serve. But I have learned no more. I cannot save you . . . free you."

Whom was he speaking to and what did he mean by . . . "save you"?

"No one will believe or remember," Ore-Locks continued. "I beg you . . . please, leave me be!"

Everything faded.

Wynn knelt in the passage, her fingers clutching Shade's face.

"No, there has to be more!"

Shade just whined, flattening her ears dejectedly. This was all she had caught. Like her father, Shade dipped only memories that surfaced—whatever rose in a person's conscious thoughts. But Ore-Locks had known what was there in the depths, in speaking to whomever or whatever.

Wynn rocked onto her heels. Was there something down there that called Stonewalkers to a life of service? The evening had ended, and that stolen memory had begun with a question.

Who is Thallûhearag?

And Sliver had spoken of a "false" ancestor.

Wynn couldn't fit it all together, but as she stared at the smithy door, she wondered how the Iron-Braids had come to such a low state. How many generations had existed this way and why? She didn't see how this helped with her own pursuit, but the memory left her pondering one person.

Ore-Locks still might be the one to help her—if she found a way to understand the memory Shade had stolen. Together, she and Shade headed out into the Limestone Mainway.

At dusk, Sau'ilahk willfully awakened from dormancy and coalesced in a shadowed side passage across from Wynn's chosen inn. It was the last place he had followed her, when she and her companions left the tram the night before. Before sunrise had forced him into dormancy, he had slipped deep into the settlement's back ways. In that desolate place, he had drained one young dwarven female caught by surprise and dragged her body into a storage chamber filled with dust-coated crates and barrels.

That one life had been strong and still brimmed vibrantly within him.

Sau'ilahk waited outside of Wynn's inn, but no one came or went. Where else might she have gone, or had she even returned from her day's wandering? He mentally recounted her visits to Sea-Side and blinked into dormancy, envisioning one place. He reemerged in the end chamber of Limestone Mainway on the lowest level and peered at the greeting house where Wynn had first met the warrior thänæ.

Why had she come back to Sea-Side? Was she seeking more concerning Hammer-Stag's death? Again he waited, sinking almost fully into the side of the end chamber's arched opening.

Business was done for the day, but Limestone Mainway still bustled with dwarves. Frustrated, he blinked out again and materialized in a dim passage beyond the Iron-Braids' smithy.

Sau'ilahk quickly conjured, hiding himself in another pool of light-banishing darkness. He heard nothing within the smithy. Then he caught a glimpse of movement, and he looked down the passage, toward the exit leading into the mainway.

Someone short, in a long robe, huddled low beside a black form.

Wynn stood up, patting Shade's head.

Sau'ilahk had wasted energies, but he slipped from his conjured darkness, letting it fade. Wynn had visited the smithy, but he was too late, missing whatever had taken place.

Where was Chane?

Wynn must be close to something, if she returned to previously visited locations.

Sau'ilahk watched her slip into the mainway, and then he glided quickly to the passage's end and halted. Too many people still wandered about for him to follow her, but he could not continue in ignorance. He needed to hear—to see—what she said and where she went. He pulled back into the passage, steeling himself and shutting out the world.

Air for sound was not enough. Fire, in the form of Light, was needed for sight, but its emanations could betray the servitor's presence. It had to be encased with Earth as well, as drawn from Stone. But a base servitor of multiple elements, in three conjuries, would cost him dearly. And a fourth conjury had to intertwine with the others. His creation would need a hint of sentience, though this would make it less subservient.

Sau'ilahk began to conjure Air first of all.

When its quivering ball manifested, he held it and reached out. Caging the warp of Air with incorporeal fingers, he began conjuring Fire in the form of Light.

A yellow-orange glow began to radiate from within his grip.

Sau'ilahk forced his hand corporeal and slammed the servitor down *into* the passage floor.

He was only half-finished. The last two conjuries had to come simultaneously while he held the first pair firm. Around his flattened hand, a square of glowing umber lines for Earth via Stone rose in the passage floor. A circle of blue-white appeared around that as he summoned in Spirit and inserted a fragment of his will.

The spaces between the shapes, glyphs, and sigils of white grew iridescent, like dew-dampened web strands as dawn first broke. He called upon his reserves, imbuing his creation with greater essence. It would be birthed closer to the edge of sentience, to serve him better.

Sau'ilahk's hand began to waver in his sight. Everything faded black for an instant. Exhaustion threatened to drag him into dormancy. He exerted more will to remain present, and he straightened, lifting his hand from the floor.

All glowing marks upon the stone vanished.

He whispered only with his thoughts. *Awaken!*

Another glow rose beneath the passage's floor.

Mute and pale yellow, it shifted erratically, darting about as if something swam through stone beneath the passage's floor. Sau'ilahk raised his hand higher, fingers closing like a street puppeteer toying with strings.

The glow halted. The floor bulged above it, like gray mud about to belch a bubble of noxious gas. And the light emerged—and winked at him.

A single eyelid nictitated with a soft click of stone as it closed and opened over a lump of molten-formed glass. Its oblong stone body holding that glass eye surfaced next and rose. Three small holes on either side of that mass were marked by small rippling warps of air where it would take any sound it heard. It stood up on four legs of thin rock, each three jointed, with pointed ends. Where those ends touched the floor, small ripples spread in rings, like those created by an insect shifting nervously upon a still gray pond.

Then it bolted for the passage wall.

No . . . no return for you . . . until I wish it!

The stone-spider skittered to a halt and began to quiver. Whirling around, that lump of glass eye opened wide, fixing upon him, and its light shifted to hot red. The servitor dashed straight at him.

Sau'ilahk curled his fingers, crushing their tips into his palm.

Obey!

The stone-spider halted, and quivers turned to shudders as that one eye burned with conscious rage.

Sau'ilahk sank his awareness into it.

Everything tinged red in the dim passage. Darker still was a black form of gently writhing cloak, robe, and cowl. He saw himself through the servitor's singular eye.

Very good . . . Follow the gray-clad one beyond the passage's end, but remain out of her awareness. You will not return until I recall you. Now go!

Sau'ilahk opened his clutching fingers, and the servitor rushed the wall once more.

It shot upward and across the passage's ceiling. Faint ripples in the stone marked its passing, like a fisher-spider darting across water.

Sau'ilahk watched it scurry out of the passage's top, and he drifted closer to the exit.

The walk back along Limestone Mainway seemed longer than Wynn remembered. But as she passed the greeting house, someone called from the mainway's end chamber.

"Wynn!"

Chane's raspy voice brought some comfort, and Wynn quickened her pace. He trotted to meet her. Noble Dead he might be, but he was always there for her.

"Did Ore-Locks come?" he asked. "How was it at the smithy?"

"Brutal," she answered. "I may have lost him, even more than Sliver."

He shook his head. "How?"

Wynn briefly recounted what had happened, and then asked, "And you?"

"The duchess returned," he answered, "as you guessed. She is lodged at an inn off Breach Mainway, near the market."

Wynn took a deep breath, though her relief was small. At least one thing had worked out this night. They might yet follow the duchess and learn more of why she was here. In turn, perhaps something useful would come of that.

"Come," Chane insisted. "I will show you . . . before we return to our lodging."

He led the way back up the curving tunnel.

Wynn was tired by the time they approached Breach Mainway, but Chane suddenly stopped short of the end chamber. He turned sharply, staring past her down the curve, and Wynn followed his gaze.

She saw nothing but the tunnel's curving dark walls. Shade had stepped beyond them but returned to Wynn's side.

"What's wrong?" she asked.

Chane's brow furrowed. He looked all around, as if uncertain what he searched for.

"I thought I heard something," he whispered. "A click on stone."

He stepped farther downslope, looking beyond the curve.

"Shade would've heard it too," Wynn said. "It was probably just an echo of her claws on the floor."

Chane glanced over at her and then turned back. Wynn fell in beside him as they stepped out into Breach Mainway.

This level looked much like the one above, where the station was. Or at least, it did until she walked into a section where the ceiling rose out of sight. A gigantic gash lunged upward into the mountain above. She'd never noticed that before in all their hurrying about.

As they reached another left-side passage, Chane stepped close to the mainway's wall. Peeking down the side tunnel, he pulled her across to its right side.

"The third frontage on the left," he whispered, and pointed the way.

Wynn peered in. About to step around for a better look, she caught sight of a flash of chestnut hair that made her freeze.

The duchess stepped out of a shop farther down the way. She carried what looked like a thick, bulky comforter and headed up the passage with one of her bodyguards. With so few others about, her voice carried all the way to Wynn.

"This should help old Chuillyon," she said. "He hardly sleeps at all on these hard dwarven beds."

The bodyguard didn't answer, and they turned into the third frontage, exactly where Chane had pointed.

"Earlier," he whispered, "her boots and cloak's hem were soaked with seawater. I could smell it."

"Seawater?" Wynn whispered.

Her head began to pound. She and Shade still hadn't eaten. But a memory stolen from the duchess, of a strange room with a grate beyond a pool, pushed itself up in Wynn's head.

As if someone else had forced it there.

Wynn glanced down and found Shade watching her.

Something had moved in that dark adjoining space beyond the grated pool's chamber.

"We should return to our inn," she said quietly. "Arrange for supper and then talk." Looking up at Chane, she added, "We have to change tactics . . . again."

Wynn paid the innkeeper for two bowls of chowder and carried them back to the room, closing the door with her hip. It was good to be alone with Shade and Chane for a little while. She set one bowl on the floor for Shade, who hungrily lapped it up, and then sat on the solid dwarven bed.

"You should eat too," Chane said, settling on the bed's end.

She was too weary to argue—or too preoccupied to eat. While Shade finished, Wynn reiterated all that had transpired with Ore-Locks. Chane listened carefully, then shifted a bit closer.

"You did as well as you could," he said. "You lured him out and may have offered something he wants, though he would not . . . trade for it. It reasons that he would place loyalty above personal desire, if he holds his calling above his family. Perhaps in dwelling on it, he may yet reconsider."

His reassurance changed nothing, but it made her feel less defeated.

"I may have broken their family," Wynn whispered.

"That is nothing. Families are destroyed every day—and some do not deserve to be saved."

His coldness stunned her. She knew almost nothing about Chane's past.

"Do any of your family still live?" she asked.

"My father, as far as I know." He looked away. "Viscount Andraso of Rùrik, halfway up the peninsula from Bela toward Guèshk. My mother took her own life shortly after I encountered Toret, my maker, who was also called Ratboy. Considering my father's treatment, death was a blessing to my mother."

Wynn was dumbstruck, uncertain what to say. Another notion occurred, perhaps to avoid his last words.

"When your father . . . passes over," she asked, "won't you inherit his title, lands . . . fortune?"

Chane laughed without smiling. His maimed voice made the sounds come out like quick, hoarse pants.

"Toret took my meager wealth, for all you saw that he owned in Bela. I am the only heir of the Andraso, but the dead don't inherit from the dead. And even if . . . I doubt I would be recognized by the nobility."

"Well, if I muck up my next idea," Wynn said, "you might at least have someplace to run when I end up in a Calm Seatt prison."

Chane's eyes narrowed. "What are you up to now?"

"In a moment," she said, glancing at Shade.

Shade had finished supper and was trying to lick the last taste from the bowl. Wynn snapped her fingers, and Shade raised her head. With one hopeful look at the bowl, the dog padded over to butt Wynn's hand with her snout.

Wynn slid her fingers over Shade's head and closed her eyes, passing memories of Duchess Reine. She followed this with bits and pieces of the dripping corridor that she could remember—the one leading to the chamber with the iron grate half-submerged in a pool of seawater.

Shade echoed the image back, and much more clearly.

"I'm seeing through Reine's memory, through her eyes," Wynn said quietly for Chane. "She is down so deep the walls are constantly damp and glistening, and the only light I've noticed is the glow of minerals coating the walls."

She began describing all she'd seen: how Reine had gone to the chamber with the pool, how it was locked, and about the side chamber Reine had never entered. She most carefully described the half-filled dark tunnel that stretched outward beyond the iron grate.

Wynn kept her eyes closed, focusing on sharp details that Shade provided. She felt the bed's stiff, padded layers flex as Chane shifted even closer.

"A pool filled with seawater . . . from a tunnel?" he asked quietly, but his voice was filled with urgency. "Fresh seawater?"

Wynn let herself sink deeper into Shade's stolen memory. She breathed in as if she were Reine within that moment, and the scent of brine filled her nostrils.

"I think so. The water seems clear and clean, not fetid, though its too dim in the chamber to be certain. It just smells like the sea. Strangely, though the chamber itself is damp, it doesn't smell moldy."

With her eyes still closed, she asked, "Do you understand what I'm thinking?"

Chane didn't answer, and Shade moved forward through the memory.

So deep inside Reine's recollection, Wynn felt sudden anguish. Again she heard something move in the dark side chamber, as before. She opened her eyes, still holding Shade.

"Clever girl," she murmured, and then turned to Chane. "This place that the duchess went to . . . it must be in the Stonewalkers' underworld."

"Another guess," he countered, but he rose and began pacing the room. "Wherever it is, the tunnel may connect to the open sea . . . and the shore."

For comfort's sake, he'd undressed down to breeches and a white shirt once they'd returned. How he could stand barefoot on the cold floor was beyond her. His feet were so pale . . . paler than his face and hands.

"We have to find that outside entrance," she said flatly.

Chane shook his head. "If the chamber *is* in the underworld, I hardly think these Stonewalkers would provide easy access. The tunnel might not be large enough—"

"Then why a grated opening into the pool?" she asked. "One obviously large enough to pass through, though it's blocked."

"The entrance could just as easily be underwater. We do not know for certain where below this massive mountain to find such a—"

"Oh, stop it!" she chided. "I know that *you* know we're going to try anyway. And . . . you want to."

Chane fell silent. Finally, he replied, "With all the insurmountable obstacles so far, we should not expect this pursuit to be any better."

Wynn merely waited—until he sighed. For the first time, she noted how odd that was, considering the dead didn't need to breathe.

"Clearly the duchess is a liaison between the royals and Stonewalkers," he said, "as well as between the royals and the guild. It reasons that she also fulfills the third side of that triangle—at least in relation to the texts. We cannot afford to lose track of her if this new endeavor comes to nothing. You stay here and keep watch on her."

Wynn jumped to her feet.

"You mean you can move faster without me," she accused. "Or you're worried it might be dangerous, and I should keep out of the way."

A flash of guilt on his long, clean features confirmed both.

"It will take some time," he added. "If I find something, I will return and take you—"

"This is my purpose, Chane," Wynn cut in. "I left the guild because I was sick of taking orders from people who thought they knew better . . . and didn't!"

Chane's lips parted, but Wynn kept at him.

"You may be more aware than they are, but that doesn't mean you understand as much as I do—and I don't take orders from you, either!"

"Fine. Then you decide," he returned. "But one of us needs to stay—and watch the duchess."

Wynn turned away, still angry, but only because he was right. "People died in Calm Seatt," she said, "because I was . . . obedient . . . and didn't resist until too late."

She heard him step closer, and his voiceless whisper softened.

"You know this part of the world. I do not. For what little success we have had, your instincts have often been better."

Wynn glanced at him, already hearing a "but" coming, though she knew the right decision.

"I have the better senses," he added, "sight and scent . . . and hearing. But I would have the harder time following the duchess, considering I tower over everyone here."

"All right," Wynn relented, "but take Shade. She has the more acute sense of smell where older scents are concerned. Two can search more quickly than one."

For an instant she thought he would argue, likely thinking she would be left unprotected. Perhaps her fixed stare made him think better of saying so.

"Can you make Shade understand?" he asked. "Make her leave you and go with me?"

"I'll try."

Chane left to gather his things, and Wynn dropped before Shade, touching the dog's face.

She began with memories of Leesil and Chap traveling together. She then turned to their own trials in Calm Seatt, before battling the wraith, when she had left Shade in Chane's company.

Shade snarled and pulled away, and Wynn had to grab her neck.

Wynn raised the image of the chamber and its pool. Working with a memory that had come to her thirdhand was difficult. She tried to focus upon the water-filled tunnel beyond the grate.

The door opened, and Chane stood in the hallway fully dressed and armed. Reaching around the door, he set the old tin scroll case on the side table, leaving it in Wynn's care.

Wynn lifted Shade's muzzle and pointed at Chane.

Shade snarled again. Instead of pulling away, this time she dropped to her haunches, grinding her foreclaws on stone.

Wynn held Shade's face and tried again.

"Please understand," she said.

Shade growled, but it quickly turned to a soft whine. She peered at Chane, swung her nose back to Wynn, and then pulled away. Shade trotted toward the door, and Chane outside. Wynn sighed in relief.

Shade swerved suddenly and headed straight for the sun-crystal staff leaning against the wall.

Before Wynn could get up, the dog rose on hind legs, forelegs braced on the wall. She clamped her jaws on the staff as high as she could reach.

"Shade?" Wynn called. "Shade . . . stop that!"

Shade twisted off the wall. The instant her paws landed, she trotted off, dragging the staff behind the bed's far side.

Wynn clambered across the bed, reaching for the staff. Shade dropped it, planting both huge forepaws atop its haft.

"What is wrong with you?" Wynn demanded, grabbing for the staff.

She jerked it from under Shade's paws and backed across the bed. Before she got halfway, Shade clamped its haft with her teeth and heaved.

Wynn flopped facedown on the bed. "Let go!"

Shade growled and heaved again.

Wynn shot headfirst over the bed's side, hanging upside down below a stubborn Shade.

"I should go alone," Chane said. "She does not want to leave you."

No, that wasn't it. Shade *was* trying to tell her something else, but at the moment, Wynn didn't care.

"Give it to me!" she growled through clenched teeth.

Wynn twisted over, slapping at Shade's legs while her own were still hooked over the bed's edge. In that upside-down tug-of-war, she finally twisted the staff out of Shade's mouth. When the dog tried to grab it again, she scrambled away across the bed.

Shade hopped up and began barking, and Wynn finally realized what this was all about.

She rarely went anywhere without the staff. Shade had pinned it down, trying to insist that Wynn "stay put" in this room.

"I'm following the duchess!" Wynn growled back. "You are going with Chane. Now get!"

With a sharp huff through wrinkled jowls, Shade bounded off and out past Chane, rumbling all the way. Wynn exhaled in frustration, though Chane just shook his head and closed the door. She got up, brushing herself off, and went to return the staff to its place.

She was sick and tired of everyone telling her what to do or not do, even a dog now. She snatched the scroll case off the table and headed for the bed. Then she froze in the middle of the room.

Wynn turned very slowly and stared at the door.

She imagined Chane following a peeved Shade. Not Shade following Chane, but rather . . . the petulant, adolescent majay-hì had been leading the way.

"Oh . . . oh, you . . ." Wynn began, unable to get the words out.

She ran for the door, jerked it open, and rushed out.

Chane and Shade were already gone, but Wynn still knew one thing: She had shown Shade what needed to be done, but the dog had given up only once Wynn had lost her temper and ordered Shade out . . . using language, not memory-speak! And how could Shade have understood what Wynn planned to do as her own task while Chane—and Shade—were away?

Wynn clutched the scroll case hard. "You little sneak . . . just like your father!"

Shade had understood words—at least enough to know exactly what Wynn planned to do.

All this time wrestling with memory-speak until her head ached—and now it seemed Shade understood at least some of what she heard. Wynn stepped back inside and slammed the door.

"Oh . . . I've got some choice *words* for you . . . when you get back!"

Sau'ilahk heard and saw through his servitor half-submerged in the ceiling stone of Wynn's room. He quickly recalled it.

The servitor rose from the inn's side wall, surfacing like a four-legged spider from mottled gray water. Sau'ilahk reached out with one solidified hand and snatched its rock body.

Wynn, Chane, and Shade were on the move again, but along separate ways.

The scroll case had also caught his attention. But it was only one text among many, a paltry resource compared to others. Clutching his conjured creation, Sau'ilahk slid out toward the mainway.

In the distance, Chane and Shade headed toward Sea-Side's entrance cavern and the lift down to its lower port. The conversation regarding one called Ore-Locks had confused him. But he had forgotten all about the Iron-Braids once he heard mention of the duchess.

An Âreskynna—"Kin of the Ocean Waves"—if only by marriage, was here in the seatt. This good fortune was almost unbelievable. Duchess Reine had acted for the royals in Calm Seatt, and they were directly connected to the guild superiors and the translation project.

Sau'ilahk half submerged into the inn's wall, pulling his servitor with him. He waited there, watching for Wynn to emerge. When she did, he merely blinked along after her, slipping in and out of dormancy as his servitor scuttled and swam high along the mainway's walls.

Wynn finally paused on the next level down and peered into a side passage.

Reine Faunier-Âreskynna stepped from a shop.

Sau'ilahk knew her face. She had helped protect his interests at the guild, keeping that city captain at bay in his investigation. The nature of the texts had remained secret, in the guild's control. The translation folios had remained scattered about the city's scribe shops.

Until Wynn had intervened.

But he no longer needed her . . . not if the duchess could lead him right to the texts.

Sau'ilahk would soon be finished with one troublesome little sage.

CHAPTER 14

Chane overtook Shade and led the way to Sea-Side's outer cavern. Passing the turn into the tram station, he headed for the main entrance. Unlike Bay-Side's larger one, there was no true market here, only a few scattered vendors with carts servicing patrons on their way in or out.

He stepped out of the huge archway and onto the mountainside street, and Shade pulled up silently beside him. The pair found themselves in the settlement's surface district overlooking the vast western ocean.

Sea-Side was less developed than Bay-Side. The narrow main street switchbacking up the mountain appeared steeper and more haphazard by comparison. Still, it was lined with varied buildings of stone, built in thin-line fitted blocks or carved from the mountain's rock. Directly ahead at the narrow plateau's edge was another crank house and lift station.

Shade began rumbling as Chane steeled his resolve. These dwarven contraptions were the most unnatural method of travel he had ever experienced.

"Come on," he rasped.

Shade's ears pricked over a wrinkled snout, and Chane realized he had picked up Wynn's habit of talking as if the dog understood.

He pulled out his pouch, pouring dwarven and Numan coins into his palm. He had no idea how much was proper for the trip down to shore level. As they approached the station, an impossibly wide dwarf waddled out of the crank house. How this whale of a stationmaster even fit through a dwarven doorway was a wonder. Wild hair tinted like redwood bark swung around his face, and a like-colored beard was dotted with oats. Perhaps he had been sharing a meal with his mules.

"Down?" he grunted. "How far?"

Chane held out his coins. "To the port."

The stationmaster grunted again and plucked a dwarven iron "slug" from Chane's palm. When he glanced at Shade, with a twitch of his bulbous nose he pecked out a copper one as well. He waved Chane toward the lift, not bothering to escort one lone passenger.

No one else waited to descend and Chane saw no passenger lift as at Sea-Side. There was only one large cargo lift, and he stepped quietly aboard. As he turned, about to close the lift's gate, Shade was lingering on the stone loading ramp.

Her head hung low. Rumbling, with every slow paw pad, she finally followed. Chane had barely closed and pinned the gate when metal clanks sounded from the crank house. At the lift's first lurch, he grabbed the rail with both hands, wood creaking under his fingers. An instant later, mountainside crags and gashes began rushing by.

Speed built quickly—too quickly—until they dropped far faster than the ride up to Bay-Side. Thunderous racket rose under the platform from its massive wheels boring along the granite road's steel-lined ruts. It was not just the sound—the vibrations shuddered through Chane's whole body. He felt as if he were being thrown down the mountain at the waiting rocky shore below. He thought he heard Shade gag over the lift's raucous noise.

He did not want to look.

The lift passed two lower settlements, but neither had a station where passengers transferred to another lift. Sea-Side's one cargo lift went all the way down, and those brief settlements blurred by in a rush.

Chane's only comfort was in knowing that—one way or another—the lift would eventually stop. When it finally slowed, then bumped into a wall-less station at the port's back, he shuddered in the silent cloud-laced night.

No one came out to check on arriving passengers. Perhaps on this side of the mountain fees were collected only above. Chane unbolted the gate with shaky hands, stepped down the loading ramp, and then stopped halfway.

Shade still stood at the lift's center. With her ears flattened and her head low and her legs splayed in a braced stance, a stream of drool trailed from her panting jaws to puddle on the platform's boards.

"It is over," he said. "Come."

Smelling sea air, he looked upward along the steep granite road. The peninsula's ocean side was more sheer and rough than the bay side. But the slant down into the open ocean was likely why full-size ships could dock here.

Other than a few warehouses framing a main avenue to the docks, buildings were sparse and deeply weathered. The shoreline, however, could never be called a beach.

Endless waves pounded and sprayed upon jagged rocks at the mountain's base. And Chane wavered at the chance of finding some small, hidden entrance in leagues of sea-battered rock. Just which way—north or south—should he begin?

Shade growled and then sniffed sharply, as she too gazed along the shore.

"A room first," Chane said, more to himself than the dog.

Shade stared upward toward Sea-Side's main settlement, probably still doubtful of leaving Wynn alone. Chane snapped his fingers to gain the dog's attention and stepped in between the warehouses.

Only a few dwarven dockworkers were about. A cluster of human sailors languished beneath a dangling lantern. He spotted only two single-masted vessels until he cleared the buildings and reached the heads of the piers. One larger ship rested farther out, near the end of the leftmost dock.

Its two masts were as tall as those of larger vessels he had seen in Calm Seatt. With all sails furled, it appeared to be quietly waiting. This had to be the duchess's vessel. If she stayed in Sea-Side, then her ship would have docked here. The other two smaller ones did not seem fitting.

Shade huffed once.

She trotted past the docks' heads, and Chane turned and followed. She finally dropped to her haunches to wait. When he caught up, she sat before a stone building, squat-looking though it was still two stories tall. Peering through the outer windows, Chane saw people inside, some with tankards in hand or seated for a meal at tables. With two stories, it might be an inn, or something like it among the dwarves.

Chane scrutinized Shade, though the dog ignored him. Perhaps she understood his intention, if not his words. It should have been a small relief, but it only made Chane warier.

What else did Shade know or understand?

Wynn returned to her room after making certain that Duchess Reine had retired for the night. Alone for the first time since Chane had reentered her life, Wynn crawled into bed early and slept hard. She needed to be up and alert by dawn, if she was to follow Reine's movements by day. In the morning, as the innkeeper's knock came at the door, she awoke feeling more herself.

She wasn't certain why, but there was something liberating about awaking in the day, even in a world without sunlight. As she rolled out of bed, stretching sore muscles from another night on a hard dwarven mattress, she wondered how to begin. She was worried about Shade—and Chane—but there was no way to know whether they'd arrived safely and acquired lodging.

Wynn looked at her gray robe lying across the bed's corner. Anyone in the duchess's entourage would spot her in an instant wearing that. But her yellow and umber elven clothing on a short human would attract as much attention. A notion came to her.

She donned the clothing, pulled the robe on as well, and then wandered out toward the inn's front room. Perhaps she could trade for or borrow something more from the dwarven innkeeper? She could then spend the day blending in with the locals—and watching for the duchess.

"Yes," she said softly to herself. "A dwarven disguise."

That night, just past dusk, Chane awoke in the portside inn. Shade sat poised at the door, watching him, as if she had done so all day. Chane scowled at her.

If Shade was as intelligent as Wynn claimed, did the dog find it strange—suspicious—that he slept all day? Young as she was, and aside from protecting Wynn, how much could Shade really know of the undead?

He rolled from bed and began dressing in salt-stiffened clothes.

The previous night they had scouted the rocky shore. Time had passed too quickly, and he had grown fearful. When he sensed dawn's approach, they backtracked to the inn, both of them soaked with sea spray. He procured a dry blanket for Shade before removing his wet clothing.

The blanket still lay in the room's far corner, only a little damp from the dog.

Shade growled and scratched at the door.

"A moment," he muttered.

An entire night now awaited them. Chane had to find the tunnel entrance—or be certain it did not exist within reach.

Wynn blamed herself for their failures, but he had not been much help to her. In truth, what little success they counted was mostly Shade's doing, ferreting out secrets from the memories of others. For the first time since reaching Dhredze Seatt, Chane was in a position to *do* something.

Between an undead and a majay-hì, he hoped the gap might not be so wide. Perhaps Wynn was enough common ground for Shade to put aside natural instinct, should she learn anything certain of what he truly was.

His clothes were not completely dry, but he would be soaked again soon enough. He donned his cloak, pulled up the hood, and wished he did not have to carry two packs. But he was not about to leave them behind.

Shade scratched the door again.

"I am coming," he said.

Opening the door, he followed as she trotted out. When they reached the common room, he paused to purchase a slat of smoked fish. He fed this to Shade as they traversed the port, passed the last pier, and climbed out onto the northward rocky shore.

It was a guess, considering he had no idea which direction was adjacent to the grate-covered tunnel of Shade's stolen memory. But north seemed more likely, by estimate of Off-Breach Market's position above in Sea-Side. It was a while before they reached where they had left off the night before.

Shade led the way, her eyes half-closed against wind that did little to ruffle her salt-stiffened fur. Soon enough, sea spray dampened them both. Chane carefully examined every inch they crossed while Shade nosed ahead.

They were utterly alone. No one else had reason to scramble across the sheer, barren edge between stone and sea. Often he had to climb or crawl on all fours over outcrops and through crags in their slow progress. His cloak grew heavy as it soaked in more spray.

When he pushed back his sagging hood and peered up, the waning moon, barely a sliver of light, had finally crested the peak above. The night was half gone. Amid the surf's noise, he had not heard any dwarven bells on the mountain ringing out the passing time.

Chane paused and looked back the way they had come.

Whatever lanterns hung upon the piers or docked ships were too far off to see, and panic crept in. The return would be quicker without searching, but if they did not turn back soon, he would be caught by the dawn. He had seen few crevices along the way large enough to hide him from the sun.

Shade barked three times from ahead, and Chane spun about.

His foot slipped on broken rocks and slid down before he regained balance.

Shade barked again, but with his sight fully widened, Chane still saw no sign of her. She suddenly appeared over the top of a steep rock backbone sloping down into the pounding surf. She stood perfectly still, waiting.

What little hope rose in Chane only heightened his fear of going farther from port, but he scrambled onward. As he climbed the backbone, Shade climbed down its far side. He crested it quickly, peering into a deep inlet, and his hopes sank.

The inlet cut so deep into the shore's steep slant that its back was pitch-black. There was no place to follow the rolling waterline. They would have to climb high upslope to get around it. The whole venture became more dangerous with half the night gone, but Shade kept crawling along the inlet's steep side.

"Get back here!" he called, though his rasp was barely audible over waves and wind.

Shade clawed along the water's edge, deeper into the inlet, and Chane dropped down the rocky backbone, boots scraping on wet rock. Waves broke and tumbled well before they reached the inlet's back, so it had to be shallow. It was still not something to wade across in the dark. Shade suddenly shuffled sideways, trying to get upslope as dark foam-laced water surged upward around her legs.

"Shade!" Chane called.

He gripped slick rock with his slope-side hand and pushed on.

Turning only her head, Shade barked at him and then gazed toward the inlet's back. As he came up behind her, the darkness in the inlet looked different. The rock above it did not meet the water's surface. A rough overhang created a low and wide opening over the undulating water.

The cave, or pocket, was half-filled by the sea.

Chane looked to the moon and then down into the water. There was no telling its depth.

Shade huffed at him, sounding impatient, and then pricked up her ears. Peering at the low cave, she cocked her head to the side and whined loudly. She barked once and began backing unsteadily across the backbone's side.

"What?" Chane called tiredly.

Shade backed another step, stopping only when she could go no farther without running into him. Clearly she had decided this was not what they sought. But Chane had to be certain and stepped down the sheer rock. He hesitated before he sank one booted foot into the dark, undulating water.

When he found his footing, he dropped waist-high into the water. Clinging to the backbone's side, he inched into the inlet until his eyes adjusted to its deeper darkness. Still, he could not see to its back, but he heard water slapping against stone somewhere deeper beneath the overhang. Shade's actions now made sense.

She had been listening for the path of the water flowing unobstructed. Even without entering, she had known there was no opening beneath the overhang.

Chane backed out in dejection and clawed up the backbone's side. Shade was already moving on. Scrabbling upslope, she began nosing out a way around the inlet, and Chane struggled after her.

They should have turned back, but the prospect of failure overrode reason.

Chane searched every nook, crack, and hollow, making certain they did not miss a single hole or odd patch of pure black. He forgot how dangerously far they had pushed on until he heard faint, distant bell tones rolling down the mountainside.

He froze, counting off the five tones.

The fifth eighth of night, by the dwarves' measure of time, and they had found nothing. Fear pulled reason back through frustration. He could push his body until morning if need be, but even now, he was uncertain whether he could reach the inn before sunrise. How could he fail Wynn in this task?

"Shade!"

He knelt on the rock as the dog paused ahead, glancing back at him. To his bewilderment, she looked up at the sky—no, up the mountainside to the moon glowing behind thin night clouds. Did she understand that they traveled by night out of more than choice? If she knew that much, then . . .

A huge wave hit the shore.

Spray rose high and slapped down around Chane, drenching him. When his sight line cleared, Shade faced him within arm's reach. One jowl twitched beneath her cold, intense gaze, and she never blinked.

"Do you know?" he whispered.

If she did know what he was, why had she never attacked him outright? If she did not, why did she always wrinkle her snout and glare at him?

Chane had to head back immediately—but Shade did not.

Indecision made him falter. Somehow, he had to make her understand. If his suspicion was correct, and she knew his true nature, then letting her see into his memories would change nothing. If he was wrong, one of them would end here—or at best, he would have to flee. What would become of Wynn without him?

Chane grew frantic.

Finding a sea tunnel to the underworld might be the only chance they had left. If he and Shade did not succeed, Wynn's mission ended in failure. There was only one way to tell Shade to go on without him—and he knew only one way that could happen.

Chane rose on his knees, his thumb already rubbing the ring on his finger. He locked eyes with Shade, but hesitated as he pinched the ring between the fingers of his other hand.

He pulled off the ring of nothing.

Shade shimmered before Chane's eyes, as did the sloped rocky shore, like an intense heat across a plain making the horizon blur. Another wave's arcing spray crashed down on both of them.

Salt water ran off Chane's face. He shuddered, not from cold but as all his awareness sharpened threefold. He had not removed the ring since first entering Calm Seatt, moons past. He had almost forgotten how much it dampened his awareness. It felt like coming alive again—or at least how he might have imagined such a thing.

And there were Shade's blue crystalline eyes, burning too brightly in his widened vision.

Shade snarled, her jowls pulling back and exposing all of her teeth. Her shoulders bunched, and even soaked as she was, her hackles rose. Shade snapped the air, her teeth clacking.

Chane went completely still—he had made a grave error.

The dog's rolling snarl took on a pealing mewl, like a cat's enraged yowl caught in its throat. Her ears flattened as her whole body quaked under that sound.

But Shade remained where she stood.

Her snarls lessened, becoming no more than low growls.

"You knew . . ." Chane whispered. "All this time."

For an instant, he could not even think how. Either Shade's own senses, so much like Wynn's old companion Chap's, had sensed he was not natural, or . . .

Had Shade caught some slip in Wynn's memories?

The dog had not attacked him, as one of her kind should. She had even fought beside him against the wraith—in defending Wynn.

How could he tell Shade what he needed her to do now?

He tried to think of memories, of any instance in which he had protected Wynn, as well as moments of *searching* since the three of them had come together. There was also the small room at the inn to which he would have to return and wait. But he had no memory like the one Wynn had spoken of—a grated iron opening that let the sea rise in an underground chamber. All he could think of in its place was the one overhang that Shade had already found, though it had proved false for what they sought.

Shade grew strangely silent, watching him.

Once Chane was clear on which memories he would have to use, he reached out.

Shade twisted on the slope and snapped at his wrist.

He snatched his hand back. He was not certain how this process worked, but Wynn had so often touched the dog that it seemed necessary.

"I must," he said, reaching out again. "I must be sure you understand! You have to go on and . . . look for the entrance, damn you!"

His head suddenly filled with a memory.

In the dwarven port's inn, in that small dark room, a lantern sat beside a narrow bed and a damp folded blanket in one corner.

Chane drew back in hesitation. He had not been thinking about that as he spoke.

Shade fell silent. Her left jowl quivered and she spun away.

Chane only watched as she clawed and hopped away, up the dark coast beneath the erratic spray of the sea. She stopped only once upon a crest of rock, and it seemed her head swung back his way.

Then all he could think of was the room at the inn.

As much as Wynn claimed that Shade was fully sentient, the truth of it had never quite settled upon him until now. She was telling him to go back.

Turning south, Chane scrambled toward the port.

Wynn heard the fifth bell of the second day—past noon—in following the duchess and her entourage. No one recognized her from afar.

She had two bedsheets tied about her waist, beneath her robe, and an oversize dwarven cloak borrowed from the innkeeper. Unless someone peered too closely, she looked stout enough to pass for a young, rather skinny dwarf. But she was beginning to regret giving in to Chane and staying behind.

In the first place, she had learned nothing. Reine spent most of her time hiding away in her inn, leaving Wynn to mill around the mainway and wait. A problematic pursuit, as no one else spent so much time loitering in plain sight. Secondly, and more important, she hated being cut off, blinded as to her companions' whereabouts and well-being.

Was Shade all right? How had Chane fared on his own among the dwarves? And had they found any tunnel entrance?

Wynn's disguise had proven adequate, but she began to think her task was a waste of time. How long could she pretend to wait for someone before anyone noticed? One set of dwarves in heavy furs had passed by more than once. The same pair of clan constables had already come and gone three times that morning. As she was about to give up and work out some other ploy, someone stepped out of the inn down the side tunnel.

Duchess Reine emerged in polished boots, breeches, and a front-split deep teal skirt. Her elven companion, as always, was nearly covered by his white robe and cowl. All three Weardas followed, and the small group marched straight toward the mainway.

Wynn ducked back and flattened against the wall, lowering her head until the cloak's hood hung over her eyes. She waited, not moving as she watched their feet tromp by. Once they were well down the way, she followed as closely as she dared.

When they turned into the passage to Off-Breach Market, she held back until they passed the first stalls. It wasn't until she caught up that she noticed the elf carrying a small piece of parchment and a sharpened stick of writing charcoal wrapped in scrap paper. Reine moved about the market, trading dwarven slugs for a blanket, a tin kettle, and a coil of stout rope.

Whatever the items were for, the elf stroked the parchment as if marking off acquisitions. Wynn slipped behind a candle maker's booth, close enough to hear them.

"Extra bread loaves would not be amiss," the elf said in his lilting, reedy voice. "Best not tax our hosts' resources, if we are to be down there several days."

Wynn stiffened, lifting her head a bit too much. They were heading below to the Stonewalkers—for days, it seemed—and she would lose them!

"I'm aware of the time," the duchess answered. "With every passing year, I can almost feel the highest tide coming."

A breath's pause followed.

"But yes," she said, "let's see about bread . . . and perhaps dried fruits."

They all headed back toward the market's entrance, where vendors of food and dry goods had set up their stalls. Wynn wove her way around the market, glancing twice toward its rear and the passages leading into the level's outer reaches.

She could think of no way to remain unnoticed in following, once they headed off for the hidden entrance to the underworld. But after acquiring several loaves, the captain turned and escorted the duchess toward the market's exit to Breach Mainway.

Wynn slipped along behind the booths one path over. As the entourage neared the exit, the duchess spoke again.

"We have everything reasonable we might need. Please make certain I'm not disturbed until tomorrow night. I need . . . time."

"Of course," the elf answered, and they all left.

Wynn didn't follow, knowing they now headed back to their inn. Apparently the duchess was holing up until tomorrow night. She would then go below for days. How many, how long—and why? There seemed no reason for it, and the only thing that came to mind were the ancient texts.

Wynn racked her brain for any way to spy on the duchess inside the inn. She needed to learn what Reine was doing here, and how she and the royal family were connected to the Stonewalkers. If they guarded the texts, and could somehow move them to and from the guild every day—over a distance of three days' shore-side journey—what purpose did the duchess serve here?

Wynn couldn't think of a way to find the answers—not without getting herself arrested. There was no point in lingering.

Grimacing, Wynn headed back to her own inn.

Chane awoke and lay quietly for an instant, uncertain where he was. The previous night filtered back into his thoughts. He rose quickly, swinging his legs over the bed's edge, and looked around, still dazed from dormancy.

"Shade?"

She was not present, but then how could she be? He had barely reached the inn on the edge of dawn, just in time to bolt into his room and fall dormant upon the bed. His clothes had dampened the blankets, as he had not bothered to undress. He picked up his cloak and left. The instant he stepped outside, he called out.

"Shade!"

Outside the inn, two husky-looking dwarves glanced his way, but Chane did not care. He looked for Shade, at a loss for how to find her, let alone whether she had yet returned.

The last of evening activities still filled the port. Another ship had docked far out on one pier. Its strange curled prow and central row of towering triangular sails caught his attention. Long ship's oars were raised upright along its rail.

Dwarven dockworkers were hauling huge bales and barrels down the pier from the vessel. Among them were short and dark-skinned Suman passengers or crew in long, flowing vestments and cloth head wraps. Though they stood a head taller than the dwarves, they were not as tall as Wynn's Suman confederate, Domin il'Sänke.

The night was even darker than the last, the moon still hidden behind the peninsula's high peak. Tomorrow, it would be invisible, even when it crested—a new moon. As the night was his world, he used to pay more attention to such things. Right now, he did not care.

"Shade?"

A low huff reached his ears.

Chane twisted left at the sound, and Shade came padding down the street. To his surprise, he felt a pang of guilt that she had been locked out all day. But she trotted right past him.

"Shade?"

The dog kept on, heading for the main road—the one that led to the lift.

"Get back here!" he called.

Shade paused at the corner, looking over her shoulder at him, and then slipped out of sight.

Chane bolted back into the inn and ran for his room. After retrieving his packs, he tossed coins on the counter for the innkeeper, waiting only long enough to see that they were sufficient. Then he rushed out.

When he rounded the corner, there was Shade, sitting at the bottom of the loading ramp.

A pack of dwarves with cargo and a pair of Sumans in garish colors approached. All of them stopped at the sight of a "wolf" in their way.

"*Dhêb!*" snarled a full-bearded Suman.

When the man reached for the hilt of an arced sword cradled in his waist wrap, Chane pushed through.

"She is mine!" he said, stepping in front of Shade. "She will not cause any trouble."

One dwarf with hair cropped to bristles grimaced at him. He whispered something to his closest companion, who in turn spoke directly to the pair of Sumans, presumably in their own tongue. Chane glanced back.

Shade wandered up to the lift under the suspicious eyes of what had to be the stationmaster. The dwarf stood silent, holding the gate open. Shade boarded with a disgruntled rumble and squatted in the platform's rear corner.

Chane stood looking at her in frustration while one Suman argued fervently with his dwarven companions. Finally, Chane boarded, stepping in next to Shade, still wishing he could somehow demand an answer. Dockworkers loaded up the platform, piling bales and barrels and crates to such width and height that Chane grew nervous about the weight. He glared down at Shade.

Had she found anything or had she given up, insisting on returning to Wynn?

Amid the fuss her presence too often caused, he had no way to find out. He would have to bear the ride up before this belligerent beast gave the answer to Wynn.

At the first bell past supper, Wynn sat on her room's floor holding the scroll's case in both hands. The duchess wasn't going anywhere tonight, and she felt at loose ends.

For two seasons at the guild she'd often sought little more than privacy. Being alone was her only relief. But a third night on her own in the seatt suddenly left her lonely. She felt strange, even incomplete.

With some reluctance, she admitted to herself that she missed Chane and Shade, that she worried for them in finding their way among the dwarves. Chane didn't even speak their language. And Shade . . .

Wynn began to feel spiteful again.

She had some choice words for that troublesome adolescent. There would be no more stubborn nonsense about *words* where Shade was concerned. Loneliness didn't break under righteous anger, but it felt like a weakness or a fault within her. She had a purpose to fulfill at any cost, even alone, if need be.

Wynn grasped the scroll case's cap but hesitated at pulling it off.

In the ice-covered castle atop the Pock Peaks, the first time she had seen this scroll, Li'kän had nearly ripped it off the shelf of the decaying library and shoved it at her. Wynn had thought Li'kän simply wished for her to read it aloud. Now she knew that was impossible.

That deceptively frail white monster had some other intention, considering the scroll's black coating over its writing. But Wynn hadn't seen inside the case that night. Li'kän dropped it, and later, Chane had found and taken it.

Why had Li'kän tried to give her this scroll case?

Wynn pulled off the pitted pewter cap and removed the contents.

The scroll itself was an ancient piece of hide, made pliable once more by Chane's painstaking efforts. But it was unreadable—at least by normal means. The inner surface was nearly black all the way to the edges, covered in ink that had set centuries ago.

Wynn carefully flattened it on the floor.

The words beneath the coating had been scripted in the fluids of an undead. Though ink and hide retained traces of the five Elements of Existence, those fluids would always be devoid of, or the negative aspect of, one—Spirit. Through her mantic sight, she could see what was missing as much as what was there. She'd already once glimpsed the ancient Suman characters beneath the coating.

This was how she'd begun her translation work back at the guild, memorizing as many of the Sumanese Iyindu characters as possible before her sight made her too sick. With Chane's aid, she'd jotted down those phrases and translated what she could. Domin il'Sänke had later assisted with corrections.

Reaching for her pack, Wynn pulled out her journals, her elven quill, and a small bottle of ink. If tonight would be spent in more solitude, she might as well do something useful. The poem hidden on the hide had been written by one of Li'kän's companions, either Häs'saun or Volyno. More likely Häs'saun—a Suman name.

Wynn reviewed her notes on the few phrases she'd glimpsed in the scroll:

Children . . . twenty-six steps

To hide . . . five corners

To anchor amid . . . the void

Consumes its own

Of the mountain under . . . the chair of a lord's song

Domin il'Sänke had corrected her translation of *min'bâl'alu*—"of a lord's song." What she'd thought was prepositional was actually an obscure Iyindu syntax with no comparison in her native Numanese. By context, it was pronounced differently than what was written, sounding like "min'bä'alâle." As well, the term *maj'att*—"chair"—should actually be translated as a general "seat" of any kind. Stranger still, its correct spelling didn't end with a doubled "t," as found in the scroll. The combined changes produced a startlingly familiar though all-but-forgotten Dwarvish term approximated in an ancient Sumanese dialect.

Min'bä'alâle maj'att . . . Bäalâle Seatt.

At the guild, she'd been given one day's access to translations so far completed. Through a very long day, and later realizations, she had uncovered other possible hints of meaning behind the poem's strange metaphors.

"Twenty-six steps" didn't refer to a distance but rather thirteen pairs of feet, thirteen individuals traveling. Wynn still didn't know what "five corners" meant, but she'd learned who the thirteen had been . . . or were.

Ancient vampires, perhaps the first Noble Dead of the world, called in'Ahtäben—the Children—had numbered thirteen. They'd served their Hkàbêv—Beloved—another term for the unknown being or force in the war of the Forgotten History. She knew other terms in varied Suman dialects for this forgotten enemy of many names, such as in'Sa'umar and il'Samar. . . .

The Night Voice.

Wynn had also uncovered names for at least five of the Children of Beloved. Li'kän, along with her missing companions, Häs'saun and Volyno, were among them. She only hoped, considering the white undead's long, inescapable isolation, that the latter two were somehow gone from this world. But there were others to account for, including a pair named Vespana and Ga'hetman.

So far, "to hide" *what* wasn't clear, but the Children had scattered near the end of the war. In the frozen castle an "orb"—for lack of a proper term—had been discovered. But where had the other ten Children gone, if any still existed, and why hadn't they accompanied Li'kän and her companions? What had "consumed its own" beneath lost Bäalâle Seatt? And more immediately, why had the wraith committed murder for the translation folios?

The wraith had attacked Wynn on several occasions, after Chane had brought the scroll to her. Had it known what was hidden therein?

Perhaps she'd overlooked *something* in her one brief glimpse of the scroll's content. But attempting to see the poem again meant raising her mantic sight. Tonight, she didn't have Domin il'Sänke or Chap—or even Shade—to help rid her of the sight, should something go wrong.

Wynn sat there, staring at the scroll's blackened surface and teetering between sensibility and overwhelming desire. As usual, curiosity tipped her one way. She set the scroll aside, extended her right index finger to draw a mental circle upon on the floor, and—the door burst open.

Chane rushed in behind Shade. Both halted at the sight of the scroll and Wynn's finger poised over the floor stones.

"What are you doing?" Chane demanded. "Are you trying to summon mantic sight all alone?"

The odor of the sea filled the room from her returned companions. Chane's clothing was stained in faint white shadows of dried salt, though much of him still looked damp. His hair was a mess, as was Shade's crusted charcoal-colored fur.

Shade crept over, sniffed the scroll, and wrinkled her jowls. Her glittering eyes narrowed on Wynn—the suspicion there was too much like what Wynn remembered from Chap.

She searched her companions' faces, caught between relief and trepidation over their venture.

"Did you find it?" she blurted out.

Chane scowled, matching Shade's disapproval over what they'd caught her doing.

"Maybe," he answered, and glared at Shade.

Wynn went numb. "What does that mean?"

"What are you doing?" Chane repeated. "I thought to find you near the market or the duchess's inn."

"Pointless," she answered, rolling up the scroll and tucking it back in its case. "Reine has retired until tomorrow night. Everyone with her is apparently waiting for something. They're going back down for days. I have no idea what's so special about tomorrow night."

"The new moon," Chane said, and before she asked, he shook his head. "Something I noticed while onshore. The moon will be invisible tomorrow night."

Wynn pondered this, though it didn't seem to mean anything. Stonewalkers would rarely see the sky or the moon.

"Never mind . . . did you find a way in or not?"

"Ask her," Chane replied, jutting his chin toward Shade.

Wynn blinked rapidly. How could Shade know but not Chane? Upon seeing her confusion, he explained all, up to the point when Shade led him back to the lift.

"She clearly wanted to return to you," he added.

Wynn put aside Shade's sneaky reluctance for language and crooked a finger at the dog.

"All right, you," she said. "Out with it, now!"

Shade approached and Wynn reached for the dog's face. At the touch, she raised a memory that Shade had shown her—of the grated opening beyond a sea pool in the sealed chamber that the duchess had visited.

In answer, Wynn's head swam with new images, scents, and sounds.

The smell of the sea was overpowering, as if it clogged her whole nose. She felt cold and damp all over. Even high up the shore's slope, the surf's spray kept hitting her. Her feet hurt, as if she'd been walking barefooted—bare-pawed—on broken stone all night.

Inside Shade's memory, Wynn looked down upon rock as she sniffed her way along the shore. Wet crags, cracks, and crevices glittered in her sight. She—Shade—glanced up.

The sky over the ocean was dimly lit. Dawn wasn't far off, though the sun couldn't have yet crested the eastern horizon beyond the mountain. Only Shade's superior sight allowed Wynn to see as much as she did. She felt and heard herself whine, and the sound was so frustrated and tired.

In the distance, too far off, she made out the port by its tallest buildings and the few moored ships. Instead of dipping her muzzle in continued search, Wynn turned back toward the port. Her pace quickened as much as shifting rocks would allow.

Wynn's own frustration and misery mounted on top of the memory. She let her hands drop from Shade's face at her own weak whisper.

"No . . . no."

"What did she find?" Chane rasped.

Wynn was too crestfallen to face him. Shade had found nothing. But when Wynn tried to lift her head to answer, Shade huffed. The dog dipped and wriggled her muzzle until Wynn's fingers slid down her neck.

The memory began again.

Down the shore, the port seemed nearer, but not by much. And Wynn—Shade—climbed higher up the shore to pass over a deep inlet. Then she stopped, pricked her ears, and listened. The sound of the water below seemed wrong.

She heard the undulating sea breach the inlet's shallows, and she crept dangerously close to look down. Waves broke out near the inlet's mouth, and below, she couldn't quite see the inlet's back.

A second memory flashed over this moment, from sometime much earlier during the night.

Wynn saw an inlet from along its southern-bordering rock ridge. At the back was a wide overhang barely a few feet above the water. She—Shade—listened as the water hit the cave's back somewhere in that deeper dark.

Then she was back in the previous memory.

She stood atop the overhang, and the sound had changed. It echoed. Not the soft reverberation of water undulating against the cave's back, as in that second overlaid memory. It was more rolling and extended, amplified in the space below.

The water in the inlet was shallower now, revealing the inlet's rocky floor.

Wynn scrambled across the inlet's top and down the backbone. She didn't stop until she was all the way along its inner slope and staring into the inlet. At low tide, the overhang was now well above the water's shifting surface. The change of the waves' sounds increased, becoming clearer. Wynn leaped off the backbone's edge into the cold water.

She sank chest-deep as all four paws fought for sure footing, and she heard . . .

A soft trickling, water flowing . . . *out* between sluggish inward surges.

She froze, waiting as water rolled inward, rising halfway up her hips and soaking her tail. When it receded, again she heard the hollow echo of water trickling out—as if from a deeper space.

Wynn lunged in beneath the dark overhang. When her nose finally struck the back wall, she recoiled, snorting and shaking her head. The dim light of predawn wasn't enough to see, but the water was now only halfway up her legs. She nosed carefully along the rough stone until . . . it wasn't there anymore.

Wynn—Shade—pulled back, startled, but the echo of trickling water was now loud in her ears. She glanced back to get her bearings and found she had shifted far to the right of the overhang's opening. Whatever space she'd found would never even be seen from outside.

She extended her snout.

Poking about, she found an opening's edge. One careful paw step after another, she crept inward.

It was a tunnel. By her best guess and the echoes of her splashing steps, the passage was not tall. The farther she went, the less water surged inward, until it barely splashed under her paws. Then her head bumped sharply against something hard. Somehow it had missed her nose and caught her on both sides of her face. She retreated as the thump echoed, sounding dully metallic.

Wynn sniffed about until she found something.

It was upright and round, thicker than her foreleg. She carefully closed her jaws on it. Indeed, it tasted like metal. The next vertical bar was too close to slip her head between them.

Shade had found a hidden passage, but it was barred against entry.

She was already shivering from cold, but it didn't matter. She had found what Wynn needed.

Shade wheeled about, lunging back down the passage, into the ending cave, and out from beneath the overhang. By the time she scrabbled over the rocky backbone, she was hurrying for port as fast as her footing allowed. When she reached it, full daylight had arrived.

Fishermen and sailors glanced over as she trotted between the buildings, but none approached, giving her no reason to growl. She was alone and cold, longing for the blanket at the inn. She stopped outside the door, hesitated, and turned aside. Then she spotted a small shed filled with netting and piled canvas.

Shade slipped inside and burrowed into the pile.

The memory ended suddenly.

Wynn's head ached from such a prolonged exchange, but she knew the rest of what had happened. Shade had waited out the day, having no way to reach Chane. Close within sight of the inn, she had watched for him and led him back to the lift.

Wynn was shaking, and not just from memory of drenching cold water.

"Oh . . . oh, my Shade!"

"What did you see?" Chane asked.

"She did it! She found it! Shade, you clever girl!"

Wynn told Chane all she'd experienced. His eyes widened at her mention of the inlet, and he shook his head, as if denying it was true.

"The tide," he hissed. "Why did I not think of that?"

At Wynn's silence, he explained how he and Shade had first stumbled upon the inlet and found nothing.

"We must check the tides," he added, "and return when it is low or at least receding."

"And find a way through those bars," Wynn returned. "It may be another grate, like the one in the pool's room."

Then she faltered. One puzzle remained concerning her companions' venture.

"How did you make Shade understand what to do . . . on her own?" she asked. "She can memory-speak only with me."

Chane hesitated and then raised his hand directly before Wynn's face—the hand with the brass ring.

He pinched it with his other hand.

"No . . . don't!" Wynn gasped.

Before she could stop him, Chane pulled off the ring.

Wynn heard Shade's quick snarl behind her, but that was all.

"She *knows,*" Chane said. "Perhaps has known all along."

Wynn twisted about.

Shade still sat on the floor, but her ears were flattened. Her jowls curled at Chane before her crystal blue eyes turned back on Wynn. Shade grew quiet once more.

"I knew the risk," Chane whispered. "It was the only way for her to see my chosen memories and hope she understood."

Wynn studied Shade, still unsure what this really meant. One thing was certain—Shade was aware of much more than she let on. Without warning, Wynn whispered one sharp word at Shade.

"Chane."

Shade's gaze wavered, flickering briefly toward him.

"I saw that!" Wynn accused. "You little sneak!"

"What are you talking about?" Chane asked.

"Her!" Wynn jabbed a finger at Shade.

With a throaty whine, Shade cocked her head.

"You're not the only thing she knows about," Wynn accused. "All this time, twisting my head apart until it aches, trying to use memory-speak, because it was all she understood . . . and she's been lying to me! She knows *words!*"

Chane let out a tired groan that sounded more like a hiss. "Names, perhaps . . . only because she has heard them, connected them to someone."

Wynn didn't believe it, but it was easy enough to test. Keeping her thoughts clear of memories, she scanned the little room. She spotted the sheathed sun crystal where she'd left it.

"Staff!" she said pointedly.

Shade started to turn her head but halted. In barely a blink, her ears lowered and she didn't look back up at Wynn.

"That's it!" Wynn growled. "Get over here, you . . . you obstinate . . . adolescent!"

With one quick step, Wynn made a grab for Shade's scruff—and missed.

Shade scooted her butt back across the floor. One snort and a huff, and she made a face at Wynn, wrinkled and repugnant, like she'd tasted something foul.

"Wynn, this is not the time," Chane warned.

"Oh, yes, it is!" Wynn shot back, still eyeing the dog. "If we're headed into more trouble, I've no time to constantly wrestle with memories. She's going to stop being stubborn and start doing things my way. Now . . . come here, Shade!"

This time, Shade spun on her butt. She pushed off from a squat and leaped straight up and over the bed's foot. The sight would've scared most people, but not Wynn.

"Don't you run from me!" she ordered, making another grab.

Her hand slipped too quickly down Shade's rising back and haunches. When her fingers crossed the dog's tail, she clenched her grip.

In the years to come, Wynn would look back on this moment and cringe. Snatching the tail of a now panicked wild animal taller than any wolf would be one—among many—of the stupidest things she'd ever done. But in the moment, she didn't care, until . . .

Shade yelped and twisted her head back with a snarl. Standing on the bed, she leveled her eyes with Wynn's—and Wynn balked.

"Stop it!" Chane said sharply. "She will turn on you!"

"No, she w—"

A squeak of shock was all Wynn finished with, as Shade lunged away.

Chane rushed by as Wynn's legs caught on the bed's foot, and her feet left the floor. Still clinging to Shade's tail, she shot forward and landed facedown on the hard pile mattress. Half of Wynn's breath rushed out in a grunt, and Shade's tail slipped from her hand.

Wynn rolled onto her side, trying to sit up. She heard Shade utter a vicious snarl and shrank away, flopping over on her back.

"Get back!" Chane hissed, and his hand shot out above Wynn.

She saw him try to shove Shade away.

"Chane, don't—" she started to warn.

Shade had already wheeled upon the bed.

Chane's hand barely lighted on her shoulder when she twisted her head and nipped him. He snatched his hand back, clutching it in shock. Before Wynn could react, large forepaws landed against her side and shoved.

With another squeal, Wynn slid sharply across the bed, over its side, and straight into Chane's legs. He toppled as she flopped on the floor and quickly scrambled over onto her hands and knees. Chane sat on his rump, staring at his shaking hand.

"It burns," he whispered, "like . . ."

Like Magiere's blade, Wynn thought, though Chane never finished. Then Wynn saw the smudge of oily black fluid above the base of Chane's thumb.

As far as Wynn knew, the only other things in this world beside Magiere's falchion that could sear an undead with a wound were the teeth and claws of a majay-hì. Shade had broken Chane's skin, and though she obviously hadn't intended serious harm, she'd gone too far.

"Damnation!" Wynn swore, clawing up and over the bedside. "How many pain-in-the-ass majay-hì do I have to fight with in one lifetime?"

Shade wasn't there—not exactly.

The tips of two tall, dark ears peeked above the bed's other side. For Shade's size, it was ridiculous for her to think she could hide there.

"Shade," Wynn said, "I'm your elder, no matter why your father sent you!"

The dog's head rose just enough to reveal her yellow-flecked blue eyes. She blinked slowly with mocking, sleepy-eyed disinterest, and swung her muzzle over to rest upon the bed.

Then she snorted.

Wynn lost her last grain of calm. "You *will* learn more words . . . if I have to pin your ears back and shout them into that stubborn head!"

Shade wrinkled her jowls—and her tongue flicked out and up over the tip of her nose.

Wynn stiffened. That impudent gesture was all too familiar—like the one Chap always used. She stabbed a finger across the bed, straight at Shade's nose.

"Don't you sass me, young lady!"

CHAPTER 15

The following night, Chane trailed Shade up the jagged shoreline and helped Wynn along behind as often as she would let him. With her pack over one shoulder, she gripped both her staff and cold lamp crystal on that same side, leaving one hand free for climbing. The crystal's light leaked between her clenched fingers.

Chane was little burdened by his two packs, though he had lashed his broken long sword over his back. He also carried a long steel pry bar in one hand. This had cost all of their dwarven slugs and two silver Numan pennies. Hopefully, it would be stout enough for him to breach the tunnel's two grates.

Since Shade's revelation of the hidden tunnel, and the subsequent dispute over her awareness of language, Wynn had barely spoken to the dog. This, more than need of Shade's lead, was the reason for their procession's present order.

They had left the upper inn following Shade's tantrum, hurrying to prepare. While in the market, Wynn had tried several times to speak simple nouns to Shade, pointing to associated objects. She urged the dog to identify similar items in their surroundings. Shade complied a few times and then ceased altogether. She repeatedly tried to shove her head under Wynn's hand, likely to use memory-speak instead. Wynn always pulled her hand away.

As they had finally headed for the lift, Shade tried again to duck under Wynn's hand. When she failed, two steps later Wynn halted, turning on the dog in angry astonishment. Chane had not really wanted to ask, but he did. It seemed Shade had raised one of Wynn's memories about creatures seen in the Elven Territories—something called "fra'cise."

"She thinks I jabber like a monkey!" Wynn fumed, and stormed off toward the lift.

For Chane, dealing with those two was becoming exasperating. His hand still burned lightly from Shade's bite, and Wynn was being as obstinate as the dog. From what Chane gathered, Shade's memory of rediscovering the inlet had been more vivid than Wynn could verbally describe. But amid the pair's nearly silent form of bickering, Chane did have one realization.

Shade and her kind converted experience into memory more quickly and completely than other sentient beings—certainly more than humans. It made sense, considering their form of communication, and might well be the better way, given time, ability, and skill.

Perhaps it was Shade who expected Wynn to improve in that.

When they had finally headed for Sea-Side's lower port, arriving before dawn, they went to the same inn that Chane had used before, and slept away the day.

Now that they were out on the rocky shore, the black sky was moonless, and though the waves were calmer this night, salty spray still crashed with force. For some reason Wynn ended up more soaked than anyone as she struggled along last.

Chane could see that she was cold and exhausted.

"Take my hand," he said, reaching back.

Wynn was trying to clamber over a barnacle-covered shelf. Too winded to argue, she grasped his hand, letting him pull her up. Her cloak's hood had fallen back, and she kept trying to pull it up. Soaked hair clung to her cheeks and forehead. Fortunately she chose to wear her elven clothing in place of her longer, traditional robe, making climbing a little easier.

"How much farther?" she breathed tiredly.

"Not far," he answered. "But we must move quickly. Low tide came just past dusk, and it is already rising."

Wynn nodded and followed after him.

Shade barked loudly from ahead, and Chane paused.

"Is that it?" Wynn asked.

The dog stood atop the long rock backbone. Chane grabbed Wynn's hand, pulling her along. As they climbed up, Shade scrambled down the far side. Chane crested the rock and Wynn held up the cold lamp crystal.

Light exposed the inlet's overhang and the dark space beneath. Shade already picked a precarious path inward along the water's rolling edge.

The tide was higher than Chane had hoped. He had no idea how long the tunnel would be. Even looking up the massive peak to where Sea-Side was situated inward on the peninsula, he could not begin to guess. Another wave rolled in, breaking near the inlet's mouth.

He waited for it to pass before stepping down. When sure of his footing, he reached up for Wynn and helped her follow.

"Wait here while I look," he said.

Setting down the pry bar, Chane stripped off his packs, sword, and cloak.

"I don't think even you can see much in there," Wynn said. "You'd better take this."

She held out the cold lamp crystal.

Chane hesitated, but not because he had never held such a thing. Since following Wynn to the guild's founding branch, he had never been so aware of what the crystals represented. They were bestowed only upon sages who had reached journeyor status and above—those who had proven themselves superior to all others. This one crystal represented the world Chane wanted to be a part of, but it was also like holding a piece of Wynn.

He took it, watching it glow softly in his pale palm.

"Wait, on second thought," she said, and reached out to take it back.

Chane was confused, even hurt by this—until she briskly rubbed the crystal. She opened her hands, and it burned bright with the heat of friction and her own warmth.

"The water's cold," she said. "You might have trouble brightening it . . . especially once you're wet."

She placed the crystal back in his palm.

Beneath its strengthened light was Wynn's own warmth. That sensation in Chane's palm washed away doubts. But he felt something else, something more, which brought a new fear.

He smelled Wynn—her *life*—as if her warmth in the crystal accentuated it, even under the cold shore breeze. The beast within him stirred slightly in its perpetual appetite.

"What's wrong?" she asked.

Chane closed his hand, clutching the crystal, fearful it might be taken again—even as its incidental warmth faded against his cold flesh.

"Nothing," he whispered, and stepped into the water.

The ocean's true chill was not as cold as he felt inside.

He sank only to his knees, relieved that the tide had not risen as high as he had first thought. Shade barked at him, but he ignored her and waded in under the overhang. Wynn had said the opening was hidden at the far left. He worked his way to the back wall and followed it.

The round opening was no more than a shadow in the rock until he stepped directly in front of it. He had to duck to step in, but the curved floor inside was smoother than the inlet's bottom. The tunnel was fully round as far as he could see, like a great stone pipe surging into the mountain's base. There was no doubt that the passage was unnatural. It had been excavated long ago. Algae and the remains of other dried growths spread halfway up its curved sides.

Soon, he could stand upright, though his head brushed the tunnel's top. It widened as well, until he could only just touch either side with outstretched hands. As he sloshed up its center, the incline was so gradual that he never noticed it, until the water undulated only to his ankles. Then he spotted the grate ahead—or rather a gate.

Vertical bars filled the tunnel from top to bottom. Its outer frame was mounted in the circumference by massive rivets. But the gate's condition surprised him more.

The iron bars were not new, but neither were they wholly rusted or worn. Continual exposure to salt water and air should have eaten at them more. The gate was either newer than the tunnel excavation, or it had been replaced repeatedly over the years. Then Chane noticed the lock plate level with the one horizontal slat of iron through which all vertical bars passed.

The plate was larger than a flattened hand. There was no handle or keyhole. Only a palm-size oval, slightly domed, appeared on the plate's surface. Even obscured by grime and salt crust, its tone was lighter than the surrounding iron.

Chane held the crystal close, and light sparked a vague sheen from the oval. He rubbed it, scraping with his fingernails, until the reflection brightened.

Nearly white metal, pale but bright as silver, bounced the crystal's light about the tunnel. That one clean patch was smooth and perfect, unmarred by salt. It was the same metal he had seen in the floor portal to the Stonewalkers' underworld.

Chane quickly headed back, emerging in the inlet to find Wynn and Shade crouched at the water's edge on the backbone's steep side.

"Did you find it?" Wynn called.

"Yes. Hand me my packs and the pry bar. Make sure your pack is secure. The footing is rough until we get inside the tunnel's mouth."

"What about the grate?" she asked, handing him the pry bar first. "Can you break it open?"

"Perhaps. It is actually a gate, but . . ." He hesitated. "Better you see for yourself."

They paused to tie up their cloaks above their waists, so the bottoms would not take on water and weigh them down. It was only then that Chane noticed a long sheathed dagger tucked in the back of Wynn's belt cinching in her tunic.

When she turned about and found him looking at it, she frowned but handed over his packs. He hooked one over each shoulder by its outer strap, so they hung together behind him, and then grasped his sword, holding it along with the pry bar.

"I will hold the crystal, so you can keep your staff above the water," he instructed. "Grip one of my packs if you need to steady yourself."

Chane turned to Shade and pointed beneath the overhang. The dog hopped into the water and waded inward. Wynn climbed down to join them and sucked a sharp breath as a cold roll of the ocean surged to her thighs.

"Stay close," Chane whispered, heading after Shade.

By the time they gained the tunnel, Wynn's teeth were chattering with shivers, and their splashing footfalls echoed off the curved walls. When they approached the gate, Shade was already waiting there. The dog appeared better than Wynn at withstanding the cold.

Chane was not certain, but it appeared the water in the tunnel had already risen slightly.

"Look here," he said, holding the crystal above the gate's plate.

Wynn crept closer, wide-eyed as she studied it.

"Have you seen this metal used like this before?" he asked. "Do you know how it is operated?"

"Chein'âs metal again?" Wynn shook her head. "I've only seen it used for portals and some weapons, such the Anmaglâhk's, Leesil's new blades, and Magiere's dagger."

Chane had seen these weapons for himself in the castle of the white undead.

"Oh, and the head of my elven quill," she added.

"A lock of some kind," he returned. "But we do not have time to guess its function without a place to insert a key . . . if we had one."

"Magic?" she asked. "You know conjury. Can you see or sense anything?"

"It does not work that way, by my experience. Magic cannot be sensed, even if I were a full mage. That is wishful folklore and nothing more. And in artificing, not all mages mark an object. In alchemically created items, component materials are sometimes imbued before or during preparation and assembly."

Wynn scoffed. "I've felt something whenever I've called up my mantic sight."

"That was *not* magic you felt. Rather the impending change in the natural order of existence, the change within yourself. Did you feel anything when you first held or used the staff with its crystal?"

"No," she admitted, then sighed through her little nose. "Well, we're no worse off for it."

Shade pushed in and shoved her muzzle between the bars, peering beyond it. Chane held out the crystal through the gate. As far as the light reached, he saw no sign of the tunnel's end. He worried about Wynn's already worn condition, especially in not knowing the tunnel's full length. He needed to get her beyond the water's reach before it rose further.

"I will break through," he said.

He handed off the crystal to Wynn as she leaned her staff against the tunnel wall. Then he stripped off one pack at a time, switching the pry bar and sword between his hands. As Wynn took the packs, he hoped she could keep all three above the water. He restrapped the sword to his back as she slung one of his packs over her shoulder. She stumbled briefly under the added weight but clutched the second pack in her arms as she kept the crystal extended for light.

"Both of you stay back," he said.

The two most feasible ways through were either to pry at the lock side until the bolt snapped or bent, or attempt to lever out the hinge pins. The latter would take considerably longer, as the pins' heads were hammered, sealing them in place.

Chane set the pry bar's beveled end into the space beside the lock plate.

He put his back against the wall on the same side and pushed the bar outward with all his strength.

Iron creaked and groaned under the pry bar's steel.

Pain stopped mortals from injuring themselves. He had no such limitation, so long as he retained enough life energy. He had not exerted much since his last feeding, but that had been a while ago. Still, there were only two gates, and he could easily last long enough for that.

Chane watched the space widen between the lock panel and the outer frame, but the bolt within the crack never moved.

"Crystal . . ." He grunted. "Bring it closer."

Wynn's feet splashed as she shuffled in with her burdens. But the crystal's light shifted enough to pierce the narrow space.

Chane threw his full effort against the pry bar. Though the gate shifted slightly from the frame, the bolt still did not move. Rather the lock plate moved to expose a bit of it, and its metal had a sharp glint.

The bolt was thick steel, not iron.

"*Odsúdýnjè!*" Chane hissed in his native Belaskian. He released all effort and slumped against the wall.

"What's wrong?" Wynn asked. "Why did you stop?"

Chane slowly shook his head. "The bolt is steel . . . and not attached to the lock."

Wynn's brows gathered in puzzlement.

"The bolt comes out of the wall," Chane tried to explain, "and into the lock plate. I will never pry the gate out far enough for the lock to slip free of it. There is not enough give between frame and gate."

"What about the hinges?" Wynn asked.

Chane looked back down the tunnel at the softly undulating seawater. "No, that would take too long."

"Then bend the bars."

Even Shade could not worm her head between those. Chane scanned all the way around the gate's circumference.

"The steel pry bar should hold," he answered. "But the iron bars are thicker."

Frustrated, he clutched one upright bar in silence.

"Heat," Wynn suggested. "You can conjure fire around one bar, make it more pliable."

Chane shook his head. "I cannot make conjured flame defy the earth and hang in the air . . . no one can."

"Then what? There has to be something!"

There was, now that the idea had been broached. But it was not something he was comfortable trying, considering Wynn's past reactions to the origin of his brass ring. He tucked the pry bar under his arm and unlashed the flap of his pack in Wynn's arms.

"What are you looking for?" she asked.

Chane pulled the etched steel hoop out of Welstiel's belongings.

"Where did that . . . come . . ." Wynn began, but trailed off, and she raised her eyes in accusation. "More of Welstiel's toys? Just how many of that madman's things did you take?"

"Everything he had," Chane returned flatly.

He had no time to deal with Wynn's distaste. He was not even sure that what he had in mind would work. The hoop's outer circumference was encircled with one etched black line no more than a hair's breadth. Similarly delicate and swirling marks and symbols covered the rest of it. Though it had the feel and weight of steel, a faint scent of charcoal rose from its etchings.

Chane stepped to the gate's center.

Crouching below the cross strut, he slipped the pry bar's end through, along one iron bar's side, and then reached through and hooked the loop over its end. The hoop slid down, resting against the gate's bar.

He had barely fathomed the hoop's operation. Whereas Welstiel had called up intense heat within the item, even handled it while hot, Chane could barely get it to glow. And once it was activated, he dared not touch it, always waiting long, until it cooled enough to pick up.

Chane waved Shade back as Wynn watched in silence. With a hoarsely whispered chant, he traced his index finger around the hoop and jerked his hand back.

Red pinprick sparks rose within the hoop's marks. They spread until all the etchings glowed like the coals beneath a fading fire.

"Is it doing anything yet?" Wynn asked.

Chane carefully touched the gate's bar in contact with the hoop. Barely any heat had penetrated. He needed more. But how?

He made a blind choice.

Dropping his free hand into the water, he drenched it. He then raised and extended his index finger as he began to chant again.

"No, it's too hot!" Wynn warned.

Chane quickly traced his finger another time around the hoop. A sizzle of water rose from the contact. He felt his fingertip begin to sear as he finished and thrust his hand down into the water.

The hoop's marks glowed with a sudden intensity. Red light became ruddy orange.

Pronounced heat radiated upon Chane's face. He heard Wynn suck in and hold a breath as he repeated the process, once, twice, three times more. The scent of seared flesh became distinct in the air. With his hand submerged the last time, Chane let hunger rise enough to eat away the small pain.

The hoop's markings turned pale orange-yellow, and the pry bar's steel began to grow hot.

He untied his cloak and wrapped a corner of it around the pry bar's nearer end. Even with protection, he felt heat grow beneath his grip. Vapor began to rise off the wet wool, but he focused only upon the gate's bar in contact with the hoop.

The barest dim red had spread into the black iron. He tipped the pry bar forward.

The hoop fell on the gate's far side and hit the water with a sharp hiss. As a cloud of steam erupted on its impact, Chane threw all his force against the pry bar's cloak-wrapped end.

Without a wall to brace his back, his boots slipped on the tunnel's submerged floor, but the one heated bar bent away from its nearest neighbor. He twisted back, levering the other way. The other central bar barely gave, but the heated one bent a little more.

"That's enough," Wynn said. "You've got it."

Chane pulled the pry bar out and splashed water against the gate's heated bar. Once it stopped steaming, he knew it was safe enough to pass through. He tossed the pry bar to the other side and took his packs from Wynn. He held hers as she struggled through the widened space, and then Shade wriggled after her.

Chane passed Wynn's pack and staff through. When she was ready, he shoved his own belongings through the tight space. Getting through himself was more trouble, and he ended up soaked to the shoulder on his left side. The last thing he did was fish out the pry bar and use it to hook the hoop out of the water.

The etchings still glowed. Not as brightly as when he had dropped it, but more than in the first pass of his finger. He had not yet learned how to dispel its heat and would have to carry it on the bar for now. He crouched down a bit.

"Warm yourselves," he said, nodding to the hoop.

Wynn waved Shade closer, though the dog was hesitant. Both took a moment of much-needed heat. Then Chane noticed the water on this side of the gate.

It reached above his ankles.

When he looked up, Wynn was staring up the tunnel. With a nod from her, they resettled their gear and moved on. Shade took the lead, and Wynn stayed close behind on Chane's right, holding the cold lamp crystal as he kept the dimly glowing hoop suspended ahead of him. It was a while before their feet stopped splashing, and they were walking on only damp floor. More than once, Chane glanced back, listening.

"What's wrong?" Wynn asked, watching his face.

"You and Shade are cut off," he answered. "If we reach a dead end, you cannot get back out until the tide recedes. It will be too far to submerge and swim."

Wynn grew very still. Perhaps she finally caught what he heard—the soft shift of the undulating ocean creeping up the tunnel.

"Come on," she breathed.

Chane pressed forward, but it was not long before they both heard Shade's growl, followed by a huff and a snarl. They quickened their pace until the crystal's light illuminated the dog ahead.

Chane nearly groaned.

Just beyond Shade was another gate.

Beyond that, the tunnel stretched into the pitch-dark distance.

They were nowhere near its end or the final gate Shade had seen in the duchess's memory. And the tide was still coming.

Sau'ilahk patiently waited in a dim side passage beyond the turn to the Off-Breach Market. A narrow place, it was little more than rear access to a few shops carved into the mainway.

Wynn had vanished beyond his reach, but he did not care. She and her companions had likely embarked on another pointless foray. He had overestimated the sage's intelligence, but she had served one purpose in the last few nights: Sau'ilahk had found a better link to the texts' whereabouts.

Duchess Reine Faunier, Âreskynna by marriage, would go below tonight. He would follow, finally gaining a way to the underworld.

Come, he whispered with thoughts.

An orange-red glow rose in the passage's side wall.

His stone-spider surfaced, its single glass-lump eye radiating bloodred. It clung there, watching him, as ripples spread in the rock beneath each point of its four legs. Another ripple snaked along the floor. This one rose at his feet.

It broke the floor with more ripples in stone, arching upward like a rope-size worm of rock-plated segments. Its round mouth oscillated, tasting the air that filled its limbless body.

Neither of these two was the one he had sent to track the duchess.

He had left more than one corpse in the seatt's forgotten corners in order to call and keep all of his compound servants active. At halfway to midnight, a curling twist of black smoke rolled in under the lip of the passage's ceiling. It spread along the high stone, clinging to that surface in its progress, until it hung above Sau'ilahk's cowl.

It gathered itself into a mass, and like black steam, it spread over his cowl.

Each of his trio of servitors was endowed for its special purpose, couched within a spark of sentience. The spider of Stone, Fire, and Air could see and hear. The worm made of Stone, Water, and Air could smell and taste. And the smoke, that blending of Air, Fire, and Spirit . . .

Show me, he commanded.

It curled over his cowl, into its opening. Within the black robe—within Sau'ilahk's incorporeal form—it spread.

The passage vanished from his awareness.

He looked *down* upon the wide columned tunnel of Breach Mainway from high above, hanging somewhere within the great crag by which it had been named. Below, the duchess and her people turned into the passage toward Off-Breach Market.

Sau'ilahk, submerged in his third servitor's recordings, drifted out of the high crag, curling along the passage's ceiling, and followed. The market was closed, empty and quiet, but the duchess passed all the way across to one rear tunnel. He followed inward, wafting along the new path's side wall.

The duchess walked amid her entourage with slow, sluggish steps.

No one spoke. It was a strange, silent procession.

Sau'ilahk's servitor flowed down the wall and surged forward along the dark passage's floor. It—he—spread around the rear guards' clomping feet and gathered about the duchess's smaller ones. All Sau'ilahk could see in the servitor's recording were the swish of the elf's white robe and the pounding of the captain's boots. But he felt . . .

Fear clung to Duchess Reine.

More than that, there was the pain of loss. Two emotions matched and joined to Sau'ilahk, as if one led to the other and back again. She feared the loss might repeat, all the worse for it.

Sau'ilahk did not understand and wished someone had spoken during his creation's surveillance. Anything to illuminate this clinging odor of dread and remorse might have proved useful.

The duchess coughed, slowing. Ahead, the elf's footsteps drew to a stop.

Sau'ilahk's smoke servitor slipped away along the floor. As it rolled up the side wall to the ceiling, he saw the duchess turn with her hand over her nose and mouth. The elf sniffed the air twice and wrinkled his long nose as he looked up and down the passage.

"Someone passed this way with an open torch," he said. Before he expressed more, she waved him onward, and the procession continued.

Soon, Sau'ilahk saw a passage wall of cut stones roll inward after five touches from the duchess. He would not need to deal with the passage as she had.

Banish!

The smoke within him thinned to nothing. He no longer needed that one and, unlike the other two, it could not swim through stone to keep pace with him. He now knew where to go and carefully envisioned his destination.

Follow, he commanded, and winked through dormancy.

Sau'ilahk reawakened before the passage wall, its fitted stones returned to their proper place. He waited only long enough for his two remaining servitors to catch up.

Wynn clenched her chattering teeth. Her feet were numb inside her boots as she slogged through knee-deep water. Shade's breath, like her own, echoed in the tunnel in shudders. Wynn tried not to look back too often.

The encroaching tide gained on them every time they stopped to face yet another gate. So far, Chane had broken through five more. Though these hadn't been as stout as the first, it took him longer each time. He hadn't used the hoop on the first three. When he did so for the last two, it took him longer to bend the heated bars. She worried that even his strength wouldn't hold out if they ran into another. The last one had taken great effort, and he'd faltered three times.

Wynn couldn't fathom why the Stonewalkers bothered creating and maintaining this hidden way if it needed to be so impenetrable. Every gate had an oval of Chein'âs metal in its lock plate.

She forced one foot after the next, with no idea how much time had passed. It felt as if they'd been struggling up the freezing tunnel for half the night. She and Shade were now trapped by the tide. But all that mattered, if—when—they made it through, was locating the texts.

"Have you been counting?" Chane suddenly asked, his voice a hoarse whisper.

"Five gates . . . since . . . the first," she managed between shivers.

"Paces," he corrected.

Wynn sighed in exhaustion. "More for me . . . your legs are longer."

"We have traveled almost a league, at a guess."

She didn't need to hear that.

"Do you need to rest?" Chane asked, glancing sidelong at her.

He stopped walking. His face looked even paler in only her crystal's light, and the anxiety on it was smothered under a wrinkle of anger.

"Your lips are blue!" he hissed, and then shook his head. "This was foolish . . . foolish! I never should have allowed this."

"You? Allow?"

How many times had she reminded him that this was her mission? Even if he found the texts on his own, he certainly couldn't read most of their content.

Shade whined up ahead. Much as Wynn empathized with Shade's suffering, she couldn't stop shaking herself. Shade huffed twice more.

Chane turned and took a few more steps.

"*Odsúdýnjè!*" he cursed.

Wynn didn't have to ask. She sloshed forward and peered around his side . . . at another gate.

Sau'ilahk watched from a far vantage point as Duchess Reine stepped into the lantern-lit end chamber of the downward-curving tunnel.

The two dwarven guards above in the entrance room had not been an issue. He had simply pushed his cowl through the wall of moving stones until he saw the hidden space. He quickly withdrew before the guards noticed a subtle change of shadow on the inner wall. That brief glimpse had been enough to judge distance and position for whatever space lay beyond the door within.

He had waited for the duchess and hers to move on, and then blindly slipped through stone around the room. Lost for only a moment in groping to an exit, he emerged slightly below the head of the downward-curving tunnel.

Once his servitors followed, he trailed the duchess, remaining out of sight around the tunnel's wide curve. She finally reached the end chamber, and he was forced to remain far back. She faced two more armored dwarves framing another door, and Sau'ilahk barely contained his exhilaration.

Had she reached the underworld?

The door was unimpressive, unlike the iron panels in the entrance chamber, and doubt dampened his excitement. It could not possibly be a portal into the Stonewalkers' realm.

"Welcome again, Highness," one guard said, and pulled a heavy key ring from his belt. Neither dwarf appeared surprised to see her.

Sau'ilahk again wondered why she chose to go below at night.

The first guard unlocked the door and stepped aside. The duchess and her people passed onward. Sau'ilahk caught only a vague glimpse through the opening.

Light beyond it was brighter than in the end chamber, and the elf pocketed his crystal as he entered. As the last Weardas followed, Sau'ilahk was too far off to spot any passage beyond. The guards pulled the door closed, locking it again, and Sau'ilahk began to panic.

He had not seen enough to blink into that space beyond the door. Even so, he could never emerge in plain sight if the duchess lingered. All he could do was gain the door, prepared to slip through when he was certain no one on the other side would see him.

This left him an obvious dilemma.

How to kill both guards, quickly and quietly, so that no one beyond the door was alerted? If there was another passage—or more than one—he might lose the duchess.

Sau'ilahk glided back up the tunnel and drew his servitors with him.

Rise, he commanded, and the segmented stone worm arched out of the floor.

He snatched its head, squeezing its round mouth shut, and began to conjure something more into its body. Pale yellow vapors leaked from the worm's mouth to escape between his solidified fingers.

Hold, he commanded. *Expel only when you smell life before you.*

He pulled the worm from the floor, placing it against the side wall. Once it submerged, he pointed to the ceiling directly above. The stone-spider scuttled across the ceiling above his fingertip.

Tap until someone approaches, he instructed. *Then open your eye, burning brightly.*

And last, Sau'ilahk raised another pool of light-eating darkness. He sank through it, halfway into the wall, until only his cowl's edges remained surfaced as he watched.

The spider's *click-click-click* began.

"Did you hear that?" one guard asked the other in Dwarvish.

"Hear what? There's nothing . . ." the other began, and then, "Oh, Eternal's mirth! Some rat sneaked in again!"

The first grumbled. Leaning his iron staff against the wall, he trudged up the curving tunnel. Sau'ilahk remained still, letting him pass along the curve, just beyond sight of the end chamber.

A red glow appeared upon the ceiling.

The dwarf froze, staring upward. Before he uttered a puzzled exclamation, the worm snaked out of the wall near his head. He flinched away, but not far enough.

A soft crackle of grating rock came as the worm's mouth snapped open. Pale yellow vapor erupted in the dwarf's face, and a startled suck of breath did the rest.

The dwarf choked once, never gaining breath to cough. He crumpled in a dull clatter of armor and heavy bulk.

"Guster, what are you doing?" the second called from the end chamber. "Guster? If you cannot find the vermin, stop fooling about!"

No answer came, and the second guard hefted his iron staff. He stepped cautiously up the tunnel, and Sau'ilahk grew anxious.

This was taking too long—long enough that the duchess could be well ahead of him. He had no way to dispose of bodies in this place, though he had hoped to feed on a guard before moving on. He waited only until the second guard stepped through the pocket of banished light.

Nothing but a black silhouette showed against the tunnel's far wall, marking the dwarf's presence.

Sau'ilahk thrust out both hands, and his forearms sank through the thick chest.

He felt the dwarf turn toward him, gagging and shuddering in the pure darkness. Something long and narrow toppled across the light from the spider's eye. The dwarf's grip had loosened on the iron staff. It was falling.

Sau'ilahk whipped his left arm sideways through the dwarf, keeping his right encased. Willing both solid, he snatched the toppling staff as the dwarf stiffened around his forearm. He tried to wrench his hand out, tearing the chest open—but it would not come. What had been easy with humans, such as the city guard of Calm Seatt, was nothing like this—like trying to pull free of half-hardened clay.

The dwarf's hands slapped upon the wall's surface, shoving hard. Sau'ilahk felt himself being dragged out of the wall.

In panic, he struck the staff sharply into the guard's head. At the dull thump, massive weight jerked his arm downward. He quickly released his will, his forearm turning incorporeal.

As the dwarf's body slumped to the passage floor, Sau'ilahk heard the thick blood spatter upon it like sudden rain as it fell through his ghostly arm.

Leaning the staff against the wall, he let his hand become incorporeal, and rushed to the end chamber. He hesitated there, not daring to slip through, but in the silence, he heard the duchess's voice beyond the door. His instant of relief passed quickly.

Sau'ilahk was at a loss as to why she had not moved on.

CHAPTER 16

Reine stepped into the domed chamber and halted as the door closed behind her. She stared at the floor's white metal portal, smoother than a mirror—or a still pond. The last comparison made her feel worse. She rarely thought of water without an anxious twinge, though that old fear had become small compared to others.

She didn't think of the dwarves' honored dead, now at peace in the Stone-walkers' care. Nor did she think of ancient texts heralding sinister days to come—or to come again. She thought only of that strange white metal, and how such simple beauty could seal in torment.

The underworld waited.

Chuillyon came up beside her, following her gaze. At his light touch upon her shoulder, she stepped onward.

"Welcome, Highness," said one thänæ bearing a long-hafted mace. All four about the chamber nodded sharply to her, and Chuillyon went directly to the bell rope.

One long, deafening tone shivered through Reine's flesh—one ring would call Cinder-Shard. When the Âreskynna's tall elven advisor glanced back, his amber eyes filled with concern. Reine didn't acknowledge him. His counsel and care were welcome, but not his pity.

Captain Tristan stood eternally attentive, occasionally eyeing the four thänæ. She didn't know him well, in spite of his years serving the royal family. He rarely spoke except for a question or an order. As a leader of the Weardas, his ability was beyond question. So was his loyalty, considering the secret she'd borne from the day she had married the one man she loved.

Her other two Weardas, Danyel and Saln, stood at attention, awaiting orders. She knew them even less, though they'd been handpicked by Tristan.

A rhythmic grinding began to build inside in the chamber, becoming a vibration in the floor. The white metal portal split along its thin seam, the halves sliding apart, and the lift rose through the opening.

Master Cinder-Shard stood alone upon the platform.

His gray-streaked black hair hung loose, and he wore no hauberk of steel-tipped black scales. In only charcoal-colored breeches and a bulky shirt, he looked much as Ore-Locks had a few nights ago. But his dark eyes were far more challenging.

"My lady," he said in his cracked-gravel voice.

He often avoided either of her titles—one by marriage, and the other she preferred by birth. One he acknowledged; the other he ignored. Titles meant nothing here. No bloodline or royal bond would see her through a night like this. If she saw it through again.

Cinder-Shard took a half step, then paused, and his craggy face tensed. He cocked his head, peering about the domed chamber, as if trying to find something only he heard.

"What?" Tristan barked.

Exchanged glances passed between the four thänæ as they watched Cinder-Shard. The master Stonewalker's tension appeared to spread among them. They followed his roving glare—as did Reine—and Chuillyon moved closer to her.

Cinder-Shard rolled his massive shoulders and shook his head.

"Nothing," he muttered. "Let us go."

Reine willed herself numb as she followed him onto the lift.

Sau'ilahk listened intently outside the door. The soft grating of sliding metal was followed by stone grinding out a rhythm—like the gears of a dwarven lift. When all noise died, a gravelly voice rose. It did not belong to anyone in the entourage.

A dwarf, most certainly, but that voice pulled a twinge from Sau'ilahk, as if he still had true flesh and muscles that could spasm. So few words, but that voice made him anxious. He faltered, uncertain why, and then heard the lift's grinding begin again.

Sau'ilahk could not bear ignorance. He pressed his cowl slowly through the door until the blindness of submerging in wood faded. He glimpsed beyond the door, then quickly drew back. It was enough to leave him astonished, hopeful, and frustrated all the more.

Duchess Reine descended through a central shaft in the chamber's floor. All her companions were with her, as well as some elder dwarf in dark attire.

Sau'ilahk had found the duchess's entrance into the underworld, and the texts waited somewhere below. But more guards stood within the chamber.

His patience thinned.

The two outer guards would be found sooner or later, but living ones left behind would quickly betray an invader's presence. Four thänæ could never harm him, but he could not kill them all before one raised an alarm. Already weakened by conjury, he lacked strength to fill the chamber with conjured noxious mists.

And the duchess was slipping away.

Sau'ilahk slid back from the door. Was his one glimpse enough? The shaft lay directly inward. If he could only keep a straight course, he could reach it.

Follow, he whispered to his servitors, and he sank through the end chamber's floor.

The lift settled at the shaft's bottom, and all Reine could do was retain her composure. Cinder-Shard opened the gate, but she barely took two steps before he paused, blocking the way.

The grizzled master peered down the rough passage ahead. Far away, past where the path split in three directions, Reine saw dim phosphorescence in one natural cavern at its end.

Cinder-Shard spun about toward the lift, glanced up the shaft over Reine's head. He then lowered his gaze, scowling in uncertainty. He spun back to stare down the way ahead.

Danyel and Saln both put their hands to their sword hilts. Tristan remained still, watching Cinder-Shard. But the master Stonewalker said nothing. He finally stepped off the platform, turning to usher Reine out.

"Do we have your leave to continue?" she asked, hoping he might offer a hint for his behavior.

"Of course," he said absently. "You know the way. . . . My thoughts go with you."

More pity.

"Thank you," she answered coldly, hoping he said no more.

At the tunnel's branching, Cinder-Shard followed the main path, but Reine turned left, to the west. Somewhere in this direction, beyond the mountain, lay the ocean and a rising tide.

"What was that about?" she whispered to Chuillyon.

The tall elf shrugged with a lazy roll of his large amber eyes. "I could not guess. Perhaps the old tomb tender has spent too much time in silence down here."

Tristan said nothing—probably because he had nothing to say. He, Danyel, and Saln brought up the rear. This was one of the few places where the captain never required that he take the lead, entering the unknown before her.

Reine made her way as Chuillyon dropped back behind her.

This side tunnel was nearly as old as the first castle of Calm Seatt, and its walls grew damper the farther she went. Tiny beads of water glistened dully upon their faint yellow-green phosphorescence. She heard soft, erratic patters as the droplets fell. But the tunnel grew dimmer the farther she went. Entering the passage's last leg, she stopped before a lone door, and Chuillyon pulled out his cold lamp crystal.

The stout wooden door showed signs of decay. Rust stained the hinges pinned into stone with steel spikes. The door would need replacing again in a year or two.

Reine peered at the handle and the lock plate with no keyhole. Only an oval of the white metal domed slightly from the plate.

She reached up and pulled one sea-wave-shaped comb from her hair. In its back was a small spot of white metal, as if a silvery molten teardrop had fallen there to bond with the mother-of-pearl. She placed the comb's back side over the lock plate's white metal oval. The steel bolt instantly grated away into the wall.

Reine shifted her other comb to hold back her falling hair. As she cracked open the door, she handed the first comb to Chuillyon. When he turned to pass it to the captain, she stayed his hand.

"Keep it," she said.

"You do not wish me to come with you?" he asked.

"Just . . . wait out here. I'll call if I need anything."

"But the goods we purchased . . . Should you not—"

"Later, Chuillyon."

"Highness—"

"Leave me be!"

She slipped inside, shutting the door. With her hands pressed against the damp wood, Reine heard and felt the bolt slide back into place. The sound still made her stomach clench, no matter how many times she heard it. All of this had begun a moon after she'd been found drifting alone in the boat—the night she had lost Frey.

Reine leaned her forehead against the door, and looked down at another white metal oval on the lock plate's inner side. Twice per year, the highest tides were the worst.

She always left the one comb with the white metal teardrop behind, locking herself in. Without it, only Chuillyon—or Cinder-Shard—could let her out. Nothing could escape this place. She rolled her head upon the door and peered toward the rough opening in the far-right wall.

The space beyond it was nearly pitch-black.

Reine took a long breath, straightened, and headed for that opening. She tried not to look upon the pool's invading seawater, even as she stepped along its rear stone shelf. Too many times, she'd stared blankly across it at the iron gate, waiting for something to come. Half-submerged by the rising tide, the gate, its every detail, had already been branded into her mind. So much so that it had worn away even her fear of the ocean. This "cell," as she'd come to know it, had been excavated so long ago that not even Cinder-Shard knew when.

The tide's welling stench intensified, making it hard to breathe, as Reine stepped into the adjoining dark chamber. She reached out and slid her hand along the opening's inner right side. Her fingers caught on tiny crisp edges, and she stroked them three times.

Dim light rose from the thumb-size crystal resting on a ledge. It was a small gift she clung to in this place, passed to her privately by Lady Tärtgyth Sykion, high premin of Calm Seatt's sages. Reine peered about the space.

A blend of fixtures turned the place into a tight and cluttered cross between a sitting room and a study. Its major furnishings were a small scribing desk, a wooden couch with aging cushions, and a book-laden stone casement chiseled into the opposite wall. She'd tried to soften its nature with tapestries, blown-glass fishing floats of varied hues and such, but nothing changed what it was.

There was no end in sight to this repeated torture, and still she refused to give in. She glanced reluctantly to the right. There was another opening in the sitting room's rear.

"I'm here . . ." she said flatly, but bitterness leaked in when she added "again."

She heard the rustle of fabric from that next room. That one didn't even have the dim glow of phosphorescent walls. Uneven shuffling footfalls upon stone echoed from it.

A dim, tall figure took shape in the doorway.

Head low, dark blond hair draped around his face. One of his hands clutched the opening's edge.

Reine saw sallow fingers with faint undertones of sickly green. Or was that just the light in the sitting room reflected by mineral-laced walls?

"It will pass," she whispered, stepping closer. "Just one more night."

She would never cry in front of him. He didn't need that further burden.

"I'm here now. Everything will be all right . . . my Frey."

The seawater reached Chane's knees, and even he grew hard-pressed to advance. He could only guess how bad off Wynn must be.

The steel hoop had long ago cooled and been stored away. The more gates they reached, the more the tide gained on them, until the bars were too deep in cold water to heat up. He had to force them by sheer strength. The last—the sixth—had taken too long.

Shade suddenly vanished in a splash.

Wynn grabbed his arm, about to shout, and Chane quickly hooked the pry bar in his belt, ready to jump in. But Shade resurfaced and paddled back until her forepaws caught on something. She rose, standing only chest-deep.

Chane looked beyond her, clenching his jaw. There was a dropoff beneath the water.

Wynn's forehead pressed against his arm.

"Damn dead deities!" she whispered. "If they don't want anyone to get in, why not just trap the place, kill us off, instead of these endless—"

Chane clamped his hand over her mouth.

He had already wondered about the same thing, thinking that perhaps the tunnel had other uses than simply to let in the sea. But right then, he looked ahead, uncertain of what he saw.

A faint light glowed somewhere down the tunnel.

Glancing down at Wynn, he laid a finger across his lips and slowly lifted his hand from her mouth. He leaned close to her ear and whispered, "Look."

Wynn lifted her head, eyes widening.

Chane glanced down at Shade, once more laying a finger across his lips, and then he peered down the tunnel again. Perhaps twenty, maybe thirty yards ahead, he thought he saw vertical lines of black over the light.

Another gate.

He tried to release fatigue and sharpen his sight, but he still could not be sure. The opening looked smaller than any they had breached . . . or maybe the bars were just thicker?

Had they finally made it all the way?

Chane carefully slid his boot along the tunnel's submerged floor. His toe slipped off an edge, and he lowered his foot over. He sank above his waist, soaking his tied-up cloak before hitting bottom.

Perhaps it was a reservoir, keeping the end pool filled longer than a high tide. Wynn would sink to her chest. Their packs might get wet, and he would not like that for all the precious books he carried. There was little to be done for it.

"Hold your pack over your head," he whispered. "I will try to lash the staff to your back, crystal upward."

Wynn slipped her pack's straps off, so he could secure the staff, but he was still worried about his books. The ones from the healers' monastery might survive, but Welstiel's journals had some entries made with charcoal sticks. He slipped a pack off his shoulder and pulled out those journals.

Wynn scowled at them, and then at him.

She knew what he intended and did not like it or the sight of them. But she took the journals and roughly shoved them in her pack.

Chane knew better than to thank her and hoisted on his packs.

"We go slowly—silently," he whispered. "And Shade *must* let me hold her afloat. We cannot have any splashing."

Wynn nodded and touched the dog's face. Whatever passed between them, the meaning must have been clear. Shade only twitched a jowl as he wrapped one arm around her chest. Wynn stepped over the dropoff, and he grabbed hold of her belt.

Chane waded forward in slow steps, flinching every time water splashed even slightly. How would he break through the last gate in silence? With his strength waning, the prospect was almost more than he could face.

This had to be the last one.

Reine sat upon the couch holding Frey reclined in her lap. He was thin and pale, and it didn't matter how many times she'd seen him like this; each time was worse, because each time he looked worse.

At least he was dry, so he hadn't tried to drown himself again. Still, everyone around her—from Chuillyon and Cinder-Shard to all of the family—said he must have seawater to touch as well as gaze upon. It was all that kept him from slipping into pure madness.

But Reine saw the hunger in her husband's aquamarine eyes.

It was worse than that first night she'd met him, when he'd stared out the castle window. Now and then, in his quieter moments, she still saw the semblance of thought in his frail features. His eyes would shift, and suddenly he'd glance up, seeming to notice her for the first time.

"Yes, it's me," she said calmly, again and again. "Just me, Frey."

He squinted as if recognizing her only then. But any turn of his head exposed his throat.

Triple sets of faint creases marked both sides, like the faint beginnings of wrinkles that would deepen with age. But these were too perfect, too straight and parallel, placed so high near his jawline. They appeared only at the highest tides each year, vanishing again as the tide receded.

Frey suddenly rolled his head toward the opening to the pool's outer chamber.

Reine felt him go rigid in her lap. His eyes didn't blink.

"They're coming," he said hoarsely.

Sick of the terror, Reine couldn't hide it anymore and began to shake. Not because of what might—or would—come . . . but because he longed for it.

"No," she whispered, and then more sharply, "No!"

Frey rolled from her lap, though she tried to hang on to him. By the time he gained his feet, she'd already blocked the opening. How many times had she stopped him from beating himself nearly unconscious upon the pool's gate?

"Frey, stay," she ordered.

He held his place, staring over her head.

"Listen to me, love," she whispered, hanging on to calm. "The water can wait . . . until the tide passes. Then you can . . ."

She lost her voice as his head cocked. His brow creased in concentration as he swayed slightly with effort to stay on his feet.

"Not . . . them?" he croaked.

Frey's lost gaze drifted down to Reine and then rose beyond her again. Puzzlement in his expression shifted first to suspicion and then hardened to anger, enough that Reine hesitantly glanced over her shoulder.

The outer door was still shut tight, but she heard the softest scrape of metal. Its echo in the quiet left her uncertain where it came from. She backed one step through the opening, glancing toward the pool. . . .

Reine toppled aside as Frey knocked her out of his way. Her back hit the pool chamber's rear wall, stunning her as she heard the splash. She went cold with fright.

Beneath the pool's rippling surface, a mute wavering form moved along the bottom toward the gate.

Reine leaped off the edge and sank to her chest. She thought she heard another splash, but as her feet hit bottom, she was clawing into the water, trying to find a grip on Frey.

"Chuillyon!" she screamed.

At the tunnel's end, Chane looked through stout vertical bars. Beyond the gate, seawater collected in a wide pool within a roughly hewn chamber. What light filled the space came from the glittering walls and more from an opening in the right wall's far end. Whether someone was in there, he could not tell, but he spotted a stout door in the rear wall's left side. Worse was that it held a white metal oval in place of a lock.

This last gate was smaller than any others, and its bars were not as thick as he had first thought.

"Can you do it?" Wynn whispered.

Her voice startled him, and then he noticed her blue-tinged lips. He had to succeed. They would never make it out of the tunnel any other way.

Wynn mouthed the word "staff" and turned her back to him.

Chane untied it, and she leaned it against the tunnel wall. But how was he going to keep Shade afloat? They could not have the dog treading water.

Wynn placed her pack behind her head, atop her shoulders, and backed up to pin it against the tunnel wall. Her lips quivered again as she mouthed, *Shade*, and held out her arms.

Chane carefully glided the dog into Wynn's grip. Shade sank a bit in Wynn's arms, struggling for an instant. Once the dog settled, Chane pulled the pry bar off his belt.

Shade twisted sharply and growled.

Her sudden splashing made Chane stiffen. Wynn struggled to keep Shade still, but the dog kept wrestling to get free. He reached instinctively to grab Shade's snout but stopped.

Shade looked down the tunnel and snarled again.

The water's surface rolled, nearly churned, as if the tide had suddenly surged up the tunnel.

A grip latched around both Chane's ankles. He heard Wynn suck a loud breath as his feet were pulled from under him.

Chane lost sight of Wynn as he was jerked beneath the water.

Wynn's hold on Shade broke as the dog thrashed around. Shade clawed the tunnel's side wall as she tried to put herself between Wynn and the churning water. Wynn's breath came hard and fast.

"Chane!"

She pinned the pack to the wall with one hand and groped wildly beneath the surface for Chane. Shade snarled and snapped, but she was struggling to remain afloat. Something light-colored stretched out beneath the water's surface.

Wynn tried to grab for it, but it broke the surface beyond reach, and it wasn't Chane.

A barbed spearhead rose.

She snatched her hand back. The spearhead was nearly white, like Chein'âs metal. Water erupted beyond it as Chane thrashed to the surface.

Shade pushed off the wall, treading water as she moved in front of Wynn.

Wynn barely caught a glimpse of a dim form behind Chane, holding on to one of his packs. She heard another splash behind her, but she reached out wildly for Chane.

"Chuillyon!"

Wynn flinched at that scream from beyond the gate but kept her attention on Chane.

His features twisted in rage, and his eyes had lost all color. He swung back at his attacker as another set of hands rose from the water and latched around his waist.

Chane vanished beneath the surface in a splash.

"Let him go!" Wynn shouted, and reached behind her back, pulling Magiere's old dagger.

Shade suddenly sank with a yelp, and Wynn let the pack drop as she lunged for the dog.

Another spearhead thrust up, driving straight for her face. She toppled backward, pushing with slipping feet, and her back hit the gate's bars. The spearhead on its long shaft halted, level with her throat.

Two slender arms shot out through the bars behind her.

"No, Frey!" someone shouted behind her. "Get back!"

The arms latched around Wynn, pinning her against the bars.

Trapped by the hovering spearhead, she didn't dare try to slash herself free with the dagger. A third arm reached past her head and a small, delicate hand snatched her wrist.

"Release the blade . . . *now*," someone commanded.

Harsh as the voice was, it was clearly a woman's, though the arms around Wynn's chest were those of a man. Wynn slowly opened her hand and felt the dagger being ripped away.

Shade splashed to the surface, hacking and coughing. She paddled to the tunnel's wall, clawing for any grip to anchor herself.

"Please," Wynn begged. "Let me help her!"

"Silence!" the hidden woman snapped.

The spear's shaft before Wynn tilted as water rolled around it. Its wielder began to rise. The first of it that she saw was a row of pale spikes.

Slowly breaking the surface, webbing followed at their bases, stretched in a crest over a bald scalp. Black-orb eyes, fully round and too large to be human, watched Wynn. Translucent membranes in place of lids nictitated over them.

The being was covered in slick, smooth skin tinged blue or perhaps more teal. Its face appeared distended, making the orb eyes look slightly pushed to either side of the hairless head. Its nose was only two vertical slits. When its lipless mouth parted, Wynn saw needle-sharp opalescent teeth like those of a sea predator.

When it—he—stood to full height, he was long and slender, but as solid as a full-grown male elf. More web-separated spikes ran along the outside of his forearms to match those cresting his skull. Wynn's breath caught as three slits on each side of his throat flexed like gills beneath a long jawline.

The strong hands and arms that held her suddenly slackened.

"Frey, please," the woman whispered, and then cried out, "Chuillyon, Tristan . . . help me!"

Wynn didn't know who held her. With the spear aimed at her throat, she couldn't twist her head to look.

"We're coming!" someone called, and more splashes came from the pool's chamber.

Chane erupted from the water again, just beyond Shade.

Before cascading droplets settled, three teal-skinned beings burst up and were on him. With a grating hiss, he shouldered one into the tunnel's wall. Shade twisted back, lunging and snapping at the first being's forearm. That one turned at the dog's assault, and his spear wavered.

Wynn jerked free and spun partway, groping for her staff. Then her gaze caught on a man's face pressed hard between the gate's bars.

The anguish there made her falter.

His half-mad eyes might've shed tears, but any such were obscured by water running down his face from his drenched dark-blond hair. His mouth gaped as he stared into the tunnel, but not at her. He looked only at the teal-skinned being holding off Shade with a spear.

Wynn had seen that expression, or ones so similar.

It showed on the faces of peasants in the worst corners of this world, such as Leesil's birthplace in the Warlands. Starving, dying of thirst, or beaten down, for them hope had become a lie. Worse, the man looked at the teal-skinned being as if his relief dangled tauntingly just beyond his reach.

The woman's voice shouted, "Chuillyon! Get the gate open!"

A woman had her arm wrapped over the madman's shoulder and across his chest, pulling on him to no effect. When she turned her head back from crying out, Wynn looked into the panicked face of Duchess Reine.

"Frey, stop it!" the duchess ordered.

"Wynn . . . get away from them!" Chane rasped.

He slapped away his assailant's spear. Shade clawed along the tunnel wall, floundering as she tried to get around her own opponent. With two companions desperate for help, Wynn could only try for the closest. She took a step to grab for Shade.

The point of a long, narrow blade struck the tunnel wall before her eyes.

Wynn's feet slipped as she tried to duck. She toppled against the curved wall to keep from sinking. The long blade levered in, and its edge set against her throat.

Duchess Reine had her arm thrust through the gate, pinning Wynn in place with a saber.

Shade let out a wild snarl, and then all sounds of struggle quickly lessened.

The duchess's enraged eyes turned away.

Wynn could barely move with the sharp edge at her throat, but she followed that gaze to Chane.

"Yield or she's dead!" the duchess commanded.

Chane froze in place, surrounded by the trio of strange beings, while a fourth held Shade off with its spear.

Wynn nodded once at Chane and turned only her eyes toward the gate.

As the duchess withdrew her saber, the white-robed elf tried to pull the wild-eyed man away. The captain, sword in hand, jerked the gate open, forcing both to retreat a little.

"Inside," he ordered, leveling his long sword at Wynn.

Wynn hesitated. Amid the confusion, her pack had sunk. She wasn't sure she'd be allowed to fish it out, but she wasn't leaving the sun crystal's staff behind. She reached for it.

The captain surged in, grabbed her tunic front, and jerked her through the open gate. She floundered, swallowing a mouthful of water, and another Weardas dragged her to one side. Shade came splashing after her, snarling and coughing. The captain ducked into the tunnel, sword out toward Chane, and grabbed the staff.

Chane came through next, all the teal-skinned newcomers herding him. He paused, raising one open hand as he pulled Wynn's pack from the water. He was soaked from head to toe, and his colorless eyes shifted rapidly as he watched everyone. As he passed through the gate, another Weardas snatched the pack away and herded him at sword point to the pool's far side.

Then the wild-eyed man tore from the elf's grip, lunging for the tunnel opening.

The duchess threw herself on top of him, screaming, "Freädherich, no!"

They both toppled and sank, but that name overrode Wynn's fear for an instant. She recognized it.

The pair heaved up, splashing water everywhere.

Wynn sucked in a panicked breath as the captain flung the staff onto the pool's far edge. And the bodyguard before her flattened his sword in warning against her chest.

The captain and the elf rushed toward the duchess as the third Weardas circled around, blocking off Chane. Like Wynn, Chane watched everything in complete confusion.

The closest teal-skinned being stepped to the half-open gate.

The wild-eyed man shrieked like a mourner, reaching out to it. Even with the duchess atop him, and the elf and captain trying to get a grip on him, his fingers kept clutching the air toward the visitor.

The visitor slowly stretched out its hand in turn. Long, narrow fingers, ending in claws, were webbed in the spaces between.

"Get away from him!" the duchess shrieked. She rolled off the madman, ducked around the tall elf, and slashed her saber. Its blade clattered across the gate's bars.

But the being in the tunnel didn't even lift its spear. It just slowly lowered its hand.

Duchess Reine threw her whole body against the gate. It slammed shut with a clang that reverberated through the chamber.

"You're not taking him!" she hissed, backing away with saber held out. There was less rage than terror on her face.

All the being did was quietly grip one iron bar and gaze through the gate with its black-orb eyes.

The duchess whirled in the pool as the captain and the tall elf heaved the whimpering man onto the pool's rear ledge. She looked as if she might break right there, collapse, and sink beneath the water.

"Highness?" whispered the bodyguard before Chane.

With a convulsive shudder, Reine straightened and turned her eyes on Wynn. In place of the whimpering man's madness, some fear-driven rage filled her features. She surged through the pool straight at Wynn with the saber thrust out.

"What are you doing here?" she demanded.

Wynn might've come up with something if she weren't so overwhelmed. Her gaze flicked erratically about. She knew of only one man named Freädherich, though she'd never seen him up close.

The younger prince of the Âreskynna, thought dead for years, was locked away in the Stonewalkers' underworld.

Wynn couldn't get out one word.

CHAPTER 17

Reine stood numbed by shock, barely aware that she shivered in the pool's cold water. The chamber was half-illuminated by light leaking from the sitting chamber. On the side nearer the door leading out, a dark and dripping wolf stood upon the pool's edge above the sage.

Reine couldn't believe anyone, less that Wynn Hygeorht, had found their way in here.

Better that the sage and her companions had been drowned in the rising tide. It would have made things simpler. No one in the outside world must ever know Frey still lived.

Yes, it would've been easier on Reine if Wynn had simply died by her own fault. But the sage hadn't come seeking Frey. That she'd found him was just the worst happenstance.

How had Wynn known where the texts were being kept? Was this why she'd schemed her way into speaking with Ore-Locks?

Reine lowered her saber slightly as she backed away.

"If you've nothing to tell me," she growled at Wynn, "then you and yours will remain silent!"

Wynn nodded slowly.

These outsiders had already seen too much to ever leave this place. But the longer temptation remained in the tunnel, the worse Frey would suffer. Reine turned at the pool's center.

Tristan and Chuillyon crouched upon the pool's rear ledge, holding down Frey's limp form.

"Release him," she said.

Chuillyon quickly raised his head, glaring sternly at her—something very rare for the old one. The captain's expression mimicked the elf's, with a more frustrated anger.

"Highness—" he began.

"Do it!" Reine ordered.

With a grimace, Tristan took his hands away, as did Chuillyon. Frey's haunted eyes roamed about the chamber.

"Frey," Reine whispered gently, "come."

His gaze lifted beyond her, fixing upon the gate, the tunnel, or whatever waited there.

"Frey!" she said more sharply, and held out her hand.

He scrambled over the ledge's lip, slipping into the water with barely a splash.

Danyel and Saln were still in the pool, along with Wynn and her tall guard. Both half turned, trying to keep their captives in sight. Like her, they tensely eyed the rippling form beneath the water as it slipped along the pool's bottom.

Saln swallowed audibly, but Reine kept her eyes on the approaching shadow. Tristan dropped into the pool to follow, but she raised a hand to warn him off. She hoped Frey would heed her.

The wavering shadow of her husband reached her feet.

Frey surfaced, rising tall above her. His aquamarine eyes stared over her head at the gate—at the *visitors* waiting beyond it.

Reine reached up and touched his cheek.

"Send them away," she whispered, but it came out pleading rather than firm. "Frey, you must . . . please."

He blinked in confusion, and the hurt in his eyes flooded through her. She didn't know if his pain came from her request or realizing he'd forgotten her amid mad obsession.

"Please," she repeated.

Frey closed his eyes. His head dropped until it rested heavily against her hand. He submerged, and Reine's hand followed upon his shoulder into the water. She forced herself not to clench his shirt and hang on. She didn't need to turn, to look into the tunnel. She knew the *visitors* had sunk beneath the water as well.

Faint pulsing tones rose in the pool. They filled the chamber dully, as if coming from somewhere far off.

Frey had once tried to describe whale song and the utterances of dolphins. She still didn't know how he'd learned of such things. She felt the sounds through her legs and through her hand upon his shoulder. Any ignorant unfortunate who heard them would've thought them beautiful, like horns and reed flutes blown beneath the sea amid rolling staccato clicks.

Every tone made the pool's surface shiver subtly.

Every sound made Reine cringe, knowing they came from her beloved Frey.

He rose up before her, his eyes vacant, and stepped slowly toward the tunnel. Tristan waded forward, poised to grab him, but Reine shook her head.

There was nowhere for Frey to go, now that the gate was shut and the visitors were gone. Cinder-Shard called them the Dunidæ—the Deep Ones.

Only the Stonewalkers knew of their existence, along with the Âreskynna and a few others trusted with such a secret. They appeared only here, or where the ocean crept in beneath the mountain to meet the underworld. No one knew why, and it happened only after one of the Âreskynna "vanished"—like Frey. As with his ancestors, perhaps the change in him at the highest tides was what summoned the Dunidæ.

Every generation was tainted with this "sea-lorn" sickness, but there was always one who suffered worst. The last had been Frey's aunt, King Leofwin's sister, Hrädwyn. To public knowledge, she'd died of a fever at fourteen.

Hrädwyn had lived past twenty-three, though she'd never left this place in those nine years. Sea-lorn madness had finally killed her. And from what Leofwin had told Reine, Frey was more afflicted than his aunt, though it had set upon him later in life.

Reine clamped a hand over her mouth, refusing to cry.

Without the comb with its hidden droplet of white metal, Frey could never open the gate or the door. She'd become his prime jailer—for his safety, for the future need of him, like some tool or weapon harbored in secret for fear of a long-forgotten enemy.

Unless the Dunidæ let him out, and that would happen only if he asked for it.

How many times would his love for her keep him from doing so?

"Danyel!" Tristan barked, shifting toward Wynn and gesturing across the pool. "Make certain the gate is locked."

Reine came to her senses.

Danyel was nearest to Wynn, but when he began moving, the wolf snarled and clacked its teeth at him. He stopped, raising his sword for a thrust at the animal. Wynn reached up quickly and clamped her hands over the wolf's muzzle.

Danyel took a step closer to the sage.

"Get away from her!"

Reine and Tristan both turned at that maimed voice.

Wynn's guardian stood with Saln's sword point pressed against his chest. Pale skinned and pale eyed, the tall man bore a scar that ran completely across his neck. Some old battle wound had taken his true voice forever. More disturbing was that he never even glanced down at Saln's sword.

What had Wynn called him—Chane?

He ignored the weapon as if it weren't there. But the expression on his face, as he looked between Wynn and her captors . . .

Reine read it clearly, like a finely inked letter. She caught his tone beneath the written words. Chane was no mere guardian. And if she knew one thing intimately, it was the pain of impossible love—and the lack of awareness to escape it before it was too late.

Again, it made everything worse for what had to be done.

Reine turned on Wynn as the sage shook her head at Chane, warning him off. It didn't matter. At the slightest flinch, Saln or Tristan would kill him without hesitation.

But then, Master Cinder-Shard's massive form appeared in the doorway, and Wynn's wolf spun, snarling at him.

He ignored it, demanding, "Who opened the tunnel gate? Where is the prince?"

"I opened it," Chuillyon answered. "We have visitors. . . and not the usual ones."

Cinder-Shard's eyes fixed on Reine and then drifted beyond her. He relaxed just a little upon spotting Frey, but his expression darkened when his gaze fell upon the young sage.

"Princess . . ." he began, turning his cold eyes to her.

"Highness?" Tristan asked.

The captain stood halfway to Chane with his sword poised. Danyel and Saln waited as well.

Reine knew what was expected. They held back only for her command to confirm it. Suddenly all she could think of was Frey, somewhere behind her.

No one must ever learn he was alive or where he was. But he would never approve of what she had to do—for his sake and the family's ancient secret, for a world's hope—or for all that was hinted at in Wynn Hygeorht's damnable texts.

Reine looked up to Chuillyon standing on the pool's rear ledge.

The elder elf took a visibly hard breath. He dropped his eyes, as if whatever he might say wouldn't matter. No trace of sly humor remained on his old face.

"Your order, my lady," Tristan said, and it wasn't a request.

Reine retreated one step. A few quick sword thrusts and it would be over. Then her back bumped into someone, and she dropped her saber. As it sank in the pool, she whispered too faintly to be clear.

Tristan's eyes widened. "Highness?"

"Arrest them," Reine said clearly, anger rising to choke off fear. She spun, wrapping her arms around Frey as the captain's voice grated in her ears.

"My lady, we cannot—"

"Do it!" she ordered, and buried her face in Frey's back. "Get them out of here!"

Amid splashing, barked orders, and the wolf's growls, Reine slid her hands around and over Frey's chest. She felt one of his hands settle over hers.

"It'll be all right," she whispered. "It will pass . . . again."

But those weren't the words filling her head, the ones that made her small fingers curl in his wet shirt until the fabric began to tear.

Don't you ever leave me!

Sau'ilahk slid slowly down the lift's shaft wall, pausing often to listen and peer into the depths below. He waited until any light at the bottom faded before he completed his descent.

The duchess, her entourage, and their Stonewalker guide were gone, but she had led him far enough. That assistance was all he required, for he was here, in the underworld.

By all Wynn's bumbling efforts to locate this place, the texts had to be here as well. What would be safer for the guild than to hide them in the hands of the Stonewalkers?

Ahead . . . and see!

At his command, the stone-spider clicked down the passage's roof.

As he waited, he called the stone-worm out of the wall, making certain it had kept up. Once the spider returned, confirming that the way was clear, he slipped onward. But when he came upon a three-way branching of the passage, he halted to study each path.

He could not linger long enough for his servitors to scout all three. There was no knowing when someone might come back or the lift would be called for others to descend. Before long, the outer guards' bodies would be discovered.

Straight ahead, down the main passage from the lift, he spotted a faint glow.

Sau'ilahk turned full circle, examining all ways, and finally pushed on toward that dim light. Finding just one lone Stonewalker seemed the only way to learn what he needed. Soon, the rough-hewn tunnel spilled into a natural cavern.

Aside from the dull glimmer of phosphorescent minerals in glistening walls, there were smaller, steaming orange crystals dotting the cavern. Their light broke upon merging stalactites and stalagmites. Shadows cast every which way made the place a maze of dark columns. He could just make out other black openings to other places.

The underworld looked—felt—so different from what lay in the seatt far above.

Less excavated, it was a realm of natural spaces rather than those expanded and formed to meet the will and need of the dwarves. Some might have found the place unnerving, but it left Sau'ilahk melancholy with its sense of permanence. As if it had been, would be, always here—like him.

He drifted in a straight line, slipping through natural columns toward one opening better lit than the others. The hollow beyond was smaller than the main space, and only dripping stalactites hung from its low ceiling. Some had been broken off for clearance, and the floor had been cleared and leveled. In its center stood a stone rectangle chiseled perfectly smooth. In repose, atop it, lay the corpse of a warrior thänæ in full battle dress.

Sau'ilahk slipped in, briefly lingering over Hammer-Stag's body.

The dwarf had been washed and dressed in clean clothes and a polished hauberk, but his pallid features still held a trace of his last moment of fury and agony. Strangely, his eyelids were open. The great ax that had given Sau'ilahk moments of trouble was clutched to the thänæ's chest in his large hands.

A stone trough filled with murky water rested against the platform's side.

Sau'ilahk spotted a pallet leaning against the far wall, made of a wood frame and interwoven leather straps. Four long iron bars leaned near it. He was familiar with dwarven cairns for their dead, but he had no notion what was taking place here. Did Stonewalkers immerse their dead before final burial? Were they preserving the body?

He needed a live Stonewalker, not a dead thänæ. And whoever had been preparing the body, where had they gone? He returned to the main cavern, but had barely reached its center when a thunderclap rolled through the underworld.

Sau'ilahk froze as it echoed off of stone.

Between glistening natural columns he spotted a hulkish dark shadow. It stood in one of the far openings and stepped into the main cavern. Orange light caught on the dwarf's thick red hair and glinted upon a thôrhk around its neck.

Sau'ilahk rushed at it, straight through the wet columns.

The dwarf drew a wide dagger from his belt. His other hand swung wide and slapped against the cavern's wall.

Another thunderclap rose from stone.

Sau'ilahk halted upon hearing a grating beneath the noise. At a shift of shadow, he whirled to see the cavern wall bulging.

Darkened stone formed into a wide face and a body that followed.

A second Stonewalker emerged straight out of the cavern wall.

Wynn tried to regain her wits as she was herded down the passage. She held on to Shade's scruff and glanced back for Chane. One young Weardas flicked a sword point at her in warning. Beyond him, Chane was disarmed and driven forward by the other bodyguard and the captain.

And the captain held her staff.

Wynn panicked for an instant. To use the staff, she needed her pewter-framed glasses. Her thoughts scrambled back over the wild struggle at the gate before the sea tunnel. She dug into the pocket of her elven pants, and when she felt the rims of her spectacles, she drew a minor breath of relief that she hadn't lost them. Hurrying on, she looked back once again.

A glimpse of white at the rear told Wynn the elf followed, but she couldn't tell whether the duchess was there. The only person ahead of her was the master of the Stonewalkers.

Wynn was lost as to what had happened in the pool chamber. She'd blundered into more than just the hiding place of her texts. A dead prince was locked away in the Stonewalkers' underworld, and Duchess Reine was with him. Foreign beings had risen in the tunnel's water, clearly having some affinity for Prince Freädherich. And the prince had submerged to utter unimaginable sounds.

Whatever it all meant, Wynn realized that none of it was intended for the world outside. And the only reason she still lived was because the duchess had faltered.

Even if she was left alive, she'd be locked away where no one would ever find her. There would be no charges, no trial, no chance to justify how and why she'd forced her way in here. Wynn Hygeorht would simply disappear.

She still couldn't get it all straight in her head.

The duchess had nearly stood trial for her husband's disappearance and assumed death. If she'd known he was alive, why hadn't she spoken up at the time? The answer was partly here, but how was the prince connected to those beings in the tunnel?

A single memory lingered in Wynn's mind. It complicated all other questions.

Half a world away in Droevinka, Leesil had uncovered a hidden chamber beneath the keep near Magiere's home village. There, Ubâd had engineered her unnatural conception and birth. In that chamber, they'd found the remains of those slaughtered for the ritual.

Elves and dwarves were known, one of each present among the desiccated bones. But the others were like no beings Wynn had ever seen—until later. A séyilf, one of the Wind-Blown, had appeared at Magiere's trial before the Farlands' elves. In the search for the orb, Magiere, Leesil, and Chap had been taken into the depths before the Chein'âs, the Burning Ones.

The Úirishg—five races associated to the Elements—were only a myth.

But not to Wynn—not after all she'd been through in the last two years. Elves and Dwarves, Séyilf and Chein'âs races stood for Spirit and Earth, Air and Fire. That left only Water. Even knowing the other races existed, the impact of what—who—she'd seen in the pool chamber's tunnel was more than she could take in.

Wynn had seen the people from the sea, the last race of the Úirishg.

But right now, she had to focus. She, Chane, and Shade were in deadly trouble, and not from the undead or the agents of a long-forgotten enemy. They'd stumbled into a tangled secret, one the duchess seemed ready to kill for to keep hidden.

"Where are you taking us?" Wynn finally asked.

No one answered.

She glanced back at Chane and scowled as a Weardas tipped a sword at her face. Chane looked coldly unconcerned. That didn't worry her as much as his eyes.

His irises were still colorless, glinting like crystals. She still didn't fully understand why and how that happened, except that it occurred just before he did something unnatural—something undead-like. He was waiting for a moment to attack and get his hands on a weapon.

Wynn shook her head at him emphatically. Injuring or killing royal guards would only make things worse. When he didn't even blink in acknowledgment, all she could do was move on, watching the master Stonewalker's wide back.

Then she thought she heard thunder.

Shade halted, lurching Wynn to a stop. The bodyguard behind her stumbled and cursed. Master Cinder-Shard grew still in the passage ahead.

"What was that?" Chane asked.

Shade snarled loudly, and Wynn stroked the dog's back. Instantly, her head began to ache. A memory swelled, nearly bloating the passage from her sight.

A black shadow coalesced like a column of night in a street sparsely lit by lanterns. The wraith stood between Wynn and the guild's keep. It was the night she'd first gone to meet Chane.

Wynn took a sharp inhale.

Cinder-Shard glanced back, one hand on a sheathed blade at his waist. But Wynn teetered as Shade called up one memory after another—always of the black wraith.

It burst out through a scriptorium door. . . .

It escaped the Upright Quill with a folio. . . .

It tore out a city guard's chest.

"No!" she whispered sharply. "You're wrong. I saw it ripped apart . . . like smoke. It's gone!"

Shade clacked her teeth, snarling so loudly it reverberated.

Cinder-Shard's craggy features filled with suspicion.

"Wynn?" Chane called.

Another boom like thunder rolled down the tunnel, and the master Stone-walker whirled about, facing the path ahead.

"What is it?" the captain barked.

Cinder-Shard took off at a run, his heavy boots hammering the passage floor.

"Stop!" Wynn shouted.

"What is he doing?" Chane hissed.

"Shut it!" the captain ordered, and then shouted, "Cinder-Shard?"

Wynn turned toward Chane but faltered. Still gripping Shade's fur, she looked down. Shade stood rigid, hackles raised. A mewling rumble began pouring between her bared teeth.

Wynn still didn't want to believe. She shriveled inside, trying to hide from Shade's truth. If that *thing* had survived, after all it had done to get the folios, there was only one way it could've known to come here.

It had followed her.

When Wynn looked to Chane, she was choking in misery. She had led that monster in here.

"Wraith!" she whispered sharply.

Silent malice washed from Chane's features, replaced by startled disbelief. He began to shake his head. And Shade suddenly ripped free of Wynn's grip.

The dog bolted down the passage and cut loose an eerie wail that echoed. Both young Weardas behind Wynn winced at the deafening sound. Chane wasn't shaking his head anymore.

"The staff!" Wynn shouted, looking to the captain.

"Tristan, follow Cinder-Shard!" the duchess ordered from somewhere at the rear. "Don't lose sight of him."

Chane spun about, blocking the captain. "Give Wynn the staff. Do it, or you are all dead . . . even your precious noble!"

"I told you to keep quiet," barked the captain, shoving Chane forward.

"Duchess!" Wynn called. "Tell him to give me the staff. Not even the Stone-walkers can face this."

The pair of Weardas charged her. One grabbed her soaked tunic's shoulder and shoved her on. Before she turned, she looked to Chane and flicked a quick glance toward the staff in the captain's hand.

Chane nodded once.

CHAPTER 18

Sau'ilahk had no time to ponder how the second Stonewalker came out of a cavern wall. The thunderclap raised by the younger, red-haired one had to be an alarm. He needed to end this and slip away before being forced to flee. And he needed life to feed on.

He rushed the second Stonewalker, as it slashed at him with a wide dagger. Gray-blond hair hung wildly about the elder dwarf's bony face. The blade swept through unimpeded, and his expression shifted to surprise.

Sau'ilahk sank his incorporeal hand through the dwarf's black-scaled hauberk. Elation rose at the tingle of life as the dwarf's mouth gaped.

The old one tried to back away, and Sau'ilahk paced him, wanting to leach as much life as possible. He had not had enough time to memorize this cavern. If exhaustion forced him into dormancy, he would rise in the last place he had awakened.

The elder Stonewalker backed against—into—the wall.

The tingle of life vanished, and Sau'ilahk froze, staring into his victim's face, which was half-submerged in glistening stone.

The stone's texture and phosphorescence flowed over the elder dwarf's features. It began covering his form, armor, hair, and eyes. He became a likeness seemingly carved from the rock.

Sau'ilahk's hand began to harden, as if solidified against his will, trapped inside the stone.

Nothing could hide its life from his touch. Nothing could grip a spirit, especially one such as him. Stunned and horrified, he willed his hand to return to its spiritual state and jerked free, retreating in a rush. He whirled at the sound of grating boots, and the red-haired young one closed quickly.

Sau'ilahk could not help recoiling as another dagger slashed through him.

The young one's eyes widened when the blade did not even ruffle the black cloak. Sau'ilahk swiped at him in turn, hoping to consume this one's life. The dwarf slapped his free hand against a stalactite.

Sau'ilahk's black-wrapped fingers passed straight through his red hair and his face. The young one did not flinch, and Sau'ilahk did not even feel a brief tingle.

"Meâkesagh, yaittrâg vuddidí maks! Chleu'intag chregh; chleu'intag hìm!"

He twisted at the elder's deep voice, catching the meaning of those barked commands too late.

Ore-Locks, block the far exit! Keep to stone; keep to me!

The gray-blond elder stepped forward, his still-carved face pushing from calcified rock. Glistening stone flowed from his features, until he stood fully distinguished from the cavern wall. A rush of booted feet made Sau'ilahk whip the other way.

The red-haired one dodged between half-lit columns and deep shadows, always keeping one hand upon a stalagmite or stalactite. He regained the far opening where he had first appeared.

Sau'ilahk turned fear-fed anger on the bony-featured elder.

. . . keep to stone . . . keep to me.

He hissed, and his cloak began to rise. Even if he blinked across the cavern by line of sight, he could not feed on the young one. The elder was the key to Sau'ilahk's failure. That one somehow protected himself and the other through contact with stone. And there was stone here everywhere.

Sau'ilahk had to force one of them to lose contact between flesh and stone.

If the elder died, the younger would be helpless, but turning fully corporeal to fight them would deplete Sau'ilahk's energy. He would not last long. Even if he killed one, to do so quickly would not feed him enough.

He surged rearward, rushing back through three calcified columns.

"Bulwark?" the young one called.

"Hold!" the elder shouted, swerving around a lumpy column.

Sau'ilahk spread his arms wide.

His servitors could do little against enemies who became one with stone. A pure conjury was too slow, and a base summoning was the only choice.

He arched his arms forward as the elder Stonewalker rounded another stalagmite. Sigils and shapes formed in Sau'ilahk's sight, but not fixed upon his assailant.

He held them within the vacant space between his arms, and the cavern's air began to shift.

Wind raced in through openings as if the cavern sucked it in. It built into a whirling core within the half circle of Sau'ilahk's arms. The elder dwarf faltered, slapping at hair whipping across his bony face. He growled unintelligibly and charged.

Sau'ilahk clapped his hands together.

A crack shook the cavern as churning air exploded outward. The elder Stonewalker skidded back, and his heavy body slammed into a joined stalagmite and stalactite. The column shattered under his bulk, chunks scattering all about.

The brief hurricane died just as suddenly as it came. Not one fold of Sau'ilahk's robe had been ruffled, but the elder dwarf lay prone and still in the column's rubble.

Sau'ilahk glanced aside in growing fatigue. The younger one was gone from the far opening, perhaps flattened as well. Satisfied, he slid toward his unconscious victim.

The elder rolled over. Shaking off shattered stone, he heaved himself up, not even bleeding.

Sau'ilahk halted in frustration.

At a clatter and scuffing of boots, the younger dwarf clambered back into the far opening.

"Hold!" the elder shouted. "The others are coming!"

An eerie wail rolled into the cavern.

Sau'ilahk peered at every opening, searching for its origin. He knew that sound, and hope drained like his strength. He had been detected. If the black wolf was here, so was Wynn. How had she found her way into the underworld? Had she learned the location of the texts, or even beaten him to them?

Something moved beyond a wide-based stone cone to his right. It was neither of his opponents. It slipped around that tall and broad stalagmite, taking shape in the wall crystals' orange light.

A third Stonewalker, a female, watched him with unblinking pellet eyes.

Sau'ilahk's hiss shifted to a moan. He did not have the reserves to engage three. All he need do was to sink into dormancy and vanish. But he had come so close to his desire.

Another form rushed out of the wall behind the gray-blond, bony-faced elder.

It shot from solid rock like a broad shadow and landed on heavy boots, sending vibrations through the cavern floor. This fourth Stonewalker seemed vaguely familiar, with black hair streaked by gray, and a beard of steely bristles.

Sau'ilahk slowly rotated, tracking his four opponents as they shifted about the cavern. Again he should have fled. But the texts were here, containing secrets he needed—for the means to regain flesh.

The black wolf rushed in beyond the two elder Stonewalkers.

Another warning to flee, but Sau'ilahk's long suffering smothered him.

He would not let that whelp of a sage steal the texts, steal his hope, no matter what it cost him.

Wynn stumbled out of the main passage into a long, low-roofed cavern filled with twisted light. One Weardas bodyguard shoved her against the side wall, and, as the others came through, she looked frantically about for Shade. The dog had bolted ahead, wailing her alarm, so she must be here somewhere.

Shade reappeared, circling back to a protective stance before Wynn, and her eerie wail lowered to a snarl.

Small dwarven crystals spread pockets of wispy orange amid the walls' dim yellow-green glow. Shadows multiplied into a forest of dark silhouettes between the glistening wet columns. Some of those shadows moved.

Wynn spotted two, no, at least three dwarven shapes. One passed into the light of a nearby crystal.

Cinder-Shard stepped into view as all four Stonewalkers faced toward the cavern's midpoint. Wynn followed their attention, and her stomach tightened.

A black figure floated there, garbed in a flowing robe and cloak that shifted and swayed upon a breeze she couldn't feel. It raised one arm, and its sleeve slipped down, exposing its forearm, hand, and fingers all wrapped in black cloth strips.

Wynn had believed Shade and had known what they would find. But to actually *see* it made her choke.

The wraith slowly turned, watching the Stonewalkers. Shade suddenly lunged at a break between the dwarves.

"No!" Wynn shouted. "Stay!"

Shade halted short but didn't retreat.

The wraith's cowl turned at her voice, its opening darker than any cavern hollow.

The captain shoved Chane aside, and the second Weardas took his place as guard. Wynn tried to remember what the captain had called that one. Was it Danyel?

The captain dropped the sun crystal's staff and stepped out.

"We're here!" he shouted.

"Stay back!" Cinder-Shard returned. "Keep your people out of our way!"

The wraith's cowl cocked slightly, fixing on Wynn.

"The staff!" she shouted, and tried to step out for it. "Give it to me!"

The captain cast her a hard glare and set his boot on the staff. The third Weardas shoved Wynn back, pinning her to the wall with one hand. She heard a guttural rumble, but it hadn't come from Shade.

Chane's face twisted in his own snarl. The guards had taken his sword, but he could fight without it. His colorless eyes shifted from Wynn's assailant to the captain's exposed back.

Reine ignored Wynn and stood staring beyond Tristan and Cinder-Shard at a tall, black-robed figure. She'd heard scant details of a "mage" who'd murdered sages for translation folios. Through all of it, Wynn had insisted that it was something else. . . .

What had she called it—an undead?

Reine hadn't read Captain Rodian's final investigation report, but she'd been told that he claimed the perpetrator had died. Yet here was a likeness that could be no other. The culprit lived and was here in the underworld.

Wynn Hygeorht's follies mounted by the moment. She'd repeatedly muddled Rodian's investigation in trying to get access to the texts. There was only one way this interloper could've found the underworld.

Reine's fright turned to anger.

Wynn had led a murdering mage into the place of Frey's safekeeping.

Sau'ilahk fixed on Wynn; then his attention shifted again.

Beyond the black wolf, a tall royal guard in a helm and red tabard had dropped the staff and now held it down with his boot. Its upper section was enclosed in a leather sheath.

Sau'ilahk knew it even with its crystal hidden. That crystal had nearly burned him into oblivion the last time he had hunted Wynn. But she was pinned against the wall, and her ignorant new companions would not let her have the staff.

He took a fleeting instant of joy before spotting another small woman.

The duchess stood with saber in hand before an overly tall, white-robed figure. Though an Âreskynna only by marriage, she was still a royal. If the elder gray-blond dwarf could make the other Stonewalkers as impervious as himself, killing so many would be impossible, let alone taking one to torture for information.

Sau'ilahk's attention shifted erratically between Wynn and the duchess.

Could he seize someone more susceptible, someone he might even exchange for the texts? Tormenting Wynn would please him most, but even if she knew the texts' location, would the others sacrifice her and move the texts as a precaution?

He lost his train of thought as all of the Stonewalkers became still. They spread their arms wide and began a low, guttural chant in unison. It thrummed throughout the cavern as they stepped inward, closing around him.

Sau'ilahk did not know what they attempted, but their lack of fear concerned him.

Then Chane lashed out at one Weardas.

Sau'ilahk knew Chane would fight to get the staff into Wynn's possession.

Too many sides were coming at him at once. He wanted to screech in frustration at more lost strength as he crouched and solidified one hand.

Sau'ilahk slammed his palm against the cavern's floor.

Chane could not believe the wraith had survived—not after all they had been through to destroy it. There was only one way to drive it off and give them time to learn why. Swords were worthless; regaining the staff for Wynn was all that mattered.

A Weardas still held her against the wall, but Chane needed to put his own guard down and reach the captain.

The Stonewalkers suddenly halted, and their chant rose. At the distraction, Chane twisted and slammed a fist into his guard's face.

The man teetered as his head whipped back, but he still managed to slash out with his sword. Chane felt the blade's point tear across his chest. Hunger rose quickly to eat that small pain. He crouched and drove his other palm into the man's gut.

The guard toppled, and Chane lunged for the captain's back.

"Tristan, behind you!"

At the duchess's shout, the captain started to turn, and another blade slashed across Chane's back. It failed to penetrate his cloak. Chane grabbed the captain's wrist above the sword, ready to strike the man down and snatch up the staff.

The cavern's glow brightened sharply with orange-red.

Chane hesitated as the Stonewalkers' chant died. He saw fire erupt from stone around the wraith's crouched form.

A line of flame spread from under its flattened hand and shot outward, racing and twisting around the wide bases of stalagmites. Cinder-Shard lunged out of the fire's path as the other Stonewalkers scattered.

Chane had hesitated too long.

A sword hilt struck the back of his skull—but the blow was too weak. He barely dropped his head as someone shouted, "Highness, keep away!" Chane knew who had attacked him from behind and did not care.

He wrenched the captain off balance as he thrust back with his elbow. But his arm slammed against something more solid than a small woman. He twisted his head in surprise, coming face-to-face with the young guard he had punched. Blood ran from the man's nostrils across his mouth.

"Chane, get out of the way!" Wynn shouted.

The line of fire raced toward the gathering at the entrance, steam shrieking off the wet stone in its path.

He glanced quickly beyond the bloody guard blocking him. The duchess and the elf stood in the way. There was not enough time to get through them, let alone get the staff to Wynn. The fire was coming too fast.

"Shade, free Wynn!" he ordered, hoping the dog understood.

Chane shouldered sideways into the young guard and charged toward Wynn.

Reine stiffened as the fire streaked between through the cavern. Blood ran freely down Danyel's face, dripping off his chin, and Tristan stared at the oncoming flames.

"Everyone out, now!" she commanded.

Then the wolf leaped at Saln.

He stumbled aside, fending it off, and lost his hold on Wynn. Chane slammed into Wynn, pushing her back against the wall, and he grabbed for the wolf's scruff. He tried to pull them both behind his wet cloak.

Reine took a step, and Chuillyon's light hand fell upon her shoulder.

"Be still," he whispered.

She spun, ready to grab him and flee, but faltered at his soft voice.

"Chârmun . . . agh'alhtahk so. A'lhän am leagad chionns'gnajh."

Chuillyon's large amber eyes closed as his other hand flattened over his heart.

Reine's Elvish wasn't good enough. All she caught was something about "grace," as if he'd whispered a prayer. She grabbed his robe's belt to pull him, but his grip on her shoulder closed slightly.

Chuillyon sighed, and a shallow smile spread across his thin lips.

When Reine turned her head to call the others, Tristan kicked the staff aside before he tried to leap clear. Onrushing flames raced over his boot, licking up his shin. He hadn't been wearing his cloak in Frey's pool, and the dry hem ignited. He ripped it off, letting it fall, and stomped on it. The stream of fire reached Saln, sending flames up his legs.

"Saln!" Reine cried. "Drop!"

He did, rolling on the floor as he screamed.

Reine backed against Chuillyon, shoving at him. Try as she might, she couldn't force him into the passage.

Sau'ilahk watched with glee as Stonewalkers scattered. But holding conjured fire upon wet stone while keeping his thin bond to his servitors became too much. His remaining energy was quickly draining away.

He savored only an instant of satisfaction as Chane abandoned the staff and ran to shield Wynn and the wolf. Frustration followed as the tall captain kicked the staff aside. Flames caught in his cloak. As he ripped it off, another guard was hit full on by the fire. That one cried out in pain, steam and smoke rising from his damp pants and boots.

But the white-robed elf just stood there.

He pulled the duchess back, calmly closing his eyes. His lips moved, but whatever he spoke was too soft to hear.

Sau'ilahk was sick of the unknown, from mystical dwarves and Wynn's two companions to some white-robed dabbler with the duchess. With a clear line of sight to his target, he jerked his hand from the cavern floor, releasing his hold upon the fire. He rose, preparing to blink across the cavern and snatch the duchess, for the others would trade anything for her.

Sau'ilahk halted with a shudder of disbelief.

Wynn pushed at Chane, shouting, "The staff! It'll burn!"

"Be still!" he said, holding her tight. "Stay beneath my cloak."

Wynn bumped against Shade as she craned her head halfway around Chane's shoulder. She saw the captain kick the staff aside and then gasped as fire raced over his other foot. It struck another guard dead on. Then the twisting snake of flames shot toward the duchess.

The staff lay not far from the captain's smoldering cloak.

Wynn shouted in Chane's ear, "Let me go!"

His body felt like an immovable wall.

Wynn watched Reine cringe against Chuillyon, pushing on him. The tall elf foolishly held his place with eyes closed. There was nothing Wynn could do but shout at them, "Get out!"

The fire ended in a sudden splash.

Barely a yard before the duchess, flames fanned into the air, and Wynn couldn't help a small gasp.

Fire licked and crawled, but it advanced no farther. Red-orange flickers spread over some unseen barrier. Where flames danced, they vanished, as if eaten away into nothing, until the fire's trailing end rushed in.

It fueled one last surge and then dissipated in the air, and the cavern dimmed instantly. All that remained were heated drifts of steam rising from wet stone as the burned Weardas lay gripping his legs and moaning.

The staff lay free and clear in sight.

Wynn stiffened at a loud hiss filling the cavern. Before she looked for the wraith, a dark hulk leaped out of the far wall past the captain.

Cinder-Shard landed with a thud in the dead fire's steaming path. His eyes fixed toward the cavern's center as an eager grimace spread on his wide face.

"Make me a path, you bothersome trickster!" he growled.

Wynn didn't know whom he meant until a soft laugh pulled her attention. Behind the stunned duchess, the elf in white smiled openly.

Chuillyon's large amber eyes focused toward the cavern's heart. He lifted his hand from Reine's shoulder and spread his fingers.

Wynn felt the air turn chill as it gusted suddenly, and she sucked in a frightened breath. As Chuillyon's brow wrinkled in puzzlement, and Cinder-Shard straightened in shock, Wynn knew what had happened.

She'd felt that same shift of air twice in the night streets of Calm Seatt. The wraith had vanished, but not for long.

"Where is it?" Cinder-Shard shouted, looking around wildly.

"It's coming!" she whispered sharply in Chane's ear. "Get me some time!"

Wynn pushed around Chane, charging for the staff, as she dug in her pocket for the glasses. She finished only two steps.

Coiling darkness, like black smoke, thickened on her right as two Stone-walkers came out of the walls.

The wraith materialized directly before Reine.

Sau'ilahk held the main entrance in his thoughts as he winked through dormancy. He instantly reappeared to see the duchess's face flushing white with fear.

But he was more than an arm's length away.

That was not right. He should have awakened almost atop her. Something was *pressing* him back, as if he had become partially physical.

Sau'ilahk stared over the duchess's head into large amber eyes.

The tall elf merely glared back, a soft smile upon his pressed lips.

A saber slashed through Sau'ilahk, but he did not look at the duchess, only at the elf who somehow impeded him. He needed a hostage more than ever and pushed against the resistance, reaching for Reine as he called his servitors.

Kill the white one!

Sau'ilahk heard snarls, and he felt teeth burn through his incorporeal leg.

The wraith coalesced before the duchess as Chane pivoted away from Wynn. One moment was all she needed, though he hoped she gave him warning before igniting the crystal—and that his damp cloak would be enough to protect him if he crouched beneath it.

Then Chane saw the duchess swing her saber.

It passed through the black figure as Shade scrambled in from behind. Shade's jaws clacked through the wraith's robe.

Chane rushed in on the dog's tail. Shade yelped—in unison with a wail from the wraith—but as Chane closed, the side of the entrance bulged in a fist-size lump.

A red glow swelled within that moving nodule of stone.

One burning eye, like a lump of molten glass, erupted from rock. It leaped out of the stone. The spindly-legged thing arched straight for the elf's head. The wraith reached for the duchess, but its movement was so slow, as if it struggled to get to her.

Chane senses widened as he swung at the wraith's back side.

His hand passed through the black cloak, and cold like a thousand icy needles ran up his arm as the thing with the burning eye became clear.

That fist-size stone insect, with four legs ending in barbs, shattered in the air a forearm's length from its target. The light of its eye suddenly died, and dull pieces of stone rained down. The elf stiffened as these struck his head and shoulders.

A gravelly voice shouted from behind, "*Maksag, choyll-shu'ass Kêravägh!*"

Shuddering in pain from striking the wraith, Chane felt someone grab his cloak's collar and jerk him aside.

Wynn snatched up the staff. The captain spotted her as she saw something break apart in the air above Chuillyon. Whatever the thing had been, it broke apart, showering down upon the elf, as Chane and Shade assaulted the wraith.

Cinder-Shard rushed by, shouting in Dwarvish, "Out, you dog of Kêravägh."

His last word baffled her as she shoved the glasses over her eyes. Then she faltered for one breath.

Cinder-Shard grabbed Chane's cloak collar and tossed him away as if throwing a rag.

"Chane, cover up!" Wynn shouted.

The wraith whirled around, and Shade dodged out of its reach. It froze, its dark-filled cowl centering on her as she leaned the staff's crystal out.

Someone grabbed Wynn from behind.

Strong arms forced hers down, dragging the staff as well. About to thrash and shout, Wynn stiffened at an unbelievable sight.

Cinder-Shard's large hands clenched the front of the wraith's robe.

Horror filled Sau'ilahk, as he had not known in centuries. The bristle-bearded dwarf wrenched him sideways toward the cavern wall.

"We must drive it out—banish it!" another Stonewalker shouted.

"No!" roared the one clutching him. "This mongrel of the Nightfaller is mine! I will finish it now!"

Sau'ilahk clawed at the elder Stonewalker's grip. But regardless that this one somehow held him, his own hands slid through the dwarf's thick arms, touching nothing. Fear overwhelmed him. He could not think quickly enough.

"Into stone . . . with *you*!" the dwarf growled at him.

Sau'ilahk heard Wynn and one of the Weardas shouting. But he was so weak, so depleted. Everything vanished from sight as he was pushed into the cavern wall.

He felt his form turn corporeal, almost as if he were flesh once more. Bone and sinew began to harden, like the instant he had pierced the first Stonewalker with his hand and that one had stepped back into the wall.

Sau'ilahk released a hiss but heard nothing within stone.

Terror broke his will, and exhaustion dragged him down.

He vanished into dormancy.

CHAPTER 19

Wynn ceased struggling against the captain's hold. Shade paced before her, alternately snarling at the captain and staring where the wraith had vanished. The burned Weardas was down, moaning in pain, and Danyel's nose was bleeding. Sword held out, Danyel stood angrily over Chane, who was conscious but still on the floor where Cinder-Shard had thrown him.

Wynn stared at Cinder-Shard's arm penetrating stone. He'd somehow gripped the wraith, as if it were whole and solid. Realization set in. Any doubt concerning the texts' movements was gone.

The Hassäg'kreigi—Stone*walkers*—could pass through solid stone and earth. They were carrying the texts in and out of guild grounds.

Cinder-Shard jerked his arm from the wall, and Wynn's numbed mind reawoke.

"Did you kill it?" she asked wildly. "Is it finished?"

He stood looking at his hand in bewilderment.

"Master?" a familiar voice called.

Ore-Locks stepped into sight, closing quickly on Cinder-Shard.

Another Stonewalker pushed past them and ran his broad hand over the rough, damp wall. Gray-blond hair hung around his bony face of jutting brow, cheekbones, and chin. His hand stopped, thick fingers tensed, and a seething grimace twisted his features. He shook his head at Cinder-Shard.

Wynn sagged in the captain's grip. Whatever the master of the Stonewalkers had tried, it had failed—the wraith had escaped.

Cinder-Shard stepped straight to her and jerked the staff from her grip. Before he said anything, another voice shouted out.

"You . . . *miscreant*!"

Wynn's gaze shifted instantly.

Reine stood before Chuillyon, saber in hand, shuddering in fright or rage, or both. She took a step toward Wynn, but Chuillyon restrained her. Chane immediately regained his feet.

"Who was that?" the duchess demanded.

"The wraith," Wynn answered hoarsely. "An obscure myth . . . the only one that fits it."

Reine's eyes closed in a scowl.

"It killed sages . . . for the folios," Wynn insisted, "likely Hammer-Stag, too. I thought we'd destroyed—"

"You led a murderer here!" The duchess's voice cracked with strain.

Wynn fell silent, unable to deny this. The only way the wraith would've come to Dhredze Seatt was by following her. It hadn't given up any more than she had. But if the sun crystal hadn't destroyed it in the streets of Calm Seatt, then what chance did she have now? Why did this thing seek the texts with such vicious determination?

Reine's gaze lifted slightly, perhaps to the captain. "Lock them up!" she ordered.

Chane inched forward, and Danyel pressed a sword's point to his chest as a stocky female Stonewalker pulled a wide dagger and flanked him.

"Chane!" Wynn warned, and shook her head.

The sun crystal was still their best way to hold off the wraith, and Chane's blindly assaulting Stonewalkers and royal guards wouldn't help. Even if they regained their belongings and eluded capture, they had no way out. The sea people blocked the tunnel, and warrior thänæ guarded the domed chamber above the lift.

Wynn had to prove herself indispensable before anyone here would *want* her help. As always, the texts seemed the only chance to find answers.

"We have no prison here," Cinder-Shard growled. "There is only one sealable chamber, but—"

"No!" the gray-blond elder snapped, and turned on Cinder-Shard. "The living do not belong—"

"I don't care," the duchess shouted. "Put them in some hell, if you have to. They already know too much. But keep them contained until we understand whom we're dealing with!"

Ore-Locks, the middle-aged female, and the bony-faced elder all watched Cinder-Shard expectantly. The elder one still shook his head in warning, but Cinder-Shard focused only on the duchess.

Reine shrank a little, as if reproached. Even Chuillyon looked less than pleased by what she demanded.

"Very well," Cinder-Shard finally answered.

The duchess exhaled, but Chuillyon frowned. Then the elf crouched.

Retrieving Wynn's and Chane's discarded belongings, he glanced at Cinder-Shard with clear disapproval. Cinder-Shard turned away, heading for the cavern's far-left end. The female Stonewalker lifted the burned Weardas, carrying him.

"He needs attention," she stated flatly. "I will take him to Amaranth."

Wynn had no idea who or what that might be. The captain released her, shoving her onward as Chane was herded into motion. Wynn grabbed Shade's scruff to keep the dog out of the way, but kept her eyes on Cinder-Shard, trying not to guess where they were going. Instead, she groped for any notion to pique her captors' interest. . . .

Something they might half believe, enough to want more and thereby take her to the texts. The duchess's reaction, like that of Captain Rodian of the city guard, suggested that any mention of the undead would only make things worse.

"Smarasmôy, this is not right," Chuillyon called from farther back. "You know it!"

"This is not your domain," Cinder-Shard answered.

He continued on, leading the way into an adjoining cavern. With no orange crystals in its walls, the space was lit only by dim phosphorescence. Strangely shaped lumpy protrusions rose head-high among the shadowy columns of joined stalagmites and stalactites. But they crossed too quickly, exiting into another dim space before Wynn made out anything.

Amid the rush, something occurred to her—something Cinder-Shard had shouted.

Maksag, choyll-shu'ass Kêravägh!

Out . . . Leave . . . you dog of . . . Kêravägh?

Did he think the wraith was a minion of . . . what? Wynn was sickened at the possible answer as she tried to break apart that final word.

It had to be a proper noun, but seemed older than the Dwarvish she knew. The root "kêrakst" referred to "black" or "blackness." Not in color but as in nightfall, when twilight ended and the last of daylight vanished. But the suffix was baffling, like a root word conjugated to an infinitive—then declinated into a vocative noun?

"The Nightfallen One . . ." Wynn whispered absently. "The Nightfaller?"

Cinder-Shard slowed.

Wynn clenched her mouth shut, but he resumed his pace without glancing back. She grew chill as a connection formed, though she wasn't certain of her translation.

Hkàbêv meant "Beloved" in Iyindu, an ancient form of Sumanese. Il'Samar and in'Sa'umar in varied dialects meant "the Night Voice." Most Aged Father of the an'Cróan and Anmaglâhk had a very old Elvish term for it.

Nävâij'aoinis—the Ancient Enemy.

Had Cinder-Shard spoken a lost Dwarvish title for the enemy of many names? Was the enemy known among this hidden sect of dwarves?

They twisted rightward through more columns in another low-ceilinged cavern. Cinder-Shard stepped out into a long, straight tunnel.

Chuillyon had also whispered something before the wraith's fire had raced in. But Wynn's thoughts were so wrapped around Cinder-Shard's utterance that all she remembered for the moment was . . .

Chârmun . . . Sanctuary.

This was the name of the ancient great tree within Aonnis Lhoin'n—First Glade—at the heart of the Lhoin'na's homeland. That thought vanished as Wynn saw the path's end.

Crystals in the walls illuminated an archway of heavy framestones, but its opening was nearly black. Drawing closer, she saw it was walled off with age-darkened iron. There was no lock or handle, and Wynn grew frantic.

It looked like the triple-layered portal beneath the amphitheater. Her thoughts raced for a way to reason with the duchess, but she couldn't think of anything certain.

Cinder-Shard closed on the archway's left side.

Wynn heard metal slide evenly across stone, clinking to a stop, but she couldn't see around his broad form. More grating and clacks followed, and the archway's iron wall began to move. It slid left to right, rather than splitting down the middle, and behind it was another. The second door began grating after the first.

Cinder-Shard stepped aside, exposing an open stone cubby. A three-by-four grid of iron rods was pressed or protruded at varied depths. She'd seen something similar with her mantic sight on the other side of the amphitheater's door. But here, the lock was on the outside.

Wynn realized how Cinder-Shard had opened the amphitheater doors. He'd passed right through the wall, opening them from the inside. She and Chane possessed no such ability, and they were about to be locked away.

"Please!" she shouted, trying to turn. "You have to—"

She was cut short as someone grabbed the back of her collar. A third iron door began to open, and Cinder-Shard pointed into the darkness beyond it.

"Mind the landing," he warned. "Do not slip and fall."

"Inside!" the captain ordered.

A firm hand shoved Wynn between her shoulder blades.

She pulled Shade along before the dog turned to snap. Chane stumbled in next, wheeling about, and the captain warned him back with a sword. Cinder-Shard returned to the archway's side, and Wynn heard iron rods being shifted.

"The wraith is after the texts!" she cried. "It won't stop killing until it finds them!"

The first iron door was half-closed, and she sidestepped, leaning into the narrowing space.

"Give me access to the texts!" she shouted. "Let me find out what it wants . . . or something to help us fight it!"

Chane grabbed her, jerking her back as the door clanged shut.

Wynn shuddered twice in the full darkness, hearing the duller thud of the second and third doors.

Tightly holding her sea-wave comb with its drop of white metal, Reine hurried all the way to Frey's chamber. Danyel followed on her heels. Pressing the droplet to the lock, she opened the door. All of her pent-up fear threatened to break free.

"Frey!" she called.

He stood in the pool, gripping the gate's bars, and staring into the tunnel. When he looked back, he smiled softly, sadly at her. His hair was still soaked, but his gaze was clear.

"Highness?" Danyel whispered.

Reine glanced over her shoulder. He hung in the doorway, as if uncertain whether to enter or not. His nose had stopped bleeding, though he wiped it again with his sleeve. She cared only that Frey was unharmed—and in control of his wits.

Reine stepped to the pool's rear ledge, holding out her hand.

"Come," she called softly. "Please."

Frey waded over and reached up. As he took her hand, he gently pulled. Reine shook her head, trying to smile.

"No, I have to leave again. You come out of there."

She had to return quickly to Cinder-Shard and learn how he intended to ensure Frey's safety.

Frey didn't move until she pulled. He climbed up to stand before her, and nothing remained of his brief smile.

"It's all right," she said, touching his chest. "Danyel will stay."

Frey glanced at the bodyguard and frowned. Resentment was at least another sign he was rational. She knew what this looked like—what it was—and didn't care for putting him under guard any more than he did. There was no choice.

She walked him to the sitting chamber's entrance and ushered him inside, but as she turned to leave, she hesitated. Spinning back, she grabbed his arm, jerked him toward her, and clenched the front of his shirt with both hands.

Reine pulled herself up and Frey down, until her mouth pressed firmly against his. When she let go, she kept her eyes shut until she'd turned away.

Danyel stood at full attention, his gaze averted.

As she neared the door, she whispered sharply, "Don't let him near the pool."

Danyel nodded once, seeming unaffected by all that had happened. It was difficult to shake the Weardas—the Sentinels of the royal family. Then he surprised her, asking, "Highness, what if the . . . *others* . . . return?"

He glanced toward the tunnel at the pool's rear.

In truth, Reine would've preferred leaving Chuillyon with Frey, but she needed him and Tristan at her side.

"They won't," she assured him. "Not until tomorrow's highest tide. I'll return before then."

"My lady?" someone called softly.

Chuillyon stood in the outer passage.

"We should go," he said. "I must speak with Cinder-Shard."

Reine sighed in exasperation and stepped out, shutting the door and locking Frey and Danyel inside.

"Do not antagonize Cinder-Shard," she warned as they headed off. "We are guests, and Prince Freädherich is their cherished ward. This new threat is all that upstart sage's doing!"

Even so, she hadn't forgotten Wynn trying to reclaim the staff. The sage had shouted for it, as if lives depended on that simple object. In retrospect, Reine began to wonder.

Who was this black figure that created fire from nothing and made it run at them like something alive? She trembled at a murderer with such skills learning of Frey's presence.

When she and Chuillyon reached the intersection with the main passage, Captain Tristan was waiting, his expression impassive. She'd rarely seen him without his cloak, and he carried his helm under his arm. His cropped hair made him appear more human than the coldly fierce leader of the Weardas.

"Highness," he said, gesturing ahead.

Reine strode past him. Once they reached the main cavern, she slowed, spotting Cinder-Shard near another of the cavern's openings. Bulwark, the other elder, stood with him, glaring suspiciously at the staff in Cinder-Shard's grip. A movement among the calcified columns pulled her eyes.

Balsam, one of the females, paced a winding path toward the pair. Her head thrown back, she studied the cavern's ceiling.

Reine glanced up but couldn't guess what she was looking for.

Balsam was less wide than her comrades, with straight brown hair and a nose a bit flattened yet smoothly fitted between her rounded cheeks. Reine found her refreshing. For a cloistered Stonewalker, Balsam tended toward action first, questions later. Stoic Master Cinder-Shard and acidic Master Bulwark were much harder to fathom.

"Why did you stop us from forming a barrier?" Balsam called, lowering her gaze. "Now it can attack again at any time."

"Better us than our people above," Cinder-Shard returned. "And because I failed, it may be loose among them. Guardian Thänæ and constabularies will not stop it with ax, rod, or sword."

Balsam took a breath through her nose, blatantly dissatisfied with her elder's answer.

Reine looked around the cavern. A total of six Stonewalkers lived here deep beneath Dhredze Seatt, but only three were present. She didn't see Ore-Locks anywhere.

It had all happened so fast. Perhaps Amaranth and Thorn-in-Wine couldn't reach the battle in time. Amaranth was the other female of the group—and a healer before she took up a greater calling in the underworld. She was probably busy tending to Saln. As to Thorn-in-Wine, he could be daunting, like a younger version of Cinder-Shard.

Reine wondered about the missing three, especially Ore-Locks. He had been here for the battle, so where was he now?

The murderer hadn't entered directly with Wynn Hygeorht, but it had gained the underworld undetected. The unanswered question remained, How? Rumors during the killings in Calm Seatt suggested that it could walk through walls—like a Stonewalker.

"Well, then," Chuillyon said pointedly, and pushed past into the cavern.

Reine's frustration sharpened. She rushed after his swishing white robe as he headed straight at Cinder-Shard.

"If you will not lock it out, then what *do* you intend?" the counselor demanded. "Do *something*, and soon, or I will."

Reine didn't know how Chuillyon had held off the black mage's racing fire. She knew little about him—even less about his sect among the Lhoin'na sages. Exactly what did the elder of the Pras'an je Chârmuna—the Order of Chârmun—think that he or Cinder-Shard could do about this mage?

"I did not say I would do nothing!" Cinder-Shard retorted.

He glanced at Reine and then jerked the leather sheath off the staff's top.

Chuillyon cocked a feathery eyebrow as Reine too peered at the exposed crystal. Its perfect long prisms were as clear as polished glass. Cinder-Shard leaned it out toward her.

"What is this?" he demanded. "Obviously a made thing . . . likely from the sages' furnaces. I can sense all forms of stone and earth . . . but nothing of this."

Reine shook her head. "I don't know, and I hesitate to ask. We can't give that sage more opportunity for manipulation. Domin High-Tower and Premin Sykion both implied she's irrational."

"I saw no madness in her face," Bulwark said, folding his thick arms over his scaled hauberk.

"Nor I," Balsam added, "and that thing was afraid of her wolf."

Chuillyon still studied the staff's crystal, but he rolled his large eyes. "Could we delay discussion of canines and contrivances . . . and return to plans?"

"What would you suggest?" Cinder-Shard growled back. "Do share, you sanctimonious jester!"

Another Stonewalker, Amaranth, approached through the cavern's columns, and Reine turned to greet her. For all of Cinder-Shard's and Chuillyon's sharpness, they were friends of old. It was best to leave them to their crucible of bickering until they extracted a solution.

"How is Saln?" Reine asked.

Amaranth was wider than Balsam, with heavy creases surrounding her eyes and mouth, though no gray showed in her sandy hair. She finished wiping her hands on a muslin square and tucked it into her stout belt.

"His burns are not as deep as I first believed," she answered. "But more blistering will come. If he ignores my instructions—and proper treatment—scarring and disability may occur."

Tristan stepped closer. "Can he stand for his duty?"

"I just said. . . ." Amaranth scowled and shook her head. "It is his wish, though I warn against it."

Reine glanced up at the captain towering over everyone except Chuillyon. A flicker passed across his face. Was it remorse, sorrow, or misguided shame?

The Sentinels numbered twenty-seven, almost always working in threes. She didn't know if hers were friends as well as comrades. It seemed strange that Tristan was disturbed by Saln's loss of duty more than the man's injuries. But at times, she knew duty was more precious than life.

Chuillyon's too-sharp whisper pulled Reine's attention.

"She already saw how you got your stubby fingers into that *shadow*!"

Cinder-Shard didn't lash back. His eyes flicked once toward Reine, and he quickly looked away.

What were they arguing about now—and what did it have to do with her?

"What shadow?" Reine demanded.

Chuillyon's sarcastic annoyance faded. He appeared to study her—assess her—before turning an accusing glance upon Cinder-Shard.

"I heard you shout," he said. "Do you or do you not believe it was a servant of—"

Cinder-Shard's eyes widened, and Chuillyon never finished. The old elf had almost said something the master Stonewalker disapproved of, but Reine didn't know what or why.

"Was it *Âthkyensmyotnes*?" Chuillyon demanded.

At that strange word, Reine closed on them. It sounded like something in Elvish.

"Who are you talking about?" she asked.

Bulwark shifted uncomfortably, exposing clenched teeth. Balsam glanced between her two elders, apparently as lost as Reine.

"It is old," Cinder-Shard answered grudgingly. "Very old."

"You did not deny my suspicion," Chuillyon challenged. "So, what else did you sense?"

Cinder-Shard grunted. "What did *you* sense, as you blocked its flames?"

"Nothing . . . and that frightens me."

"Someone answer me!" Reine demanded.

Cinder-Shard flexed his free hand, stared at it, then looked to the cavern wall near the main entrance. No one answered her.

"Apparently, I cannot entomb it," Cinder-Shard muttered. "What other way is there to kill what is already *dead*?"

Reine stared at him in astonishment. Surely he didn't believe Wynn's insane notions.

"We need to bind it . . . in, not out," he said to Chuillyon. "And your ways, though effective against manipulations outside of itself, will not halt it from acting directly."

Reine grabbed Chuillyon's sleeve. "You cannot bring that murderer back here, not so near Frey!"

He looked down upon her, saddening for less than a blink before his mouth set in a hard line.

"We will not have to bring *Âthkyensmyotnes*," he answered coldly. "*It* will come when ready."

Reine could don a regal air at a whim. She could match any monarch, noble, or commoner stare for stare with an outward ease of detachment. But she wavered under Chuillyon's icy gaze.

"Who are you talking about?" she asked again. "I don't know that name. Is that the man in the black robes?"

"Not *who* . . . but *what*," Chuillyon corrected, "though it may have been a man . . . once."

"Enough dramatics," Cinder-Shard grumbled. "Needlessly frightening her accomplishes nothing."

"Yes, it does," Chuillyon countered. "If I—if we—are correct about what that thing is."

Again, "thing" and "it," as if the black mage were . . .

"You cannot believe the sage's prattle," Reine returned. "Walking dead . . . spirits . . . whatever?"

The sages believed an old enemy might rise again, one connected to the end of known history in a great forgotten war. Many people—most people—thought that war was only an overblown myth. Once, she had thought so herself—until she married Frey and became tangled in the secret of the Âreskynna bloodline. Only until she had spent too much time dealing with sages.

Like the premins, Reine's new family believed the world wasn't ready to know the truth about an Ancient Enemy—and a forgotten war. In silence, the Âreskynna and even her own uncle, King Jacqui Amornon Faunier, and all of their ancestors, had been waiting and watching through generations.

She'd never known . . . until Frey.

But this nonsense from Chuillyon, the family's oldest advisor, as well as from the master of the Stonewalkers, was too much. War was fought by the living, not the dead, whether it was one of the past or one yet to come.

Still Chuillyon watched her, as if waiting to see something in her face.

Amaranth rested her fists upon her hips. "Someone please tell me what has . . . will happen."

Balsam opened her mouth, but Bulwark cut in.

"Soon," he rumbled, and turned indignantly to Cinder-Shard. "You want to trap it here, among our honored dead?"

Reine's attention shifted from one to the next, her exasperation growing. Had Master Bulwark succumbed to the sage's nonsense as well? Chuillyon's eyes brightened as he looked away from her, but he shook his head.

"That would require permanence."

"No," Cinder-Shard countered, "only long enough to hold it . . . to finish it."

"Can you?"

Cinder Shard took a deep, slow breath full of doubt. "I was taught the way, as was my master before me. But I fear trapping this malignant thing may take time—and the focus of all my order. This will be . . . difficult."

Chuillyon frowned. "Very well, I can think of nothing better . . . for now."

Before anyone else spoke, a booming voice echoed across the cavern: "We have other matters first!"

Thorn-in-Wine strode toward them, phosphorescent light catching upon each polished steel tip of his hauberk's scales. Unlike the other Stonewalkers, he kept his dirt-brown hair cropped. A few curling strands looped around his ears and upon his brow to match his short beard.

"The constabularies in the access tunnel are dead!" he declared. "But the portal thänæ saw no one come through."

Cinder-Shard shook his head. "It evaded the warrior guard."

Reine peered toward the entrance to the main passage. She didn't need Chuillyon's cryptic babble to frighten her. The sage-killer may have followed Wynn Hygeorht to the seatt, but if the guards above had been killed, then the mage had followed someone else into the underworld.

The murderer had followed her.

"I must warn the conclaves," Thorn-in-Wine said, "and learn whether anything has happened in the settlements."

Cinder-Shard released the staff, letting it topple into Chuillyon's waiting hand.

"My lady," Cinder-Shard addressed Reine. "Thorn-in-Wine has need of your captain, at least until more guards are placed in the tunnel. Tristan has experience with pragmatic strategy that we do not."

"Of course," she answered, waving Tristan on.

But the captain remained planted. "My duty is to the life and blood of the royal line—above all else."

"You can best protect the prince by securing the underworld," she returned. "Chuillyon can ward against this mage's skills, and as to any mundane assault . . ."

She settled a hand on her saber's hilt.

Tristan's expression didn't change, and he didn't move. Lifting one knee, Reine pulled a narrow-bladed dagger from her boot and slipped it at the ready into her belt.

"That wasn't a request, Captain," she said.

He reluctantly nodded and turned away, following Thorn-in-Wine toward the main passage. But Chuillyon headed off in another direction.

"Where are you going?" Reine asked.

He paused without turning. "To speak with the sage."

"Why? She's done nothing but lie and connive. What could we possibly gain from her that we could trust?"

"Confirmation," he answered.

Reine quick-stepped to grab his sleeve. "You are a royal counselor, not my keeper, so answer me! What are you and Cinder-Shard hiding? What is this Ath . . . Athkin . . . ?"

Chuillyon whipped around.

"*Âthkyensmyotnes,*" he hissed, and Reine shrank back.

"The sovereign of spirits," he went on, "another forgotten word, like the sage's 'wraith.' I searched it out in little-known Numan folktales, once I heard things concerning the murderer in Calm Seatt. By the time I found anything, Wynn Hygeorht and her associates had taken matters into their own hands."

Reine just stared at him.

Chuillyon's branch lay too far south in Lhoin'na lands, and she'd never gone more than two days without seeing him. If he'd gone to the Calm Seatt guild, she would've heard mention from High-Tower or Sykion. How and where had he learned this?

Or was it all some excuse? Had he learned that odd name some other way?

"There is no time for your disbelief," he warned. "Your husband's safety matters more than your own—more than the texts—and that *thing* cannot learn of him."

Chuillyon jerked his sleeve from her grip.

"My counsel, Highness, is that you keep that foremost in your thoughts." He looked to Cinder-Shard. "Are you coming? I assume you wish to hear the sage for yourself."

Cinder-Shard had watched the exchange in silence. Without a word, he fell in beside Chuillyon. Both strode onward.

Reine watched them in shock before hurrying to catch up.

CHAPTER 20

Chane shivered, though he did not feel the cold. Along with Wynn and Shade, he'd been locked away in pure darkness. He could not see anything at all.

"Open the door!" Wynn shouted. "You have to listen!"

"Enough," he said. "They are gone. Light your crystal . . . I cannot see."

"What? But . . . you're undead."

"Even our—*my*—eyes require some light."

He heard clothing rustle, and a soft glow rose in the dark, orange-red at first.

Chane watched light build, filtered through Wynn's small, rubbing hands. When she opened her fingers, her face was illuminated by the cold lamp crystal resting in her palm. They both looked around.

Shade stood nosing the stone landing's left side. Just beyond her, stairs led downward along a curved wall. The landing itself was no more than six paces square, its front and right side dropping straight off into the dark. Though the crystal lit the wall around the arch, its light barely reached the high ceiling above.

Chane peered over the landing's edge and could not make out what waited below. His thoughts were overwhelmed.

The wraith still existed. At its barest touch upon the cavern floor, fire had erupted and been *shaped* in a way he could not imagine. Dwarves had emerged from cavern walls. A small stone creature with one glowing eye had done so as well and then broken apart in midair around the disturbingly serene elf.

But worse, Chane was hungry.

The effort to gain the underworld, as well as swiping his hand through the wraith, had taken much from him. Possibilities for feeding were almost nonexistent. He feared what might happen if he grew desperate.

Glancing back, he expected to find defeat in Wynn's round face. What he saw startled him more.

In the crystal's upward light, her features looked so hard. Wynn's bright, sweet face was filled with anger unlike anything Chane had ever seen in her.

"Imbeciles and idiots!" she whispered sharply. "They don't know what they're dealing with, and they lock up those who do!"

Wynn glanced at him. The dark taint in her expression lingered an instant longer before it finally drained away.

"We have no weapons at all, if the wraith attacks us here," she said, "nothing to hold it off without the staff."

Overstating the obvious accomplished nothing, but Chane kept silent. In truth, he felt vulnerable without his sword or the treasured belongings in his packs.

"How could it have survived?" she whispered. "I watched it burn to nothing!"

She did not seem to expect an answer.

"It is more than just a spirit, especially by its actions," he said. "If it is a Noble Dead, even my kind are not easily dispatched."

Her gaze flickered to his throat. Beneath his cloak and shirt collar, he bore the scar around his neck as proof of that point. He too had risen from death a second time.

"What was that other thing . . . that leaped at the duchess and the elf?" she asked.

"I remember scant references to . . . constructs of a kind, from my earliest studies. Conjured things of the Elements with awareness of their own." He paused and shook his head. "We should survey our surroundings . . . see if there is anything of advantage."

"Why is this place so dark?" she asked, stepping past him toward Shade. "The walls don't glow like most of the outer caverns."

Much as he valued her curious nature, it now wore upon him, like the beast pacing within him, pulling against its bonds in growing hunger.

Wynn held the crystal out above Shade, illuminating the wide stone stairs, and Chane studied the wall. It was hewn smooth, unlike the caverns. This was a created rather than a natural space. No moisture crept in to coat it with glittering mineral deposits, which seemed impossible at this depth.

Chane stepped past Wynn. Only a dozen stairs down, Shade scurried into the lead, sniffing every step they took. He had not counted the steps, but too many passed before Wynn's crystal began to expose the chamber's lower reaches. If she had stumbled off that landing, it would have been a very long first—and last—step.

They passed the stairs' midpoint and circled at least halfway around the outer wall. The chamber was indeed round, though only a third as wide as it was tall. Indistinct forms took shape below, standing around the lower floor. Something in the floor's center caught the light of Wynn's crystal.

Chane felt Wynn's hand upon his shoulder.

"I've seen this place," she whispered.

"When? How?"

"Shade saw it in Ore-Locks's memories."

She pushed past him, scurrying downward, and Chane hurried to keep up. Before he reached the bottom, the erect forms already looked like mute representations of standing figures. But Chane focused on that shining disk in the floor's center.

The large plate of ruddy metal, perhaps polished brass, was at least three or four strides across. There were markings upon it. Shade stepped off the last stair and began circling the floor, but Wynn went straight for the closest tall form.

"Wait!" Chane ordered.

She stopped short, an arm's length from one strangely shaped, upright black . . . casket. At least, that was what it looked like. Drawing closer, he saw that it more resembled a stout form of iron maiden, a torturous execution device he had only read of.

Dull black, perhaps basalt, it was slightly taller but far broader than Wynn—even greater than the breadth of a male dwarf. Narrowing slightly at its base upon the floor, its bulk widened upward, until . . .

Chane's gaze came to where the plain figure narrowed into the dull, domed representation of its "head." The raised shape of a riveted band was carved out of the stone, wrapping around at jaw level. Two like bands ran around its "body" at shoulder and thigh height. But he saw no seams along its sides.

It was carved whole from one solid piece. And between the two lower bands around its bulk was a vertical oblong shape of raised stone covered in engraved characters.

Chane peered around the chamber.

Seven basalt forms—trapped and bound in place—faced inward toward the floor's central disk. But between two on the far side he spotted another opening in the chamber's wall. He glanced up, barely making out the landing above. The opening was directly below it.

Then Shade rumbled.

Chane was not the only one who did not like the feel of this place. The dog paced around the chamber, remaining equally far away from the tombs and the floor disk.

"Wynn?" he said uncertainly.

When she did not answer, he turned back. Wynn was about to touch the oblong of engraved characters on a tomb.

"No!" he said. "The floor disk first."

It was the only thing he could think of to stop her. She frowned at him and headed for the floor's center.

Chane backed up, still eyeing the mute black shapes. When he spun about, Wynn had crouched at the disk's edge, holding her crystal above it.

It was made of brass, though Chane saw no sign of tarnish. Someone must clean and polish it regularly. Not truly a circle, the octagon's sides were slightly curved outward, causing that mistaken impression. Inside each edge was an emblem like a complex sigil. In the center was a depression, akin to a high-edged bowl sunken into and melded with the disk. One larger pattern rested in its bottom.

"Arhniká . . . Mukvadân . . . Bedzâ'kenge . . ." Wynn whispered.

With each strange word, she pointed to a symbol around the outer circumference.

"These are *vubrí* for dwarven Eternals," she added in puzzlement. "Eight of the Bäynæ."

Chane knew little of dwarven saints beside Bedzâ'kenge—Feather-Tongue.

Wynn flattened her hands upon the disk and leaned out to look into the center depression. Before Chane could jerk her back, she lurched away.

"Lhärgnæ!" she whispered.

"What?"

Wynn scrambled to her feet, turning unsteadily as she looked to all of the basalt figures. She darted around the chamber, examining each oblong panel, finally stopping at one tomb.

"Sundaks!" she exclaimed.

"What are you reading?"

"Avarice . . . one of the Lhärgnæ," she answered. "Oh, dead deities! They've locked us in with their Fallen Ones!"

"What does that mean?"

"Their devils, their demons . . . cursed ones! Those who represent vice—and worse—by dwarven culture."

"So, religious representations?"

"No," Wynn answered. "They were once real, at least as much as the Eternals, though their names were stripped away. They bear only titles, chosen for their singular disgrace."

"These are not true tombs," Chane countered. "They do not open. There are no bodies here."

"Then why bother? Why the disk in the floor? Is that something of the magic discipline . . . conjury perhaps?"

Chane looked again at the great brass disk.

Mages did not call upon deities—or saints—in their arts. Formal religions were more widely spread in this part of the world than in his. Most peasants of the Farlands clung to superstitions of nature spirits and dark influences. Some practiced forms of ancestor worship.

He knew of priests—and others—who claimed to be gifted by higher powers. They had their grand ceremonies and contrivances to dazzle the ignorant.

"Some priest's supposed ward against the damned," he replied. "It is nothing more than trappings to appease the masses . . . to control them through their fears."

He was about to expound further when Wynn rounded on him. "Do the Stonewalkers look like a pack of charlatans to you?"

"You are a scholar," he answered. "Do not believe in this."

"Then why did *you* hesitate when we first entered the temple of Bedzâ'kenge?"

Chane was struck mute.

"Yes, I figured it out," she said. "You were afraid of entering a sacred space. We both know there are things beyond reason we never wanted to believe, and still . . ."

Chane looked about the chamber. She was alluding to theurgy, the supposed gain or use of power from higher spiritual forces. That was only more priestly aggrandizing—was it not?

His skin began to crawl, aggravating his nagging hunger. Had he finally stepped into a true sacred space? Was this a prison for a people who believed their ancestors, saintly or otherwise, resided in this world and not some separate realm of the afterlife?

Chane strode past Wynn to the chamber's only opening. It was too dark to see into the space beyond, until light grew behind him. Wynn approached with her crystal and its light filled a small round chamber.

One lone fake tomb of basalt stood at the back. Why was this one kept apart from the others?

Chane backed up—until he bumped into Wynn and pivoted.

"What's wrong with you?" she asked.

"Besides being locked up?"

"Yes."

He could not meet her eyes or give her the answer. "I will check the wall for any more openings, as well as back along the stairs and landing."

Chane walked away, heading along the wall behind the silent basalt forms. He was not about to tell her of his hunger. They both had enough fears for the moment, and he would not add to hers concerning himself.

But they had to escape this place, soon.

Wynn watched Chane walk away and couldn't stop worrying about his colorless eyes. She'd never seen them this way for so long. Something was wrong with him—more than just this disturbing place. But she couldn't force him to tell her.

She stepped into the small chamber, wondering why this one tomb was kept isolated. And a phrase or two surfaced from the back of her mind.

Chârmun, agh'alhtahk so. A'lhän am leagad chionns'gnajh.

She remembered Chuillyon's whisper.

Chârmun, grace this place. Fill me with your absolute nature.

What did it mean? Why had he whispered of the tree called Sanctuary at the heart of First Glade, and as if it might answer . . . his prayer?

Wynn hadn't forgotten Magiere's revelations from wallowing in the memories of Most Aged Father. Aside from hearing mention of the fall of Bäalâle Seatt, Magiere had relived far more through the decrepit leader of the Anmaglâhk.

Most Aged Father, once called Sorhkafâré—Light upon the Grass—had been alive during the time of the mythical war. As a commander of an allied army, he'd fled with straggling remainders of his forces before a horde of undead slaughtering everything in the night. They'd rested each day and run in the dark, being picked off all the way to First Glade. Less than half of them reached that place, where they discovered that no undead was able to follow.

Wynn had always known of First Glade and its great tree, Chârmun. Few people that she knew had ever traveled to see it. She certainly hadn't . . . yet. No one ever realized that it had been there since the time of the Forgotten History itself, always present; neither the Lhoin'na nor their branch of sages had ever mentioned this.

It didn't seem possible that they *didn't* know that First Glade had existed before the war. And this elf with the duchess, dressed like a sage in a robe of no order's colors, had whispered the name of the tree called Sanctuary.

And its name, which had always been known, took on a greater meaning by what Magiere had told her.

Wynn pushed such mysteries away as she faced the lone tomb in the small chamber. She wasn't certain she truly wanted to know more of this place, but she couldn't ignore an opportunity to fathom the ways of the Stonewalkers. Not if she had to work through them, and the duchess, to get to what she needed.

She raised her crystal close to the figure's oblong panel and traced its markings with her finger. It was an epitaph of sorts, but not the kind placed on the marker of a loved one or ancestor. She struggled to decipher archaic patterns constructed entirely in round dwarven *vubrí.*

. . . outcast of stone . . . deceiver of honored dead . . . ender of heritage . . . the seatt-killer . . .

The last one almost stopped her cold, and then she reached the bottom and a final *vubrí*. All of the others she'd worked out made it easier to decipher.

Thallûhearag.

As with the tomb of Sundaks—Avarice—and the others, the title was written at the bottom, not the top, as was customary in almost any culture. It was the same term she'd first overheard spoken in High-Tower's chamber, when Cinder-Shard and Ore-Locks had visited and then vanished. All that Wynn had read in the epitaph's archaic Dwarvish clarified the meaning of that title.

She jerked her finger from the cold black stone, wiping it down her tunic.

Thallûhearag—Lord of Slaughter.

Dwarves used that final term differently than in other culture's languages. It referred to killing the defenseless versus carnage or execution of food animals. She tried to understand the few earlier phrases.

"Outcast of stone" could mean an outcast of the dwarven people. "Deceiver of the honored dead" implied deceased thänæ, and perhaps even their caretakers, the Stonewalkers. "Ender of heritage" was too obscure, but "seatt-killer . . ."

Something horrible had happened at Bäalâle Seatt during the war.

Wynn backed up one step. "Lord of slaughter . . ." she whispered, ". . . seatt-killer . . ."

She suddenly felt as if she were being watched.

Wynn looked to the tomb's faceless dome of a head, which was visually gagged by its raised carving of a riveted band. Everyone in that forgotten seatt, including enemy forces, had been "lost," though no one knew how or why. She realized her first translation of epitaph's final symbol lacked the true meaning, for "heritage" was everything to the dwarves.

"*Thallûhearag . . .*" she whispered, "lord of genocide!"

Shade began to snarl from behind. Before Wynn could turn, the tomb's shadow moved upon the wall.

"His true name was Byûnduní . . . Deep-Root."

Wynn slid back a step at the baritone voice seeming to rise from the black stone. A thick hand entered the crystal's light from behind it and settled upon the tomb's shoulder. Shade lunged in around Wynn with a snap of jaws, her hackles stiffened.

Ore-Locks stepped from the shadows, his hand sliding down the tomb of Thallûhearag.

How did he know a name for this mass murderer? The names of the Fallen Ones were washed away by time. How he had gotten in here unseen, or had he simply slipped through stone, like his brethren?

Ore-Locks raised his eyes to the tomb's head, as if he saw more than that mute form's representation. He placed both hands flat upon its oval plate, as if trying to blot out the epitaph. Melancholy in his broad features quickly turned into cold resentment.

He glanced sidelong at her, the same way the duchess had in the dangerous moment in the prince's hidden pool chamber.

Wynn's head churned with frightened notions all wrapped around this dwarf who'd been her only lead to the Stonewalkers.

"He does not belong here!" Ore-Locks whispered.

Her breaths quickened until she grew light-headed. His siblings had renounced him for his spiritual pursuit. Sliver's revulsion drove her to keep the source of his calling from their mother. And in High-Tower's study, the domin's venom for his brother had been visceral in his voice.

"What do you know?" he demanded. "What did you find in those cursed texts? Where do his bones lie . . . where is Bäalâle Seatt?"

A forgotten ancestor, obscured from oral tradition, had called Ore-Locks. But it wasn't a Bäynæ or any forebearer of his people as a whole. It was one in a direct bloodline that the Iron-Braids couldn't bear to acknowledge once Ore-Locks had tried to force it upon them.

She looked at his hand, pressed firmly upon that tomb of the lord of genocide—Thallûhearag.

Wynn ran out of the small chamber's entrance, screaming, "Chane!"

Chane was halfway up the stairs, feeling along the wall, when Wynn called his name.

The beast within him threw itself against the limits of its chains. His hunger broke free amid fear for her safety. His senses widened as he took the stairs three at a time for a few downward strides.

Chane lunged off the edge into midair. His legs buckled as he landed; he was only half-aware that he crouched upon the floor's brass seal as Wynn rushed out of the opening between the tombs.

Her crystal's light flooded the space, burning Chane's sight for an instant. Shade bolted out next, snarling. The sound heated Chane's frenzy.

Something moved in the dark opening. Bits of it glinted in the crystal's light.

Chane rushed in, grabbing Wynn's shoulder. As he jerked her behind himself, the drive to hunt became tangled with his need to protect her. Something had entered this place—something he might kill and feed upon. Then he heard Wynn gasp.

Chane whipped his head around and went rigid.

The cold lamp crystal lay on the chamber floor.

Wynn stared at him, eyes wide with shock, as she gripped her shoulder. Torn bits of felt from her tunic stuck out around her small fingers. A thin scent of blood began to permeate the chamber's stale air.

Chane choked on a surge of hunger. It burned cold in his throat, and he heard Shade snarl directly behind him.

"Shade, come!" Wynn called.

He shuddered so hard, clenching both hands against the spasm, and backstepped away from Wynn. He shook his head and mouthed, *No*, over and over, but when his lips silently parted, Wynn flinched.

Chane clamped his mouth shut, hiding the change in his teeth.

The barest creases formed on Wynn's brow over her narrowing eyes. There it was again—that fear in her face, backed by wary anger. The same as on the night she had seen him emerge from a scribe shop's window behind the wraith.

"Wynn . . ." he rasped, but did not know what else to say.

Shade circled wide around him, taking a position in his way, as Wynn crouched to retrieve her crystal.

Chane gazed into its light, causing pain in his widening sight. He wished it would sear him.

"I did not come to harm you."

Chane twisted back at the deep voice.

Ore-Locks stood between two tombs before the opening. The red-haired Stonewalker was dressed in a hauberk of steel-tipped scales, with two wide black-sheathed blades lashed to the front of his belt. He did not advance but only watched those before him, as if waiting for a response.

For an instant, Chane wanted to vent all his anguish on this one.

This dwarf had frightened Wynn, caused her to cry out . . . caused Chane's momentary loss of control. The beast inside him began to wail, and he ground his jaws, beating the monster into submission.

Chane stood shuddering as he glared at Ore-Locks.

"No one has ever breached our underworld," Ore-Locks said, fixing on Wynn. "So you are not what you seem. Did you guide that black spirit here?"

"Of course not!" she answered.

Chane knew something of what had passed between these two in the Iron-Braids' home. Ore-Locks would hardly consider Wynn a friend.

"But it followed you," Ore-Locks stated.

Chane waited, but Wynn did not answer immediately.

"I've nothing to say to you," she answered. "Not with what I know. Not with what you worship!"

Ore-Locks's eyes narrowed, but Chane was confused by Wynn's words. What did she mean?

The dwarf lifted his chin, teeth clenched between barely parted lips. Chane set himself, watching for Ore-Locks's slightest move.

"That *thing* in there," Wynn went on. "Somehow, he was responsible. . . . Whatever brought down Bäalâle Seatt . . . that mass murderer did it."

"No!" Ore-Locks snarled, and took a step.

Chane instantly shifted into his way.

"Then why is he here?" Wynn demanded. "Why else would Thallûhearag's representation be put aside, separated even from the Fallen Ones?"

Ore-Locks's jaw muscles clenched in mute outrage, and Chane understood what was in that small chamber. He remembered all Wynn had told him concerning Bäalâle Seatt and a forgotten title feared by the few who knew of it and wished to forget it.

Chane tried to calm himself. He needed to wash his thoughts clean if he were to have any chance at sensing deception in the dwarf's words. Letting go of everything, trying to ignore hunger and how he had recklessly injured Wynn, he closed his eyes.

But the only thing he could find to soothe him was a memory.

There had been one brief moment when he had sneaked into the guild's library with Wynn. With her so close, guiding him into her world, he had stopped and looked upon all of the volumes placed so orderly upon the shelves.

"He is not one of them!" Ore-Locks shouted. "Not as claimed by the few who remember only his title . . . and not his name. I have known him since I was a child, though I did not understand until later who touched me—called me through blood. He cannot be what they claim . . . not as *my* ancestor!"

Chane remained placid in that quiet memory of the library, letting each word pass through him. Though the beast moaned at his complacency, no discomforting twinge rose within him. He opened his eyes and fixed his gaze on Ore-Locks.

The dwarf was not lying—or at least he believed his own words. Chane turned his head enough to glance at Wynn. He nodded at her, hoping she understood.

Wynn blinked at him, her brow wrinkling slightly.

"Now you owe me—in barter!" Ore-Locks said. "What do you know of the black spirit that followed you here?"

Wynn hesitated.

"Only that it is an undead," she answered. "One form of what is known in the Farlands as the *Vneshené Zomrelé*—the Noble Dead . . . though it isn't physical, like the type more commonly dealt with."

"Physical?" Ore-Locks repeated.

Wynn shook her head. "That doesn't matter. . . . We're dealing with a powerful spirit, which can become corporeal in part or whole for brief periods. We believe it is a conjuror, one so old its power and skill are like nothing heard of before. But like any undead—or most—it can be injured by sunlight."

"Then it is impervious in our underworld," Ore-Locks countered.

Wynn took one step forward, passing her hand before Shade's face.

"No," she returned, "not if I have the staff."

Ore-Locks cocked his head, his eyes narrowed in doubt, but Wynn quickly went on.

"The key to stopping it is to find out what it wants! Get me access to the texts you are holding for the guild!"

Ore-Locks said nothing. Chane tensed at the dwarf's steady gaze upon

Wynn—as if the Stonewalker actually considered her demand. Had Wynn finally gained them an ally here? But was it one they even wanted or could trust?

"That can wait," someone else called out.

Chane twisted about, looking around and then up.

Duchess Reine, her elven companion, and the master Stonewalker stood above, a dozen or more steps up the stairs. Chane had not heard the iron doors above slide open.

The elf stood lowest, in the lead, gazing down upon Wynn. He held the staff in his hand, its crystal unsheathed.

"I also have questions, Wynn Hygeorht," he said flatly. "But I am not here to barter."

Chane slipped in behind Wynn and gently touched her unharmed shoulder. A rush of relief came, along with guilt, when she pressed back against him. Monster though he was, besides Shade, he was all she had.

Did he too often take advantage of that?

He whispered in Wynn's ear, "Stay close. Listen for what I tell you."

Reine stood upon the curving stairs between Chuillyon below and Cinder-Shard above her. She was dazed and aching from their silent method of entrance. Chuillyon had hoped to catch whatever the captives might be discussing before revealing their presence. But the nonsense Reine heard made her want to snatch the staff from him and leave this place.

That wasn't possible until Cinder-Shard opened the portal.

She'd seen the Chamber of the Fallen only a few times, but always from the landing above. By the light of the sage's crystal, it was disturbing in its dark simplicity—more so because Ore-Locks was here. He was the last person who should be alone with this manipulative, mad sage, who'd already used him once.

"What are you doing here?" Cinder-Shard growled.

Ore-Locks rounded the great brass seal away from Wynn and approached the stairway's base. His chin lifted, but he didn't look to his master. Instead he eyed Chuillyon and the staff.

"I came for answers," Ore-Locks replied. "More than the ones you seek."

Cinder-Shard gently pushed Reine against the wall and stepped down behind Chuillyon.

"You are out of place!" Cinder-Shard nearly shouted. "The others already see to our people's defense—as you should!"

"I am seeing to *my* people!"

Cinder-Shard turned his head, looking off to the chamber's far side.

Reine tried to follow his strange shift of attention. At first she had no idea what he was doing. Then she saw a black opening between two stone figures. It was directly below the landing above.

She'd never come down the stairs before, so had never seen it. What was in there? Obviously not another way out, or Cinder-Shard wouldn't have placed captives here.

Cinder-Shard stepped off the stairway's edge. As his boots landed upon the chamber floor, a dull thunder echoed into the heights.

"What have you done?" he demanded. "What have you told them?"

"Nothing," Ore-Locks answered. "Nothing more than what the sage read for herself."

Cinder-Shard sagged under some unseen burden, almost like a mourner in a graveyard. He ran a large hand over his face and turned his eyes on Wynn.

"You . . . you can read the ancient *vubrí*?"

All this time, Wynn had merely watched and listened. The wolf stood rigid before her and Chane behind her, his cowl pulled up and his hand upon her shoulder. She drew back against him, as if seeking refuge beneath his chin.

"Yes, I can read them," she answered. "As well as some other old writings . . . like those in the texts."

"So obviously you are well studied," Chuillyon interjected. "Perhaps you even think you know more than your superiors. What have you learned of this person you call . . . the wraith?"

The change of subject threw Reine off guard, and she didn't care for his new approach.

Wynn Hygeorht had no guard on her tongue and no respect for her guild's authority. She had a way of making superiors seem at fault for the horror and death of the past half moon—which began with two dead sages in an alley. The royal family treasured the guild, and Reine had no interest in any more of this upstart's insinuations.

Still, Chuillyon, Cinder-Shard, and even bitter old Bulwark all believed this mage was something more—something out of Wynn's wild tales. Reine couldn't bring herself to think of such nonsense, not in the face of a more real threat. She had Frey to protect.

"It's old," Wynn finally replied, "perhaps older than even First Glade."

What did that mean? Another pause passed.

"Forgive me," Chuillyon answered, "but I fail to understand your comparison."

"*Lie!*"

Wynn stiffened at Chane's whisper. It was barely a shaped breath, but she'd heard it just the same. How was he doing this—and was he right? She studied the puzzled frown upon Chuillyon's triangular face, but she couldn't see any sign of deception.

Chane squeezed her shoulder lightly for emphasis.

Her reference to First Glade had nothing to do with getting to the texts, but she couldn't help that one opportune prod. There was no telling when or if she might get another chance.

She'd grown up believing elves the best of all people, of all races. But after the deceit in dealing with the Anmaglâhk of the Farlands' elves, and learning one hint of the hidden history of First Glade, those experiences had left her suspicious. How much subterfuge was there among the elves of her continent—and among their branch of her own guild?

Then there was still the issue of Thallûhearag, Bäalâle Seatt . . . and Ore-Locks.

The way Cinder-Shard's face had twisted in sudden anguish, as he looked into the mass murderer's chamber, left Wynn frightened. He clearly knew what had called Ore-Locks to service, and the master Stonewalker had still taken in the young dwarf. How many corruptions did she now face? How many enemies surrounded her, even from avenues she'd once thought beyond question?

"You have nothing to stop the wraith," she said to Chuillyon, ignoring even the duchess. "And the staff will work only for me."

Chuillyon stepped all the way down and set the staff's butt upon the floor.

"What is it?" he asked too politely. "What does its crystal do?"

Wynn looked his robe up and down, its color mockingly white and pure.

"It is imbued with the sun's power, the nature of its light," she answered. "Sunlight is . . . destructive to all undead."

"So this is what you used to face it the last time?" he asked, turning the staff in his hand.

Its crystal cast faint colored glimmers around the chamber as its prism caught light from her cold lamp crystal.

"Yes," Wynn replied.

"Then it was hardly effective," Chuillyon answered.

"Enough nonsense!" Cinder-Shard cut in. "Even if . . . How would such a thing be made?"

"You would have to ask Domin il'Sänke," Wynn answered.

"How convenient!" Reine spit. "The domin she speaks of is from the guild's Suman branch. And he has returned home, well beyond questioning."

"It was created at my guild," Wynn countered. "From what I understand, Premin Sykion nearly fainted when she learned of its cost. Ask her . . . or Premin Hawes, head of Metaology."

"And from what *I* understand," the duchess responded coldly, "the guild took you in as an orphan, raised you, fed you . . . educated you, and trained you as one of them. And you thanked them with your selfish ploys!"

Wynn couldn't help flushing with anger.

"The wraith is here for something," she said. "Until you know what that is, you won't know for certain what it will do . . . how it will act."

"And you would know of this?" Chuillyon asked.

"I can help only if you help me," Wynn answered.

Cinder-Shard raised his dark eyebrows. "In what way?"

"Give me my staff and my belongings . . . give me access to the texts."

"No!" Reine cut in.

"Then you'll die," Wynn said flatly. "You'll probably die anyway. The wraith wants those texts, and it will kill anyone in its path to reach them. But why? Unless I learn that, you're fighting blind."

She looked at Chuillyon again. "Can you read old tongues . . . Iyindu, Heiltak lettering . . . old Stravinan or Belaskian?"

He shrugged idly with a raised feathery eyebrow. "Some."

"*Lie!*" Chane breathed behind Wynn.

A lie about what? Could Chuillyon read such languages more—or less—than he implied?

"Can you?" Chuillyon challenged. "Or is this another boast . . . upon which we base our slim chance of survival?"

Wynn was careful not to show any reaction. His tone implied he did know old languages, as if he might actually be a sage. This was the only way he could ever judge whether she "boasted" or not. So if he could read dead languages, why bother with her?

He was baiting her, but to what purpose?

"Yes," she answered. "Well enough that I might find something useful. After all, I was raised . . . cared for . . . and educated"—and she cast a glance at the duchess—"inside a guild branch."

Chuillyon pursed his lips and fell silent.

Cinder-Shard seemed to calm suddenly. He glanced at Chuillyon, and the old elf merely nodded to him.

"So, you have raced this thing to gain the texts," Cinder-Shard said.

It seemed too obvious a comment, and Wynn grew warier.

"And *Âthkyensmyotnes* will continue to try to stop you," Chuillyon added, his expression growing thoughtful.

"No!" Chane hissed. "You will not—"

"No one is speaking to you!" Cinder-Shard growled.

"Wynn," Chane whispered, "they are trying to—"

"I know," she answered.

The wraith knew both she and the texts were here. It had killed to gain translations sent to scribe shops in Calm Seatt for clean transcription. But rather than searching their content and leaving them behind, it had always taken those pages. Whatever it sought, it didn't want others to find as well. Either it hadn't found what it was after, or it wanted to keep others from doing the same. It had followed her, in her search for the originals, so it had some way of tracking or locating her.

Chuillyon wasn't baiting her; he was making her *into* bait.

"Yes," Chuillyon whispered.

Wynn tensed slightly, and Chane's grip tightened upon her shoulder.

"What you learn of *Âthkyensmyotnes*'s goals may help us—or not," Chuillyon added. "Either way, you will tell us all you discover . . . in exchange for access to the texts."

"Chuillyon!" Reine gasped.

He raised a hand to silence her.

"At the least," he went on to Wynn, "if it knows you are here, it might be more direct . . . less cautious . . . in returning. Will you consent to this?"

Wynn hesitated. They offered what she wanted, but at a price.

Chuillyon had called the wraith by another term. She knew it from delving into old folktales of her people. The elf knew more of the wraith than she'd guessed—and Cinder-Shard did as well, from his shout in the main cavern.

Wynn reached up, putting her hand over Chane's.

"Later I will need his help," she said. "He knows more about fighting the wraith than any of you. Give him back his belongings . . . and his sword."

Chuillyon shook his head emphatically. "Absolutely not." He pointed at Chane. "We do not want to arm that one."

"Then delve into the texts yourself," Wynn returned. "Choose."

It was a bluff, and likely the elf knew it, but no one else did. If he called her on it in front of the others, it would simply be based on what everyone knew of her: that she would want the texts no matter what. If he succumbed to her conditions, the others might not think much of it, but Wynn would know what it meant.

Chuillyon knew less than he let on, or . . . he had more to hide with his deceptions than Wynn could guess.

She wasn't certain whether he suppressed a soft smile, but he just stood there watching her, not saying a word. Silence lingered so long that the duchess crept down behind him, a frown growing on her face. Still, Chuillyon stood poised with the staff resting lightly in his grip.

It was Cinder-Shard who finally answered, looking to the duchess.

"Have one of your men bring their gear. If they wish to survive, they will fight and do as they are told. I will take the sage to the texts . . . with your permission."

He waited upon her reply, as if all had to be in agreement. The texts belonged to the guild but were ultimately under the protection of the monarchy of Malourné. The Stonewalkers were merely guardians.

Reine appeared suddenly weary. "Do what you think best."

"Very well," Cinder-Shard replied, and without turning back, added, "and

Ore-Locks will come. He will stay with the sage and watch her while we attend to other matters."

Wynn didn't care for that. There was no telling what private agenda Ore-Locks had—let alone that his superior appeared to know of the young Stone-walker's ancestor. Cinder-Shard stepped closer.

"You will share all you learn. When you finish, you will report such findings to the princess and myself."

Wynn glanced at Reine's poorly hidden distaste. Cinder-Shard wasn't making a request, but Wynn answered.

"Agreed."

CHAPTER 21

Up on the landing, Wynn watched Cinder-Shard and Ore-Locks walk straight through the iron door. An instant later, its first outer panel began grinding open and another realization struck: Cinder-Shard had simply entered by walking through stone—or iron, as it were. Anything of the earth must submit to their passage. But that didn't explain the duchess's and Chuillyon's presence with the doors closed.

The innermost door slid away, and Cinder-Shard stood blocking the archway. He looked first at Chane.

"You and the wolf remain here until she finishes," he ordered. "I will leave the archway open if you swear to stay unless called."

Wynn glanced nervously at Chane.

His irises still lacked any trace of brown. Her shoulder was only scratched beneath the tears in her tunic, but she understood why he'd accidentally injured her. His hunger had returned, and it was growing. How many days had passed since she'd procured the goat's blood for him?

Worse, he swayed slightly, blinking slowly as he glared at Cinder-Shard. Was dawn approaching outside the mountain?

"It's all right," she told him. "I'm in no danger at present . . . you rest."

She thought he might argue, but he merely answered, "Remember what I told you."

The comment lost her at first. All he'd said to her since the duchess's arrival was one word—*Lie.* Then she understood, careful not to glance at Chuillyon, but getting Shade to wait as well was another matter.

The instant Wynn said, "Stay," Shade snarled. Wynn grabbed the dog's face, hoping no one asked what she was doing. She recalled memories of the long day in the guild's catacombs, when she'd first gained the codex and translations. She hoped Shade understood what she was going to do. She finished by saying, "Stay with Chane."

Shade curled her jowls, sneering at their captors, but she didn't try to leave. Or rather she dropped to her haunches, planting herself dead center in the archway. Shade licked her nose at Cinder-Shard.

Wynn stepped out to face the master Stonewalker.

"I'll send your packs and sword," she called to Chane, not taking her eyes off Cinder-Shard, "before I go anywhere else."

Cinder-Shard scowled at the insinuation. "Leave the staff. It cannot be taken where we go."

"I do not remember agreeing to return it!" Chuillyon sniped from somewhere behind Wynn.

"This is my agreement," Cinder-Shard growled.

Wynn heard the tall elf muttering as he pushed past her. When she glanced back, Chane held the staff, its crystal sheathed once more. She would've preferred to take it, but leaving it with him was the next best thing. At least their packs, weapons, and her companions would all be in the same place.

Cinder-Shard turned down the passage, but Ore-Locks stood waiting. Wynn didn't move. She wasn't having him at her back. With a derisive grunt, he headed off and she followed, Reine and Chuillyon falling in behind her.

When they reached the main cavern, Reine sent Wynn's dagger, Chane's packs, and his sword back with a female Stonewalker named Balsam. Reine then left, perhaps to look in on her husband.

Why had the Stonewalkers hidden the prince here? Had he gone mad, his death faked to hide the truth? If so, then why had they chosen a lie that so obviously implicated Reine?

Wynn had watched the prince sink beneath the pool. The people of the sea had done likewise in the tunnel. The chamber had filled with dull clicks and melodic tones rising from the water.

It seemed like he'd *spoken* with them.

"Take only what you need," Cinder-Shard said.

Wynn started from the distraction. He was holding out her pack, and again she wondered exactly where she was being taken. She dug out her elven quill and a wax-sealed vial of fresh ink. Though she rummaged to the pack's bottom, all of her journals, even a new blank one, were soaked. Wynn took the one from her day in the catacombs, with her notes from the translations. She looked up, prepared to ask for spare paper or parchment.

Cinder-Shard was staring at her hands.

"Where did you get that?" he demanded.

She looked down at the quill with its white metal tip. "A gift, during my travels among the elves of the eastern continent."

"So that is how you breached the tunnel," he growled.

She didn't understand what he meant, but she had more immediate concerns.

"I need paper or parchment," she said. "Something for notes."

Cinder-Shard sighed. "Chuillyon . . . is there anything of use in the prince's quarters?"

"No need," the elf answered, and began digging in his robe's deep pockets.

He pulled out a small multifold of paper stitched into a makeshift pamphlet slightly bigger than his palm. Chuillyon leafed through it, tore out two "pages" of markings, and handed over the remainder.

"Will this do?" he asked.

Wynn took it without answering. It wasn't much to write on, perhaps four sheets' worth of space all totaled. If she had to, she could write in her journal, hoping the ink didn't run too much.

Then her fear and excitement began to build again over what was to come. Not since the day she'd returned home had she held the texts themselves. Would she find the answers she needed?

Cinder-Shard was about to set her pack near the main passage's opening.

"Send it back with the rest," she said.

Irritation amplified the crags of his features.

"I will see to it," Chuillyon interceded.

"No!" Wynn snapped. She could just see him digging through her possessions and more of her journals vanishing.

"There is no one else," Cinder-Shard stated flatly. "Or would you rather leave it here?"

Wynn clenched her jaw. "Fine!"

Chuillyon offered an annoyed raise of one eyebrow as he took the pack and headed off. Cinder-Shard turned across the cavern, and Wynn followed.

Ore-Locks suddenly caught up, stepping in beside her. She had to force herself not to shrink away. The wraith wasn't the only minion here of some forgotten abomination, and she kept her eyes on Cinder-Shard's broad back.

The first time she'd seen these two was in the doorway of High-Tower's office. Did they share a bond beyond their calling, something deeper, fouler than with the others of their caste? No doubt Cinder-Shard knew what had brought Ore-Locks to "service," so was the master Stonewalker as corrupt as the outcast of the Iron-Braids?

"He is my mentor," Ore-Locks said. "He has taught me from my earliest days."

Wynn said nothing to this. Cinder-Shard didn't glance back, though he must have heard.

Ore-Locks's declaration only heightened Wynn's suspicion of his mentor. She'd become blindly entangled in unfolding events and couldn't abandon her path. In that moment, she almost wished she hadn't taken on this shadowy purpose—to halt the wraith, to learn the texts' secrets, to know for certain if the fears of Most Aged Father and others were true.

Was the Ancient Enemy returning soon? It appeared that its servants were already on the move. Cinder-Shard halted and turned to face her.

"We enter a place kept safe," he declared in warning. "You will swear never to speak of what you see . . . nor scribble about it."

Steel streaks in his black hair glinted like fire strands by the light of the walls' orange crystals.

Wynn flushed with fresh anger and swallowed hard. She was sick of this, always shackled by truth itself against the integrity she'd once thought the guild stood for.

"Agreed," she finally answered.

"Swear it . . . by your honor to the sages!"

His demand went against the very thing he expected her to swear by.

Truth through Knowledge . . . Knowledge through Understanding . . . Understanding through Truth . . . Wisdom's Eternal Cycle.

But how many times since she'd returned had she lied, manipulated, held what she knew like a tool, a weapon, or a chain upon others? Oh, she could always claim a reason to uncover what others refused to acknowledge and to save them from themselves. But even that seemed a hollow excuse sometimes.

Was she even a sage in anything more than title?

Yet there were still a few who'd put their faith in her, from Domin il'Sänke and perhaps Tärpodious, to young Nikolas Columsarn and others. Even High-Tower in his bitter way.

"I swear by the creed of my guild," she answered.

Cinder-Shard led the way into a new cavern. Wynn breathed in, held it as she followed—and then exhaled and scowled.

It was just another cavern. No orange crystals lit the space. By only the far wall's glimmer, she walked a wide, cleared path between calcified, shadowy columns. Here and there, thickened protrusions rose between those. Then she caught a looming shape in the corner of her sight.

Wynn sidestepped in reflex, glancing as she walked on.

A hulking stalagmite rose from the cavern floor, thick and fat all the way up to head-high. Its top joined the narrower end of a descending stalactite, but that faintly glistening bulk was too big to have formed from just drizzling, mineral-laden water. Some boulder or outcrop had once stood there, now buried beneath decades of buildup.

Cinder-Shard veered off the path, directly into the forest of columns.

Wynn stepped carefully, for the floor was rough and the way narrow and erratic at times. Ore-Locks fell back behind her. As Cinder-Shard made a sudden turn around a thickened protrusion, Wynn's boot toe caught on something in the dark.

As she toppled sidelong, her shoulder struck another broad outcrop. When she recoiled, finally regaining her footing, she squinted at the dark shape. For an instant, it looked too much like a rough mockery of a Lhärgnæ's false tomb.

Wynn's jaw locked, and the closer she looked, the more every muscle tensed. There was a resemblance.

At the top of the wide protrusion, it narrowed over rounded "shoulders" to the bulk of a "head" melding into the tip of a descending stalactite. Wynn shoved her hand into her pocket, digging for her crystal.

"No!" Ore-Locks said—and his thick fingers closed on her wrist.

Wynn spun toward him and lurched back, bumping straight into the calcified dark form.

"Get your hand off me!"

Ore-Locks's grip remained, and she hadn't managed to grasp her cold lamp crystal. Cinder-Shard loomed into sight beside her.

"Do not bring light in here!"

Wynn barely made out his scowl in the dark. Ore-Locks slowly released his grip and held up both open hands.

"Do not disturb their rest," he added.

Wynn glanced frantically between them and then into the dark forest of glistening columns. She spotted at least six more protrusions nearby but couldn't see farther, not even back to the path they'd left. Her gaze fell on one hulk half-hidden beyond a stalagmite's upward spike.

Pale phosphorescence illuminated its features.

The female's eyes were perhaps open, though there was no way to be certain. Even her clothing was nothing more than ripples of calcification. She gripped something in her hands, long, narrow, and slightly slanted. Beneath clumped mineral deposits coating its whole length, it could have been a thick staff. The buildup had turned her hands into lumps where they held it.

Wynn saw other dark shapes about the cavern's silent stillness. Comprehension lessened her tension but didn't bring ease.

She was standing among the dead.

Was this what it meant to be taken *into stone*? No coffins or even tombs, the Hassäg'kreigi entombed their honored dead in stone itself. Left here for years, decades, perhaps more, they would become one with the earth and stone their people cherished. But the number of them was disturbing at a guess.

In the rush when she was locked away in the Chamber of the Fallen, she'd passed too quickly through at least two other such places. Wynn turned all the way around, a wild notion rising in her thoughts.

"Is Feather-Tongue here?" she breathed, about to backtrack and search.

Ore-Locks blocked her way.

"Bedzâ'kenge is in his temple," he answered. "As are all Bäynæ who live on among us."

Wynn's eyes narrowed. That was impossible, though she now knew she wouldn't find Feather-Tongue's remains here, Dhredze was the only known seatt still in existence, but likely not as old as the mythical war. By the tales of Feather-Tongue's life, he'd lived at a time when there were others, perhaps back beyond the war and into the Forgotten History. This left her wondering about the great statues of the Bäynæ in their temples.

Did those statues truly hold the bones of the Thänæ who'd become the dwarves' Eternals? Or was Ore-Locks's claim just a spiritual metaphor?

Wynn looked once more among the honored dead slowly turning to stone through the ages. She wished she hadn't sworn to keep all of this to herself.

Cinder-Shard pulled her onward, and then stopped before the cavern's back wall. It was so dark that she couldn't be certain, but there didn't appear to be any door or opening. Was it hidden, like the one the duchess had used to come here?

Cinder-Shard turned to her. "You have audacity. Do you also have courage?"

She didn't know what he meant, but she answered, "Yes."

Cinder-Shard held out his hand. "Take it."

Wynn did so with slight hesitation—then panicked as she realized what would happen. She had seen Cinder-Shard force the wraith into the wall, perhaps trying to entomb it in stone. He knew what had called to Ore-Locks and had still taken the man in. And she had blindly gone alone with both of them.

It would be so easy to be rid of her. No one would ever know what became of her.

Cinder-Shard's face sank into the damp wall.

Wynn stopped breathing as the texture of glittering rock spread down his hair and across his back. She tried to jerk free but was dragged toward the wall. A sharp voice rose behind her.

"Do not breathe!" Ore-Locks warned. "Not until you hear him speak to you!"

Wynn sucked in a breath and her world went black and cold.

Chane hung near the archway behind Shade. Like her, he kept watch down the empty passage. He did not like sitting idle, feeling useless and incapable. He was so drained that he could not stop the beast's hungry mewling within himself.

Though he had given his word to remain until Wynn's return, a promise to enemies meant nothing. There were too many tangles, hidden alliances, and secrets in this place, and all seemed to grow more complex with each night spent in this dwarven seatt. Ore-Locks seemed to genuinely believe his own denial of Wynn's accusation—that he was intricately connected to a long-dead mass murderer. And Chane was anxious that she had gone off with Ore-Locks and his master.

He waited, trying to be patient . . . not to worry . . . and to push down the hunger.

He was failing at all three.

No one came down the passage, but he could not tell if anyone waited in the cavern at its end, the only exit along the path. He almost slipped out to inch down the way when a stout dwarf in black stepped through the passage's far end.

A female Stonewalker approached carrying two packs, but she paused partway as someone else called out. The tall elf in white came in behind her and handed off a third pack. Then he turned back to vanish out the end. When the Stonewalker reached the archway, she held out all three packs with one hand—and his sword and Wynn's dagger in the other.

Chane took them, offering no thanks. Then she pulled a bag off her shoulder, dropped it, and left without a word. She never looked back.

He set the packs next to the staff leaning inside the archway and strapped on his sword. Opening the bag, he found a water skin, a loaf of bread, some jerky, and a wooden mug within it. He took out some jerky, poured a mug of water, and brought them to Shade.

"Here," he said, kneeling down.

She did not growl at him and lapped the water briefly. He set the jerky on the floor and moved away. Shade snapped it up, barely chewing, and returned to her vigil.

He could not help but admire her patience. She had thrown herself at the wraith more than once, always protecting Wynn without hesitation. She had found the shore entrance to the underworld when he could not continue the search.

Shade was a better companion than most Chane had known.

"She will come back," he said.

Shade's ears twitched, but that was all.

He hoped Wynn would return with some answers, perhaps even concerning the scroll. In her absence, he hoped Shade might grow more used to his presence. Natural enemies or not, they were stuck with each other in a common purpose. But even that had become too complicated, from the elf's indiscernible lies, to the master Stonewalker's seeming acceptance of Ore-Locks . . . and the madman hidden away in the pool's locked chamber.

Worst of all, the wraith still existed. It had gained the underworld before raising any alarm or awareness—even his own.

Chane looked down at Welstiel's ring of nothing on his finger. He had worn it so long, so often, he sometimes forgot it was there. It was necessary, or had been. But if he had not been wearing it when they had entered this place . . .

Even Shade had not sensed the wraith until too late. Chane had not sensed it at all, not while wearing the ring. The wraith would come back, and he needed to know when, if not where.

Chane gripped the ring with his other hand. "Shade?"

She twisted her head up and back, looking at him. He showed her what he was about to do, but she merely returned to her vigil. In one swift movement, Chane pulled the ring off.

For an instant, the world rippled like the surface of a disturbed pond. His senses sharpened slightly as his awareness expanded, free of the ring's influence.

Chane smelled—*felt*—Shade's life and the brief twinge of someone else beyond the passage's end. Then it was gone, though the beast within Chane lunged to the end of its bonds.

Shade remained silent though Chane thought he saw her hackles prickle.

Between them, he hoped one would know if—when—the wraith returned.

Chane slid down the archway's side to settle beside the packs and the staff. Hunger kept eating at him, as if it turned upon him with nothing else to sate it. He closed his eyes, thinking of anything else. . . .

Of Stonewalkers . . . and their secrets . . .

Of white-clad, false elven sages . . . and their secrets . . .

Of beings of the sea and a prince believed dead.

There were moments he wished none of this had begun. It would have been so much better to slip into the guild library for the brief part of any night with Wynn, even if he spent his days hiding in some hovel. But what he had seen could not be ignored, even as he felt himself drifting at the dark edge of dormancy.

A dead prince of this foreign land appeared to have spoken to people of the sea that Chane could never have imagined. Among other puzzles, that one lingered upon him now. What did it mean? It seemed a very desperate secret, dangerous enough that the duchess might yet kill for it.

Chane found himself standing among the guild library's shelves.

He tried to pick a first book to pull out. He knew there was one he needed to find, but could not think of what it was. When he turned to ask Wynn's advice, he was looking at the pool through the bars of the sea tunnel's last gate. Face-to-face, he stared at a man soaked to the skin, who reached through those bars.

A dream . . . and even within it, he wondered why.

Dormancy held no dreams for the dead. But a few times before, they had come to him.

He heard something that made him turn, waist-deep in the tunnel's freezing water. But Wynn was not there, nor was Shade. The long darkness behind him, filling the tunnel to its round walls, seemed to twist . . . like black coils with soft glints of light.

Crushing cold . . . suffocation . . . pure darkness that brought utter silence . . .

Wynn felt stone's chill over her whole body and couldn't move. The pressure threatened to grind her into nothing as the heat in her flesh rapidly leached out.

She was buried alive.

In terror, she tried to scream, but her mouth couldn't open. Even her jaw and lips wouldn't move. Her lungs began to burn, wanting to expel used-up air.

"It will pass quickly," someone said.

That sudden voice in the silence made her flinch in panic, and she collapsed. Her left arm felt instantly strained, but the darkness began to lighten.

"Breathe," someone ordered in a gravelly voice. "Open your mouth and breathe, fool!"

Wynn did so, in one tearing, heaving gasp. She grew faint, but something held her up by her left wrist and wouldn't let go.

"Do not succumb to what you feel, or it will linger!"

Wynn opened her eyes.

In the dimly lit dark, Cinder-Shard was watching her. Her left shoulder ached, and she finally realized he held her up by her wrist. The few items she'd brought lay on a damp floor of dark stone below her buckled legs. She struggled to regain her feet.

"Let go of me," she said, but it came out hoarse and broken.

"Not until you can stand," he answered.

Ore-Locks stepped into view, blocking off more of the surroundings.

"The first time is the worst," he said, "though few have ever traveled this way."

Wynn wheezed and coughed, and Ore-Locks glanced at Cinder-Shard, as if in concern. She finally planted her feet firmly on stone.

"She will recover," Cinder-Shard said.

When he released her wrist, her arm flopped numbly against her side.

"Come for me when she is finished," he added, stepping around her.

Wynn slowly wobbled around, still shivering, but all she saw behind her was the cave's rough wall. Cinder-Shard was gone, and she was alone with Ore-Locks.

"Why did he . . . bother coming," she got out between breaths, "if you're staying?"

"I cannot yet take another with me . . . as he can."

Wynn began to breathe normally and turned back, trying to make out her surroundings.

She found herself inside a large, slanted pocket of rough stone. The ceiling was low, but she could stand upright. And half blocked by Ore-Locks's bulk was a pool near the cave's left side.

There were no other openings besides the pool in the floor, its water likely held down by air pressure of the pocket itself. She had no indication of where or how far she might have come—only that she was still under the earth and near the ocean, by the smell of the water.

She froze upon seeing what waited at the cave's far end.

Three small chests were stored in a space below a set of short stone tiers.

Something very familiar lay on the first deep shelf. It was a sheaf of stiff hide plates bound between two squares of thin, mottled iron. It was the first text that she and Chap had discovered, the night Li'kän had caught her amid the blizzard and dragged her to the ice-bound castle.

Wynn was still in too much shock to even feel relief. Digging in her pocket, she pulled out her crystal. It didn't even start to glimmer upon her chilled hand.

She rubbed it clumsily, until its light began to grow. When she bent slowly to retrieve her fallen items, Ore-Locks was quicker and picked them up. She took them, ignoring him, and stumbled across the cave. She was halfway to the shelves when she heard a soft splash.

Wynn teetered as she turned.

Rippling rings spread on the pool's surface as a white-tipped spearhead rose at the center of the water. It was quickly followed by a row of spikes upon a hairless, teal-tinged scalp.

Large, round black-orb eyes broke the surface, and Wynn stared eye-to-eye at one of the sea people.

In the crystal's light, she saw the slits for a nose and translucent membranes spread between the ridges of head spikes. He rose enough to expose webbing between clawed fingers, and between the spikes running along the outsides of his forearms. His stomach muscles appeared strange, different somehow, and he had no navel.

Then his lipless mouth parted slightly over interlocked needles of teeth. Without distinguishable irises, it was impossible to follow his gaze until he actually turned his head toward Ore-Locks.

Ore-Locks crouched and patted the floor, nodding. The sea man sank until the water covered the slits of his throat and his mouth—but not his eyes.

"Why is it . . . he . . . here?" Wynn asked.

"He is a guardian," Ore-Locks answered. "I cannot speak to him, but I reassured him that your presence is sanctioned."

"Who are they . . . and where are they from? Why did they come to the prince?"

Ore-Locks left her, heading to the shelves. "Where do you wish to begin?"

Wynn hesitated, still watching the hairless head of webbed tines and those round black eyes. She backed away toward the shelves.

"Bring all three chests out, so I can use one as a desk," she said, buying a few moments.

Until seeing this place, she'd entertained a few notions. Perhaps she could steal a few crucial pages or even one whole text. Or maybe she might spot another way in—or at least gain some sense where the texts were located, so she could find them on her own and retrieve them.

None of this would ever happen.

Only a Stonewalker could bring her and take her back out. She'd bought her way in here on a bluff, and now she needed to produce results. Her heart pounded in her rib cage.

"Haste is necessary," Ore-Locks said, sliding out the first chest. "We do not know when the . . . the spirit—"

"Wraith," Wynn corrected.

"Yes, as you say . . . and we do not know when or how it will return."

"I'm well aware of that. This isn't like looking up something in a library volume. Just get the other chests out. Search for freshly scribed folios of translations so far."

Ore-Locks dragged out the second chest.

"And the codex," she added. "It's a large volume laced together with waxed string. I need something to help decipher the originals, and their order, without my . . ."

Wynn went silent as she opened the first chest.

"What?" Ore-Locks asked. "Did you find it?"

Resting atop the piles therein were five volumes she hadn't seen in half a year. Their soft leather covers were lashed closed with wrapped leather laces. They looked rather worn and even travel-weary to her eyes.

"My journals," she whispered. "My *stolen* journals!"

Ore-Locks peered into the chest. "You wrote those?"

When she didn't answer, he turned away and hauled out the third chest.

For a moment all Wynn wanted was to gather those five leather-wrapped volumes, leave this place, and hide them where no one could take them from her again.

"Is this it?" Ore-Locks asked.

Wynn looked up.

He held up the thick codex where he crouched. Inside the third chest were piles of bound sheaves, translations like the ones she'd seen at the guild. There were so many—but maybe she'd forgotten how much work had been done. It had taken her a whole day to just scan quickly through them.

"What about this other one?" Ore-Locks asked.

"What other one?"

He reached into the chest and held out a thinner volume than the first—but it had the same temporary wax stitching.

"Give it to me!"

Wynn snatched it from him and slapped it open upon the chest's edge. Inside were entries of completed or ongoing translation work, like the ones she'd seen in the first volume that day in the catacombs. She looked at all the sheaves, even a few folios, stacked inside the third chest.

"*Valhachkasej'â!*" she cursed.

Thoughts of Sykion—and especially High-Tower's resentments toward her—began to build until she stammered in anger.

"You . . . you two . . . !"

Wynn couldn't think of anything vile enough to call them. She was holding a second codex.

They hadn't shown her everything. Only what they thought she'd believed was all the work so far, just enough that she might lean their way, in their urgency to keep all of this a secret.

"What is wrong?" Ore-Locks demanded.

Wynn tried to regain her self-control. "Nothing," she hissed.

"Truly? You are this upset by nothing?"

She wasn't about to explain herself to him. He and Cinder-Shard had both expressed opposition to the translation project in High-Tower's study. She doubted he would empathize with her bitterness. But more important for now, she had more to work with—more translations—to help her fight her way through the original texts.

Wynn dug through the second chest to gain an idea what it held, as well as the first, which had contained her journals. She set those aside for use and looked up to the shelves filled with all the varied books, tomes, and sheaves she'd taken from Li'kän's library.

"What was it like," Ore-Locks asked, "the place where you found these?"

Her mind flashed back to that long, sleepless night. She and Chap had carefully chosen what seemed important, readable, or merely sound enough to take from among a wealth of decaying sources. Her friends had helped her carry away so little compared to what they left behind, now half a world away.

"Older than you can imagine," she answered. "So old the only guardian had forgotten the sound of speech . . . or her own voice."

Wynn shook off the memory of that naked, deceptively frail undead with slanted teardrop-shaped eyes like no breed of human she'd ever seen.

"Stop bothering me," she said. "I need to work."

Ore-Locks stepped back as she began pulling out translation sheaves and folios and made a quick mental account of the other two chests' contents. They contained the more frail volumes versus the ones on the shelves. Where should she start first?

At present, information concerning the wraith was most dire. It seemed to have targeted folios mentioning the Children, the Reverent, and the Sâ'yminfiäl—the Eaters of Silence. From Wynn's encounter with Li'kän, she knew it was possible that minions of il'Samar, Beloved, the Ancient Enemy by whatever name or title, still existed to this day.

Cinder-Shard had called the wraith the "dog" of Kêravägh—the Nightfaller.

Apparently he believed it was, or had been, a servant of the enemy. Li'kän, Häs'saun, and Volyno had been three of its thirteen Children, all Noble Dead but vampires. So if the wraith was a servant as powerful as they were, she reasoned that it may have been someone just as important. Perhaps someone who'd once held a position of note as part of one of the other two groups.

But Wynn had little idea what the titles "Reverent" or "Eaters of Silence" actually meant. All she had were lists of names from one day of reviewing the translations. She'd found only hints that the Reverent might be a religious order.

For survival—for credence in being here—she first had to find solid information for Cinder-Shard and the duchess. Second, she needed answers for herself on anything regarding Chane's scroll, and thereby any mention of Bäalâle Seatt.

She almost glanced back at Ore-Locks, growing sick inside at the thought of that thing—that lone tomb—separated from the Fallen Ones. Then it dawned on her that of all the Stonewalkers, if she must have a guard, Ore-Locks might be the most useful.

His eyes had lit up at mention of Bäalâle Seatt, though she hadn't fully known why at the time. Perhaps, his interest was a way to gain his compliance, if and when she needed it.

Third and last, with little time for it, she hoped for any mention of an ancient elven sanctuary.

Chap—as well as Magiere—had caught some of Most Aged Father's oldest memories from the time of the Forgotten. He had seen Aonnis Lhoin'n—First Glade—the place where no undead could enter. The place the Lhoin'na had left hidden in plain sight since that time.

Members of the elves' guild branch sometimes visited the one in Calm Seatt, yet not one had ever mentioned the great age of First Glade. At its mention, Chuillyon had feigned ignorance, according to Chane. Why would they keep this a secret?

Wynn needed to know. If the undead could not enter the glade, then such a place, such a haven, might be indispensable in days to come.

"Why do you hesitate?" Ore-Locks said. "Is something missing?"

Wynn realized she'd sat too long doing nothing. "No, I'm deciding where to begin."

"Were the texts not in your possession for some time? Did you not study them on your journey home?"

"Not enough," she whispered. "My domin, Tilswith, suggested I wait to rejoin my peers—more experienced cathologers. It made sense . . . because I was a naive girl! But I don't think even he expected the texts to be confiscated."

As soon as her mouth closed, she regretted telling him anything.

Yes, she'd perused some of the works on that journey. Curiosity had gotten the better of her more than once. But events in the Farlands had been fresh in her mind, along with losses. Some days of the journey, the texts had been too much of a reminder of what their acquisition had cost.

Then she remembered something she and Chap had chosen.

Wynn stood up, searching the shelves. When she couldn't find it, she dug in the chests. In the second, she found a flat volume, its two hide-coated wood covers held on with gut-thread lacing grown brittle with age.

Wynn looked more carefully at it.

Someone had removed the old lacing and rebound the volume with fresh, waxed hemp string. The cover had been rubbed with something that had revivified the leather, though it was still terribly marred by age. When she and Chap had chosen this one, she hadn't yet known about the scroll.

Ore-Locks appeared at her side, apparently unable to stay out of her way.

"Why that one?" he asked.

Like Cinder-Shard, he opposed the guild's project, but now he showed quite a bit of interest in the texts themselves.

"Because it may have been written by one called Häs'saun," she answered. "Another forgotten minion of a forgotten enemy. He was part of a group called the Children—all vampires, another kind of Noble Dead besides the wraith. In Calm Seatt, the wraith seemed especially interested in folios concerning them."

Ore-Locks watched with intensity as Wynn opened the thin volume. She'd tried for so long to tell her superiors the truth of these texts. She felt dull surprise that Ore-Locks didn't even question her words.

"What was Häs'saun's reason?" he asked.

High-Tower would've roared for silence.

"Three vampires," she said, "along with followers, took what we call an 'orb' all the way to the Farlands. In its highest desolate range, the Pock Peaks, they built a castle. Their purpose seemed to be guarding the orb."

"For what? What does it do?"

"We don't know."

Her denial was true. Magiere, Leesil, and Chap had all offered varying accounts of what happened in the underground cavern that held the orb. But when Magiere had accidentally activated or "opened" it, the orb had consumed all free moisture within reach.

Water dripping upon the cavern's walls, bleeding down from ice above being heated by the cavern's fiery chasm, had rained *inward* all around into the orb's burning light. And Li'kän had been there for centuries, in a place with little or no life to feed on. The orb had somehow sustained her.

Ore-Locks frowned. "If only three went to these Pock Peaks, what of the others? You said there were thirteen of these . . . Children. Where did they go?"

"That may be what the wraith wants to learn."

Just as she did, especially since it had taken a furious interest in Chane's scroll.

"Now let me read," she said.

Ore-Locks folded his hands behind his back and turned away in silence.

Wynn closed the third chest. Using it as a makeshift desk, she placed Häs'saun's text upon it. She retrieved the second codex, for if what she suspected was true, she needed to know if other translations came from work noted in the first one. Again she found references to sections in numbered volumes, but how was she to know which ones those were?

She idly flipped through Häs'saun's thin text, until she spotted an inked note on the upper inner corner of its back cover. It was marked as volume two.

Turning back to the second codex, and opening the thicker first one as well, she scanned both work schedule listings. Volume numbers between the two schedules were erratic, so the codices weren't sequential. In fact, dates of work overlapped all the way back to the first moon in which she'd arrived home. Some unknown criteria had been used to determine what translation work was entered into which codex.

Wynn didn't need to check further. They'd hidden the second codex from her. Translations she'd already seen wouldn't include those from volumes listed in it.

She immediately began pulling texts off the shelves, saving the fragile ones in the third chest for last, and searched for work entries or more volume marks. There were unseen translations to go through, but she wanted the originals at hand as she did so. She looked once to the sheaf of hide pages between old iron squares.

A tip of a parchment strip peeked out of its far side.

Wynn tugged it lightly, until its end was visible, showing it was marked as volume seven. She remembered that reference from the first codex and the translations she'd already seen. Then she came to a bundle on the second shelf wrapped in brown felt cloth. Upon unwrapping it, she remembered it well.

Atop a short pile of petrified wood planks was a strip of parchment marking this collection as volume one. It made sense that this text had been worked on early. She carefully placed the slats on the chest beside Häs'saun's thin volume. She'd chosen them, having identified the author as Volyno, the last of Li'kän's trio.

Each of the seven planks was a forearm's length and two handbreadths wide. They were covered in faded ink marks she'd recognized when she'd found them. Volyno often wrote in Heiltak, an ancient writing system and a forerunner dialect of contemporary Numanese. Wynn was most familiar with it.

She set aside the volume marker and gently separated the top three planks. The first was ragged at the ends, decayed and disintegrated long ago. She scanned what remained, searching for anything that caught her eye. Halfway down the third plank she spotted one oddity—a Sumanese term rendered in Heiltak letters.

Sâ'yminfiäl—the Eaters of Silence.

"What?" Ore-Locks asked.

Wynn hadn't realized she'd sucked in a breath too quickly. "Nothing," she answered.

She traced backward from that term and came upon mention of "thirteen" and "Children." She cracked open ink, dipped her quill, and started reading again from the plank's rotted top.

Too many parts were faded, worn, or darkened with age. She'd find those same missing pieces marked in the translation with dots for obscured words or strokes where the count couldn't be guessed. About to check the second codex for what volumes had been worked on in conjunction with this one, she paused upon a sentence fragment.

. . . âv Hruse . . .

It literally meant "of the earth" or "of earth," but the capitalization meant something more. Was it a reference to Earth, as in one of the five Elements? The sentence's first half was unreadable, as was a short bit that followed. Then she saw something more easily translated.

. . . chair of a lord's song.

It was the same phrase as her own mistaken translation from a term in Chane's scroll. And here it was again, with the same mistake, but written in Heiltak. Il'Sanke's correction had rendered her translation into a reference to Bäalâle Seatt!

Wynn scanned the second codex and found listings for work complete on volume one—sections one through seven, likely referring to the seven planks. Why this was recorded in the second codex and not the first that she'd been shown?

Something else nagged at her. She looked between both codices at the handwriting rather than the entries. There were variations in the first, different people recording scheduled or complete work. But the second was written in one hand only.

It was High-Tower's.

The implication was clear. He'd been the only one to decide on the work she hadn't seen. How many others, even those involved in the project, were unaware of whatever he was doing—and why?

Wynn slammed the first codex shut, keeping only the second, and stared at the third plank. The decayed part between the two fragments wasn't long, but she couldn't be certain they were both part of the same sentence. Digging out any completed translation wouldn't help.

It wouldn't give her useful information to feed Cinder-Shard and the duchess, but she was too obsessed to turn away. When she read onward, other fragments made her neck muscles tighten. Somewhere behind her, Ore-Locks paced intermittently.

Wynn straightened where she knelt, still second-guessing what she was about to do.

Without turning, she asked, "Has the duchess ever been down in the Chamber of the Fallen?"

Ore-Locks's shifting steps stop, instantly.

"No, not down," he answered. "Your presence there . . . was unprecedented."

That brought some relief. Aside from royal involvement in suppressing the texts' existence, perhaps they didn't know about Ore-Locks's true *calling*.

"What do you know about Bäalâle Seatt?" she asked.

A long pause followed.

"Only the lie that Thallûhearag . . . Deep-Root . . . was its final bane."

Wynn glanced over her shoulder, wishing Chane were here to confirm Ore-Locks's lies.

"I once heard that everyone there was lost," she said carefully, watching his eyes begin to widen. "It was under siege in the war . . . and even the enemy's forces didn't escape."

Ore-Locks tensed, until a vein stood out upon his left temple.

"Heard?" he whispered, as if he couldn't get a full breath. "Where could you have heard anything of that place?"

Again, she wouldn't give him any more than she had to. Turning back to Volyno's text, she began reading aloud.

"'. . . of Earth . . .'" she began, then tried to fill in, "'beneath the chair of a lord's song . . . meant to prevail but all ended . . . halfway eaten in beneath.'"

That last part didn't make sense, but she read onward to what truly mattered.

"'. . . even the *wéyelokangas* . . . walk in Earth . . . failed Beloved's will.'"

At Ore-Locks's puzzled expression, she explained.

"Beloved is how the Children referred to the Ancient Enemy, the one your master calls Kêravägh."

His brow furrowed. "What is *wéy . . . lok* . . . ?" he began, faltering on the word.

"It's Numanese, my language," she returned, "but so old that few would recognize it. It means 'war lockers' or 'war sealers.'"

Still she saw no understanding in his face.

"Traitors!" she snapped. "Oath breakers who change sides amid a war, giving advantage to the enemy. And they walked in earth . . . or stone!"

"Lies!" Ore-Locks breathed, as his face flushed in anger.

"They were Stonewalkers!" Wynn shouted back, though obviously he understood. "Your precious Thallûhearag . . . was Hassäg'kreigi . . . like you!"

Ore-Locks took a quick thundering step toward her as the sea man rose in the pool, leveling his spear. Wynn was frightened, but she'd never let it show.

"Don't even think of threatening me," she warned. "I'd wager Cinder-Shard doesn't even realize all that you are . . . not by the way he went after the wraith, one of the enemy's own."

Ore-Locks held his place only an arm's length away. He could kill her quickly enough, but he wouldn't.

She was playing a dangerous game, one Leesil or even Magiere might have tried: Make an enemy afraid of being exposed for worse than anyone suspected. Wait for him to make a mistake he couldn't erase in the sight of others—and finish him.

But just how would she do that when the time came?

"Cinder-Shard is waiting for me," she added coldly. "As is the duchess."

Ore-Locks paled, anger draining.

Wynn began to worry. Did he know what she was up to? Then he raised his hand toward the being in the pool.

That one settled once more, immersed to his slitted throat, just watching her.

"Return to work," Ore-Locks breathed.

Wynn stood her ground, not breaking eye contact, until he finally stepped back. Her hammering heart made it almost hard to breathe as she turned away. She was careful to take every step slowly, as calmly as she could, until she knelt before the chest.

One more question remained, concerning Ore-Locks's brother.

High-Tower had left home—after his brother—to take service at the temple of Feather-Tongue. In the end, that hadn't been enough for whatever drove him. It obviously wasn't some spiritual calling. He'd abandoned that place for a life in the guild—the life of a "scribbler"—a peculiar choice for any dwarf steeped in oral tradition.

Wynn looked at the second codex, written entirely in High-Tower's hand.

Certainly others had been involved in its listed translation work, but all under his direction. Was he trying to find the truth of a tainted ancestor—or hiding his family's shame from anyone outside of the guild's walls?

Wynn returned to Volyno's writing, hoping an ancient Noble Dead could speak across centuries to give her answers. It took longer before her hands stopped shaking, so she could turn to the next plank.

Sau'ilahk wallowed in dormancy, drained and beaten down until night came again. Awareness slowly returned, as did memories of recent events.

He had felt his *body*—as if unwillingly manifested in full—when the dwarf had forced him into the wall. Stone's crush had sent him into terror, and he instantly fled into darkness. But Beloved had been silent amid Sau'ilahk's dormancy, offering no words of assistance or rebuke.

Those black-clad dwarves—Stonewalkers—had power he did not understand. They had power over him!

Sau'ilahk wanted to wail his anger, his fear, to rend and tear those who reduced him to cowering flight. He wanted to make Wynn Hygeorht suffer for this. How had she breached the underworld at all?

He could go nearly anywhere, anyplace he knew of and could remember. She was a witless, confused young woman, even with her staff and its crystal. Impudent Wynn Hygeorht saw herself as his opponent, his equal.

These Stonewalkers would die soon enough. He would find a way to kill them one by one. But Wynn would be last. Let her watch every ally fall before her eyes. She would die alone, slowly enough to remember the faces of the dead around her.

A soft hiss entered his thoughts.

Do not expose yourself—us—and give the sage's rants credence. Remain hidden . . . keep all in the dark.

Sau'ilahk's awareness fell to cold stillness at Beloved's words, so filled with new urgency. Was there something more beneath them, as if his god were . . . panicked?

He waited to see dormancy's darkness break with the appearance of stars. Each point of light would turn to a glint upon black scales, until those rolled and twisted all around him in turning coils of his Beloved's presence.

But not a single glint appeared.

True consciousness began to tingle and stir inside him. With it, rage reawoke. He quickly focused upon memory of the underworld's cavern, trying to scratch together its details and shapes. He had to remember . . . he had to return there and nowhere else.

And when chance comes . . . sever the kin from the sea!

Beloved's final words pierced Sau'ilahk, flooding his whole being. With them came a wave of hate that drowned his own anger for an instant.

Sau'ilahk materialized, quaking—and Beloved's fading hatred left only confusion.

He tried to fathom those last words, but he needed to hunt, to put an end to these centuries of searching—to put an end to that sage. And he found himself at a sudden loss.

He looked across a deserted cavern of tall and wide dwarven columns—the marketplace. He stood somewhere at its rear, where he had followed the duchess to the hidden entrance into the mountain's depths. He was not in the underworld.

Sau'ilahk had awoken in Sea-Side!

With an angry hiss, he turned down the rear tunnel. Why had he returned here? Had he not remembered the underworld cavern well enough—or had Beloved done this? What had his god meant by . . . *sever the kin from the sea*?

Those words worked upon him as he glided along dim passages. Did it mean "kin of the ocean waves"? But the only Âreskynna here was the duchess, and she bore the name by marriage, not blood. She was not truly one of them.

Rumbling voices carried from ahead, and he slowed. At the passage's branching, he slipped along its left arc, sinking halfway into the wall. Everything dimmed for an instant, almost taking him to the blackness of dormancy.

Sau'ilahk fought exhaustion, willing his awareness to clear, and peered around the curve to where the passage straightened. Six dwarves stood before the wall of blocks where the entrance was hidden. A few murmured to one another, as all kept looking along the passage.

Sau'ilahk sank fully into hiding within stone.

These were not constabulary. They were armed and fully armored in steel-reinforced hauberks and helms with heavy iron bands. An iron tripod had been placed before them, its basin filled with orange crystals that lit up the space.

The dwarves had been warned.

In his current weakness, he could not kill six quickly enough, let alone feed to satisfaction. Was his remaining servitor still within the mountain? Would it be enough for an instant's advantage?

Beloved had commanded that the knowledge of his return should be hindered. Rampant slaughter and reports of a black figure would heighten any state of alarm. Much attention would turn his way.

Sau'ilahk did not care anymore. He was tired of hiding within shadows. He needed to kill, feed, and grow stronger with every death.

The Stonewalkers worked in unison, so he would scatter them like rats in the mountain's bowels. Let them blindly pursue him, uncertain where he might strike next, and he would take them one by one. There would be no more waiting, wandering in frail hope of flesh.

And he would find Wynn—or the duchess—and torment her until she relinquished the texts' true location. Perhaps he would learn as well the meaning behind Beloved's final demand.

Sau'ilahk tried calling his last servitor.

Come to me . . . come to the target of my intent.

He fixed upon a point down the passage beyond the dwarves and waited, holding that one spot upon the floor with his full awareness.

The stone-worm rose there.

Liquidlike ripples spread through the floor's stone around its trunk. One dwarf shouted, pointing at it, and the others turned that way.

Sau'ilahk shot across the passage into the far wall and sank only halfway.

Two dwarves raced toward the worm, one raising a mace to shatter it.

Sau'ilahk flowed rapidly along the wall, his black-cloth-wrapped hand extending toward the first dwarf's exposed back.

Left in silence, Wynn ignored Ore-Locks and the sea guardian as she lost herself in research. Switching between chest tops as a desk, she had carefully arranged every text or translation listed in the second codex all around her. Now she tried to find references to the Children, the Reverent, or the Eaters of Silence.

She struggled through ancient languages and letter systems, some too obscure to fathom more brief phrases. Others were utterly unknown, including a system of ideograms she'd never seen before. Those might've come from Li'kän, perhaps well after she was alone, drifting into madness amid isolation. But Wynn found no further mention of traitors, warlockers, those who "walked in earth," or even Bäalâle Seatt.

So why had the last been found in Chane's scroll?

Volyno's work was the easiest to read, but it held little that was useful. She often referred to notes of names taken from direct translations she'd read in the guild's catacombs. She was halfway through another book, its pages made from some thin animal skin. The content was in Iyindu, an old Sumanese dialect, so likely written by Häs'saun. Occasional words were written with characters similar to what she'd learned of Belaskian and Old Stravinan in the Farlands.

And then she stumbled upon mention of the Reverent.

That term was recorded in her notes, though this was first time she'd seen it here.

Wynn ran her fingers over the page's surface. She was holding the actual text from which that translation had been taken, containing that term and unknown names. And here were the names she'd written in the same paragraph.

Jeyretan, Fäzabid, Memaneh, Creif, Uhmgadâ, Sau'ilahk.

She still hadn't come across a clear definition for the Sâ'yminfiäl, or the Eaters of Silence. If the Children were powerful servants to the ancient enemy, the offspring of a perceived god, and the Reverent were its priests, then who or what were the Eaters of Silence? She read on and came to a passage concerning Vespana and Ga'hetman, two of the other Children. It seemed an account of a journey.

It couldn't have taken place after the Children "divided," as mentioned in the scroll. Häs'saun would've been off on his own trek, and therefore couldn't have learned the details. Wynn made out only a few terms, and quickly searched for translations from this text. There were some, but they didn't help much.

. . . to the west of the world's fulcrum . . . [symbols obscured, possible number] *long nights from K'mal . . . Khalidah grew tiresome . . . though eluded the tree-born . . . many tainted-blood died . . . a few filled our ranks . . .*

The place references were baffling, but she copied everything word for word, even the dots indicating missing or untranslated parts. Some of it was clear. "Tree-born" had to mean the elves, likely ancestors of the Lhoin'na and the an'Cróan. "Tainted-blood" might be humans, and among the dead the few who "filled our ranks" meant only one thing.

Vespana and Ga'hetman had raised them as undead.

. . . were one's forces over and over . . . by the Sâ'yminfiäl . . . their mad thoughts consuming weak earth-born minds . . . waking slumber and . . . the rituals of Khalidah . . . that trio with their twisted whispers of thought . . . promises and fears . . . the walkers in earth, guided the anchor of Earth . . . eating up through the mountain's root . . .

The pieces hinted at strange things. Wynn lingered most over mention of "walkers in earth" and "guided the anchor of Earth." The latter was baffling, perhaps some siege engine used against the seatt. Whatever it was, it seemed the Stonewalkers had aided in this. But other parts took more time to connect, and when they did, it was so much the worse.

"Oh, no, no, no," Wynn whispered, and then quickly went silent.

The rituals of Khalidah . . . the trio with their whispers of thought . . . consuming weak earth-born minds . . .

Wynn understood what Sâ'yminfiäl, the Eaters of Silence, meant. They were sorcerers.

A trio of them had been part of the siege upon Bäalâle Seatt, along with Vespana and Ga'hetman.

Chane had deduced that the wraith was a conjuror, so it couldn't be one of them. That meant this Khalidah wasn't the wraith. One more name had now moved to one of her three known groups, but it still left too many others unclassified. She had nothing to truly support her notion, but she felt more and more certain that the wraith had served among the Reverent.

For whatever reason, it—he—was obsessed with seeking where the thirteen Children had gone. But also, much as she was now, had it been seeking what had happened at Bäalâle Seatt?

She was onto something, but what?

Wynn returned to Häs'saun's text, struggling with an ancient dialect she hadn't mastered. Almost as cryptic and secretive as the hidden writing in Chane's scroll, what little she fathomed was often condensed. She opened her journal to entries of names taken from the translations.

Jeyretan, Fäzabid, Memaneh, Creif, Uhmgadâ, Sau'ilahk.

The wraith had to be one of them. She didn't know what use might come of knowing its name. Perhaps it was just the need to know anything, any scrap concerning her enemy. But it might also help her understand any other references to the Reverent, anything they'd done . . . anything the wraith knew.

She read on, catching only every third word and doubtful of her translation, but she used these to guess at the others. She came upon a strange series of fragments that seemed connected.

. . . by the priest's jealousy of us . . . prayers like begging . . . with Beloved's three-edged boon . . . the joy of his petty vanity . . .

It was the closest she could translate, though she could be wrong. From Domin il'Sänke's comments concerning the scroll, it might be Pärpa'äsea rather than Iyindu, or even some other tongue. But it seemed that one of the Reverent had made a bargain with his Beloved to fulfill a vain wish.

What could an ancient Noble Dead have that anyone would envy for the sake of vanity? And why had Häs'saun claimed the boon was "three-edged"?

The metaphor of "two-edged" was part of almost any culture. It referred to a benefit that could be a downfall as well. "Three-edged" implied something worse, as if deficit outweighed any gain twofold.

. . . by beauty . . . frail the high priest was and is . . . his wish fulfilled . . . cheated with eternal life . . .

Wynn went cold in the pit of her stomach.

Not just one of the Reverent, but their very leader had asked for and received eternal life, but it didn't make sense. How could one be "cheated" by such a gift? And the Children were not alive; they were undead, Noble Dead.

And "was and is"? When had Häs'saun written this? How could he know what had happened, or would happen, to Beloved's high priest, considering Häs'saun had gone off with Li'kän, Volyno, and the orb?

. . . not mortal . . . not in young eternity . . .

Wynn sighed. That translation couldn't be right. She closed her eyes, reworking the phrases in her mind.

. . . never immortal . . . never eternally young . . .

"Three-edged" and a high priest's "vanity" began to connect. He hadn't just been after eternal life but eternal beauty. So why wouldn't eternal life provide that?

. . . Beloved's vain first [something] *knew not what he would lose . . .*

Whatever trick had been played on the high priest hadn't come to pass at the time of the siege.

. . . eternal being, Sau'ilahk shall never be . . .

Wynn came to a frantic halt.

She had found the name of the tricked priest, the last one among those identified as part of the Reverent. But it wasn't enough, and the rest of the page wasn't readable. She flipped to the next, but it started with an account of something else. There was no mention of Beloved's high priest.

"Eternal being but never be . . . what?" she whispered.

Or was that all there was to it? No eternal youth, no immortality, but eternal life just the same. What was the result of such a mistake in Sau'ilahk's shallow longing for beauty?

Wynn knew the answer, slowly rising to her feet.

"Ore-Locks," she said slowly, "I think I know who the wraith—"

"Someone comes," he cut in.

Wynn turned to find him facing the cave's far wall. She backstepped at the sight of a hulking figure emerging from stone and grew wary as it took form.

It wasn't Cinder-Shard.

"Master Bulwark," Ore-Locks said in equal surprise.

Wynn recognized his bony features and gray-blond hair. Her crystal's light glinted on the steel tips of his black-scaled hauberk.

Master Bulwark appeared equally surprised, then angrily suspicious. He glanced once at the guardian in the pool as he strode forward.

"I could not believe Cinder-Shard sent you here with the sage!" His eyes narrowed on Ore-Locks. "What have *you* been doing?"

"What I was told," Ore-Locks returned, though resentment leaked into his voice. "To wait until the sage finished and then notify Master Cinder-Shard to retrieve her."

Wynn took only a grain of comfort in the exchange. Bulwark didn't trust Ore-Locks. Perhaps he didn't even approve of Cinder-Shard taking in the outcast of the Iron-Braids. Did Bulwark know something about Ore-Locks's connection to Thallûhearag? Had Ore-Locks ever come to this cave before, trying to delve into the texts on his own?

The elder Stonewalker glowered at Ore-Locks and stepped past toward Wynn.

"Have you discovered anything useful?" he demanded.

"What?" Wynn sputtered. "Possibly . . . but I've barely begun. I need more time."

"The day has passed. Night has come again," he said. "You will return to your companions, as Ore-Locks is needed elsewhere. If you have something to report, I will inform the duchess, and she will come to you."

Wynn backed away. Apparently Bulwark was second only to Cinder-Shard. He was going to pull her through stone whether she wanted to go or not. She had little to tell, so little that she might never see the texts again.

"I can tell the duchess what I've learned," Wynn bluffed. "But she will want to know more once she hears it . . . as will Cinder-Shard."

Ore-Locks was already packing the texts away with great care. Bulwark merely stood waiting, speaking only to Ore-Locks.

"You may go. Find Amaranth and assist her until you are called."

As Ore-locks turned across the cave, Wynn sagged. She crouched to gather her things, never seeing him step into stone. One desperate notion struck her.

The wet journal she'd brought lay within reach of five more—her older ones, from her time in the Farlands. Travel-worn as they were, they couldn't be mistaken for part of the ancient texts. Bulwark wouldn't know what she had brought with her or what she found here.

Wynn closed the wet journal, sliding it onto the top of the other five.

Deceptions and lies, threats and coercion—now she could add thievery to the lot—but these were hers, stolen from her in the first place.

Wynn snatched up her quill and ink, and shoved these with her crystal into her pocket. With all six journals bundled under one arm, she rose in the cave's near darkness. Master Bulwark grasped her other wrist and dragged her toward the wall.

Wynn quickly sucked in a breath for what would come next.

CHAPTER 22

Reine reclined numbly on the sitting chamber's couch while Frey rested in the adjoining bedchamber. Chuillyon stood before the stone bookshelves, but he wasn't looking for something to read.

Reine knew the family relied on him for more than wisdom and insight; whenever possible, he accompanied any who left the royal grounds. But until the black mage had appeared, she hadn't fully understood why. Seeing Chuillyon halt the racing fire left her wondering who and what he really was. But she started from contemplation when Tristan appeared at the sitting chamber's opening.

Beyond the captain, Danyel stepped back out into the passage, closing the pool chamber's outer door. Strangely, she was relieved to see Tristan again. He was like her homeland's eastern stone steppes, immovable and permanent. He was the heart of the Weardas . . . he was *the* Sentinel.

"Were you able to assist Thorn-in-Wine?" she asked.

"Uncertain," he answered. "A Stonewalker appearing before clan leaders overrode most doubt or disbelief. Word was sent to other settlements. Six warriors guard all portals to the underworld. More patrol Sea-Side, keeping people inside. The display of numbers may give the black mage pause."

His passivity might've fooled others, but Reine knew better. What could he or any of them do against an assailant who could appear anywhere? Even here, in the pool's chambers, Frey wouldn't be safe until it died.

Tristan exchanged glances with Chuillyon. The captain subtly shifted his weight from one foot to the other—very uncharacteristic—and Chuillyon cleared his throat.

Reine didn't like these signs.

"My lady," he began, "the captain feels it's best that he stay with the prince. Danyel and I will take you—"

"No," she cut in.

"Highness," Tristan tried in turn, "I can protect the prince from himself. Your safety matters. The family cannot afford to lose—"

"I'm not leaving," she warned. "There's more to protecting Frey than—"

"You are needed!" Chuillyon snapped. "If you were lost within scant years of the prince's apparent death, how could it be explained to the people?"

Reine scoffed. "Many of the *people* still think I'm guilty, no matter what Captain Rodian reported. I'm less benefit than burden to all of the Âreskynna. Let's hope, for the future, that this doesn't affect the alliance with my country."

"Faunier and Malourné are old allies," Chuillyon said, "almost from their founding days. Your status as scapegoat will not alter that. You and the queen are the only ones—"

"Who can't become sea-lorn?" Reine finished bitterly. "Who will never succumb to a mad longing eating our wits and will? All the more reason—more than ever—that I will not leave my husband!"

Chuillyon's mouth opened once more, and Reine sat upright.

"*Don't!*" she whispered.

He shut his mouth in a frustrated frown. Tristan still bore no expression, but it was obvious he agreed with the advisor. Getting her out of harm's way had probably been his idea.

Someone knocked at the pool chamber's outer door.

Relieved by the interruption, Reine was already up by the time Danyel opened the outer door and leaned in.

"It's Master Bulwark, Highness," he called.

Why had he come? She stepped across the chamber and looked out through the partially opened door. Master Bulwark waited with arms crossed.

"The sage has been returned," he said.

Hope and dread flooded Reine. "You didn't bring her here?"

"I assumed you wished to question her away from the prince," he said quietly. "She is with her companions."

Reine moved into action. "Danyel, stay with the prince. Watch him carefully. Tristan, Chuillyon . . ."

They were already joining her.

Reine hesitated, looking to the sitting chamber's opening. She'd never left Frey alone so much on a rising tide, especially not the highest of the year. She turned once more to Danyel.

"If the prince wakes, tell him I won't be long . . . and keep him away from the pool."

Danyel glanced at the pool's rear gate. "What if *they* come again?"

"Drive them off!" she ordered.

"Reine!" Chuillyon said sharply, and he rarely used anything but her titles in front of others. "Do not jeopardize an older alliance through bitterness!"

"You have your orders," she told Danyel, holding out her hand.

With one curt, sure nod, Danyel handed over the comb with the white metal droplet, though Chuillyon expelled an exasperated sigh. Reine swept out, following Master Bulwark, with Tristan and Chuillyon close behind.

Nothing Wynn Hygeorht said should be trusted, but Reine hoped the sage had discovered something in the texts. They needed any slim advantage before Frey was exposed to something worse than the burden of his heritage.

Sau'ilahk stood among the ashen-faced bodies of only five dwarven warriors. Two had died before any realized he was upon them. The fifth had taken too long to put down. For all his efforts, and the need for expedience, he had barely consumed the sum of one whole life. And the sixth warrior had escaped.

But Sau'ilahk was fixed upon a course, and nothing would turn him.

The placement of new guards meant warning had spread. Others would soon learn he had reappeared. There would be no more peeking through walls, surprising anyone who waited in the hidden room.

A distant bell's clang reverberated through the mountain's passages—over and over.

Sau'ilahk focused hard on the downward passage that lay beyond the hidden room. It was the only place he could remember clearly along the path to the underworld. He blinked through dormancy and stood in the tunnel's head.

Any guards bypassed in the hidden room would be alerted soon enough. He drifted down the tunnel's gradual curve, listening carefully along the way, until he finally spied the ending alcove.

Four armed and armored dwarves stood guard before the lower door.

Sau'ilahk slipped into the tunnel's sidewall. Only his cowl's opening protruded as he watched. If he faced them openly, any inside the domed chamber beyond would hear their shouts. Another alarm would sound, indicating his new location and further cutting into his time to find what he sought. But without at least a glimpse through the door, he had no sight line by which to slip through the floor to the lift's shaft.

His choices were frustratingly inadequate. If he used a servitor for another distraction, not all of the four new guards would come after it or any at all. If he had to fight, it was better to get as far as he could. He fixed upon the door—or rather the sense of open space just beyond. And he tried to remember the one glimpse through its opening he had ever had.

Sau'ilahk blinked again, awaking in the domed chamber, surrounded by six dwarves. Four wore spike-ended circlets around the raised steel collars of their armor.

The nearest shouted a warning and leveled his iron staff in a swing.

Sau'ilahk lashed out as he summoned his servitor.

Hinder those outside the door! Distract them!

The dwarf's staff whipped through him as his own fingers slashed through a helmet and wide face. The dwarf yelped, and Sau'ilahk blinked out.

All it would take was just one reaching the bell rope to warn of his presence. A thrust of incorporeal fingers could put down a human, but it would only weaken a dwarf. He materialized instantly before the bell rope as the other five dwarves spread out, closing from all around.

Sau'ilahk saw his tactic would not work.

Not one had even hesitated as the first slumped against the wall. They were willing to die so that one could get to him. It would take only one to grip the rope as the last fell. Sau'ilahk had to leave this place in silence, no matter what it cost, but he had so little to expend. Barely one life taken, and now he would lose even that. Why had he not reawakened in the underworld?

He raised his arms, robe sleeves sliding down over limbs wrapped in black cloth.

Sau'ilahk began to conjure, more strength draining away.

Wynn followed Balsam until the Stonewalker stopped at the final passage and pointed onward. She rushed on alone with her regained journals clutched in her arms. Shade sprang to all fours, barking excitedly as she lunged forward from the archway. Wynn hurried straight past, looking about the landing for her pack.

Chane was slouched beside their belongings with his eyes closed.

She was surprised to find him still dormant. Bulwark had said night was upon them. Was Chane's hunger becoming too great? Had he slipped into some other kind of unconsciousness?

"Chane?" she said in alarm.

His eyes opened as he sat upright, but he appeared disoriented. "Wynn?"

In relief, she dropped to her knees, dumped the journals, and began pulling everything out of her pack.

"When did you return?" he asked, blinking. "Where did you get those?"

Wynn didn't answer. She didn't know whether the duchess had ever seen the texts or knew of the old journals among them. She wasn't about to find out. Pulling out her tightly folded robe and spare shift, she reached for the pile of journals.

Chane grabbed her wrist. "What have you done?"

"They're mine!" she shot back. "*My* journals . . . from the Farlands!"

She jerked free and shoved them in the pack's bottom.

"What if their absence is noticed?" he asked. "At least portions of the texts are taken to the guild each day."

"These journals hold everything that happened to me. Every detail of what I learned . . . and they're mine. I don't care who finds out, because no one will get them back!"

She began stuffing her belongings on top. Chane craned his head, looking over her and out the archway.

"Hurry!" he urged. "If you are here, others will come soon." He paused as if remembering something, and pointed at a bag on the floor. "There's food and water."

She hadn't eaten all day, hadn't even thought of it. She finished lacing her pack closed and hurried over, helping herself to water and a torn hunk of bread. Then she felt suddenly guilty.

Nothing here would sate Chane's hunger.

He stood up, bracing against the wall, and his other hand clenched into a fist. He stepped into the archway, watching down the passage.

"Did you learn anything?" he asked.

Shade pressed in, nosing Wynn's cheek. Still chewing, Wynn wrapped her free arm around the dog's neck. Then she began recounting what little she'd uncovered.

Chane crouched before her, listening intently, and then he glanced out the archway.

"What is it?" she asked.

Shade pulled from Wynn's arms, her pointed ears rising.

Duchess Reine, Chuillyon, and Captain Tristan strode down the passage toward the archway.

Wynn stood up beside Chane. Without even thinking, she took the staff and held it firmly, fearful it might be taken again.

"What have you learned?" the duchess demanded, still a few strides off.

Did she wish to hold this discussion from the passageway?

Chane wrapped his near hand around his sword's sheath, just below the cross guard. He pocketed the ring, freeing his sword hand if needed.

Why had he taken the ring off? If the Stonewalkers, especially Cinder-Shard, could sense the wraith as an undead, would they sense him without the ring's protection?

Chuillyon slowed, almost falling behind the other two. He arrived three steps after the duchess and the captain, eyeing Chane.

"Well?" the duchess asked more sharply.

"A little," Wynn returned in kind. "Master Bulwark interrupted me too soon. I need more—"

"Do not play me!" The duchess took two rapid steps closer.

Wynn forced calm, though one bitter thought escaped. "It's regrettable you were less interested back in Calm Seatt. Several people might still be alive."

"Enough!" Chuillyon said, pulling back his cowl.

The passage's orange light accentuated the lines around his eyes. Wynn couldn't help wondering at his age.

"Please continue," he instructed.

Wynn knew she had to share her meager findings but still hoped for more time with the texts.

"I didn't uncover the wraith's specific goal . . . yet," she said. "But I believe I have *his* name . . . and something of the part he played in the war."

"The war?" the duchess echoed with disdain.

"What name?" Chuillyon demanded.

"The Ancient Enemy had three distinct groups of followers," Wynn began. She briefly recounted the Children, the Eaters of Silence, and lastly the Reverent, a religious caste. She left out what little she knew of a bargain with Beloved, adding only . . .

"His name was—is—Sau'ilahk, high priest of Cinder-Shard's so-called Nightfaller."

Chuillyon's large eyes lost focus. His gaze dropped, staring at nothing, and then shifted erratically. Wynn wondered what thoughts came so quickly, one overwhelming the next.

"Liar!" Reine accused, pulling Wynn's attention. "I'm sick of your schemes. To suggest that this mage has been around since—"

"Silence!" Chuillyon ordered.

The duchess spun on him. "You cannot possibly believe—"

"I have told you there's no time to cling to disbelief!" He turned back to Wynn. "You learned nothing more . . . of what it wants . . . how to deal with it?"

Wynn hesitated at Chuillyon's so quickly accepting her words without a shadow of the duchess's doubt. She'd been dismissed so often, so few believing a grain of what she said, that his acceptance made her more suspicious. She had a very disturbing sense that he was looking for *untried* tactics, which would only mean . . .

Had he tried others, sometime before . . . in facing this monstrous spirit?

And there was one other thing the wraith might be searching for, just like her.

"It may be searching for—"

"The last locations of others among the Children," Chane cut in.

Wynn regained her senses in shock. He never spoke to anyone but her of such matters. When he glanced down, she caught the slightest, almost imperceptible shake of his head. She'd told the duchess and Chuillyon nearly everything pertinent—except Sau'ilahk's bargain for eternal life. She still wasn't certain of her conclusions on that, and it would've only aggravated the duchess even more. So what else was there to hold back? Only one thing . . .

Chane wished her to keep silent about Bäalâle Seatt.

"Nothing more?" Chuillyon asked again.

"No," Wynn answered. "I had too little time. Translation is painstaking work."

"But it thinks you know something." The captain's sudden words were almost as out of place as Chane's.

"Pardon?" Wynn asked.

"It must believe you *know* of what it's after," the captain said, calm and cold. "Or it wouldn't have followed you." He turned to Chuillyon. "She offers nothing of use, so we must fall back on Cinder-Shard's plan. Let the Stonewalkers trap it . . . using the sage as bait."

"I do not think so," Chane hissed.

Wynn had to grab his arm, as both he and the captain reached for their swords.

"Journeyor!" the duchess snapped, and then briefly closed her eyes, as if struggling to regain composure. "In Calm Seatt, you and Captain Rodian seemed to have vanquished this . . . perpetrator . . . or in retrospect, at least injured it. How?"

Wynn studied Reine's face, not as lovely as some, but fetching in its clean simplicity surrounded by thick chestnut hair.

"Rodian had nothing to do with it," Wynn answered. "Chane and Shade kept the wraith at bay long enough for Domin il'Sänke to hold it for an instant. In fact, the captain and his men nearly ruined our one chance. But I managed to ignite the staff's crystal anyhow."

She paused, anguished again over so many lost lives.

"Our plan should've worked—I watched the *wraith*," she said with force, emphasizing what it was, and looked at Chuillyon. "I watched it tear apart in the light. But we merely beat it down enough to save ourselves that night."

Everyone—most especially the captain—listened in silence. He eyed the staff she held.

"The sage should be kept at hand," he said flatly. "Even if the staff proves less than she claims."

Wynn felt Chane reaching around her waist, pulling her back.

His arm tightened, and Shade began snarling. The dog inched through the archway, ears flattening as her hackles rose.

"Too late!" Chane whispered. "It has come!"

Sau'ilahk settled upon the shaft's bottom and peered along the underworld's main passage. Yellowed wisps of vapor drifted down the shaft to coil around him, as if dragged by his descent.

Once his conjured gases had filled the domed chamber, there had been only a brief moment to feed before the last dwarven warrior died. Not one had laid a hand upon the bell rope, but that one taken life was too little. He raised his hands and watched them turn translucent for an instant.

The tip of a steel blade thrust out of his chest.

It flashed aside in a speeding arc as Sau'ilahk whirled about, facing an older female dwarf in black scaled armor. But the lift had not come down.

This Stonewalker had stepped out of the shaft's wall behind him.

She held two long, triangular daggers at ready. Dark blond hair hung around her wide face, which appeared unsurprised that her blade never connected. The chance to feed again made Sau'ilahk lunge.

She did not move until his hand neared her chest.

The instant his fingers penetrated, she struck the shaft's wall with the back of her right hand, still gripping one broad blade.

Sau'ilahk saw stone flow across her body and face.

The feel of her life vanished from him, and he panicked, remembering his arm solidifying when he had tried to take the old one in the main cavern. Sau'ilahk jerked his hand free before the flow of stone reached his wrist. He slid back, out of the shaft into the passage's head.

The Stonewalker had not even flinched, but her face now wrinkled in spite, her eyes glaring.

"Come on!" she challenged in deep Dwarvish. "Take my stone, if you can . . . you soot-wisp!"

This could not be happening. This was not the way things should be.

She lunged at him.

Sau'ilahk raised a hand to strike and then saw what she did. At each hammering step, the back of her hand holding a dagger grazed the passage wall on either side. The space was too tight. There was no way to get to her so long as she could touch stone.

He spun, fixing on the passage's far end, and blinked.

The instant he appeared there, he flew into the glistening cavern, looking for any near path. The black-haired elder leaped out of the wall on his right.

Sau'ilahk had barely turned when two heavy footfalls slammed the cavern floor behind him. As he spun, a rising deep chant erupted around him. The elder female closed at full speed down the passage, no longer bothering with her staggered wall-touching advance.

He had no time for them. Where was Wynn?

Desperation made him latch upon the only way to find her—the wolf. All he need do was raise the beast's awareness of him. Wynn would follow its lead soon enough.

Sau'ilahk gathered lingering energies to conjury, twisting the air within his form, and created a *voice*. He shrieked his rage, letting it echo through the cavern.

A long, pealing wail answered.

Sau'ilahk rushed toward the cavern's left opening, and then slowed.

A faded, nearly forgotten memory came to him. He struggled as if trying to advance against a desert windstorm. In place of a wind's whistle and moan, he heard the Stonewalkers' baritone thrum.

What were they doing?

Drawing more power, he burst forward, breaking whatever impeded him. He sailed through the cavern, into the tunnels, following the sound of a majay-hì's hunting cry.

Wynn heard the distant shriek.

Even the duchess twisted about as the captain spun and jerked out his sword.

Less than a breath passed before Shade threw her head up. Her eerie cry exploded at full volume.

Wynn grabbed Shade by the scruff, shouting, "Hold . . . wait!"

"Make her quiet, now!" Chane rasped.

"Shade, stop it," Wynn urged.

"No . . . let her howl," someone said, and Wynn looked up.

Cinder-Shard stood in the passage. How had he arrived so suddenly, and from where?

"My brethren heard the black one," he added. "If it runs toward the wolf's noise . . . so much the better."

Wynn understood—they all thought the wraith would come for her.

"Everyone up the passage and into the next cavern!" he ordered. "Until I am certain where the intruder is, all of you stay near. Do as I command, and do not get in our way."

Wynn released Shade, who ceased howling but still rumbled. Chane pushed past, signaling her to follow.

They hurried down the passage after him, leaving the Chamber of the Fallen behind, and emerged in a cavern lit only by dim phosphorescence. Wynn knew what those dark forms were in that place. Light suddenly erupted behind her.

A cold lamp crystal blazed in Chuillyon's outstretched palm. He closed his hand over it, crushing out the light.

"Do likewise," he told her. "But toss your crystal when I cast mine."

Wynn dug in her pocket, first pulling out the pewter-framed glasses. She tucked these into her grip upon the staff and then retrieved and prepared her crystal. In its briefly escaping light, forms moved among the cavern's columns and the calcified remains of the honored dead.

Bulwark stepped around a figure barely recognizable beneath crusted minerals. Another Stonewalker at the far end moved inward. Both stared toward the cavern's left side, but Wynn couldn't see what they watched through all the obstructions.

She closed her hand, snuffing the crystal's light, as a thrum began to build from two, and then three deep voices. The last, somewhere off to her right, had to be Cinder-Shard.

Chane stood tense before her and reached back, pulling her as he stepped inward and away from the walls around the entrance.

"No!" the duchess whispered.

Wynn glanced back as Reine pulled free of the captain's grip and followed.

Chuillyon advanced behind her with a scowl, and the captain hurried out ahead of them.

Shade's rumble rose to a pealing whine. A shout echoed from the cavern's left, sounding far off.

One dimly glowing column off to Wynn's left went black—then returned. Two more did likewise, one after the other, as if something dark passed quickly before them.

Light erupted behind Wynn. The bright spark of a cold lamp crystal arced past her between the columns, and fell to the cavern floor.

Wynn shuddered at a grating hiss rolling throughout the space.

The wraith stood in the cavern's heart and twisted toward the crystal's light.

Wynn quickly threw her crystal to the other side, filling the cavern with more light, and the black figure turned toward her. Every time she saw it—him—her stomach wrenched like that first night in the streets of Calm Seatt. It was nothing but black robes and cloak, sagging faceless cowl, and cloth-wrapped hands that weren't truly whole and real.

"Chuillyon, get them out, now!" Cinder-Shard yelled.

The wraith lurched around, turning every way.

All six Stonewalkers shifted among the columns and the still, stone forms of the dead as they circled inward. Those who'd just arrived joined the others in the thrumming chant, doubling its volume. Wynn still didn't understand their utterances as they raised their palms outward.

The wraith pivoted back to fix upon her.

His hiss seemed to form into words she couldn't quite catch—and he rushed straight at her.

Shade lunged out as Chane reversed, grabbed Wynn's arm, and thrust her aside before she could speak. She spun into a column, tripping on its wide sloped base, and he stepped straight into the wraith's path.

"No, get to cover!" she shouted.

The wraith never slowed.

Shade backpedaled, hopping aside with a failed snap at it, as Cinder-Shard shouted, "Balsam, cut it off!"

The Stonewalkers' rhythmic chant faltered the instant Chane collided with the black spirit.

The wraith dissipated like smoke on a wind gust, and Chane stumbled through, nearly collapsing.

Those shredded black vapors coalesced again with a hoarse scream. At first, both the robe and cloak trailed wisps of black dust or smoke in the air—as if the wraith struggled to regain its presence.

Then it rushed on. Wynn had barely gained her feet when its black-cloth-wrapped hand swiped at her.

She flopped back against the column, rolling around it, out of reach. The wraith's hand closed on her staff, just below the crystal. But the staff passed straight through those clutching fingers.

For an instant, Wynn thought she saw the glow of Chuillyon's crystal behind the wraith—through it.

The wraith seemed weakened—it couldn't solidify even a hand. With a soft hiss, it whirled, its cloak's wing passing straight through the column. Wynn ducked away from the flailing, ghostly fabric.

The wraith went straight at the duchess.

"Get her out!" Wynn shouted, raising the staff again. "Shade, go . . . attack!"

Chuillyon didn't move, not even when Shade wheeled, her claws scrabbling on stone. He stood there, eyes closed, lips silently moving. Reine backed against him, eyes wide in shock, though she had her saber out. The captain lunged in front of her, straight into the wraith's path.

Something wide and dark came at them from the side, near the cavern's back.

Balsam reached around a column and latched onto the captain's wrist.

Wynn thought she saw the woman's face change. It darkened, glittering like the column's stone. But Balsam never had an instant to pull the captain aside.

The wraith swung as Tristan slashed with his sword. A black hand whipped down through Tristan's face and chest as his blade passed straight through the cloak and robe.

The captain flinched, eyes widening, and that was all. Nothing happened to him.

The wraith halted, frozen in place, and Shade closed from behind.

Rising on rear legs, she snapped her teeth through its wrist, and they both screeched. The wraith slapped down at Shade, but she wheeled out of reach.

Wynn pulled her glasses out of her grip upon the staff, trying to get them on her face.

The wraith crouched, flattening its hand against the floor.

Chuillyon's soft laugh startled Wynn.

The elf's eyes opened, his left arm wrapping around the duchess and holding her close. He peered down at the wraith's wavering form.

"Oh, no . . . *Sau'ilahk*," he whispered.

The wraith snapped to full height at its name.

"No tricks for *you*!" Chuillyon added with a slow shake of his head. "Not again."

Balsam reached out for the wraith. Her other hand was fastened around a column, and the wraith retreated in a gliding rush, searching in all directions.

Wynn finally shoved the glasses over her eyes. But the wraith began to fade, becoming a pale shadow in her sight as she grew frantic. Then the Stonewalkers' thrumming chant rose again, and it instantly reappeared.

It appeared to shudder, its fingers twitching before its chest.

"Chane . . . cover up!" Wynn shouted, tilting the sun crystal outward.

In her mind, she formed the outlines of shapes, each one appearing within the last as the pattern overlaid her sight of the long crystal. Circle then triangle, another triangle inverted, and a final circle.

"Mên Rúhk el-När . . ." she recited—*From Spirit to Fire . . .*

The sagging cowl's empty pit whipped toward her—then the wraith rushed straight at Balsam.

Balsam faltered in her chant. Before Wynn could even shout a warning, the female Stonewalker slapped her palm against a column.

The wraith slammed through her and onward, and it vanished through the cavern wall.

Wynn's frustration choked off her voice, though she heard Chuillyon cursing in Elvish over the growl of Cinder-Shard.

CHAPTER 23

Sau'ilahk groped through stone. Despite Beloved's demand that he not further expose himself, the entire settlement might be alerted to his presence.

And they had learned his name. There was only one way that could have happened.

Wynn Hygeorht had seen the texts.

He was failing, yet the sage had touched the very things he desired. And he had sensed a difference in Chane, leaving no doubt—that one was a vampire. But too many opponents had appeared, and he was so weak that he had not even manifested one hand. He had failed to snatch the staff and shatter its crystal once and for all.

At each more desperate tactic, he had been hindered or halted. The Stonewalkers' chant somehow barred him from dormancy, even to blink elsewhere. One had shielded the tall captain with her connection to stone, and again the white-clad elf had interfered with his conjury.

Sau'ilahk tried to call his remaining servitor, but it never came.

He arced through rock, groping toward one long passage glimpsed beyond the duchess and the elf. The passage's far side suddenly appeared, and he instantly withdrew. Only his cowl's opening protruded as he listened to shouts and whispers among his enemies.

"*Malhachkach thoh!*" snarled the elf.

"Where?" a dwarf shouted. "Where did it go?"

"Through the wall behind me," another returned. "Master, I am sorry . . . I should not have—"

"Quiet!" another barked like cracking stone. "None of us knew what it would do."

"Stay away from the walls," Wynn called out. "Everyone get between the two crystals, so we aren't blocking their light."

"Do as she says—now!" the elder Stonewalker shouted. "All of you, face outward and watch!"

Sau'ilahk fumed as he listened to them repositioning to spot him the instant he tried to attack. Behind all of the voices he could hear the wolf rumbling and mewling in agitation.

"Reine, stop!" the elf shouted.

"Let go of me!" she commanded. "I have to get to—"

"Silence!" he commanded.

Sau'ilahk grew attentive, but all he heard was the wolf snarling. What had the duchess been about to say?

"It's gone!" she cried out. "It could be anywhere . . . even in his—"

"No, it is still here," someone rasped.

Sau'ilahk knew Chane's maimed voice but puzzled over how the vampire could sense him. Throughout his time trailing Wynn, only the wolf reacted when he drew too close. And the duchess had said "his" . . . *his* what? Of whom was she speaking?

"Listen to Shade," Wynn called. "She knows."

"Highness, please," the captain demand. "You must remain—"

"Stand off, Tristan!" she ordered. "If the mage can't be contained, I will not leave him alone."

Sau'ilahk fixed upon those words. The duchess feared for someone's safety—someone elsewhere in the underworld. But his own fears were growing.

In the next day's dormancy, he would be alone with his Beloved. His impudent disobedience would bring suffering amid failure to serve his own need. Could he find a way to appease his god and lessen his punishment? Beloved's cryptic warning filled his thoughts.

When chance comes . . . sever the kin from the sea!

Whom did the duchess fear for above all others?

Sau'ilahk suddenly understood the possibility stretched between duchess's slip and Beloved's demand.

Another Âreskynna was in the underworld, one of true blood.

"Follow me," the duchess shouted. "Obey me!"

Quickened footsteps followed.

"Duchess, please don't," Wynn called.

"Get out of my way!" the duchess snarled.

"Remain where you are! All of you!" the elder Stonewalker countered.

They were breaking in chaos and fear, and Sau'ilahk slid into the passage.

Light diminished and shifted beyond the passage's opening, as if the two crystals were being moved. Illumination faded toward the cavern's far side, where he had first entered. Was Wynn, or even the duchess, on the move? Then he spotted Chane and Shade as they rounded a far column.

The wolf wheeled, staring straight at him, and its bellow pierced the air.

Sau'ilahk flew into the cavern as the crystals' light vanished. The only adversaries remaining were all six Stonewalkers, and they circled around him.

"Seal it in!" shouted the elder.

Sau'ilahk could not allow them to interfere with his task, his salvation from Beloved's wrath. And he still had hope of stealing Wynn or the duchess to learn of the texts.

The Stonewalkers raised their hands, their palms out. . . .

Sau'ilahk blinked through dormancy to the cavern's far side and fled.

Wynn raced through the passages after Reine and the captain, with Chuillyon obscuring a clear view of them. She knew where they were headed and glanced back once. Chane was close behind, and she heard Shade's scrambling claws farther back.

But it all felt wrong.

Intuition and reason told her that Chane's awareness and Chuillyon's warning were both right. The wraith was still near. After all it had done to follow her, it would not give up so easily. If Stonewalkers couldn't stop or hold it, even slow it, there would be only one defense left for a dead prince.

Wynn wasn't certain that even the staff's crystal would work. In these tight spaces, all the wraith had to do was slip into a wall, wait for her to weaken and for the sun crystal to go out. It could come again—and again.

Doubt told her that she should've stayed with the Stonewalkers to face it.

As Reine reached the turnoff toward the prince's chamber, a shout echoed from behind them. Chuillyon halted and turned, blocking the way, and Wynn heard the duchess's footfalls fading ahead.

"What?" Tristan called from beyond the elf.

"Take everyone onward!" Chuillyon ordered.

"No!" Wynn countered. "You can't stand alone against it . . . if it doesn't just slip past you!"

Chuillyon grabbed her tunic collar, ignoring Chane's warning hiss, and jerked her past himself.

"Go, and keep your staff ready. The chamber is the safest place now. I will delay or hinder it if possible . . . *move!*"

Wynn stared at him in disbelief. How could the prince's chambers be safer than anywhere else?

But Chuillyon's intense gaze was set in conviction. Wynn backed down the passage as Chane and Shade came through. The captain remained for an instant.

"What are you doing?" he asked.

"Take them onward, Tristan," the elf insisted, and he stepped out into the main passage, heading back the way they'd come.

The captain backed down the passage.

Shade turned, taking two slow steps toward the exit into the main passage.

Wynn grabbed the dog's neck fur and locked eyes with Chane. They had to remain together in whatever they chose to do. Did they stay to fight, or fall back, knowing the wraith would likely get past and follow? What did Chane want to do?

"We go," he said.

Wynn thought she heard Chuillyon's whisper echoing to her as she pulled Shade and ran on ahead of Chane.

Sau'ilahk rushed into the underworld's main cavern and paused. He looked all ways for a lingering hint of light from a sage's crystal. He saw nothing but the orange glow of dwarven crystals on phosphorescent walls.

Sensing life in the mountain's dense depths was more difficult than in the open, and he was so weary. Hunger obscured his awareness—and Stonewalkers would come at any instant.

An unintelligible whisper reached him, and he turned.

It came from the mouth of the underworld's main passage. Had his prey run for the lift? If they reached further help above, it could slow him more. He surged into the main passage.

A white form stood only a stone's toss down the way.

The elf had his hands clasped, his eyes closed. His thin lips barely moved in a narrow face so calm and serene. Sau'ilahk heard a whispering like prayer—or was it more like a nearly voiceless song?

"Chârmun, agh'alhtahk so. A'lhän am leagad chionns'gnajh."

One life, even so old and spent, would still serve Sau'ilahk's need. He flew at his prey.

The elf's large eyes opened without surprise.

Sau'ilahk slammed against invisible resistance and shuddered as if struck.

It was not the same as the Stonewalkers holding him in this world, barring him from dormancy. He felt as if he had become wholly solid in an instant. He clawed toward the elf beyond his reach, and resistance grew—like being submerged in mud.

"No farther, Sovereign of Spirits, by Chârmun's presence," the old elf breathed. "You end here . . . Sau'ilahk! We have your true name . . . for an epitaph no one will ever read. This time, you *will* be forgotten!"

Sau'ilahk faltered—did this withered old one know him from somewhere?

The elf's clasped hands, with fingers laced, clenched tighter.

Sau'ilahk's thoughts went numb as he looked into his adversary's eyes. Those amber irises appeared to shift hue, brightening to the tawny glistening of bare wood. Every bit of distance Sau'ilahk gained, he lost more quickly, leaving him more drained. And his true quarry was getting farther beyond reach.

Did they have an escape route wherever the other Âreskynna was hidden? Any moment, the Stonewalkers would find him again. They would bind him from dormancy as the elf held him at bay. And then . . .

This delay had to end!

Two side passages lay beyond the elf, one toward the ocean and the other landward. Which way had Wynn and the duchess taken?

Sau'ilahk shifted left to the passage's landward side. When the elf stepped to block him, he rushed the passage's seaward side.

Everything went dark.

He tried to veer left again inside the mountain's stone, but that hidden pressure still stalled his advance. He surged deeper to the west, deeper into the unknown, his awareness of sight and sound still blinded. As he tried again and again, the resistance began to weaken.

He found the limits of the old elf's reach.

Sau'ilahk broke through, pushing onward in silent darkness, but he wallowed in the mountain's bowels, trying to find his way out.

Wynn had lost sight of the duchess as she ran for the prince's chamber, but she could still see the captain ahead. What had become of Cinder-Shard, Ore-Locks, or the other Stonewalkers—or Chuillyon?

The captain swerved through an open door near the passage's dead end.

Wynn heard a high-pitched screech rise inside the chamber as she raced for the door.

Chane grabbed her arm from behind. Without a word he pushed past, sword in hand, and lifted its broken tip as he entered. In spite of everything, what Wynn saw through the opening still shocked her.

Tristan threw his sword aside and leaped off the pool's rear ledge. The blade clanged against the wall as he splashed down and thrashed toward the commotion at the pool's gate.

Prince Freädherich had one hand latched upon a gate bar as he fought to get Danyel off his back. A line of blood ran down the young bodyguard's left cheek, as he struggled to pin the prince's free arm. Reine was soaked as she pulled at her husband's grip on the gate. Tristan closed from behind, wrapped his arms around the prince, and wrenched the young man around.

Wynn couldn't believe Freädherich's state. He barely resembled the lost man she'd first seen in this chamber.

Shirt torn by his struggles, he craned his head back. His features contorted in horrid misery as he tried to cry out. But his voice broke, and he choked as if drowning, even as he gasped for air. When his frantic eyes opened, they were nearly fully black. His face, his skin, was paler than before—and tinged beneath with the taint of teal.

That taint was almost the color of the sea people.

The duchess collapsed against the gate. Wet hair matted to her forehead, neck, and cheeks. She was too wet for her tears to show as she sobbed.

Wynn began to suspect what had driven Reine to let the world believe her husband was dead—and why she silently suffered lingering suspicion as his murderer.

Reine couldn't think as Frey twisted within Tristan's hold. In the worst times in memory, the hints of Frey's change had come and gone with the tide. And now . . .

Danyel waded to the pool's edge, catching his breath as he wiped blood with the back of his hand. Reine realized he'd dropped her comb with the white metal teardrop in the water and it was floating. Danyel scooped it up.

"*They* came," he said, panting. "They tried to open the gate. I shut them out, but . . ."

Frey thrashed halfway around toward the bars, but Tristan's hold wouldn't break.

"Must go—go now!" Frey choked out. "They wait . . . for me . . . and *it* is coming!"

The pool's chill broke through Reine's anguish.

How did he know what was happening? How had he learned of the black mage? She swiveled, backing toward him as she looked down the tunnel beyond the gate, and then quickly closed on her husband.

"No, we can protect you—"

A splash and clank pulled her around again.

Two male Dunidæ stood beyond the bars. One had his white spear tip tilted toward the lock's outer side. He pushed with the spear, and the gate swung inward through the water.

At the sight of them, Frey began choking as if he were drowning in the chamber's dank air.

They had come, and Reine reached back, flattening a hand against his chest.

"Highness?" Tristan asked, panting.

She stared at the visitors. Her other hand slipped unconsciously to the saber's hilt.

"It must . . . not . . . find me," Frey whispered.

Reine looked up into her husband's face. His black eyes almost broke her again, but she saw his full recognition of her. He struggled to speak, as if his throat hurt with every word.

"It speaks . . . to the enemy," he gasped out.

She knew this fear that he mentioned. The families, hers and his, had feared for generations what might come again.

"You . . . are my world," Frey said so softly with effort. "And I . . . cannot lose . . . that world. I must hold . . . our oldest alliance."

His glistening eyes were so fully black—or perhaps such a deep aquamarine that they seemed so in the dim chamber. He lifted his face toward the Dunidæ in the tunnel and then returned to her.

"I must survive if . . . *my* world . . . is to survive."

Reine shrank, muffling a sob, as three creases split on each side of his throat. They flexed like the gills of the Dunidæ. He choked hard, and they quickly closed.

Sorrow drove Reine into panic with the fright of losing him, and this fed her anger. The cascade of emotions overwhelmed her like an ocean swell, until she couldn't see any shore to swim for.

He grew still, no longer trying to break free.

"Frey?" she whispered.

He didn't need any shore to swim to. She couldn't watch what she had to do and closed her eyes.

Reine pulled Tristan's hands until he let go of Frey.

She felt her husband's fingers on her cheek, sliding upward, until her soaked hair dragged against the shallow webbing between them. His mouth pressed on hers, his lips too chilled, and then his touch was gone.

She heard only a soft splash in his wake.

"Highness!" Tristan shouted.

Reine blindly held out a hand to stop him. She couldn't even look when she heard the gate clang shut. She stood there, growing more numb by the moment.

Frey was gone, free, safe—and she had nothing left.

Wynn watched a once-dead prince vanish into the dark tunnel. Of all things, she thought of Leesil.

Born of an elven mother and a human father, he was one of the few mixed-race beings she'd ever met. Yet here was a man of royal blood bound by the tides of the deep ocean. There was only an old name and long-lingering rumors among her people.

Âreskynna—the Kin of the Ocean Waves.

Tales of their obsession with the sea went back many generations, though the accounts varied so much they were little more than gossip and folk legend. What had happened—when had it happened—that the Âreskynna carried within them the blood of the Deep Ones? The mere thought of such an ancient mating seemed impossible.

Wynn thought of Reine, whose marriage to a prince of a neighboring country affirmed a long-standing alliance. Wasn't blood also a like bond? Was the one within the Prince even older than that of Faunier and Malourné? Did it go back to the very war against an enemy she hadn't yet come to understand?

She had blundered in here, leading the wraith to the haven of this secret. She had endangered allies mistaken as adversaries in the pursuit of her answers. Even as Shade began rumbling and then snarling, finally lifting her voice in a keening yowl, Wynn couldn't stop looking into the darkness beyond the iron bars.

There was nothing left to see.

"It is coming," Chane warned, as Shade's noise grew deafening in the chamber.

Even the captain thrashed to the pool's edge and grabbed his sword as the other guard climbed out.

But Wynn kept staring across the pool at the duchess.

They had no time for pity.

"Wynn!" Chane snarled.

She stiffened, blinked, and shoved her hand in her pocket, pulling out the large pewter-framed glasses.

"Get the duchess," she told the captain. "Chane and Shade will hold off the wraith for me to prepare—and stay out of our way! If it touches any of you, you're dead."

The captain glared at her, then turned to Danyel. "Give me the comb and take the duchess into the other room."

Tristan went straight for the door to the outer passage and grabbed hold of it to slam it shut.

"Don't!" Wynn ordered as she jerked the sheath off the staff's crystal. "Chuillyon or anyone else won't be able to get in."

"And a closed door will not stop the wraith," Chane added.

The captain hesitated, then closed the door only partway. He returned to the pool's edge. He took the comb from Danyel and leaned over, stretching out his hand.

"Highness!" he barked.

The duchess didn't even raise her eyes as she sloshed over and let him pull her out.

Chane urged them off with his broken blade. The captain took Reine into the far chamber and guarded the archway while Danyel stood a few paces farther out front. To Chane's relief, Wynn abandoned her useless concern for these arrogant Numans and focused on their task. She put the glasses over her eyes.

"Get it as far inside as you can," she told him. "Then bolt for the other room. Don't wait, Chane; just go!"

"I will," he answered.

But not until the last instant—not until he was certain she had finished preparing and could ignite the crystal. Since their arrival in Dhredze Seatt, nothing had gone the way he—or she—had envisioned. Here and now, Chane could do what no one else could—face another Noble Dead, regardless of its unique state.

Shade's voice dropped to low mewling, almost that of some large cat. She began pacing along the chamber's far wall beyond the half-open door.

Chane glanced quickly about, searching for the best positions. He pointed Wynn toward the pool's ledge, farthest from any wall without stepping into the water. He backed partway toward her, giving Shade room as he watched.

If Shade did sense the wraith's direction, she could harass it when it appeared, and he was free to flank it from either side. If she was wrong, he would be ready to take it first, and let her box it in.

Shade suddenly stopped. Charcoal fur rose on end along her neck and shoulders, and Chane slid his sword back into its sheath.

"Get ready," he warned.

Shade backed along the pool's edge.

A patch of wall blackened.

The stain quickly spread upward and downward and then bulged. Shade's jaws clacked as the wraith pushed through at the pool's far side. Its black robes began floating on the air.

Chane leaped from the ledge to the pool's far side, boxing the wraith as he heard Wynn begin whispering. He swung his hand straight at the wraith's cowl.

It instinctively flinched aside, nearly sinking into the wall, and Shade rushed it from the other side, snapping and snarling.

Wynn's repetitious whispers grew to a voiced chant.

The wraith halted, its cowl turning at her voice. That black opening swung quickly both ways, as if taking in the whole chamber.

Chane could not let it rush Wynn, and swung at the cowl again with his other hand.

The wraith vanished, sinking into stone, and Chane's hand slapped against damp wall as he heard Shade's jaws snap closed. He quickly pivoted, watching the whole chamber as Wynn's voice stopped.

"Shade?" Wynn whispered, and glanced at Chane.

The dog turned about, sniffing the air with her ears pricked up. She raced past Chane, pacing back between the chamber door and the ledge Wynn stood upon.

"Where is it?" the captain shouted from inside the far chamber.

And the black-robe winked in, directly before the archway.

Danyel drove his sword at it, but in the same instant, its hand reached out, passing through his chest.

Chane bolted around the pool as Danyel's blade's tip slipped out the back of the black cloak. Shade charged, snapping at it from behind. Wynn spun, aiming the staff and chanting once more as Chane ran by her.

The wraith vanished.

Chane skidded to a halt behind Shade, both of them snarling in frustration.

Danyel just stared blankly at them.

Chane did not notice how pale Danyel looked until the young guard simply crumpled.

"Danyel!" the duchess shouted.

His knees hit stone, his eyes still locked open, and he fell forward. Shade sidled quickly away, and the man's chest and face slapped the floor.

He was dead.

Chane spun, keeping Wynn in sight as he watched the whole chamber. He knew what the wraith was doing. That one pause before it sank into stone had been enough. It had taken the lay of this small space and all who were in it. Now it had even gained a glance at the next room.

"Get out of there!" he told Tristan and he sidestepped toward Shade.

The captain came out, sword in hand, and hauled the duchess along. She pulled her own saber, and Chane hissed in disgust.

How many times had they been told, and still they clung to their useless weapons. Even so, the wraith would not be coming through any wall.

It had taken a life, at least a taste, and Chane felt his own hunger gnawing at him. It gained strength, while he slowly weakened further. It would keep up this tactic, disappearing and reappearing, breaking Wynn's focus over and over, and exhausting and disorienting all of them.

Until it pulled them down, one by one.

"We go now!" he snarled at Wynn.

Racing to the door, he snatched up their packs, tossing one at the captain.

"Put it on and carry the other," he ordered, handing off the second. "And put your weapons away!"

He shoved Wynn's pack at the duchess.

"Go where?" Wynn shot back. "We can't let that thing come at us in some narrow passage!"

Chane dropped off the edge into the pool and looked up at Wynn.

"Down the sea tunnel," he said. "You use the staff to threaten it off while we run for the outside. We keep moving, changing locations. . . . We must make it out by dawn."

Her eyes widened—then her young face wrinkled in anger. She looked about the chamber, perhaps wishing the wraith would come once more. It was obvious she did not want to run.

Chane was about to pull her down when she let out an exhausted breath. She stepped off the ledge, sinking to her waist in a splash.

Shade snarled and barked at her from the pool's edge.

"No . . . come," Wynn said.

"What are you doing?" the captain demanded.

"We run for daylight," Wynn said.

"Or at least somewhere the wraith has not been," Chane added. "By its tactics, it cannot appear in any place it has not first seen. Now open the gate!"

The captain still hesitated. The duchess stared at the body of her dead guard, her expression slack. Chane had no interest in either of them, but he empathized with the captain's dilemma.

"Into the tunnel," Reine whispered, almost too low to hear. "Chuillyon knew . . . he knew we could escape from here."

All Chane cared about was getting Wynn—and Shade—out of here before the wraith reappeared. They could not defeat it in this place.

The captain stepped off the edge, followed by the duchess, and waded toward the gate. He reached into the back of his surcoat and handed off a sea-wave-shaped comb to the duchess. In turn, she placed it over the gate's white metal oval.

Chane heard grating as the bolt slid open. When the duchess removed the comb, he saw a small pellet of white metal on its underside. She had barely begun to open the gate when . . .

"*Valhachkasej'â!*" Wynn cursed under her breath.

Chane glanced at her. She was staring in fury at the white metal lock.

Wynn closed her eyes and shook her head. She stepped forward and jerked the gate open, muttering angrily under her breath.

Chane had no idea what she had said, though her tone was full of venom. Whatever bothered her, it could wait.

Shade was about to jump off the ledge and swim across, but Chane held her back with a raised hand. He and she had to take the rear for when the wraith finally followed. And it would.

Chane motioned the duchess and captain into the tunnel after Wynn.

Sau'ilahk lingered in the outer passage, three strides from the chamber's door. Then noise echoed up the passage from behind him. He quickly sank into the passage's wall.

He had fed only a little, not nearly enough. Killing so quickly did not allow for a proper meal. But the suddenness of his tactics, the helplessness fostered in Wynn and her companions, was a gain in the balance. He would give them a little longer to wonder, let uncertainty feed their fears. Not knowing when and where he would reappear would consume them. And a body lying dead among them was more fuel for that fire.

Bit by bit, he would break Wynn before he even touched her. A grip on her, or even the duchess, and the staff would come next. No one would risk either life if he demanded it in exchange. Once the crystal was shattered, he could drag off his hostage, and slip into hiding. He would learn where the texts lay before he fed more properly.

And his prey had nowhere to run.

A brief glimpse into the adjoining chamber had shown no other exit. The gate beyond the pool was shut, an oval of white metal in place of its lock. As with the portal above the shaft into the underworld, at a guess, only the Stonewalkers could open either. Otherwise those trapped within the chamber would have already fled.

But night was slipping away too quickly, and he had to finish this.

Sau'ilahk blinked, materializing before the opening to the second chamber—the last place he had appeared, and so the last place they would be watching for him.

The pool chamber was empty.

He rushed into the adjoining room, and on through a rear opening he had not seen the first time. It was only a bedroom with no other way out. He flew straight through the wall, back to the pool's side.

The chamber was still empty—and he looked toward the shut gate at the pool's back.

Sau'ilahk sank halfway through the floor as he angled down into the pool and approached the iron bars. Distant footfalls echoed up the tunnel.

How could they have opened the way?

Wynn had eluded him yet again—and she was running for the dawn.

Wynn slogged down the tunnel, seawater sloshing inside her boots. Once they'd waded beyond the pool's outer reservoir, the tunnel floor was clear for as far as her cold lamp crystal's light could reach. Fortunately the tide was either falling or hadn't fully risen. But amid fear, she was fuming inside at what she'd seen the duchess do.

Reine's comb had a small white metal nub on its back that tripped the gate's lock.

All the struggles that she, Chane, and Shade had gone through to get in hadn't been necessary. She'd had a *key* all along. The tip of her elven quill, gifted by Gleann in the lands of the an'Croan, was made of Chein'âs metal.

All she would've had to do, it seemed, was touch it to any white metal oval in a gate.

Wynn cursed under her breath again. Once they were far enough down the tunnel, she handed the cold lamp crystal to Tristan. The duchess took the lead with the captain behind her, holding the crystal high so its light spread ahead and behind. Wynn fell back with Chane and Shade.

She felt like a coward.

Others had stayed behind to face the wraith instead of her. There was no telling what had happened to Chuillyon. Much as she disliked him, suspected him, it worried her that he'd never made it to the prince's chamber—nor had Cinder-Shard or the other Stonewalkers.

The pressure of her failures grew.

A woman had lost her husband. A kingdom had lost its prince a second time, trapped in isolation for the burden of mixed blood. And Wynn had brought the wraith in among the unaware.

All because she wouldn't let anything get in her way.

What had she gained for it? She had her old journals, a brief glimpse at the texts, and had unmasked the worshipper of an ancient traitor taken in by the dwarves' secret guardians of the honored dead.

Wynn tried to clear her mind. The wraith would come, and if Chane was right, the only thing to hinder it might be the inability to see far enough down the tunnel to close upon them instantly.

Shade inched forward on her right, and Wynn glanced back at Chane. He'd left his sword sheathed and only kept watch, alternating between behind and ahead. His irises glinted colorlessly whenever the crystal's light touched them.

He had stood by her as had no one else but Shade. She wished she could tell him how grateful she was, but this wasn't the time. If she died this night, would she regret never having told him?

Shade slowed and turned.

Wynn halted, following the dog's gaze. Chane already faced back up the tunnel. She didn't need Shade's rumble to warn her.

"It's coming," she said.

Tristan backed Reine against the tunnel wall and pulled his sword. Perhaps that was his only comfort in not being able to do more. Wynn silently held out her open hand toward the captain and then clenched.

He closed his fist around the crystal, and all light vanished.

Wynn fumbled in her pocket for the glasses and pushed them onto her face.

Shade began mewling, and the sound shuddered in the tunnel.

"Shade, no," she whispered, and the dog quieted.

In the silence, she heard the duchess's low, quick breaths, and longer, even ones from the captain. Right in front her, Shade hissed in suppressed growls. But she heard nothing from Chane, no breath, no movements, and something else now frightened her.

"The sun crystal . . ." she whispered, hoping only he heard. "You can't hide here."

"My cloak will be enough."

Would it? In her guild room, he'd dropped and covered himself, but il'Sänke had left the sun crystal lit for only an instant. It would take much more to put the wraith down and not just drive it off for the moment.

"Start your preparation," he whispered.

"Can you see it?" she asked.

"Listen to Shade," he answered.

Wynn felt him brush past and crouch behind her. One of his arms wrapped lightly around her waist. What did he think he was going to do, pull her to safety if this didn't work?

"All of you, close your eyes!" Wynn whispered. "Chane, keep . . . Pull your hood down over your face."

She heard him struggling, but his arm never left her waist.

In the dark, she felt along the staff with one hand to get a mental fix upon the sun crystal's position. She focused upon it and began as Domin il'Sänke had taught her. The nested circles and triangles came more quickly, in pairs this time, as she uttered phrases spoken in old Sumanese. Wynn held off the last utterance, just listening.

Shade snarled loudly.

Wynn nearly shouted the last words: "*Mênajil il'Núr'u mên'Hkâ'ät!* . . . for the Light of Life!"

Light erupted before Wynn's eyes, and the glasses went black for an instant. A shrieking hiss tore at her ears over Shade's yelp. The lenses cleared, and she saw . . .

Beyond the blinding crystal, the wraith thrashed in the tunnel.

Had she caught it so off guard? Had luck finally turned in her favor? Wynn took a half step and thrust the staff, trying to spear the wraith with the crystal's searing light.

The wraith fragmented like soot in the air, spreading in all directions. Its hiss faded and those wisps dissipated under the sun crystal's intensity.

Wynn just stood there—then she was startled from inaction as Chane's hand tightened on her waist. She quickly wiped the pattern from her mind, as well as the triggering utterances lingering in her thoughts.

The crystal went out, and she fumbled to get the glasses off her face.

"Some light!" she shouted.

It came as Tristan opened his fist around the cold lamp crystal.

"Is it gone?" he demanded. "Is it finished this time?"

Wynn looked up the empty tunnel.

She didn't know how to answer; she'd hoped for some better hint. Everything had happened much the same as when they'd faced it outside the scribe shop. But this time . . . it had burned away so quickly. And she smelled something strange, just a hint over the odor of seawater.

"Wynn?" Chane whispered.

"I don't know," she answered. "Are you all right?"

"Yes."

She held her hand back toward Tristan—who passed off the cold lamp crystal. With the crystal in hand, she tried taking a step up the tunnel.

Chane let go of her waist, rising, and grabbed the back of her tunic. It startled her. Then something else caught her eye.

The tunnel's roof began to stain black.

"No!" she whispered.

"Run!" Chane hissed, pulling her back as Shade lunged in front of her.

Wynn tried to set her feet. The wraith, torn by the light, had simply retreated into the walls. She couldn't destroy it in here, where it could take refuge in an instant. But she wouldn't let this thing get to the others.

There was only one way to halt it—to give it what it wanted.

"Sau'ilahk!" she shouted, snagging Shade by the scruff. "I know what you want . . . I know where they are!"

This was a lie; she didn't know what the wraith sought in the texts, let alone where they were.

"What are you doing?" Chane asked in alarm.

Between his pulling, and Shade wanting to lunge, Wynn held her ground.

Even if the wraith took her bait, tried to make her answer, she couldn't reveal where the texts were hidden. But if it had to deal with only her, the others might escape.

The ceiling's black stain began to drip—to slowly drizzle downward like twisting smoke. Vapors swirled into a column as others took the shape of a cloak's wing.

The wraith stood before Wynn in the tunnel.

It remained too still compared to other times she'd seen it. No invisible breeze lifted its cloak to climb the curved walls. She glared into its cowl's pit.

"Take me!" she challenged. "And I'll show you."

"No!" Chane snarled, and his other hand clamped across her mouth.

Wynn lost her hold on Shade as Chane jerked her back. The dog lunged forward as Wynn's eyes widened.

Still clutching the staff with one hand, she tried to pull Chane's hand from her mouth without dropping the cold lamp crystal. Suddenly she was spinning away, her feet barely touching the tunnel floor. Someone grabbed her before she hit the tunnel wall.

Captain Tristan hefted her up. He tried to advance and join Chane, but Wynn blocked him with the staff, and then . . .

"Did you believe it was that easy to evade me?"

Wynn glanced at Chane's back as he stood with Shade before the wraith. But the voice she'd heard wasn't some hiss of wind. It couldn't have been the wraith.

"I cannot move from place to place at a wish," it went on, calm and light, almost mocking in tone. "But neither will you."

Wynn took a step, raising the cold lamp crystal as the wraith twisted away toward the tunnel beyond it.

Around its black form, a flash of white showed up the tunnel. Chuillyon stood no more than a spear's reach beyond the wraith, the barest smile upon his thin lips.

Chane lurched back toward Wynn as something came out of the wall beside him.

Cinder-Shard's boots barely hit the tunnel floor before he lunged at the wraith's exposed back. Another Stonewalker, the older female, came through the tunnel's other side. Chane grabbed Shade, startling a snarl from the dog, and heaved her back.

Wynn saw Cinder-Shard's thick fingers catch in the wraith's cloak and she heard Chuillyon speaking softly.

"*Chârmun . . . agh'alhtahk so. A'lhän am leagad chionns'gnajh.*"

The wraith's hiss turned to a shriek.

Wynn rushed in behind Chane. His right hand gripped his sword hilt in reflex, the same hand that he'd used to hold her waist. It was seared.

She wasn't certain what to do, or whether to just stay out of the way. . . .

And yet another Stonewalker appeared. Their chant began drumming along the tunnel as the wraith tried to swipe back at Cinder-Shard. The elder Stonewalker snatched its wrist.

"I'll make you a tomb, you dead dog!" he shouted. "Let Kêravägh try to find you then!"

Wynn couldn't believe it would work. Too many times the wraith had slipped away, even from Chuillyon and the Stonewalkers. She couldn't let it happen again, and jerked on Chane's cloak.

"Take Shade and get the duchess out," she whispered.

Cold fury glowed from his colorless eyes. "No!"

"Do it . . . please!"

She didn't want him here when the sun crystal ignited again. She would burn it longer this time, and Chane had shown too little regard for his own safety.

Wynn grabbed Shade's face, shoving the dog back.

"Go . . . guard!" she ordered, pointing at the duchess.

Shade went mad, snarling and snapping as she tried to get in front of Wynn.

Chane reached down and grabbed the dog, half shoving and throwing her back. He paused only an instant, glancing once toward the wraith and then at Wynn. He turned and ran, grabbing a shocked Reine around the waist before Tristan knew what was happening.

The captain ran after Chane and Shade.

Wynn shoved her glasses on and dropped the cold lamp crystal at her feet.

The wraith thrashed, swinging wildly in Cinder-Shard's grip. Its one free black-cloth-wrapped hand passed through the master Stonewalker like shadows of no substance.

Chuillyon stood beyond them with hands clasped and his head slightly bowed as if in prayer. The other Stonewalkers' chants built, and Cinder-Shard surged forward, pressing his captive into the tunnel's floor.

"No!" Wynn shouted. "Lift it up!"

He glared once over his wide shoulder, the creases of his face deepened by fury. Wynn thrust out the sun crystal, already forming the shapes in her mind.

Cinder-Shard rose up, heaving the thrashing wraith high overhead.

Wynn finished brief utterances in thought only. She poured all of her will into those words as she thrust the sun crystal upward. Its light erupted—then winked out as it sank into the cowl's dark space.

Her breath caught as sunlight exploded in the tunnel, and the glasses' lenses blackened to shield her eyes. The Stonewalkers' chant broke as several barked startled exclamations. The lenses began to clear as a shrieking wind filled the tunnel.

Wynn saw the long crystal burning brightly at the staff's top. She stood fast, willing the wraith to die . . . and its form began to waver.

The shrieking wind grew louder.

The wraith's cowl burst.

Its black cloak began to shred apart in Cinder-Shard's great hands.

The shreds turned into smoke.

The thinning ring of smoke spread out around the crystal, dissipating as it splashed against the tunnel's walls.

Everything went silent.

"Enough," Cinder-Shard growled.

He'd retreated to one side, shielding his eyes, as had Chuillyon out ahead. Wynn quickly wiped the pattern from her mind, and the sun crystal went out. The glasses were too dark for only the cold lamp crystal at her feet. She pulled them off, and it took a moment before her eyes adjusted.

Chuillyon lowered his hand from his eyes. Likewise, Cinder-Shard stared up into the air where he'd held the wraith but a moment ago. Both had managed to hold it in place so it couldn't escape.

Wynn gazed up wildly, her heart beating fast.

There was nothing to see in the air above the master Stonewalker. Had she finally done it? She'd burned the wraith from within, but had she finished it this time? Was it gone for good? She looked to Cinder-Shard.

He scowled, eyeing the staff's crystal, and stepped to the spot where the wraith had appeared.

"Well?" Chuillyon asked, closing on him.

Wynn waited anxiously as Cinder-Shard turned about. He ran his hands down both walls, across the floor, and even looked to the ceiling.

"Nothing," he whispered absently. "I . . . feel . . . nothing but our own honored dead."

Chuillyon heaved deeply, letting out an overly dramatic sigh. "Well, that's that . . . finally."

It seemed so—Wynn hoped so—though she saw no pride or victory in Cinder-Shard's face.

"Where is the prince?" he asked flatly.

Wynn faltered in guilt. "Gone," she answered weakly. "Gone . . . with the sea people."

Chuillyon's old eyes widened as he sucked in air and then choked it out. He cringed, closing his eyes, and shook his head so slightly that his cowl didn't shift.

Cinder-Shard's cracked face, full of suppressed rage, seemed to break. He sagged in weariness, or loss, his gaze wandering. But then his eyes raised, glaring at Wynn as he pointed straight at her.

"Get out!" His loud voice echoed in the tunnel. "Leave . . . leave the seatt . . . and do not return!"

His manner struck Wynn harder than his words. She'd helped them destroy the wraith, and this was his response? But what should she expect, for all the damage she'd done? It was unlikely she would ever see the texts again.

Wynn went numb.

Dawn would come soon. Chane and Shade were waiting. And there were more preparations to make. Even more secrets than before waited to be unearthed.

Cinder-Shard turned away up the tunnel.

"See to the honored dead," he told the others. "Return peace to their rest."

He didn't look back at her as he stepped through the tunnel's stone wall. All of the other Stonewalkers followed likewise—all but one.

Ore-Locks stood just beyond Chuillyon, watching Wynn intently. Then he too vanished into stone.

Wynn was left alone with the tall, duplicitous elf, who stepped quietly toward her.

She stood her ground, waiting for whatever half-truth he might try this time. She was too weary and hollow to put up with anything from him. Everything had ended in loss. Even this final moment had come and gone so quickly.

Chuillyon merely passed her by, heading down the tunnel's faint slope.

"Are you coming?" he asked.

Wynn picked up her cold lamp crystal and followed him toward the ocean shore.

CHAPTER 24

A whole day passed, and the sun had set.

Wynn climbed the boarding ramp of a two-masted Numan ship in Sea-Side's lower port. The ship would leave at dawn and round the point below Dhredze Seatt into Beranlômr Bay, for the short journey back to Calm Seatt. She dropped all three packs near the rail.

So much had happened since Wynn had left the guild. Only bits and pieces lingered in her exhausted mind. She tried to push even these aside, to gain a moment's respite from worries, mysteries, and guilt. But her thoughts slid back to the previous morning.

They had all stumbled from the tunnel's mouth, wet and exhausted, with dawn approaching. Chuillyon offered passage to Calm Seatt. He seemed the only one to openly acknowledge that the duchess's life had been saved by Chane's decision to flee and Wynn's hand in finishing the wraith.

But morning was not far off, and they headed quickly down the rocky shore toward the port.

Wynn had been forced to tell another lie, while asking Tristan to hold the ship another day. She had to get Chane inside as soon as possible and see to his hunger. Even a voyage belowdecks during the day wasn't possible yet. She'd used the same excuse of a skin reaction to harsh sunlight as they had with the wagon driver on the way to Dhredze Seatt.

No one questioned her weak explanation. The captain recognized Chane's efforts and did not press the matter. The duchess merely walked away toward the ship.

They hurried to the same inn Chane used during Shade's extended search for the sea tunnel. Falling through the door, he'd collapsed into dormancy just barely before the sun rose. Wynn set aside trying to find him blood and fell into a deep sleep herself.

This evening, she'd awoken to see Chane crack open the little room's door. He wore his cloak, with the hood pulled up. She'd sat up quickly.

"Where are you going?"

"I need . . . to purchase a new shirt . . . and some things for myself."

Wynn knew better, and that he didn't like to discuss it, but she wouldn't let it pass.

"I can get you some blood," she said, as if it were nothing extraordinary. "There might be a cold room or slaughterhouse here . . . before the meat is taken up to market."

"No," he answered. "I will see to it myself. Meet me on the ship."

"Give me moment to dress, and I'll come with you."

He slipped out and shut the door.

"Chane, wait!"

By the time she'd reached the common room and stepped outside with Shade, he was gone.

Chane was in a bad state. She'd seen hunger in his face after they'd breached the sea tunnel's many gates. It had only worsened from there. He'd faced down the wraith more than once, exchanging injuries with it that no one else could see—that no one else would've survived. He'd done it all on one urn of goat's blood she'd bought in Bay-Side.

That act had caused him embarrassment, resentment, or maybe both.

Now he wanted to find a butcher and see to his need on his own. She understood and simply returned to the room and gathered their things. He would find her later. He always found her.

Now, aboard the ship, Shade padded out across the deck. As Wynn followed, she spotted Captain Tristan by the forward dockside rail. She thought he was looking at her but noticed his gaze was too high. Wynn followed it.

The duchess stood near the stern. By the slight turn of her shoulders, she was looking past the southern tip of the Isle of Wrêdelîd, and out to the open ocean.

Wynn leaned over the rail and scanned the shore for Chane, but the waterfront was empty of any tall humans. Left with Shade for company, she couldn't help glancing toward the duchess. It wasn't a good idea, but she went aft, slowing cautiously in approach.

"May I join you?" she asked.

The duchess didn't answer or even turn. Wynn settled on a storage trunk to the port side. Reine wasn't wearing a cloak. Tendrils of chestnut hair quivered in the evening breeze, lashing across her profile and vacant expression.

"What happened to the prince?" Wynn asked suddenly.

Impertinent, especially for her hand in his loss, but she couldn't help it. She already knew too much, as far as the duchess and her people were concerned. Yet her reasoning, her guesses about the youngest Âreskynna, needed confirmation in some small way.

"He went home," Reine whispered.

It wasn't an answer, but Wynn waited.

"Have you ever wondered how I know your premin?" Reine asked.

The sudden change of topic confused Wynn at first. "The royals have always had close ties to the guild."

"Closer than you think," Reine said, spite creeping into her voice. "I asked her to look into a certain matter . . . what might be *known* rather than rumored . . . concerning my new family. The Âreskynna told me what they knew, but it wasn't enough . . . not nearly enough for me. I sought help from the guild."

Wynn shifted to the trunk's edge, her fingers clutching the edge of its lid.

"I learned nothing more than what the royal family told me," the duchess continued quietly. "Lady Tärtgyth, your premin, found only hints that a marriage was arranged between a 'lord of the waves' and a forgotten female ancestor of King Hräthgar."

Wynn's mind was already filled with previous assumptions.

"You know that name?" the duchess asked.

"Yes . . . Hräthgar is attributed with uniting territorial factions in what later became the Numan Lands. Supposedly, he became the founder and first king of Malourné. It's said that event marked the beginning of the Common Era, as measured on our calendar from the Lhoin'na. But how far back was this ancestor who married a—"

"A lord of the waves?" Reine cut in. "What a veiled reference to a Dunidæ, even from history."

That quizzical reply, sharply edged, didn't need a response. Even Wynn had never understood where the name Âreskynna—the Kin of the Ocean Waves—had come from. Not until she'd seen Freädherich.

"No one knows when she, this ancestor, lived," Reine went on. "Perhaps even in the time of the sages' Forgotten History . . . during or before the war. I pity her, whoever she was, being used for such an alliance . . . and I hate her for the legacy she left to Frey."

Wynn understood the pity, but the hate would gain nothing.

"For all your learning, you couldn't understand such things," Reine added.

Oh, yes, Wynn could, though she wouldn't say so to this woman. She had lost three friends, each oppressed by a heritage they hadn't asked for. But she also wondered . . .

Why did the unique in this world always seem to suffer the most?

"But . . ." she began, struggling in hesitation. "But why Frey? Or do others of the royal family face this same affliction?"

Reine gripped the aft rail with both hands, taking long, hard breaths.

"They all suffer, but each generation, one is worse. That one feels it most . . . and can never be allowed to take the throne. Do you know of Hrädwyn, King Leofwin's sister?"

Wynn nodded. "Yes, she succumbed to illness when she was young."

"No!" Reine snapped. "She drowned herself . . . in that pool . . . after nine years of imprisonment."

Wynn looked to the open ocean, suddenly as chilled as she'd been upon emerging from the tunnel. All she could think of was a prince's desperate, pale features.

"Caught betwixt and between," Reine went on, "unsettled on land and longing for the sea, that sickness drives . . . that one . . . to greater desperation than the others. The tides began to change . . . *him.* I thought he had drowned that night, when he vanished from our boat. Something made him return to shore, where Hammer-Stag found him."

Wynn knew why in watching Reine—watching Frey's one reason to fight his heritage, his affliction . . . his taint, so much worse than Wynn's own.

"Cinder-Shard came to me soon after," Reine continued. "Even Frey's deceased aunt wasn't the first Âreskynna whom the Stonewalkers had taken in . . . though none before Frey had ever lived long enough to leave. But while alive, they were still necessary . . . to maintain a hold on some ancient blood-bound alliance! I stayed with Frey during the tides, especially the highest. I would've stayed always if my prolonged absence under the people's suspicions would not have cast further doubts upon the family. And each year, Frey's changes grew worse before they passed."

She finally turned, and Wynn fell victim to Reine's gaze.

"The terror of your *wraith* . . . and the Dunidæ's persistence . . . forced his change too far!"

Reine's voice broke. Though tears ran down her face, they didn't match the cold anger in her features.

Wynn sat silenced, her thoughts filled with memories of half-breeds. So rare, even unique, yet they'd all come into her life. All had appeared within this generation, after a millennium, and in these new days of history.

Magiere . . . half mortal, half vampire, some would say, though it wasn't accurate.

Leesil . . . half human, half elf, a wanderer outside of all peoples.

Chap . . . part Fay, though physically pure majay-hì, equally an outcast of eternity.

Then there was Shade, descended of a Fay-born father and majay-hì mother.

And now a prince of Wynn's own land whom all had thought dead.

Why now? What did it mean? And how much ruin had she brought down upon the last?

"I'm sorry," she whispered.

Reine merely returned to staring across the water, until the wind dried all of her tears.

"What now, sage?" she asked. "For such a price . . . what have you gained?"

How could Wynn answer? Swirling questions wrapped in secrets hidden beneath myths already overwhelmed her. One place in the world had lain hidden for centuries in plain sight. Another had been lost beyond remembering. And a traitor, remembered by only a few who wished to forget him, had gained a worshipper in the dark among the honored dead.

First Glade . . . Bäalâle Seatt . . . Thallûhearag . . . Ore-Locks . . .

"It's too much to consider," Wynn finally said. "More answers must be found."

And she had to face it all without the texts.

Reine shook her head. "In the few years since Frey's 'death,' we learned nothing more concerning the family's heritage, though Lady Tärtgyth Sykion has kept watch for anything to help me . . . to help Frey."

Reine turned, and in two quick steps, she hung over Wynn, her voice a harsh threatening whisper.

"And you will do the same!"

A snarl rose in the dark. Shade closed, head low and jowls quivering in warning.

Reine's gaze never left Wynn, and Wynn quickly waved Shade off.

"You will keep watch for anything to help," Reine went on. "Whatever you do, wherever you seek, this as well as your silence is what your life depends on. You owe your people . . . you owe my husband . . . you owe *me*!"

Reine walked away, never looking down as she passed Shade.

Wynn sat in the dark, listening for the sound of Chane's footsteps.

The following night, Wynn walked through the gates of the Guild of Sagecraft with Chane and Shade.

She'd sat up late the night before upon the ship, waiting for Chane, but then she grew tired and went to a cabin that Captain Tristan had assigned. It wasn't until the next day that she learned Chane had finally arrived at the ship just before dawn. Perhaps it had taken longer for him to find blood than she'd imagined.

At least he'd arrived and taken cover on board before the ship sailed.

Now . . . they were back in Calm Seatt, back at the guild.

The guild courtyard was empty, but by now her superiors might have heard she was returning. If they hadn't, at the moment she had little desire to tell them herself. High-Tower would want a word with her—and she with him concerning the second codex. He would be more than relieved that she was leaving again soon, and less than pleased that she would expect more funding.

Shade trotted straight to the door of the southeast dormitory. By the time Wynn shut the door of her old room, Shade had bounded onto the bed and dropped in a huff.

"Don't get too comfortable," she said. "We're not staying long."

She'd barely leaned the staff in the corner as Chane set their packs by her desk, when someone knocked at her door.

Wynn almost groaned. Someone had spotted them and told High-Tower or Sykion. She wasn't ready to face either but opened the door just the same.

A young man stood in the passage wearing the midnight blue robe of the Order of Metaology. He thrust out something flat, wrapped in plain brown paper.

"I was ordered to place this directly in your hands," he said, already turning to leave.

Wynn took the package. There were no markings upon it, and she leaned out the door.

"Wait . . . ordered by whom?"

The messenger had already rounded the passage's far end and gone down the stairs. Wynn stepped back and shut the door. Considering the messenger's robe color, she wondered if this was something from Premin Hawes, head of Metaologers. But that didn't make any sense.

"What is it?" Chane asked.

"I don't know."

The flat, flexing square hadn't been bound with twine, but every edge of the paper wrap was sealed with glue. Its contents were completely enclosed. With no name or hint of the sender, she carefully tore one corner until she could unwrap it safely.

Inside, atop a folded parchment sheet, was a note—from Domin il'Sänke.

Wynn, if you are reading this, it means you are still alive. A relief, I am certain, though a surprise to me, considering your nature. . . .

Wynn wrinkled her nose at this poor humor.

The enclosed may be of interest in your pursuits, though it is incomplete. I can do nothing more, since I have not seen the whole of the original from which it is translated. Make of it what you will, and as always, keep your secrets.

With hesitation and affection,
Domin Ghassan il'Sänke, Order of Metaology
Guild of Sagecraft in Samau'a Gaulb, il'Dha'ab Najuum

In the brief days she'd been gone, he couldn't have returned home, let alone sent this all the way back. He must have left it before he departed, with instructions for its delivery if and when she returned. Wynn unfolded the parchment, and there was il'Sänke's scrawl upon it.

The Children in twenty and six steps seek to hide in five corners
The anchors amid Existence, which had once lived amid the Void.
One to wither the Tree from its roots to its leaves
Laid down where a cursed sun cracks the soil.
That which snuffs a Flame into cold and dark
Sits alone upon the water that never flows.
The middling one, taking the Wind like a last breath,
Sank to sulk in the shallows that still can drown.
And swallowing Wave in perpetual thirst, the fourth
Took seclusion in exalted and weeping stone.
But the last, that consumes its own, wandered astray
In the depths of the Mountain beneath the seat of a lord's song.

Wynn recognized some phrases. But the impact of what she read, yet didn't understand, overwhelmed everything but her academic nature. She knew nothing of Suman poetry, let alone whatever ancient forms it took on. Likely the translation had broken much of its structure.

"This here . . . and that," Chane said, pointing at the parchment. "Those are close to phrases you already translated."

Wynn hadn't even realized he was reading over her shoulder.

Compared to what she'd worked out, incorrectly or not, il'Sänke had revealed much more. She'd have to check her journals, but his translation appeared to be all of what she'd blindly copied from Chane's scroll. Even il'Sänke had stumbled over the few phrases she'd first shown him. He must have worked furiously trying to finish the rest before he left.

"Eternals bless you!" Wynn whispered.

After all she'd been through, all the damage she'd done, she desperately needed something of worth . . . something to guide her next steps. Certain phrases upon the parchment began to nag her—like ants in her skull searching erratically for something she'd forgotten. . . .

Something right before her—something she unconsciously hadn't wanted to recognize.

"What are the five corners?" Chane asked. "It is a lead phrase, connected to the thirteen Children. You told me they divided . . . and here are five cryptic entries."

"Destinations," Wynn whispered absently.

Chane was silent for a long moment.

"Why?" he asked. "Your white undead and her companions took the orb into the Pock Peaks. Where did the others go? I cannot even tell which one of these nonsense lines relates to her or that place."

And Wynn scanned each line again.

. . . the fourth took seclusion in exalted and weeping stone.

Did "exalted" mean "honored"? Was "weeping stone" like wet walls . . . natural columns . . . ages of mineral deposits built upon the erected bodies of the honored dead? Was it a reference to the Stonewalkers' underworld? Then Wynn remembered Leesil's tales of what had happened in the orb's cavern.

High in the Pock Peaks, the orb had rested over the cavern's molten depths. Rising heat warmed the place enough that perpetual snow and ice above seeped downward—"weeping" along the cavern walls. When Magiere had mistakenly opened the orb, Leesil claimed all the moisture in the cavern began raining inward toward the orb's burning light.

Could "exalted" merely be a metaphor for a high and lofty place?

But what of . . . *swallowing the Wave in perpetual thirst . . .*

Wynn scanned again. Her eyes caught the words that il'Sänke had capitalized. Those had to be vocative nouns. Among them were five that made her think upon the domin's lecture in a seminar she'd overheard.

Each of the Elements was represented three ways, according to the three Aspects of Existence. Spirit was also known as Essence and . . .

Tree . . . Flame . . . Wind . . . Wave . . . Mountain . . .

There were five *places* hinted at by reference to the Elements, but that fourth kept sticking in her head.

. . . swallowing the Wave . . . like an orb consuming a cavern's dripping moisture.

She connected the physical Aspects in the poem to their corresponding mental . . . intellectual terms of the Elements.

Spirit . . . Fire . . . Air . . . Water . . . Earth . . .

Wynn felt a wave of drowning fatigue as she stared at the first lines—*to hide in five corners the anchors amid Existence, which had once lived amid the Void.*

These were not just destinations, and she knew why the Children had "divided."

Wynn sank upon the bed's edge next to Shade and began to cry.

Chane knelt before her, his pale face filled with concern. He touched her hands still holding the parchment.

"What is wrong?" he asked.

She couldn't take another burden like this. The weight was too much.

"Five . . . not one," she answered weakly. "Not just the destinations . . . there are five orbs."

Chane's brow wrinkled. He carefully slipped the parchment from her fingers, his eyes shifting back and forth as he read it again.

"What are they?" he finally asked. "What are they for?"

Wynn slowly shook her head and couldn't even guess. The orbs must be something the Ancient Enemy had once coveted, perhaps used to some purpose in the great war or before it. The only line that made any sense was the last, its ending reference having a far different meaning.

In the depths of the Mountain beneath the seat of a lord's song.

Il'Sänke had worked out the written ancient Sumanese word for "seat" and found it had been misspelled with a doubled ending consonant—as in "seatt." And "a lord's song" was an old Suman tribal ululation for a leader, but the word was spoken differently by context versus the way it was written. When spoken, it gave the name of a lost place.

In the depths of the Mountain beneath . . . Bäalâle Seatt.

Another thread, another chain, pulled Wynn toward that place, where Thallûhearag's treachery had claimed uncountable lives. Beneath a long-lost seatt lay another orb, the one of "the Mountain" . . . the one of Earth.

Shade rose up, rumbling. Wynn tiredly raised a hand to quiet the dog.

The wall's stone beside the door began to bulge.

"Chane!"

She tried to lunge off the bed for her staff in the corner, her mind filled with one screaming thought. *It can't be happening . . . it can't be. . . .*

A black hulk took shape, and Chane shoved her back toward the bed's head. He jerked out his broken sword as Shade leaped over the footboard, circling in on the invader's far side.

Wynn clutched Chane's side, ready to push him out of the way . . . but she stopped and stared at . . . not at the wraith.

Ore-Locks stood glowering before the wall.

Dressed in a dark cloak and a plain black hauberk with no steel-tipped scales, he still had two wide battle daggers lashed to the front of his belt.

Wynn was about to order him out and alert anyone nearby. Then her attention caught on what he held in each hand.

One sword was longer, narrower of blade, while the other was short and wide, suitable to his own kind. Both had the mottled gray sheen of the finest dwarven steel. Wynn knew where she'd seen them—in Sliver's forge room.

"Why are you here?" Chane rasped.

He tensed, raising his tipless blade as the dwarf held up the longer sword. Ore-Locks snapped his arm straight, opening his grip in the last instant.

The sword clattered at Chane's feet.

"What is the meaning of this?" he demanded.

"My barter," Ore-Locks growled, and looked to Wynn. "I know where you go next, and I come with you."

Wynn went mute in the room's silence. Somehow, he'd known what she would do next. She was going to find Bäalâle Seatt. And this worshipper of the worst of the traitors intended to follow her to the bones of his cursed ancestor.

Wynn stood there, staring into Ore-Locks's hard, black-pellet irises.

EPILOGUE

Darkness . . . awareness . . . dormancy . . .

These realizations came, each one feeding upon the previous.

Sau'ilahk wanted to wail out the horror he had swallowed at the moment of his second death.

So why was he now aware of anything at all?

Over a thousand years had passed since his first death and the anguish it had taught him. He would linger forever without flesh—without beauty. For an instant, that remembrance tore away relief amid confusion.

Death is not punishment . . . enough.

Sau'ilahk's fears welled as he felt Beloved's presence.

It is release . . . it is freedom.

He found himself standing in a desert night. Uncountable stars glinted in a clear black sky. He shielded his eyes, as if every point of brilliance shone only upon him.

And he saw his hands.

No longer wrapped in black cloth, they were whole and tan, as they had been in life. But this was not real. It was only to torment him.

Why should an impudent servant, my priest, gain freedom so easily . . . when his god remains the first slave of all?

Sau'ilahk watched stars fall.

They struck dark dunes, and he whirled, about to run, but they were all around him. Great mounds of sand shifted, growing black beneath pinprick glints . . . like a glare reflected upon black scales. Beloved's roiling coils turned endlessly around him, closing as they twisted tighter upon themselves.

Sau'ilahk had failed in the one task given to him. He had disobeyed a warning. And more of his god's enemies knew of his existence. But surely his destruction had erased that transgression. Surely that was enough for leniency, if his god had saved him.

"Pity, my Beloved!" he cried out with the memory of a voice he had raised in supplication a thousand years ago. "Forgive . . . I beg you!"

The wall of coils closed, blocking out the sky, as he heard them grinding the dunes.

You remain my tool, like all who step beyond life yet linger, dead but not dead.

One black scale, as large as a mounted rider, caught the edge of Sau'ilahk's cloak. It dragged him into those coils as the fabric tore and shredded.

You will serve. . . .

Sau'ilahk screamed as flesh tore from his remembered bones.

Your release comes only when Existence ends . . . and I am free.